THE FRONTLINE FUGITIVES

NICK JACOBELLIS

BOOK II COPS IN A COMBAT ZONE

The Frontline Fugitives Book II: Cops In A Combat Zone

Cover photographs by: Alex Landeen of Landeen Photography

Book design by www.StoriesToTellBooks.com

E Mail: badgepublishing@gmail.com

Website: www.badgepublishing.com

CONTENTS

INTRODUCTION

The Frontline Fugitives is a plot driven historical fiction story about the search for two 18 year old fugitives, who join the U.S. Army to avoid arrest, after they rob a bank that results in the death of a New York City Police Officer. Their escape plan is both daring and ingenious. While being assisted by an aging retired gangster, the two fugitives change their appearance as best as possible and use fictitious identities to get through the Selective Service induction process. Once the two fugitives are inducted into the U.S. Army, the wanted men "blend in" with millions of troops and look forward to the day when they can live on foreign soil as free men when the war is over. Even if the two fugitives don't survive the war, dying in battle seems like a much better alternative than being arrested and convicted in a New York court for murder, bank robbery and other serious crimes.

The readers of The Frontline Fugitives Book I and Book II will follow the adventures of a fictional New York City based U.S. Army CID Task Force that is responsible to investigate black-market activities and conduct other criminal investigations during World War II. When government officials learn that the two fugitives joined the U.S. Army as a way to facilitate their escape, law enforcement officers from various agencies join forces with U.S. Army Investigators to pursue the fugitives identified as Ivan Larson and Francis Shorty Mc Ghee.

The hunt for the two fugitives is complicated by the fact that the wanted teenage felons have no prior criminal history. The investigators working this case are also unable to find any personal photographs of the two fugitives. Without photographs or fingerprints of the two subjects, the civilian and military investigators are unable to prevent the fugitives from being inducted into the U.S. Army.

The fact that the main witness in the case is a Negro Police Officer, also creates certain operational problems for the two primary law enforcement characters of this story. This is the case because it is no easy task for a Negro Police Officer (Patrolman Al Parker) and a white U.S. Army CID Agent (Major James Beauregard) to travel together in a segregated society while searching Army bases for two fugitives. Even more bizarre is how U.S. military personnel during World War II were segregated, despite the fact that white troops and African American soldiers were killed and wounded on the same battlefields without discrimination. The insanity of it all is mind-boggling, yet it happened.

Finding the two fugitives among the millions of men who are serving in the U.S. Army during World War II proves to be no easy task, especially when months pass and the members of the CID Task Force have to face the possibility that Ivan Larson and Shorty Mc Ghee could be serving overseas. This concern places tremendous pressure on the members of the U.S. Army CID Task Force as they race against time to locate the two fugitives.

The Frontline Fugitives Book I and Book II also lives up to the definition of good historical fiction by accurately describing what it was like to be a black market operator, a violent criminal, a fugitive, a police officer, a police detective, a police captain, a federal agent, a Provost Marshal, a military policeman, a U.S. Army CID Agent, an infantry soldier fighting in the jungles of Guadalcanal, a combat medic, a C47 pilot, a glider pilot, a U.S. Army Glider Infantryman and a U.S. Army Paratrooper during World War II. This includes characters from different ethnic backgrounds. Last but not least, this story also includes a number of named and unnamed characters who represent the forces of evil.

A NOTE FROM THE AUTHOR

I began writing The Frontline Fugitives Book I and Book II before the new Millennium. In between working on other projects, I finished Book I and Book II in the summer of 2016. One of the reasons it took so long to complete Book I and Book II, is because I was determined to make The Frontline Fugitives as historically accurate as possible, while supporting a "believable" fictional plot and a cast of "believable" fictional characters.

In order to complete this process, I had to learn as much as I could about various subjects to include, life in New York City from the early 1900s to the 1940s, life in southern states during World War II, the history of the New York City Police Department and other law enforcement agencies during the early and mid 20th Century, the history of racism, segregation, ethnic rivalry and the assimilation of various ethnic groups in the United States, life in Nazi Germany before and during World War II, rationing and black market activities in the United States and in Europe during World War II, the Selective Service induction process during World War II, as well as information about basic training and life in the U.S. Army during World War II.

I also had to become familiar with The Punitive Expedition into Mexico in 1916, trench warfare and combat actions during World War 1, the duties of the military police, the U.S. Army's Provost Marshal's Office and the U.S. Army Criminal Investigations Division during World War II, U.S. Army glider training and various battles including, The Guadalcanal Campaign, The North African Campaign, The Invasion of Sicily, The Italian Campaign, The D Day Invasion of Normandy, France on June 6, 1944, Operation Market Garden – The Invasion of Holland in September of 1944 and The Battle of the Bulge in December of 1944.

One of my greatest sources of information for this book was my father, Benedict Jacobellis, a member of The Greatest Generation who was born and raised in New York City and served in the U.S. Army during World War II. As a boy growing up in the Flatbush section of Brooklyn, my father told me a seemingly endless number of stories about life in New York City before and during the war, as well as about life in the U.S. Army during World War II. These stories included information about rationing and black-market operations in New York City during the war years.

I also relied on my father-in-law, Louis Evangelista, a U.S. Army veteran who served as a member of the Allied Occupation Force in Germany, who at 88 years of age is able to remember details from the 1930s and 40s as if it was yesterday. In addition, I had several uncles and cousins who served in World War II.

While conducting research for this book, I also interviewed World War II veterans who served as U.S. Army Flight Officers and flew CG-4A Waco Gliders on a number of combat missions in the European Theater of Operation. Interviewing former U.S. Army glider pilots gave me a much greater insight into what it was like to fly an aircraft that had no engine in combat. Even some of the more personal tidbits of information that World War II veterans shared with me, helped to bring this historical fiction story to life.

Being an Italian American, who grew up in New York City in an era when different forms of ethnic rivalry and racism were prevalent, also enabled me to create certain characters from a historically accurate perspective. Some of the observations that I made while traveling and working in different parts of the country, also made it possible to develop a realistic fictional story line.

Over the years I also became familiar with various World War II era military and law enforcement firearms. This included field testing many of the law enforcement and military revolvers, pistols, rifles, carbines and submachine guns that are featured in The Frontline Fugitives. In addition, I became familiar with World War II era U.S. Army and German uniforms and equipment. I accomplished this by collecting military clothing and equipment, by attending one of the largest and most elaborately planned World War II reenactments and by visiting museums and other venues where antique military uniforms and equipment were displayed and sold.

Driving a World War II era Jeep around the U.S. Navy Base in Guantanamo Bay, Cuba, when I directed and participated in covert operations during our nation's Drug War, made it possible for me to experience what it was like to operate the most famous compact 4x4 vehicle of the 1940's. This is an important point because World War II era Jeeps are featured in a number of critical scenes in this series of books. Over the years, I also became familiar with other World War II era military, civilian and law enforcement vehicles.

I also became considerably more familiar with the capabilities of the twin engine DC3/C47 that was used to tow GC4A Waco Gliders during WWII, when my colleagues and I in the U.S. Customs Service used one of these amazing aircraft in one of our covert air operations during the Drug War. Learning how to fly and safely land a small single engine aircraft, with and without the engine operating, also made it possible for me to accurately depict certain flying scenes in this book series.

The fact that I survived the crash landing of a large twin engine (ex military) undercover aircraft, was a life changing event that had a significant impact on my ability to describe certain critical aviation scenes in Book I and Book II. During this in flight emergency I volunteered to serve as the co pilot and assisted the Contract Pilot in Command, even though at the time I had an expired student pilot's license and very limited flying experience. Serving as a co pilot during such a serious inflight emergency, also contributed to my ability to develop certain characters from a personal perspective.

My experience as a federal agent, uniformed police officer and New York (Manhattan) District Attorney's Office Investigator also enabled me to accurately develop the "police procedural" aspects of this story. I also relied heavily on my experience as a law enforcement officer who recruited and directed a number of reliable informants to develop characters such as Tony G., a colorful mobster who volunteers to assist military and civilian law enforcement officers investigate black market operations during World War II.

In order to make The Frontline Fugitives Book I and Book II as accurate as possible, I also included a number of footnotes to credit the research sources that provided the copyrighted information that was used to support aspects of the plot and aid in character development. *A list of general references sources and footnotes can be found at the end of the book.

I especially wish to thank Dr. Don Abbe, the Director of the Silent Wings Museum in Lubbock, Texas, for the assistance that he provided when I was putting the finishing touches to sections of this book that involve glider training and glider combat operations during World War II.

Two contacts in Belgium also assisted me when I put the finishing touches to the section of Book II that involves the GC-4A Waco glider resupply mission to a landing zone near the Village of Savy (a little over one mile northwest of Bastogne) on December 27, 1944. One particular photograph and one map that was provided by a contact from Belgium enabled me to complete a critical fiction aspect of this fugitive manhunt story, while making every effort to remain as true to actual terrain features as possible.

While every effort was made to make The Frontline Fugitives as realistic and historically accurate as possible, it is important to remember that this is a fiction story set in the 1940s when the world was at war. As a result, certain liberties had to be taken in order to combine fictional characters and a fictional plot with historically accurate events that occurred during the early and mid 20ᵗʰ Century.

*The names that were used in this book to identify different primary and secondary fictional characters were selected because the author liked the sound of these names. It is also important to remember that certain fictional characters included in this book are portrayed performing duties that were performed by real people who served with distinction in civilian life, in law enforcement positions, as well as in the U.S. Armed Forces during World War II. This includes enlisted men, non commissioned officers and commissioned officers who served in different training commands, support units and combat units. There is also no connection between any of the fictional characters in this book and anyone who lived in the past or is alive today. This includes individuals who served in the same or similar capacities as the fictional characters in this book.

*In order to be historically accurate this series of books uses the words Negro and colored to refer to African Americans because these words were commonly used in the early and mid 20ᵗʰ Century. Even though the "N Word" was used sparingly, this word was used in certain key scenes because it is historically accurate to do so. This book also includes other slang words and language that was commonly used in the early and mid 1900s.

This book series is dedicated to those who served in military and civilian positions and protected the United States and our allies during World War II. Clearly, the victory that was achieved during World War II, was made possible because decent law abiding human beings from different backgrounds banded together to fight the forces of evil.

Special thanks to my grandmother Fanny Budani for encouraging me to live my dreams in life and to my grandfather Nick Jacobellis for all that he taught me about life and my Italian heritage. Last but not least, I thank my wife for cheering me on and being incredibly supportive, while I completed this and other writing projects.

CHAPTER 1

THE BATTLE OF THE BULGE INTENSIFIES

As far as the Allies were concerned, the lull in the fighting presented an opportunity to get some badly needed rest while trying to enjoy the holiday season. In contrast, the Germans used this time to their advantage to plan a winter offensive that would become known as The Battle of the Bulge.

The Christmas Holidays in Bastogne in the winter of 1944 was by no means a season to be jolly. Between the record low freezing temperatures, the snow, the shortage of food, ammunition and medical supplies, as well as the intolerable living conditions, most men were in no mood or condition to fight a war but they did. In addition to receiving wounds from shelling and close contact with the enemy, American troops also suffered from frostbite and trench foot. Clearly, many of the battles that took place in the Ardennes in December of 1944 were some of the fiercest of the entire war.

Until the weather cleared and U.S. Army aircraft were able to air drop supplies into Bastogne, the American troops in forward areas lived on a limited quantity of food that included cold C&K rations, tins of sardines, a few pancakes without maple syrup per day and black coffee when they could get it. The American troops fighting in the Ardennes also had to contend with shortages of tobacco products. Even the brands of tobacco that U.S. troops had access to was an issue that caused controversy. This was the case because troops stationed in rear areas generally had greater access to the premium brand of cigarettes such as Lucky Strikes and Camels, while the men closest to the front had to settle for the less popular brands.[1]

During the German offensive in the Ardennes a commando operation called Operation Grief was expected to create havoc behind the American lines and help pave the way for the advancing units to capture key Allied positions. In order to accomplish their mission, English speaking German commandos under the command of SS Colonel Otto Skorzeny infiltrated the American lines while dressed as U.S. Army personnel, including as Military Policemen. Following behind the lead element of Skorzeny's commando unit, was a heavily armed mechanized contingent that was designated the 150th Panzer Brigade.

Once the word went out that Germans were masquerading as American MPs, the U.S. Army tightened security and began to establish checkpoints at key positions using real MPs. Even though some of Skorzeny's men spoke English, the average German had difficulty responding when real American MPs and G.I.s started firing questions at the infiltrators about baseball, comic book characters, movie stars, the capitol of certain U.S. states etc. One of the U.S. Army checkpoints was established on a bridge over the Ambleve River near the town of Aywaille on December 17, 1944. This particular checkpoint was manned by a contingent of American Negro Military Policemen.

As soon as Sergeant Calvin Parker spotted a jeep carrying three American soldiers approach his position, he removed his M1 Carbine from his shoulder and retracted the bolt a fraction of an inch to make sure that the chamber of his weapon was loaded. Just like white MP units, Cal Parker and his men were under strict orders to properly screen anyone trying to pass through their checkpoint, regardless of their rank. Cal was personally told by his Commanding Officer to detain anyone who appeared suspicious or failed to pass muster, even if they were wearing the uniform of a general officer (full Colonel or above).

As Sergeant Cal Parker stood off to the side to provide covering fire for his men, one of his MPs held up his hand just as the jeep approached the checkpoint. Even though Cal and his men had been through this numerous times before, they took their mission seriously and conducted themselves like true professionals whenever they screened civilian or military traffic that crossed through their checkpoint.

While one of the MP Privates in Cal's unit engaged the driver in conversation, Cal Parker slowly strolled around the vehicle to see if his presence made any of the occupants act nervous as he remarked, "Remember what Army Intelligence said about English speaking Krauts wearing our uniforms and trying to infiltrate our lines. Check these men out real good, then check 'em out again."

When the occupants of the vehicle failed to know the proper password, the African American MP Private handling the stop, waited until his partner finished examining the dog tags of the soldier sitting in the right front passenger seat, before he called out to his sergeant and said, "These guys don't know the password, Sarge. The one they're using is a few days old."

Rather than take any chances, Cal Parker pointed his M1 Carbine directly at the occupants of the jeep, as he ordered the three men to exit the vehicle and stand on the side of the road with their hands on top of their heads. The moment Cal relayed this order, two of his well trained MPs reacted by blocking the bridge with their Jeep that was armed with a belt fed M1919 .30 caliber machine gun.

As soon as Cal Parker searched the Jeep and found several foreign made pistols, a supply of ammunition, hand-grenades, a radio transmitter, explosives and an unusually large amount of American and British currency, the American Negro MPs at the Ambleve River checkpoint had more than enough probable cause to suspect the three men of being German agents. After Cal tucked one of the captured German pistols in his M36 OD Green Pistol Belt, he instructed his men to cover him while he thoroughly search the prisoners.

The moment Cal found German Army Pay Books, that served as an official form of identification for enemy soldiers, on all three men, Sergeant Calvin Parker turned to his corporal and said, "Lock 'em up...they're Krauts." As Cal Parker and his men would later find out, all three German infiltrators were executed by firing squad.

Once Cal Parker had a chance to write his father, he made sure to let his dad know that he was following in his footsteps by being a good police officer. Cal also let his Dad and his brother know that he was bringing home two German pistols and a few other souvenirs that he picked up while serving in the ETO.

When Ivan Larson learned that Lt. Gloria Rutherford was listed as killed in action he went for a long walk by himself. The moment Shorty Mc Ghee went to go after his buddy, Lt. Jimmy Donnelli held out his right hand and said, "You better let him work this out on his own, Gus."

As cold as it was, Ivan walked the entire length of the flight line as if he was out for a stroll on a beautiful spring day. It was amazing how your mind could take you to a place where the human body felt no pain from the elements when you were in some form of shock.

Unlike other folks who lived through the war, Ivan Larson had no one to mourn for until he heard that his girl Peaches was killed in action. With the exception of the time that he spent with Sister O'Rourke, Mike Connely and the members of his gang, Ivan Larson was a loner who never let anyone get close to him. Losing Gloria was like sustaining a self inflicted gunshot wound because Ivan accepted her advances in the first place. Instead of saying that there was someone back home waiting for him, Ivan melted into her arms and tried to take as much of her love and affection that he could, even though he knew that it could never last. Unfortunately, the end result was a self fulfilled prophecy.

While Ivan headed back to his quarters, he knew he was coming back to reality when he began to feel the effects of walking in freezing temperatures. Being a fugitive wasn't easy, even when things were going as planned and you were eluding the police. No matter how hard Ivan tried to go straight, his troubled past had a way of preventing him from ever living a normal life. As unrealistic as it was to think this way, Ivan found himself wishing that the police would simply go away and stop looking for him. It took another blast of ice cold air to make Ivan realize that he was living in perilous times for more reasons than one.

By the time Ivan was finished having a long talk with himself, he knew that his life would have to be lived one day at a time. Ivan also knew that he had to stick to his original escape plan. This meant that Ivan had to take his chances with the enemy, if that's what it took to ensure his long term survival.

In a strange sort of way it felt good to know where he stood in life. Even though he screwed up royally by thinking that he could have anything to do with a decent girl from a good family, Ivan was back to normal by the end of his walk. With no one else around, Ivan wiped his runny nose with his gloved hand before he looked up into the overcast sky and said, "I'm sorry, Peaches." As soon as Ivan returned to tent, he looked at Shorty Mc Ghee and Jimmy Donnelli and said, "I needed that."

CHAPTER 2

THE PLOT THICKENS FOR ALL PARTIES INVOLVED

After his meeting at the CID Office, Captain Pat Murphy Sr. knew exactly what needed to be done to motivate the War Department to draft Al Parker to serve with Army CID on the fugitive investigation. Thanks to Johnny Mc Donald and Frank Angelone, a page from Andy Gooding's ledger book was carefully removed before any of these records were entered into evidence. To the average person who reviewed these ledger books, the two names on the missing page had no special significance. Fortunately, the two detectives knew otherwise, and wasted no time in delivering this page from one of Andy Gooding's ledger books to their captain.

It took a year for Captain Murphy to collect on this debt. When the Captain informed the two influential New Yorkers, who were spared embarrassment for their involvement in violating federal rationing regulations, that it was time to pay up, they agreed to do so without reservation. Once Captain Murphy witnessed a series of phone calls being made, he used his lighter to burn the page that was removed from the ledger book in their presence. As he left their spacious office on Wall Street, Captain Murphy knew that this was one of those instances when the end justified the means.

The same War Department that expressed reservations about allowing Patrolman Al Parker to be "drafted" for limited national service, had a last minute change of heart and approved the request. Once this request was approved, arrangements were made to induct Patrolman Al Parker into the United States Army as a Military Police Staff Sergeant assigned to CID. Staff Sergeant Parker's orders assigned him to serve under the command of Major James Beauregard for the duration of the fugitive investigation.

The only question that troubled Captain Patrick Murphy Sr. was if he was allowing a police officer who was also a family friend, to go above and beyond the call of duty in order to try and capture the two fugitives during a world war. Despite, his personal concern for his friend's safety, Captain Murphy knew that Al Parker would never know another moment of peace in his life, if Ivan Larson and Francis Shorty Mc Ghee were able to evade capture.

While no one ever found out if the President was involved in approving this plan, it was well known that the Commander in Chief had a soft spot for any dangerous operation that had the potential of being successful. It was also suspected but never confirmed, that the First Lady supported the idea of authorizing a white Army Major from CID to work with a Negro New York City policeman to hunt down two fugitives in the European Theater of Operation.

The officials who were directed to approve this request suspected that the First Lady was supportive of this unorthodox plan, because she was a major proponent of allowing patriotic Negroes to serve in combat units. The fact that the two fugitives were wanted for committing several heinous crimes, including the killing of a policeman, bank robbery and the sale of black market merchandise also helped to motivate support for this unusual request.

As far as Jim Beauregard was concerned, Al Parker's police department personnel file did not come close to reflecting his actual accomplishments on the job. Even Al's decision to violate department policy and capture Amos Washington was viewed as an excusable act, because he had the common sense to bring Captain Patrick Murphy Sr. along when he made this arrest.

It was also clear to Jim Beauregard that Al Parker was an excellent investigator, a fact that was established when Al interrogated Amos Washington and Rudy Mueller. Al also made other noteworthy contributions to this investigation during the search of Johann Miller's office and when he and Frank Angelone worked as a team to locate small pieces of an unburned handwritten letter from Ivan Larson in the incinerator at Mike Connely's apartment building. This evidence enabled the CID Task Force to focus their efforts to pursue the two fugitives by inspecting air bases in France. In addition to his accomplishments during his police career, Al Parker was also a decorated combat veteran of the World War I. As far as Jim Beauregard was concerned, these credentials made Al Parker well suited for the mission at hand.

Even though the Germans were able to surround Bastogne, they were never able to capture the town and use the vital network of roadways that passed through the area. This happened because American paratroopers, glider infantrymen, tank crews, artillerymen, military police, cooks, anti aircraft crews and other G.I.s put up a heroic defense of the towns in an around Bastogne.

The fact that the weather finally cleared on December 23rd made it possible for the Americans fighting in the Ardennes to be re-supplied by air. The first air drop involved 260 C47s that flew through a gauntlet of enemy anti aircraft fire to deliver over 330 tons of supplies into a well marked drop zone located west of Bastogne.[2] In addition, U.S. Army Ground Forces would also receive air support from Allied fighters and bombers that were biting at the bit to strafe and bomb German positions ever since the enemy launched their offensive on December 16th.

Being stranded on an American Air Base in France during a blinding snow storm was not helping the war effort as far as Captain Billy Davis was concerned, especially when American soldiers were fighting and dying all along the front. With his plane covered with ice and snow it was anyone's guess when they would be able to fly again.

So far Hitler's gamble was working out. Everyone knew that a German victory was possible in the Ardennes, as long as the Americans were unable to use their command of the air to their advantage. With nothing else to do but try and stay warm, Captain Davis played cards with his crew while they waited for the weather conditions to improve. When the weather finally cleared, many considered the presence of excellent flying conditions a sign of Divine Intervention, especially since the winter of 1944 in Europe was officially designated the harshest winter in fifty years.

After days of inclement flying weather, Billy Davis and his crew were going into harms way to help turn the tide of the German offensive. While his C47 was being loaded with ammunition and rations, Captain Davis and his co pilot attended a briefing that included an updated weather report and the flight plan for the upcoming mission. After devouring a breakfast of cold army rations and a few cups of hot coffee, Captain Davis and his crew boarded their C47 and prepared to fly into the jaws of death to drop badly needed supplies to the American troops in Bastonge.

For units like the 81st Troop Carrier Squadron, the flight would take three hours and would be flown at an altitude of 1500 feet until the time came to descend to 300 feet to execute the air drop of supplies.[3] As an experienced C47 pilot, Billy Davis instinctively knew when the time was right to deliver the critical supplies of ammunition and rations over the drop zone that was selected by the 101st Airborne Division.

After leveling off at 300 feet and maintaining the proper separation between his plane and the lead aircraft in the formation, Billy Davis told his crew to get ready. The moment Captain Davis observed the C47 in front of his aircraft jettison its load over the drop zone, he instructed his co pilot to signal the crew chief that it was time to do the same. Without wasting any time, Lt. Archer looked into the cargo bay of the aircraft and lowered his left hand to signal the rest of the crew to push the crated supplies out of the open cargo door. While the supplies left the aircraft, enemy small arms fire could be heard striking the undercarriage of their C47.

Once the cargo that was carried inside his plane was dropped and the parapacks that were fixed to the bottom of the aircraft were jettisoned over the DZ, Captain Billy Davis fire-walled the throttles and executed a tight left turn. With their mission accomplished, Billy Davis and his fellow crew members were free to return to base. All they had to do to survive this mission, was to climb to a higher altitude and avoid getting shot down as they returned to the safety of the Allied lines. The fact that the enemy gunners failed to lead their plane properly became evident, when a long stream of enemy tracer ammunition was spotted by another C47 crew arching up and falling short of hitting the tail section of Billy's C47.

After turning the controls over to his co pilot, Billy Davis called out, "Let's go home." Now that this resupply mission was completed, Billy Davis and his crew would be returning to the 440th Troop Carrier Group for reassignment to another squadron.

When news of the Allied plan to use gliders to re-supply Bastogne reached the 439th Troop Carrier Group in Chattendun, France everyone braced for action. While the other men in their unit gathered in the mess hall to talk shop and wait for the order to fly a mission, Shorty Mc Ghee and Ivan Larson remained in their temporary quarters to discuss their situation in private.

As tough as he was, Shorty Mc Ghee was very concerned about Ivan's escape plan. If it worked they would survive the war and live happily ever after in Europe. If Ivan's plan failed, they would be doing exactly what the N.Y.P.D., FBI and Army CID was trying to accomplish, only they would die in battle and not in the electric chair.

While Shorty paced back in forth in front of Ivan's cot, he began to ramble on about the the massive effort that was being made by Army CID to hunt them down. For some reason Shorty had lost the confidence that he gained after making it through the investigation into the death of Lt. Perkins. The second that Ivan got tired of listening to Shorty ramble on, he tried to sound as reassuring as possible when he said, "Will you relax. The Krauts just handed us the answer to our prayers."

The thought of flying a combat mission in a GC4-A Waco Glider and intentionally surrendering to German troops made Shorty feel uncomfortable, not because he was patriotic but because he was worried about the way that he would be treated by the enemy. After Shorty took a quick look around to make sure that they were still alone, he leaned closer to Ivan and sounded as if he was pleading with his friend when he said, "Why don't we go AWOL? I heard there's thousands of guys hiding out all over France. Some of them are making a fortune selling stolen Army supplies on the black-market."

As soon as Ivan laid back against his pillow, he responded to Shorty's suggestion in a very calm voice and said, "I heard the same thing but that's not for me. I'd rather take my chances in combat and get picked up by the Krauts." The minute that Shorty started to speak and said, "But," Ivan cut him off as he laced into his friend in a low but stern tone of voice. "But nothing....there isn't a cop in the world who's gonna find us in a German POW Camp, especially if we use the other dog tags that I made up. Even the Red Cross won't have any record of Danny Gannon or Gus O'Malley getting captured. As far as the Army is concerned, they'll think we got killed in action or list us as MIA."

After pausing long enough to light a cigarette, Ivan continued and said, "Even if we get captured using the names Danny Gannon and Gus O'Malley, what cop is gonna find us at the end of the war when Europe is one big mess." Once again Ivan paused to take a drag on his cigarette before he added, "The longer we remain in Allied occupied territory, the more we risk getting picked up by the MPs. That means we have the best chance of surviving this war if we get captured by the Germans. If we can't get lost in the crowd when this war is over we deserve to get arrested."

As much as he hated to admit it, Shorty knew that there was no guarantee that just because they went absent without leave and tried to hide out in occupied Europe, that he and Ivan would be able to avoid getting picked up by the MPs or Army CID. After seeing his friend continue to appear bewildered, Ivan sat up, swung his legs over the side of his cot, stood up and said, "I know this may sound crazy but I want'a fly one successful combat mission in a glider before I pack it in. Maybe if I made it all the way to Holland I'd feel differently but since that didn't happen, I'd like to see if I have what it takes to be a real Army aviator."

As Shorty looked at his partner in crime, he could not believe his ears. This was another one of those rare moments when Ivan Larson the tough guy exposed his true feelings. While Shorty relaxed his stance, Ivan continued and said. "I'm not making excuses for the past. What's done is done. It's just that I don't want'a walk away from being a U.S. Army glider pilot until I absolutely have to." Then, after pausing for a second, Ivan stamped out his cigarette in a nearby metal ashtray as he continued and said, "Besides, I like being on the winning side."

As concerned as he was about being captured by the military police, Shorty also had moments when he regretted the past and he liked being a member of U.S. Army Air Forces. Just like his partner in crime, Shorty had to admit that despite some of the less attractive aspects of Army life, it felt good to be part of the war effort. Although he never spoke about this before, Shorty often forgot that he was a fugitive masquerading as a soldier, when he was busy performing his duties as an Assistant Glider Engineering Officer.

Since Ivan opened up to him, Shorty decided to share his most guarded thoughts as well. The difference between the two men became evident when Shorty looked down at the floor because he was too embarrassed to face Ivan when he said, "I know what you mean. I hated the Army at first but now that I got promoted and we made it to the ETO I kind'a like what I'm doing." Then, as Shorty looked up and faced Ivan, he continued and said, "You're gonna think I'm crazy but I was thinking that someday I might be able to see my Mom again. You know, after the war and once we get settled."

Even though Ivan wasn't sure if such a reunion would ever be possible, he decided to use this as an opportunity to convince his buddy to have more faith in his escape plan. While Ivan did his best to sound as reassuring as possible, he looked at Shorty and said, "I don't see any reason why you can't see your mother again. If we can make our way to Ireland, we can ask Mike's relatives to contact your mother without that piece of shit for a stepfather finding out. As long as she's willing to come to Ireland or anyplace else in Europe where we settle down, you can take care of your Mom in style for the rest of her life."

Seeing Shorty smile from ear to ear was a clear indication that Ivan hit the right cord. "I'd like that," remarked Shorty, who quickly added, "Thank God we have Mike and his relatives in our corner. Stashing a few G's in Europe was easy but there's no way we'd be able to get our hands on the rest of our cash, including the money that Mike is leaving us, if the Flynn brothers and their family members in Ireland weren't willing to help us out."

While Ivan continued facing Shorty, he did his best to sound as sincere as possible when he said, "If you can come up with a better plan I'll listen. Until that happens we do it my way and I promise you'll see your mother again." Shorty knew that it was time to shit or get off the pot as the saying goes. Ivan was a confident son of a bitch who presented his case like a skilled prosecutor. If one thing sold Shorty on Ivan's plan, it was the fact that his partner in crime always kept his word.

So far, Ivan and Shorty had successfully managed to elude capture for over one year, even though an entire unit of federal agents, military cops and city policemen were assigned to hunt them down. Shorty also found some comfort in the fact, that when their fellow soldiers read the articles that were printed about them in The Stars and Stripes Newspaper and Yank Magazine, at no time did anyone ever jump up and say, "Hey, you're the guys the cops are looking for?" Even when the Armed Forces Radio Network CID Radio Show provided its listeners with a detailed description of the efforts being made to capture the two fugitives, Ivan and Shorty often sat with their fellow G.I.s and acted as interested and as entertained as everyone else.

Despite the fact that he still had some reservations about Ivan's escape plan, Shorty decided to go along unless something happened to change his mind. After offering a cigarette to Ivan and taking one for himself, Shorty snapped open his Zippo lighter and gave his buddy a light as he said, "OK, we'll do it your way. But if the situation changes and we have to vanish in a hurry, you gotta promise that we're gonna make a run for it any way we can."

As soon as Shorty said what he had to say, he lit his own cigarette and put his Zippo back in his pocket while Ivan remarked, "Come on, let's grab some coffee and see what the rumor mill has to say about the German advance in the Ardennes."

Lt. Colonel Thomas Mason was the War Department official who was assigned to expedite the induction of Al Parker into the Army as a military police staff sergeant assigned to Army CID. As soon as Colonel Mason finished swearing Al into the U.S. Army, he presented Major Beauregard with his written orders from the War Department and remarked, "Gentlemen, there's a war on and you have two fugitives to catch."

After seeing his cue to complete his half of the transition ceremony, Captain Murphy spoke while he removed items from the desk and handed Al Parker his silver Patrolman's shield, two pairs of handcuffs, his short barreled Smith & Wesson .38 Special M&P Model revolver and two arrest warrants. "Patrolman Parker from this moment on you are officially on military leave from the police department and will assume your new duties as a staff sergeant in the military police assigned to Army CID. According to our agreement with the Army, you will revert back to being a member of the New York City Police Department as soon as you return to the United States with your prisoners in custody, or once you are transported back to New York if the fugitives are officially listed as killed in action, missing in action or captured by the enemy."

While Al finished securing the warrants and his police equipment in his attache case, Captain Murphy finished his remarks. "If you or the Major need any assistance I want you to contact me at any time of the day or night."

As soon as Captain Murphy finished issuing Al Parker his marching orders and the items that he would need to perform his duties, Colonel Mason wished Major Beauregard and Al Parker a safe and successful trip. The Colonel also warned both men that there were some high ranking Army officers who wanted this fugitive manhunt handled differently, especially if the manhunt took Army investigators anywhere near the front lines. After shaking hands with Captain Murphy, the Colonel left police headquarters in time to catch his train back to Washington D.C..

Now that this rather unusual ceremony was over, Captain Murphy looked at the newly drafted staff sergeant and said, "A day doesn't go by without me thinking about how you saved my life and my father's life and how you risked life and limb to go to the aid of my son Patrick and apprehend those bank robbers in Brooklyn. Now you're going off to war to arrest the men who killed my youngest son and committed other serious crimes." After pausing to swallow the lump in his throat, Captain Patrick Murphy Sr. looked up at his old friend then over to Major Beauregard and said, "May Almighty God bless you both with success and protect you on your journey."

CHAPTER 3

THE LONG ROAD TO SUPREME HEADQUARTERS ALLIED FORCES EUROPE

Because they were issued priority transportation orders meant that Major Beauregard and Staff Sergeant Parker were able to avoid having to make the long trans Atlantic journey on an overcrowded Liberty ship that was transporting thousands of troops to the European Theater of Operation.

In addition to traveling to the ETO on board the first available air transportation, Major Beauregard and Staff Sergeant Parker were issued orders signed by the Secretary of War that authorized them and anyone assisting them to receive any and all reasonable assistance necessary to complete their assigned mission. This included being granted immediate access to any military personnel or civilians who needed to be questioned or interviewed, along with the authority to request assistance from military personnel to assist in the search for the two fugitives, as well as authorization to requisition equipment and any form of transportation on a priority basis, including in a combat zone.

The Major's written orders also identified Alvin Parker as a New York City Police Officer on military leave assigned to serve as a U.S. Army Military Police Staff Sergeant attached to CID, for the specific purposes of assisting in the capture of two U.S. Army soldiers who are wanted by various law enforcement agencies for murder, robbery and other serious crimes.

Al Parker's presence on the B24 Liberator bomber that was converted to perform transport duty was a sight to behold, especially since he was the only Negro soldier who was traveling on the specially configured aircraft. When the B24 crew chief announced that they had reached the half way point, an inquisitive one star general by the name of Nathan Tremble leaned over to James Beauregard and spoke as if he was busting with curiosity when he remarked, "Tell me Major, what brings you and your driver to travel on a priority military flight to the ETO?"

When Jim received his orders and found out how the Army intended to transport him and Al to Europe, he knew that it was only a question of time before someone would have something to say about the presence of a Negro staff sergeant on board a priority flight to the ETO. After all, this sort of thing simply wasn't a common occurrence and everyone including Jim Beauregard and Al Parker knew it. In fact, by 1944 standards a converted B24 bomber provided first class accommodations for passengers traveling from the United States to Europe.

For various reasons, Jim Beauregard didn't like the fact that anyone, including a general officer, would automatically assume that his Negro traveling companion was his chauffeur. Without hesitating, Jim looked at the General and did his best to sound informative and respectful when he said, "Staff Sergeant Parker is not my driver, Sir. He's my partner in CID. We're investigating the whereabouts of two fugitives who are hiding out in the Army."

Immediately after a look of disbelief crossed Tremble's face, the General spoke in a tone of voice that was loud enough for others to hear when he remarked, "Your partner! What kind of crap is that, Major? I've been in this mans Army for over 27 years and I couldn't bring my aide or my driver with me on this flight. What's this Army coming to when a damn Major in CID gets to have his aide de camp tagging along on a special flight for general officers and critical supplies. Hell, I'm gonna have to talk to Ike about this."

Knowing that he was about to get the best of a one star general, Jim spoke in a matter of fact tone of voice as he removed his orders from his pocket and said, "Would you like to see our orders, Sir?"

As the cranky old general officer who began his military career in 1917 slipped on his reading glasses and barked, "I got a good mind to write the son of a bitch who gave you permission to bring your partner or whatever he is on this plane when I had to leave my aide and my driver behind. That's bullshit, son. Hell I'm a general and you're only a major even if you are in CID."

As the General removed the orders from the envelop and read the contents, Jim looked at Al and winked his right eye. While Al made believe he was asleep and rolled over facing the window, General Tremble returned the orders in a huff and remarked, "Nobody likes a smart ass, Major."

While Jim folded his orders and placed them back in the envelop, he tried not to sound like an Army officer who just got the best of a one star general when he remarked, "That wasn't my intention, Sir."

Rather than let the matter rest, General Tremble stood up and pointed his right index finger directly at Jim Beauregard and said, "You and your partner better not piss on my parade ground while you're visiting the ETO, or you boys are gonna have to deal with me and I don't care who signed those orders."

While Jim did his best not to smile and provoke the General any further, he tried to sound as respectful as possible when he looked at the superior officer and said, "Yes, Sir."

The last time that Al Parker crossed the Atlantic it was on a troop transport that ferried soldiers and equipment back to New York City from France at the end of World War I. This trip was different and proved to be a special event in his life because this was the first time that Al ever flew on an airplane. In a way Al was like a big kid out on a new adventure, even if he was a little self conscious about being a Negro sergeant traveling in the presence of a plane full of high ranking officers. Before long the excitement wore off and Al dozed off as he made himself comfortable in the rear of the plane behind the position that was normally occupied by the right waste gunner.

While Al dozed off, Jim Beauregard decided to make an entry in the journal that he was writing about his unusual wartime experiences in CID. After documenting the incident with General Tremble, Jim decided to write a letter to Bea and to each of his sons to update them about his trip to England on a B24.

As soon as Jim finished writing three letters, he sat back and thought about everything from his childhood to his police career and his current assignment. If only his grandfather could see him now. Whatever Jim thought he knew about race relations before he met Al Parker, paled in comparison to how he felt after working for the last year with the bravest Negro cop he ever met in his life. The fact that Jim had gone to the university meant that he had more of a formal education than the average policeman who served in the decades leading up to WWII.

When he combined his life experience with his education and his faith, Jim knew that even though it would be impossible for one man to right the wrongs of the past, he believed that he had to give a good account of himself or risk damnation, especially if by some ironic twist of fate Almighty God turned out to be colored.

While Al Parker drifted back and forth between a rather peaceful nap, he periodically peaked through a partially opened eye lid to see if his commanding officer was still writing his memoirs or letters to his loved ones. After all of their time together, Al Parker had come to know that James Beauregard was a decent man who was torn between wanting to do the right thing and feeling hopeless that he was powerless to change the way that society handled racial issues. If anything, Al knew that Jim Beauregard had the more difficult job because white officers who commanded colored troops, with the exception of General Black Jack Pershing, were rarely remembered in history. Al also knew that Jim Beauregard was a good man, a good cop and a good Army officer who preferred to lead soldiers in battle than serve as a CID Agent.

It was also obvious to anyone who paid attention, that Jim Beauregard and Al Parker had become good friends long before they stepped foot on the B24 to make their way to Europe. A great deal of water had passed under the bridge, as the saying goes, since circumstances beyond their control brought them to work together. It was also not Jim Beauregard's fault that Al Parker was not offered a commission as an officer, when the Army allowed a Negro New York City Patrolman to be inducted into the Army to assist him in hunting down Ivan Larson and Shorty Mc Ghee.

While Al rested his head up against the musette bag that he used for a pillow, he couldn't help but think of all that had transpired up to this point in their investigation. Here he was a policeman, on a military leave, flying across the Atlantic Ocean in late December of 1944, on what was without a doubt the most important manhunt in the history of the U.S. Army and the New York City Police Department.

As Al folded his arms, he felt good about his decision to enlist and go after the men who murdered his friend and robbed the Lincoln Savings Bank in Brooklyn. Even though everyone recognized his heroism during the robbery that took young Patrick's life, Al felt responsible for what happened to his young friend. Not a day went by when Al didn't relive the shooting outside the Lincoln Savings Bank and blame himself for not being able to get to Pat Murphy Jr. before he bled to death on a sidewalk in Brooklyn.

As far as Al was concerned, he wasn't coming home until Ivan Larson and Francis Shorty Mc Ghee were taken into custody. Even if they were officially listed as being captured by the enemy, Al had no intentions of returning to the United States, until he exhausted his search for the two fugitives, even if he had to remain in Europe until the war was over to do so.

As Captain Vincent Galloway turned to his co pilot he smiled coyly then said, "Well....was I right or what?"

While shaking his head from side to side, his co pilot put his right hand into his shirt pocket and pulled out a dollar bill. After handing the dollar to Captain Galloway, the co pilot remarked, "I'm impressed, you found England."

Vince Galloway was like many young military pilots who was anxious to get into combat as quickly as possible. It was also typical of Army life that many of the men flying the transport planes wanted to be fighter, or bomber pilots and almost no one wanted the reverse to be true. Military pilots also had a love hate relationship between flying "milk runs" as the less dangerous missions were called and the missions that involved going deeper behind enemy lines. In the end, with rare exception, everyone did what was expected of them, regardless of the risks involved.

Whether it was his fate, or simply the luck of the draw, his original orders to report to the Pacific were changed at the last minute. Instead of fighting the Japanese, Captain Galloway and his crew were assigned to serve in Europe over German occupied territory. After crossing the Atlantic in record time, Captain Galloway and his co pilot delivered several sacks of mail, some badly needed aircraft parts, two generals, one Colonel, as well as a Major from CID and his Negro partner to England in a brand new B24 that was slated to become a replacement ship in the 8th Air Force.

On December 24th 1944, a much smaller but nevertheless very dramatic re-supply mission was carried out by the U.S. Army Air Corps when a small single engine ·L4 spotter plane was used to fly a badly needed supply of penicillin and Major

Howard P. Serrell MD from the 4th Surgical Group into Bastogne to help with the wounded.[4] Despite the efforts of the German Army and Air Force, the American G.I.s in Bastogne were holding on by a thread. Being resupplied by the air was the lifeline that enabled the American ground forces in the encircled areas to resist being completely overrun.

After using their priority transportation orders to hitch a ride on a B24 that was converted to carry passengers, Jim Beauregard and Al Parker arrived in London at 1430 hours on December 24, 1944. From the moment they arrived in England the war took on a completely new dimension. England was one big military base where every type and rank of Allied soldier, sailor, airmen, merchant seamen and coast guardsmen was either on leave or contributing to the war effort in some way.

Since they were hoping to arrange immediate air transportation to France, Major Beauregard and Sergeant Parker proceeded by staff car to the Supreme Headquarters Allied Forces Europe, otherwise known as SHAFE before going to the CID Office in Picadilly. In an effort to try and make some conversation with the two American CID Agents, Corporal Irene Fletcher politely asked, "Will you and the Sergeant be staying in London long, Sir?

After quickly lighting a cigarette, Major Beauregard leaned forward as he put his pack of cigarettes away and said, "I hope not, Corporal."

As soon as he saw the attractive British corporal not know how to react to his rather cut and dry response, Major Beauregard leaned forward again and said, "I'm sorry, Corporal, I didn't mean it to sound like that. It's just that Sergeant Parker and I are hoping to fly across the Channel as soon as possible."

Corporal Fletcher proved that she took no offense to the Major's comment about their need to get to mainland Europe when she smiled and said, "I understand, Sir, but it's a shame that you and the Sergeant are planning to leave so soon. London is a wonderful place to spend Christmas."

While looking out the side window of the American made Army sedan, Jim did his best to sound like a much nicer guy when he cracked a smile then said, "I'm sure it is."

While Corporal Fletcher drove the khaki colored Ford sedan past a convoy of U.S. Army trucks heading to a Channel port, Al Parker produced a Hershey Bar and peeled back the wrapper as he leaned forward and said, "Excuse me, Corporal. Would you care for some chocolate?"

Smiling wide at the sight of the most famous American chocolate in the war torn world, Corporal Fletcher held the wheel with one hand as she eagerly accepted the Hershey bar and said, "Thank you, Sergeant." After breaking off a piece of chocolate and slipping it into her mouth, Corporal Fletcher paused to savor the wonderful taste of the perfect American treat.

In an effort to find out more about the war news, Sergeant Parker leaned forward and said, "Excuse me again, Corporal, but the Major and I have been traveling and are a little outta touch with the war. All we know is that the Germans launched a major offensive in the Ardennes on the 16th. Any word on how things are going?"

Corporal Fletcher waited until she changed lanes to respond to Al Parker's question. "From what I know, Sergeant, things seem to be going somewhat better than they were a few days ago."

As soon as Major Beauregard tapped his cigarette ash into the car's ashtray, he spoke in a rather sarcastic tone and said, "So much for the war being over by Christmas."

While Corporal Fletcher continued driving, the friendly 20 year old British corporal remarked, "Right you are, Sir," before she added, "I also know that your 101st Airborne boys are still surrounded in Bastogne but at least they're starting to get re-supplied by air."

After slipping another small piece of chocolate into her mouth, Corporal Fletcher held the remaining portion of the Hershey bar up in the air as she said, "Thank you for the chocolate, Sergeant."

While Al Parker wondered what the G.I.s on the front line were going through, he responded to the British Corporal's comment by saying, "You'd be doing me a favor, Corporal if you'd eat the rest of that Hershey Bar for me. I've had a few too many on the way over if you know what I mean."

In an effort to back up what his partner had to say, Jim Beauregard spoke up and said, "Trust me, Corporal, Sergeant Parker is telling you the truth. It's a miracle his uniform still fits after all the chocolate he put away on the way over."

Satisfied that she was being lady like enough, Corporal Fletcher tucked the remains of the luscious chocolate bar in her uniform jacket pocket as she said, "You convinced me, Sir. If you don't mind, Sergeant, I'll save the rest for later.

As soon as Corporal Fletcher reached the building that housed Supreme Headquarters Allied Expeditionary Force, she pulled the Army sedan over to the curb and said, "Here we are, Sir, Supreme Allied Headquarters."

While Al Parker picked up his musette bag he thanked the Corporal for the ride.

"That goes for me too, Corporal," remarked Jim Beauregard as he buttoned his Army officer's trench coat and retrieved his attache case from the seat of the Army sedan.

Being a well trained military driver, Corporal Fletcher wasted no time in exiting the vehicle and opening the rear door as the two American CID Agents stepped out of the sedan and walked over to the trunk to retrieve their luggage. After opening the boot, as the trunk of a car is called in England, Corporal Fletcher snapped to attention and saluted Major Beauregard as Sergeant Parker removed their bags from the staff car. As the Major returned the salute, he cracked a smile then said, "You have a Merry Christmas, Corporal and that's an order." While Jim picked up his Army issued luggage, Al Parker also wished the British Corporal a Merry Christmas as she returned to her duties behind the wheel of the car.

While the staff car pulled away from the curb, both men turned and faced Supreme Allied Headquarters. After facing his partner Jim spoke first. "We've come a long way, Al."

"We sure have, Major," responded Al.

After looking around to make sure that no one could hear what he had to say, Jim leaned closer to Al and said, "I'd appreciate it, Al, if you called me Jim when we're alone. After all, we're really just two cops wearing Army uniforms."

As soon as Al cracked a smile then said, "That would be my pleasure, Jim," Jim Beauregard picked up his bag and walked toward the entrance to Supreme Headquarters Allied Expeditionary Force (SHAFE) with his partner by his side.

The last thing that anyone at SHAFE had time for, was a Major from CID and his Negro partner seeking priority air transportation to mainland Europe so they could pursue two fugitives. The situation came to a head, when a young staff officer suggested that the Major and his partner enjoy the rest of the holiday season in England and return to SHAFE for assistance after the fighting in the Ardennes subsided.

As soon as his partner stood up, Al Parker knew the young captain was in trouble when Jim Beauregard pointed his right index finger at the staff officer's chest and said, "Captain, I'm in no mood for your rear area concern for my health. My partner and I have priority orders signed by the Secretary of War to travel anywhere we need to go, by any means, at any time, including in a forward area in order to perform our duties. My partner and I came here for some assistance and if we don't get it I'll have Sergeant Parker place you under arrest for obstructing a criminal investigation. We will then escort you in handcuffs to General Eisenhower's Christmas Party, so you can explain how you intend to plead at your Courts Martial. Do you understand?"

After hearing what the Major from Army CID had to say, the Captain swallowed hard before he responded. "Yes, Sir."

"That's better," remarked Major Beauregard while he straightened the young officer's tie before he continued. "Sergeant Parker and I require the fastest available air transportation to Paris."

As soon as the nervous Captain limited his response to a simple, "Yes, Sir," Jim added, "We also need a priority message sent to the CID Office in Paris to alert Lt. Colonel Walter Vogel that we arrived in England and will be traveling to France on the first available air transportation."

Once again the Captain sounded like a team player when he responded and said, "Yes, Sir. Right away, Sir."

After turning to face his partner, Jim sounded considerably less formal when he said, "Anything else, Al?"

Under the circumstances, Al played his part perfectly as he stood at a comfortable attention and said, "The Major covered everything, Sir."

Jim Beauregard had been a cop long enough to know how to be a hard ass one minute and a nice guy the next. After changing his demeanor, the Major continued to address the nervous Captain who appeared to be anxious to leave. "Sergeant Parker and I will remain here and have a smoke while you handle this matter for us." Without wasting any time, the Captain presented Major Beauregard with a snappy salute before he pivoted around smartly and left to complete his assignment.

The moment the Captain left the room, Jim Beauregard looked at Al Parker and smiled as he removed a pack of smokes from his pants pocket and remarked, "I said it before and I'll say it again, Al. I guess I picked up a few bad habits while working with the New York City Police Department." While Al began to puff on a freshly lit White Owl cigar, he broke out in a combined smokers cough and hearty laugh, as Jim Beauregard used his Zippo lighter to light his Lucky Strike cigarette.

Since no one else was around Al Parker leaned his chair up against the wall and assumed a comfortable position as he teased the man who was his partner and his commanding officer. "And you call yourself a gentlemen from the South."

After exhaling some cigarette smoke, Jim smiled again, then spoke with an overemphasized Southern accent as he remarked, "Only by an act of your Yankee Congress."

Even though they were under a great deal of pressure, Jim Beauregard and Al Parker enjoyed a good laugh at the young Captain's expense. As both men settled down, they looked at each other the way good friends do.

While speaking in a sincere tone of voice, Jim looked directly at his partner and said, "Maybe there's hope for this world yet, Al." Al Parker knew exactly what Jim Beauregard was trying to say and the feeling was mutual.

CHAPTER 4

I'M DREAMING OF
A WHITE CHRISTMAS

On December 25, 1944 Jim Beauregard and Al Parker woke up after a few hours of sleep and found the entire air base at Membury, England covered in a sheet of ice and snow. While Al Parker looked out the window at the winter storm all he could say was, "I thought New York had some lousy weather but this place takes the cake."

While Jim stood next to his partner and watched the snow continue to fall, he sounded just as disappointed when he remarked, "You said it." Like it or not, Jim Beauregard and Al Parker had no choice but to face the fact, that in addition to the war getting in their way, the weather was preventing the two representatives from the New York CID Task Force from traveling to France.

Although it was highly unusual for a white officer and a Negro sergeant to room together, the fact that they arrived after hours with travel orders signed by the War Department and Supreme Headquarters Allied Forces Europe (SHAFE) was ample reason to make special arrangements for the two CID Agents to be billeted for one night in an empty room at the base hospital.

The moment they arrived at the Operations Office, it was easy to tell by the lack of activity, that the U.S. Army Air Forces had the day off because of bad weather. Even two ground pounding flat foots like Jim Beauregard and Al Parker knew that Army pilots would not be allowed to fly on a day like this. After identifying themselves and stating the reason for their early morning visit, the Duty Officer promised to check the weather forecast for the rest of the day while they waited.

While the Armed Forces Radio played Bing Crosby's popular recording, "I'll Be Home For Christmas," Jim Beauregard stared out the window and thought of Beatrice and the boys. Nothing on the face of this earth gave him more happiness than watching his wife and sons open their presents on Christmas Eve or Christmas Day, depending of course on when he was off. For men like Jim Beauregard and Al Parker, the holidays usually evolved around the shifts they worked at the police department. Because the war made it impossible for most soldiers to be with their families on December 25, 1944, every G.I. in a far off land was forced to rely on their memories to get them though the day. It wasn't easy.

Once the Major took an extra moment to think of his family back home and his two sons, his thoughts drifted back to the business at hand. As an Agent with Army CID, Jim Beauregard saw Ivan Larson and Shorty Mc Ghee as the enemy long before he set his sights on the Germans or the Japanese. It was twice as frustrating for Jim to consider, that he and his partner were closer to capturing Ivan Larson and Francis Shorty Mc Ghee than ever before and their manhunt was now delayed due to bad weather.

While millions of Allied servicemen were locked in armed combat with the forces of evil, Jim and his partner were trying to bring two fugitives to justice in the middle of a world war. Their job was twice as frustrating when you consider that Jim Beauregard and Al Parker were finally making some real progress in their investigation when Mother Nature decided to side with the enemy.

Under the circumstances his prayer was short and sweet. While Jim looked out the frost covered window in the operations office, he closed his eyes and said. "They're bad men, Lord, and they deserve to be brought to justice." The moment Jim opened his eyes, he looked up into the snow filled sky and spoke just above a whisper as he concluded his prayer by saying, "Happy Birthday, Lord."

When the duty officer handed Al Parker the teletype message, Jim turned to see what was going on and said, "What's up, Al?"

With the look of disappointment on his face and the message in hand, Al Parker approached Jim Beauregard and said, "It's the weather report for England, Sir. I'm afraid it's bad news."

As luck would have it, their flight from Membury to France was grounded by the worst ice storm to hit England in recorded history.[5] Even a corporal from a family of gangsters in Chicago, who generally had no use for cops, felt sorry for the two CID Agents after hearing the reason for their presence at Membury. Robbing a bank was one thing, but killing a father of five and a New York City cop who served on Guadalcanal was something that no self respecting gangster would do and live to brag about in the windy city.

After having a private conversation with the duty officer, Corporal Anthony Lamberti approached the Major from Army CID and his Negro partner. While speaking in a respectful tone that was laced with an obvious Midwest accent, Corporal Lamberti said, "Excuse me, Sir, but if you and the Sergeant are hungry I can have some chow brought over from the mess hall?"

The thought of eating a decent meal while they waited for the weather to break sounded like an excellent idea, especially since Jim Beauregard knew that he and Al Parker would not be able to eat together in the mess hall. As Major Beauregard turned to Al and asked, "How 'bout some breakfast, Al?"

Since they weren't going anywhere and they needed to eat, Al Parker nodded his head in agreement and said, "That sounds like a good idea to me, Sir."

As much as Al Parker resented the fact that the Army treated enemy prisoners with more respect than American Negro soldiers, he appreciated the diplomatic way the air operations staff was trying to avoid having to remind a colored military police sergeant assigned to CID that he was not good enough to dine with white G.I.s of the same rank. The fact that the Corporal was a city kid seemed to help Al accept his kind offer in the right frame of mind.

Although he couldn't be sure, Al was fairly certain that the corporal was not a racist and could care less if a colored sergeant ate breakfast with white soldiers. It also became quite obvious that Corporal Lamberti was prompted by his superior officer to arrange for the special delivery of food, when the corporal turned to the duty officer and called out, "That's a roger on breakfast, Sir." As the duty officer shook his head in disgust, he picked up the phone to call in the order, while Corporal Lamberti saluted Major Beauregard then smiled and said, "I'll make sure they toss in some extra chow for you and the Sergeant, Sir."

It was moments like this that restored Al Parker's faith in mankind and gave him hope that one day all men would truly be considered equal. Even Jim Beauregard was appreciative when he returned the salute and remarked in a very sincere tone, "Thank you, Corporal. My partner and I haven't eaten much lately. We could definitely use a good meal."

Being a tough kid from Chicago, Anthony Lamberti couldn't resist and remarked, "I didn't say it would be good, Sir, just plenty of it." With that, the Italian American corporal who had as many relatives behind bars as he did in the

U.S. Army, grinned from ear to ear as he walked back to his desk and picked up the phone to call the mess hall.

After surviving the June 6, 1944 D Day Invasion Lt. Lenny Tucker and his crew participated in Operation Market Garden. Unfortunately, the C47 named Old Virginia was shot down after towing a GC-4A Waco glider to a landing zone in Holland.

When his co pilot was killed in action, Lt. Tucker along with his radio operator and his crew chief jumped clear of the flaming transport plane and evaded capture, even though they were all wounded. Fortunately, Lt. Tucker and his surviving crew members were rescued by members of the Dutch Resistance. After being transported to the safety of the Allied lines, Lenny Tucker spent the next three months receiving medical care and rehabilitation before being released for reassignment.

As soon as his father heard that his son survived being shot down in Holland, Lt. Tucker was once again a hometown hero who was secretly being groomed for a position in the state house of representatives or Congress after the war. With orders in hand to report to a Troop Carrier Squadron in the China Burma India (CBI) Theater of Operation, Lt. Tucker shocked his father when he called and said, "I've decided not to come home." After hearing his father rant and rage about all the trouble he went through to plan a parade in his honor, Lenny Tucker thought about the day he had to leave Carl Guliver in the burning cockpit of his C47 and bail out without him over Holland.

According to the crew chief's statement to air intelligence officers, Lt. Tucker refused to leave the pilot's seat until every option was exhausted to get Lt. Guliver out of the aircraft. Despite the presence of a raging fire that was spreading through the cargo bay into the cockpit, Lt. Tucker continued to hold his plane steady, while Sergeant Hathaway and the radio operator tried to move the severely wounded Lt. Guliver out of the co-pilot's seat.

The scene that followed was right out of a war movie, when Lenny Tucker and his crew ignored their own wounds and did everything possible to convince Carl Guliver that he could make it. While the seconds passed like hours, the blood soaked Carl Guliver accepted his fate. Seeing Lenny Tucker and the other crewmen hesitate to leave without him, brought Carl Guliver to speak up and say, "I'm hit pretty bad, Len. That last burst of flak ripped me to shreds. You boys better go on without me."

With tears in his eyes, a wounded Lenny Tucker patted his co pilot on the arm as he joined the crew chief and their radio operator by the emergency escape hatch. After telling the radioman and the crew chief to jump, Lenny looked up front one last time just as Carl Guliver's head slumped to the side. A second later Lenny Tucker was free falling away from the C47 that exploded in mid air, when the aircraft was hit with another burst of German anti aircraft fire. As soon as his parachute filled with air, Lt. Tucker's body received the traditional jolt as he descended to the ground below.

Lenny Tucker blamed himself for Carl Guliver's death, because he made the decision as the senior pilot on board, to fly through a wall of intense ground fire, so his crew could deliver a glider full of thirteen men to the right landing zone. When others flinched at the sight of a sky full of enemy anti aircraft fire, Lenny Tucker embraced the grim reaper as if they were old friends.

While his crew thought that Lenny Tucker was the bravest SOB they ever met, others who studied him closely thought that he had a death wish because he was raised by a man that he called judge instead of dad or father. Either way, Lenny Tucker ended up with a chest full of medals and ribbons to go along with his sterling reputation as a combat pilot, even though he had a reputation of never being anyone's friend.

It took two combat missions over war torn Europe for Lenny Tucker to realize that he wanted to be a hero for all the wrong reasons. It was almost as if the mission over Holland was a key that opened the door to a scary place in the attic of his mind, that would take him on a difficult journey, one that would eventually help change his life for the better. Although it took a while for his eyes to adjust to a new outlook on life, the day finally came when Lenny Tucker was no longer a prisoner of his past.

Up until the moment that his life changed for the better, Lenny Tucker was a scared little boy who grew up and became a man under the tutelage of an over-bearing and abusive father. Even the lashings he got as a kid turned out to be an opportunity to prove himself when his father complimented him for taking his medicine like a man. While other boys in town were being congratulated for doing well in school and doing their chores, Lenny Tucker only heard words of praise when he failed to cry after being thrashed to an inch of his life. As bizarre as it sounded to him now, Lenny knew that he had intentionally provoked his father just so he could hear him say something nice. Simply put, it was a sick way for a kid to grow up.

The more Lenny Tucker looked back in time, the more he understood why he turned out to be a pretentious snob, who behaved as if he was ordained by the legacy of his Confederate heritage to become a war hero. While other boys made friends easily, Lenny Tucker found it almost impossible to share himself with others. His life was further complicated by the fact that his father was the one of the most famous and feared elected officials in Virginia.

While on the outside it looked as if he had been blessed with a wonderful life, in reality, Lenny Tucker was raised in the presence of cigar smoking red neck politicians who drank to excess and had their way with beautiful young black women, while in public they acted like the social conscience of the community. Although it took two combat missions to make a man of Lenny Tucker, once he made the transformation he began to see things as they really are.

Although he never realized it when he was growing up, Lenny Tucker was actually quite powerful because he knew all the secrets of the political machine in Richmond. In addition to what he was privy to when he waited on his father and his entourage during their weekly card games, Lenny would sneak down the stairs and listen to his father and his cronies plot and plan their future during their more sinister meetings. Naturally, he heard things that were not meant for his ears or for public consumption. As such, he grew up in a home where substance had very little meaning. If something translated to more votes it was good. If something meant less votes it was bad. Life for Lenny Tucker became one big election where all that mattered was winning.

With no mother to raise him and put some balance in his life, Lenny learned to cope by becoming a martinet and member of his father's political machine. Even though his life was far from normal, Lenny Tucker began to enjoy being patted on the back by everyone in Richmond because he was the son of the most powerful man in town. In time, Lenny Tucker learned to play the game to get what he wanted.

By the time Lenny became a teenager he knew that he was bulletproof because of his family lineage. For the first time in his life, being his father's son meant something to him, albeit what he was feeling was the evil benefit of having power over the less fortunate. When Lenny Tucker entered college his father's wish was his command. The fact that he had no friends or fun in life was unimportant. All that mattered was that Lenny Tucker was a chip off the old block, who lived his life according to his father's master plan for his future. By the time Lenny graduated from a famous military school and he entered the University of Virginia, he was convinced, that with rare exception, everyone else was beneath him.

After listening to his father carry on about all the work that went into planning a homecoming celebration for his war hero son, Lenny spoke in a very low voice and said, "My co pilot Lt. Carl Guliver should be given a parade not me."

The moment Lt. Tucker heard his father say, "Well, bring him along if you like," he felt like a free man when he put the phone down on the receiver and walked away without looking back. That was the last time they spoke.

With his orders in hand to report to the China Burma India (CBI) Theater of Operation after the first of the year, Lt. Tucker decided to enjoy his stateside flying duties as a relief pilot with a troop carrier squadron at Laurinburg-Maxton Army Air Field. As far as Lenny Tucker was concerned, flying the mail was just as important as delivering combat supplies to the front lines, because soldiers looked forward to receiving letters and packages from home. This was especially the case over the holidays. In fact, Lenny was such a changed man after the Holland mission, he eagerly volunteered to fly an early morning run, so troops on nearby bases would receive their mail from home in time for Christmas.

As much as he was enjoying his stateside assignment, Lenny Tucker was anxious to get back in action. With his promotion to Captain expected to take place before he left for the CBI, Lenny Tucker was once again deep in thought, while he flew from base to base delivering sacks of mail and several thousand copies of The Stars and Stripes Newspaper.

After making the last delivery, Lenny and his crew headed back to the barn, as they referred to their base, to enjoy the rest of the day off. Once he leveled off, Lenny gave his rookie co pilot a chance to get in some stick time, while he accepted a cup of coffee and a copy of The Stars and Stripes from his crew chief. The second Lt. Tucker unfolded the Army newspaper and began reading the front page he couldn't believe his eyes.

Even though he could be wrong, there was something about the artist rendition of the fugitive identified as Francis Shorty Mc Ghee that made Lenny Tucker wonder if the glider pilot who was pointed out to him in Texas was one in the same man. Despite the fact that Lenny Tucker read about this case before, there was something different about the most recent set of composite sketches, that were featured in the latest edition of The Stars and Stripes, that made the Lieutenant feel compelled to contact the military police.

To convince himself that his suspicions were correct, Lt. Tucker used his pencil to draw a mustache on the face of the composite sketch of the fugitive who he believed resembled the glider pilot called Shorty. "Add a mustache and a shaved head to this sketch and this has to be him," remarked Lt. Tucker, as he showed his co pilot the latest issue of The Stars and Stripes and said, "There was a glider pilot in Texas who looked a lot like the person depicted on this wanted poster. They even called him Shorty."

"I read about those guys, remarked his co pilot, who quickly added, "They killed a cop during a bank robbery in New York."

Given the seriousness of the situation Lenny Tucker felt obligated to contact the military authorities. As their plane flew on a heading that would take them back to base, Lenny tuned to his co pilot and said, "Once we get clearance to land ask the tower to have an MP meet us on the ramp." Once his co pilot acknowledged the order, Lt. Tucker sat back in the pilot's seat and continued reading the article about the ongoing manhunt for the two fugitives who were reportedly hiding out in the Army under assumed names.

CHAPTER 5

A WITNESS WORTH LISTENING TO COMES FORWARD

A s soon as Lieutenant Pat Reilly from Army CID in North Carolina completed his interview of Lt. Lenny Tucker, he placed a call to the New York CID Office and spoke to the duty agent. After introducing himself to Investigator Sal Jacobi, Agent Reilly said, "I just finished interviewing a C47 pilot by the name of Lieutenant Leonard Tucker. Lt. Tucker believes there's a strong resemblance between a glider pilot he observed at the Advanced Glider School at South Plains Army Air Field earlier this year and the fugitive known as Francis Shorty Mc Ghee."

"That's great, Lieutenant" remarked Sal, who quickly asked a follow-up question. "What name is Mc Ghee using?"

The moment Sal Jacobi heard Agent Reilly begin to answer the question, he could tell by the sound of his voice that the CID Agent from North Carolina had bad news to report. "The glider pilot known to Lieutenant Tucker as Shorty was never fully identified to him. According to Lieutenant Tucker, his co pilot pointed a glider pilot out to him who hated to be called Shorty when they were preparing to leave Texas to take part in Operation Overlord."

Sal followup question was predictable. "What about his co pilot? Is he available to be interviewed?"

When Agent Reilly informed the New York duty agent that Lt. Carl Guliver was killed during Operation Market Garden, the New York DA's Office Investigator sounded sincere when he remarked, "I'm sorry to hear that."

As Agent Reilly continued, he informed Sal Jacobi that if it wasn't for the fact that Lt. Tucker was rescued by the Dutch Resistance they wouldn't be having this conversation. Even though Sal Jacobi was a civilian law enforcement officer and not a soldier, he was well aware of the fact that members of numerous resistance units were helping the Allies in a number of ways, including by rescuing downed

Allied air crews and escaping prisoners of war. He proved it when he remarked, "Thank God for the Dutch Resistance. Those folks do good work."

While Agent Reilly checked his notes, he continued his telephonic briefing in a very professional fashion. "Lt. Tucker also stated that the pilot he knew as Shorty was having a hard time cutting the mustard as a glider pilot and was reportedly reassigned to engineering duties. I should also mention, that based on what I was able to find out, the personnel who ran the Advanced Glider School in Lubbock, Texas in the early and mid part of this year have been reassigned and will take some time to track down."

After hearing Agent Reilly's last comment, Sal proved that he knew the significance of obtaining the necessary records from the Army Air Forces as soon as possible when he remarked, "Hopefully, we can get our hands on those records before the war's over."

When Agent Reilly continued, he informed the New York duty agent that even though there were two other glider pilots in this school who were called Shorty, Lt. Tucker is about as certain as a person can be that there's a strong resemblance between the man his co pilot pointed out to him in Texas and the latest composite sketch of the fugitive identified as Francis Shorty Mc Ghee.

When Sal asked about Ivan Larson, Agent Reilly knew that question was coming and said, "According to Lieutenant Tucker, he had very little if any personal contact with the glider pilots who were going through training at South Plains Army Airfield in Texas. That said, he seems pretty confident about being able to help identify the fugitive known as Francis Shorty Mc Ghee. The Lieutenant also wants us to know that even though there is a resemblance between the glider pilot trainee called Shorty and Francis Shorty Mc Ghee, the pilot who was pointed out to him at South Plains Army Air Field had a shaved head and a mustache."

As tempted as he was to continue his telephone conversation with Agent Reilly, Sal Jacobi decided to cut to the chase and said, "Lieutenant, you've just given our entire unit the best Christmas present any of us have ever received."

"I'm just a messenger but I'm glad I could help," responded Agent Reilly.

Sal Jacobi was an experienced investigator who knew exactly what needed to be done to move this ball forward. "I hate to ask you to keep working on Christmas, Lieutenant, but we'll need to send a copy of your debriefing report to two CID Agents from our office who are looking for the two fugitives on air bases in France. I'm also sure that Colonel Richmond will want us to interview Lt. Tucker as soon as possible. Is there any way you can have Lt. Tucker flown up to the Naval Air Station New York, which is also known as Floyd Bennett Field, either later today or in the morning? As soon as the Lieutenant lands, we can have him interviewed at the Police Department Aviation Unit."

As a U.S. Treasury Agent, who was now serving in Army CID, Lt. Pat Reilly knew the significance of this case and sounded like a man with a "can do" attitude when he said, "I'll get back to you as soon as I know how fast I can get Lt. Tucker up to New York. I'll also send a copy of my report up to New York with Lt. Tucker."

"Thanks, Lieutenant," responded Sal who quickly added, "I look forward to hearing from you."

After finishing his conversation with Agent Reilly, the Jewish American Investigator from the District Attorney's Office, who volunteered to serve as the duty agent on Christmas day, picked up the phone and called Lt. Colonel Richmond. As soon as he briefed the Colonel about his conversation with Agent Reilly, Sal was instructed to contact Captain Murphy and Andy Dubrowsky, while the Colonel called Agent Reilly to make sure that Lt. Tucker's travel orders to New York were expedited.

At 1703 hours on December 25, 1944 a khaki colored C47 transport plane landed at Floyd Bennett Field in Brooklyn and taxied over to the New York City Police Department Aviation Unit tie down area. While Pat Murphy Sr. and Andy Dubrowsky stood on the freezing cold ramp, Sal Jacobi said, "I'll get the car, Captain."

While Sal walked over to the line of cars that were parked on the side of the hangar, Andy spoke in a raised voice as the C47 taxied over to the police aviation unit. "He's right on time."

As Captain Murphy turned to face Andy, he also spoke loud enough to be heard over the sound of the radial engines. "Fred Richmond pulled some strings and got Lt. Tucker assigned to fly himself up to New York so we could speak to him as soon as possible. The Lieutenant is also bringing us a copy of Agent Reilly's report."

As soon as the C47 came to a stop and the engines were shut down, the crew chief opened the cargo door and put the step ladder in position. Once the crew stepped down from the aircraft, Lt. Tucker approached the two men wearing civilian clothes who looked like cops and said, "Lt. Tucker reporting as ordered." Immediately after Andy Dubrowsky produced his FBI credentials and identified himself, he introduced Lt. Tucker to Captain Pat Murphy Sr from the New York City Police Department.

When a car driven by Sal Jacobi pulled up and came to a stop, Captain Murphy addressed Lt. Tucker and his crew in a very friendly fashion. "Unless you gentlemen have other plans, you'll be guests of the New York City Police Department during your stay with us. While Agent Dubrowsky and I interview Lt. Tucker, Sal Jacobi from the DA's Office will take the rest of you to the Herald Square Hotel and get you checked in. As soon as we're finished, we'll join you for dinner and some Christmas cheer."

As soon as Lt. Tucker faced his crew and said, "Like the Captain said, we'll meet up later on," his co-pilot, radio operator and crew chief grabbed their overnight bags and got into the Ford sedan that was driven by Sal Jacobi.

While the CID car drove away, Andy Dubrowsky gestured toward the aviation unit hangar and said, "This way, Lieutenant."

Once they got settled in the empty briefing room, Lieutenant Tucker produced an envelope and said, "Lieutenant Reilly asked me to give this to you, Sir."

While Andy Dubrowsky thanked the young pilot for delivering a copy of his debriefing report, Lt. Tucker remembered what Lieutenant Reilly told him about the search for the two fugitives.

When Captain Murphy asked Lenny Tucker if he would like a cup of hot coffee, the highly decorated Army aviator sounded genuinely sincere when he said, "Thank you, Captain, but first permit me to offer my condolences. Agent Reilly told me that your youngest son was the police officer who was killed in that bank robbery in Brooklyn. I hope what little I know can help bring these wanted men to justice."

After thanking Lt. Tucker for his kind words and for his assistance in this matter, Captain Murphy filled three cups with black coffee.

As soon as Andy finished reviewing the well written report, he looked at Lenny Tucker and said, "Before we start I just want you to know how much we appreciate you coming forward."

"I'm glad I can help, Sir," responded the incredibly polite Army pilot, who felt obligated to come forward to help locate a fugitive who was hiding out in the U.S. Army.

After placing a coffee cup in front of Andy and their witness, Captain Murphy sat across from Lt. Tucker, while Andy sat on the Lieutenant's left side at the head of the table. Before Andy began the interview, he took a sip of coffee then said, "Lieutenant, before we go over the statement that you gave to Agent Reilly, can you explain why you are reluctant to identify the C47 Pilot who was friends with the pilot identified as Shorty. I assure you, Lieutenant, we really need to know who this pilot is."

While Lieutenant Tucker looked at Andy Dubrowsky, he answered the question in the most direct fashion possible. "I had personal reasons for not doing so, Sir." Then, after pausing for a split second, Lt. Tucker sounded as if he was being sincerely honest when he continued and said, "I'm sorry, Sir, but I thought I did my duty by coming forward to tell you as much as I could about the glider pilot, who resembles one of the fugitives depicted on the front page of the The Stars and Stripes Newspaper."

"You did, Lieutenant," responded Agent Dubrowsky who quickly added, "But if you know more, we need to know what that is."

After taking a sip of coffee, Lt. Tucker looked across the table at Captain Murphy before he faced Agent Dubrowsky and said, "The Army officer I was reluctant to identify is Lieutenant William Davis but everyone calls him Billy Davis."

As soon as Captain Murphy quickly jotted down what Lt. Tucker said, he repeated the information for accuracy purposes and said, "Lieutenant William Davis."

"That's correct," responded Lt. Tucker.

After taking a quick sip of coffee, Andy remarked, "Please continue, Lieutenant."

While speaking in a sincere tone of voice, Lt. Tucker continued with his statement. "The reason I didn't want to identify this particular Army officer is because it's well known that I did not get along with Lieutenant Davis." Even though it wasn't easy to say, Lt. Tucker quickly added, "You see, Sir, I wasn't very popular and Lt. Davis...well, he was."

In order to explain himself even further, Lt. Tucker continued, and said, "To be more specific, Sir, I was afraid that if I was wrong about this glider pilot being your fugitive, that people would think I was pulling a prank that was in very poor taste on Lt. Davis. I felt this way because according to Lt. Guliver, the pilot identified to me as Shorty was friends with Billy Davis."

After hearing what Lt. Tucker had to say, Andy nodded his head up and down before he remarked, "Even if we don't have all the details about your past difficulties with Lt. Davis, I accept your explanation, Lieutenant."

While Lt. Tucker appeared relieved that he finally divulged this information, he sat back in his chair and said, "Thank you, Sir."

When Captain Murphy asked Lieutenant Tucker to describe the relationship between Lt. Davis and the glider pilot who resembles one of the fugitives they're pursuing, the C47 Pilot responded like a man who was considerably more relaxed about being interviewed by an FBI Agent and a police captain. "Before I respond to your question I want to emphasize that Lt. Davis is a highly decorated officer who was temporarily rotated back to the states after flying combat missions overseas. As far as I know, Lt. Davis is now stationed in the ETO. I mention this because I have never heard anything of a derogatory nature said about Lt. Davis. All I know is that my co pilot who was killed during Operation Market Garden told me that Lt. Davis and this Shorty character were Army buddies."

After pausing to light a cigar, Andy Dubrowsky asked their witness if he agreed that it made sense for CID to interview Lt. Davis, to learn more about the person who resembles the fugitive Francis Shorty Mc Ghee?

Without hesitating Lt. Tucker remarked, "Yes, Sir, I do."

As Andy turned and made eye contact with Captain Murphy, all he had to say was, "Pat," for the veteran police captain to pick up where he left off.

While Andy smoked his cigar, Captain Murphy looked across the table and addressed the decorated combat aviator in a very respectful tone of voice when he continued with the interview. "Excuse me, Lieutenant, but can you go over what you heard and observed when Lt. Guliver identified the glider pilot trainee known as Shorty to you."

As soon as Lt. Tucker finished taking a sip from his coffee cup, he responded to Captain Murphy's question as if he was relaying an event that just happened. "The day that Lt. Guliver identified the pilot who was called Shorty to me, we were in our C47 at the Advanced Glider School at South Plains Army Air Field. It was early in the morning on May 22nd, the day that my crew and I were preparing to fly cross country with priority orders to get to England as soon as possible.

Just before take off I was standing by the open cargo door when a jeep pulled up and Carl Guliver said, "That's the guy I was telling you about. The guy who hates to be called Shorty." As soon as I turned around and looked, Lt. Guliver pointed and said," "There he is. The worst glider pilot in the U.S. Army."

After pausing long enough to take another sip from his coffee cup, Lt. Tucker completed his statement by saying, "Sure enough, there was a glider pilot trainee of short stature standing by a jeep outside my aircraft showing Lt. Davis a nasty looking cut that he had on his head.

As soon as Carl yelled, "Hey, Shorty, wreck any gliders lately?" Lt. Davis and the glider pilot who resembles one of your fugitives turned and looked directly at me and Carl. Lt. Davis appeared to be a bit upset and gave Carl the finger. This glider pilot also looked pretty upset as well and said something to Billy Davis, before he put his cap back on his head and stormed off in an obvious huff." Then, after pausing for a split second, Lt. Tucker added, "A few minutes later my crew and I took off for the east coast on our way to England. After flying cross country and across the Atlantic, my crew and I were assigned to tow a glider into Normandy, France."

When Captain Murphy asked if Lt. Guliver ever mentioned anything about the glider pilot called Shorty on any other occasions, Lt. Tucker responded and said, "The first time Carl mentioned anything about this pilot, was when we were getting ready to fly a training mission on Friday, May 19th. It was during this training mission that Carl and I were assigned to tow Major Mike Kirby and Chalk 30 to a landing zone on the outskirts of Lubbock, Texas. During this training mission, Carl Guliver told me that we were towing a glider that was being flown by a pilot who was and I quote, "The worst glider pilot in his class."

After pausing briefly, Lt, Tucker continued and said, "I should add that this pilot also had another nickname. According to Carl, this particular pilot was also called Skinny because he was so worried about being grounded he stopped eating. When we were flying cross country, Carl also mentioned that after this pilot cut his head while recovering a crash landed glider, Lt. Davis wanted to start calling him Stitches. When I heard this I told Carl that this particular pilot had more nicknames than anyone else in the United States Army."

While Captain Murphy continued to take notes, Lt. Tucker apologized for getting ahead of himself and returned to discussing the day when his C47 crew towed the "worst glider pilot" in the class on a training mission in Texas. "As soon as we delivered Chalk 30 to the release point, we could see that the LZ was filled with twenty nine other gliders. Once Chalk 30 cut lose and made its decent we broke off and returned to base. After we landed we didn't hear anything about the outcome of this mission until later that day. When we did get briefed on the results of this training mission, we heard that the glider pilot trainee that I believe may in fact be one of your fugitives, crashed his glider on top of one of the other gliders, then flipped his GC4A over onto the another glider. We also heard that Major Kirby sprained his ankle when he was removed from the wreckage. After he was helped over to a Jeep, Major Kirby had a heart to heart talk with this Shorty character while a medic waited to transport the Major to the hospital."

With his pen and paper in hand and ready to write, Captain Murphy asked the Lieutenant if he could identify the medic." After hearing the question, Lt. Tucker responded in an apologetic tone of voice when he said, "I don't know his first name, Captain. All I know is that he was called Doc Keller."

When Andy Dubrowsky asked Lt. Tucker why a poorly rated pilot would be allowed to continue to fly, Lt. Tucker looked at the two investigators and said, "The simple truth is that not everyone graduates at the top of their class. Major Kirby was also as strict as he was fair. I mention this because the Major was probably giving the pilot who I believe resembles one of your fugitives every opportunity to prove himself."

After pausing for a second to take a sip from his coffee cup, Lt, Tucker continued and said, "According to Lt. Guliver, Lt. Davis had some influence over the Major's decision when it came to deciding the fate of his friend Shorty. You see, Sir, it was common knowledge that Lt. Davis and Major Kirby were good friends ever since they served together during the Invasion of Sicily. Carl also said that based on what he heard, the pilot called Shorty and Skinny did know how to fly. His problem was that he wasn't as comfortable in a glider as he needed to be. This was especially the case, when he had to fly a mission by himself and when he had to land in a landing zone that was filled with a number of crash landed gliders."

While Andy Dubrowsky used a box of matches to re-light his cigar and Captain Murphy continued to take notes, Lieutenant Tucker went on to say, "Making an emergency landing in a small single engine observation aircraft on a long runway, or even in an open field after you lose an engine is one thing, but flying a combat glider in formation and having to land under fire in an LZ that's already filled with other gliders is a horse of a completely different color. Based on what I was told, your fugitive is a capable single engine pilot, who had difficulty judging how to land in a location that was jammed packed with other crash landed gliders."

As soon as Lt. Tucker thanked Captain Murphy for refilling his coffee cup, the C47 pilot took a quick sip before he continued and said, "According to Carl Guliver, Major Kirby wanted to push the pilot called Shorty to his limits, because he was the only glider pilot in his class who had difficulty dealing with the more complicated landing scenarios. This is why Major Kirby scheduled him to fly the tail end charlie position in the formation that day."

Once again Lt. Tucker paused briefly before he continued with his statement. "The Major also knew that the day could come when a glider pilot will have to fly a combat mission without the assistance of a co pilot. This is exactly what happened during Operation Market Garden."

After turning to look at Agent Dubrowsky, Lt. Tucker continued and said, "Lt. Guliver also said that Major Kirby decided to let the pilot called Shorty request a transfer to glider engineering duties with the rank of Warrant Officer. The Major reportedly made this man this offer, because this individual proved to be better at fixing gliders and other equipment than flying gliders."

"This is all very helpful," remarked Andy Dubrowsky. "Please continue, Lieutenant."

After taking another sip of coffee Lt. Tucker picked up where he left off. "To be quite honest, Sir, at the time I had a serious problem with Lt. Davis for interfering in this matter. I felt this way because I believe that any man who is unable to meet the basic standards of any training program should suffer the consequences." After lowering his head for a second, Lt. Tucker continued as he looked back up and said, "Then again, Sir, I never had a friend that I was close enough with, who I would go to bat for the way that Lt. Davis reportedly helped the young pilot who I believe looks like one of your fugitives."

In order to confirm that their witness was confident about what he had to say, Andy Dubrowsky pointed to the front page article on the latest issue of The Stars and Stripes and said, "And you're as sure as you can be that the pilot called Shorty, who was friends with Lt. Davis at South Plains Army Air Field, looks enough like the person depicted on this wanted poster for us to pursue this matter further and confirm his true identity?"

Without hesitating Lt. Tucker sounded completely sure of himself when he responded to the FBI Agent's question. "Yes, Sir, I am, Sir. However, I'm sure that you and Captain Murphy would like to know that while the overall likeness is accurate, the pilot known as Shorty who was pointed out to me in Texas had a shaved head and a mustache. I also need to add, that the pencil sketch of the fugitive called Shorty, that you published in the most recent issue of The Stars and Stripes, looks a lot more like the pilot who was pointed out to me at the glider school in Texas, than the sketches that were published in earlier issues of Stars and Stripes and Yank Magazine. I should also mention, that according to Lt. Guliver, there were two other pilots in the Advanced Glider School at South Plains Army Air Field in May of this year who Billy Davis called Shorty Number 1 and Shorty Number 2. The person I believe you're interested in was called Shorty Number 3."

As Andy leaned forward in his chair, he asked Lt. Tucker if he had anything else to say that might help them locate either one of the two fugitives. When Lt. Tucker responded and said, "I can't think of anything else to say, Sir," Captain Murphy stood up and remarked, "How 'bout some dinner, Lieutenant?"

Outside of eating breakfast and a sandwich on the plane ride to New York, Lenny Tucker missed out on the usual feast that the Army cooks were famous for making available to troops on Christmas Day. As the soft spoken Army officer responded, he looked at the two veteran lawmen who just interviewed him and said, "I guess I could use something to eat, Sir."

As soon as Andy stood up he spoke as he looked at Captain Murphy then over to Lt. Tucker. "After we grab some chow, I'll draft a message that Colonel Richmond can send to the CID Office in Paris. I'll also make arrangements for Lt. Tucker to sit down with a sketch artist in the morning, so we can have new drawings prepared that includes the addition of a shaved head and a mustache on Francis Shorty Mc Ghee's likeness."

While Andy put on his trench coat and hat, he faced Lt. Tucker and tried to sound as upbeat as possible when he addressed their very cooperative witness. "I hope you're hungry and thirsty, Lieutenant because tonight dinner is on the FBI and the drinks are on the New York City Police Department."

By now the rumors were beginning to become a reality for the men in the Troop Carrier Squadrons who would be flying badly needed supplies to the U.S. troops who were surrounded by the enemy in Bastogne. While Shorty paced back and forth, Ivan studied a map of Bastogne and familiarized himself with the area.

After looking up at his buddy, Ivan spoke up and said, "Will you settle down. I got homework to do." Without saying a word Shorty stopped pacing and stood by the stove to warm his hands.

Even though Shorty agreed to go along with Ivan's escape plan, he was not looking forward to stowing away on a combat glider mission, especially when the plan was to intentionally surrender to the enemy to avoid being arrested by the military police and Army CID. Shorty was also having some serious regrets about helping Ivan kill Steve Perkins and make his death look like a suicide. As someone who knew how disappointed his own mother was when he became a street hoodlum, it bothered Shorty to no end that Steve's mother would have to go through life believing that her son took his own life.

After putting the air chart down, Ivan stood up facing Shorty's back and said, "I know you're anxious about taking the next step but this may be our only chance to make a clean break without a squad of MPs on our tail." While sounding incredibly sure of himself, Ivan went on to say, "Just because no one suspects who we are today doesn't mean that can't change tomorrow. As long as CID prints stories about us in Stars and Stripes and Yank Magazine and they continue to broadcast those radio shows, the more the Army cops increase the odds that some G.I. who met us, or knows us, will get suspicious and turn us in."

As soon as Shorty turned around and asked if Ivan was worried about anything like that happening, Ivan remarked, "Worried no, concerned yes. In fact, I'm concerned enough to be grateful that Colonel Kirby loaned us both out to 439th because the rumor is that plans are in the works for us to fly a resupply mission to Bastogne any day now." Then, after pausing for a split second, Ivan continued and said, "Even though we both ended up finding a home in the Army, my instincts tell me that it's time for us to leave home, so the Krauts can put us in a place where Army flatfoots will never find us. As soon as this war's over, we can get lost in the crowd and make a new life for ourselves in Europe."

After crashing down on a nearby bunk, Shorty looked at Ivan and said, "OK, I'm ready to do some flying but before we go any further I have one question.

"Ask away," said Ivan.

"Did Steve Perkins really have to die?"

Under any other set of circumstances Ivan Larson would have lost it. Instead, Ivan stepped closer to his partner in crime and responded in a tone of voice that was laced with some regret. "I didn't like killing him anymore than you but it had to be done. Steve Perkins was a smart guy. If anyone could figure out who we really are it was him."

As Ivan became dead serious he continued and said, "Besides, you're the one who screwed that up so stop complaining."

After lowering his head, Shorty looked up and responded in a tone of voice that was laced with regret. "You're right, I slipped......I just wish things were different."

Shorty Mc Ghee wasn't the only one who had regrets. Ivan also had reasons to wish that he wasn't wanted by the police. The moment Ivan's expression changed and he seemed lost in thought Shorty knew his buddy was thinking about Peaches. While Ivan and Shorty looked silently at each other, it became painfully obvious that they both had their own reasons for wishing that things were different. Shorty proved that he was a true blue best friend, when he looked directly at Ivan and said, "I'm sorry about Gloria. I know how much she meant to you."

After devouring a huge breakfast with extra portions and a pot of piping hot coffee, Major Beauregard and Sergeant Parker were invited to attend a Christmas party for orphans that the Army Air Forces had planned to host before the shooting started in the Ardennes. Seeing truck loads of English kids being delivered to the snow covered base was food for the soul for every homesick American servicemen at Membury.

Shortly after the party started Al Parker was parading around like a gentle giant with two British orphans held tightly in his arms. Even Jim Beauregard forgot about their efforts to hunt down two fugitives and got into the Holiday spirit, when he spotted a quiet little boy off on his own in the corner of the room.

After picking up one of the many presents that the G.I.s had prepared in advance for the orphans, Jim approached the young boy and asked, "What's your name?"

While the shy little boy who lost his mother in the bombing of London and his father to a German U Boat looked up, he responded in a low tone of voice and said, "My name is James."

As Jim remembered the times when he brightened the spirits of his own sons, he smiled wide then said, "That's my name as well but my friends call me Jim."

In that instant James Beauregard made a friend for life. After using his handkerchief to wipe the tears from the little boys rosy red cheeks, Jim smiled as he held out the present and said, "Look what Santa left for you." As little Jimmy slowly reached for the gift and began to tear off the wrapping paper, he periodically looked up at the big American Major to make sure that he was still there. Soon the boy's eyes were wide open at the sight of a liberal supply of American chocolate, chewing gum, cookies, soap, a pair of gloves and a warm G.I. issue brown woolen scarf.

Since no child could resist the taste of a Hershey bar, young Jimmy wasted no time in tearing back the wrapper and taking a bite as he smiled from ear to ear. Then, the child who had lost everything of importance in his life, stopped chewing and remembered his new friend. At no other time in his life was James Beauregard more touched, than when the British orphan stopped devouring his very own American candy bar and offered him a bite. As Jim Beauregard thought of Beatrice and his sons, his eyes began to swell with tears of joy as he accepted the invitation and broke a small corner off the candy bar for his own consumption. Seeing a tear of joy trickle down the side of the Major's clean shaven face, brought the loved starved orphaned to slip into the American officer's arms for a badly needed hug. It was something that the both of them needed.

While Al Parker sat at a table full of happy children, he also remembered his family and thought of his two sons who were serving in a segregated Army to help free the world of the forces of evil. Seeing so many children who had nothing except each other made Al feel like a rich man, even though he came from a country that still had a few problems of its own to work out. When a smiling Jim Beauregard walked over, while carrying a happy orphan with a chocolate covered face, Al Parker knew that it wasn't such a bad thing to be delayed in Membury, England because of bad weather.

At four o'clock in the morning the operations officer for the 440th Troop Carrier Group, 96th Troop Carrier Squadron at Orleans, France woke up Lieutenant Charlton W. "Corky" Corwin Jr. and his co pilot, Flight Officer Benjamin F. "Connie" Constantino to ask for volunteers to fly a mission of mercy into the beleaguered town of Bastogne. Never before in the war was a single glider sent on a more perilous combat mission.[6]

On December 26, 1944 the sun came up at exactly 0814 hours in Orleans,

France. With the situation considered desperate in Bastogne, VII Corps Headquarters and the 50th Troop Carrier Wing approved a request that was sent on Christmas Day by General Anthony Mc Auliffe of the U.S. 101st Airborne Division to use gliders to deliver a badly needed surgical team, medical supplies, gasoline and artillery shells into Bastogne as soon as possible. It was necessary to use gliders because most medical personnel were not trained to use a parachute. It was also more effective to deliver gasoline by glider than by parachute.[7]

The first glider lifted off from Orleans and flew to a fighter base in Etain, France where Lt. Corwin and Flight Officer Constantino picked up Major Lamar Soutter MD and eight other volunteers from the 4th Auxiliary Surgical Group.[8] After being towed back into the air, the two glider pilots completed the sixty mile trip to Bastogne in less than an hour.

As soon as the co pilot spotted a yellow smoke grenade, the pilot hit the tow line release and cut away from the C47 that delivered them to the landing zone. After landing in a snow covered field, the medical team was whisked away to help the wounded. Once the medical team was taken care of, Corky Corwin and Benjamin F. Constantino were taken by jeep to the 101st Airborne Division Headquarters in Bastogne.[9] With this mission completed the U.S. Army planned to step up the pace and send in dozens of GC4-A Waco gliders and hundreds of C47s to help re-supply General Mc Auliffe and the U.S. Army troops known as The Battling Bastards of Bastogne.

After asking for volunteers, twenty American glider pilots of the 96th Squadron of the 440th Troop Carrier Group assembled for a briefing before departing on phase two of the first glider re-supply mission to Bastogne. As Lt. Colonel Mike Kirby walked into the briefing room with the aid of a pair of crutches, his Operations Officer called out, "Attention!" and brought the roomful of U.S. Army glider pilots to their feet. While dressed for combat and standing at attention in front of their chairs, the twenty glider pilots remained standing until Lt. Colonel Kirby reached the front of the room, faced the assembly and said, "At ease, men. Smoke 'em if you got 'em."

While Flight Officer Pete Peterson and his co pilot Flight Officer Russ Shultz sat down with the other pilots, Lt. Colonel Kirby addressed the roomful of Army aviators in a concerned and fatherly tone of voice. "Men, you all know that two of our pilots transported a surgical team into Bastogne earlier today. Those doctors and medics were needed to help care for several hundred wounded G.I.s because the Krauts captured one of our field hospitals. Your job will be to fly a follow-up mission to deliver gasoline, artillery shells, additional medical personnel and other supplies into a landing zone that will be surrounded by the enemy. Additional air drops and glider flights will follow at day break and will continue until Bastogne is fully relieved. The 101st knows you're coming and will do everything possible to cover you once you land. Naturally, you can count on the Germans to contest your presence over Bastogne."

As soon as the Commanding Officer of the 440th Troop Carrier Group faced his Acting Operations Officer and nodded his head, Captain Perry stepped forward and addressed the pilots in a more business like fashion. "Gentlemen, departure time is set for 1500 hours. The flight to Bastogne will cover 265 miles. Sunset is expected at 1658 hours. If all goes well you should all be on the ground before it gets dark."

As the twenty pilots began to calculate the odds of making it to Bastogne in one piece, Captain Perry stood to the side as Lt. Colonel Kirby checked his watch before he looked at the faces of the men who volunteered to fly another dangerous glider resupply mission. After pausing long enough to admire the faces of twenty very brave men, the Colonel sounded sincerely concerned about his pilots when he remarked, ""Good luck, men."

As Lt. Colonel Mike Kirby started to leave the briefing room, the men snapped to attention when Captain Perry yelled, "Ten shun!" While the Colonel walked out of the briefing room with the aid of a pair of crutches, Captain Perry announced that Chaplains of every faith would be available in the back of the briefing room to hold a brief service before takeoff.

At 1100 hours on December 26, 1944 Major James Beauregard and Staff Sergeant Al Parker boarded a C47 on the air base in Membury, England. As soon as Jim Beauregard and Al Parker boarded the aircraft, the crew chief took their USAAF issued B4 garment bags, while the Major carried his attache case and his partner carried a musette bag around his shoulder.

Even though the U.S. Army Air Forces was unable to place a plane at the disposal of CID, arrangements were made to transport Jim Beauregard and Al Parker to Le Bourget Airport near Paris, on a C47 that was being used to ferry badly needed supplies to Allied air bases in France. In fact, the cargo bay was so jammed packed with spare aircraft parts, including sheets of aluminum for patching bullet holes and flak damage on damaged Allied planes, there were very few places for the two passengers to sit.

Once the pilot in command of the C47 entered the cargo bay of his aircraft, Lieutenant Christopher Mills sounded sincere when addressed his two passengers and said, "I'm sorry about the last minute change in plans, Sir, but orders are orders."

After nodding his head in agreement, the Major remarked, "I know, Lieutenant. Sergeant Parker and I could cover a lot more territory if we were able to fly from air base to air base to look for the two fugitives we've been hunting since 1943. Thanks to the German offense in the Ardennes we'll have to conduct our search the old fashioned way."

Despite the last minute change in plans, Jim Beauregard and Al Parker knew from experience that it was part of the job to experience the good with the bad. Jim Beauregard and Al Parker also knew, that in a few short hours Lieutenant Mills and his crew could be killed, injured or captured if anything went wrong on their next combat mission.

When the co pilot quickly climbed up the ladder with the extra air charts in hand, Lt. Mills checked his watch then spoke with the confidence of an experienced aircraft commander as he said, "Sir, if you and Sergeant Parker will have a seat we'll be taking off as soon as we crank her up."

While the crew chief pulled up the ladder and closed the door to the cargo compartment, the radio operator assumed his position in the aircraft, while the two pilots made their way into the cockpit. Within a matter of minutes, the C47 piloted by Lt. Chris Mills and Lt. David Pratt taxied out to the active runway and took off on a flight plan to France.

CHAPTER 6

PIT STOP IN PARIS

After arriving at Le Bourget Airport, Jim Beauregard and Al Parker were immediately transported by Sergeant Hank Blair to meet Lt. Colonel Walter Vogel, the Commanding Officer of the CID Office in Paris. According to Fred Richmond, Walter Vogel is a well respected police captain from Colorado, who continued to retain the demeanor of a policeman, even though he had over twenty years of service in the National Guard and was on active duty ever since the war began.

As soon as Jim Beauregard and Al Parker were introduced to Lt. Colonel Vogel. the Commanding Officer of the CID Office in Paris instructed Sergeant Blair to keep checking on the cable traffic from New York. Once Sergeant Blair acknowledged the order and left the Colonel's office, Walter Vogel continued addressing his guests while he stood behind his desk and pointed to the door. "Out there we're soldiers. In this office we're cops. Now that we got the formalities out of the way, have a seat and smoke 'em if you got 'em. We have a lot to discuss."

While Jim and Al sat in comfortable chairs in front of the desk and produced their favorite tobacco products, Lt. Colonel Vogel took his seat and removed a document from the case file that was marked New York Fugitives. As the Colonel held the document in his hand, he proceeded to brief the two representatives from the New York CID Task Force. "While you were on your way across the Channel, I received some good news from Colonel Richmond."

After hearing what the Colonel just said Jim wasted no time in responding. "We could use some good news, Sir."

Colonel Vogel proved that he was very familiar with their case, when he spoke from memory without referring to the report that he held in his hand. "On Christmas morning a C47 pilot assigned to the 438th Troop Carrier Group contacted the MPs at Laurinburg-Maxton Army Air Field, after he read the recent issue of The Stars and Stripes that features the updated wanted posters of Ivan

Larson and Francis Shorty Mc Ghee. All we know at this time, is that a Lieutenant by the name of Leonard Tucker observed a pilot going through glider training in Texas who was called Shorty, who bears a strong resemblance to the fugitive Francis Mc Ghee. After being interviewed by a CID Agent in North Carolina, Lt. Tucker was scheduled to fly up to New York to be interviewed by an FBI Agent and a New York City Police Captain. According to Colonel Richmond, Lt. Tucker sounds like a credible witness."

As Lt. Colonel Vogel continued to brief his guests, he rose out of his chair and handed a copy of the cable traffic to Jim Beauregard. "As you can see, Colonel Richmond ended this message by stating that specific details regarding Lt. Tucker's interview with our agent in North Carolina and his interview in New York will follow."

While Jim handed the message to Al, the Colonel sat back down and said, "Unfortunately, we haven't received any other messages from your office in New York or from CID Headquarters but I'm not surprised given the current state of affairs here in Europe now that all hell has broken loose. The other bad news is that the Army Air Corps has started using gliders to resupply our troops in Bastogne. If Ivan Larson and Shorty Mc Ghee are serving as pilots, including as glider pilots, there's a good chance they've already been in action, or will be flying in the next few days."

After pausing to light his pipe, the Colonel continued with his briefing. "Unfortunately, ever since the Germans went on the offensive in the Ardennes, this entire theater of operation has been jumping through hoops to turn the tide of their advance. We can also blame the German offensive for keeping the most recent issue of The Stars and Stripes on bases in England, while more critical supplies and equipment are being flown across the Channel. This means that with the exception of a few copies that are floating around, it will likely take several days before your front page feature article that describes the raid on Mike Connely's apartment and the connection between the two fugitives and this retired gangster will be distributed to troops on mainland Europe. The same goes for your next broadcast on the Armed Forces Radio Network."

While Lt. Colonel Vogel leaned forward and put both elbows on his desk, he went on to say, "For the record, I agree with your assessment that the information in the latest issue of Stars and Stripes, as well as your next radio broadcast, has an excellent chance of breaking this case wide open. All it will take is one soldier or airman to remember that two G.I.s in his unit talked about their Uncle Mad Mike Connely, or received mail from their Uncle Mike to expose Larson and Mc Ghee for who they really are. The fact that Lt. Tucker came forward after reading the latest issue of Stars and Stripes proves that point."

After seeing the look on Al's face, Jim addressed the Colonel and said, "Excuse our disappointment, Sir, but we purposely timed the release of that information to our arrival in the ETO."

"I agree," it's a bad break for our side but don't take it so hard," remarked Colonel Vogel who quickly added, "The simple truth is, there's no way that you and Sergeant Parker or anyone else in CID could have predicted that the Germans would mount such a massive offensive in December of 1944." Then, after pausing briefly to relight his pipe, the Colonel continued and said, "In fact, there are some very high ranking officers in this man's army who thought the war would be over by Christmas. A number of these officers are still surprised that the Germans were able to launch such a massive attack at this stage of the war."

While Al leaned forward and rubbed his tired face with both hands, Jim did his best to console his partner by saying, "I know how you feel, Al. If it's not the weather, the war is definitely holding us back."

As soon as Al sat back up in his chair, he regained his composure after being let down by the news and said, "I'm sorry, Sir."

"No need to be sorry, Al," remarked Colonel Vogel who quickly added, The Major's right. This lousy winter weather and the war are getting in our way, which is why we need to make our moves in this case as if we're playing chess not checkers. Remember, once the word gets out that CID is hot on the trail of the two most famous fugitives in the United States Army, Larson and Mc Ghee would be fools to hang around and wait to get arrested. This is the main reason why I thought we should hold off on inspecting air bases in France until we receive more information from your office about Lt. Tucker's interview.

As anxious as they were to proceed, both Al Parker and Jim Beauregard knew that Lt. Colonel Vogel was right. The simple truth was, they could easily end up wasting valuable time by traveling to the wrong air base, if the information provided by Lt. Tucker enables them to go in a much more productive direction." After seeing Al nod his head in agreement, Jim looked at the CO of the CID Office in Paris and said, "You're right, Sir. We better sit tight and wait to hear from Colonel Richmond. We can always change the plan if we don't hear anything by tomorrow morning."

Since there was nothing else to do at this time, Colonel Vogel stood up and said, "I say we take a break and grab some lunch. I'll let Sergeant Blair know where we're going, so he can contact us if any additional information arrives while we're gone."

As soon as Jim and Al stood up and grabbed their coats, Jim asked the Colonel if there was anyway that someone in his office could find out which hospital his wounded son Michael was in, so he could visit him while he was in France. "No problem, Jim. I'll put someone right on it." responded the Colonel as he left his office with his guests.

While Jim and Al sat at a quiet table in the corner of the Colonel's favorite French restaurant, the Commanding Officer of the CID Office in Paris leaned closer to the table when he continued addressing his guests. "There's something else you need to know." After casually looking around to make sure no one was paying attention to their conversation, Lt. Colonel Vogel spoke in a low tone of voice when he said, "The current situation in this theater of operation is further complicated by the fact that Army Intelligence has determined that the Germans have mounted an operation using English speaking troops dressed as U.S. Army personnel, including as MPs, to infiltrate our lines and create havoc. This additional thorn in our side has put a tremendous strain on manpower. As a result, I'm supposed to have all of my agents assigned to assist a small army of MPs protect a number of General Officers. Even though this is the case, I have no intention of sending the two of you off on this manhunt without help."

After removing a folded report from his uniform jacket pocket, the Colonel handed it to Jim Beauregard as he said, "Speaking of German infiltrators, I thought you and your partner would like to see this." While Jim reviewed the file, he cracked a smile before he handed the report to Al Parker. As Al read the report, the Colonel sat back in his chair and said, "It seems a Sergeant by the name of Calvin Parker was commanding a detail of MPs at the Ambleve River Bridge, that was responsible for capturing three armed and well equipped German infiltrators who were dressed as American G.I.s."

While Al Parker was beaming with pride, both Colonel Vogel and Jim Beauregard praised Al's son and his men for a job well done. When Jim Beauregard told the Colonel that he had the opportunity to meet Al's youngest son before he shipped out, he added that Cal is a definite chip off the old block.

After hearing what his partner and commanding officer said, Al smiled then said, "Don't say that to his mother, Sir, 'cause she thinks Cal takes after her."

As all three veteran law enforcement officers who were now serving in the Army had a good laugh, a waiter delivered their lunch. Even though things were not moving as fast as they preferred, there was no reason to go without eating, especially when they had the chance to enjoy such a fine meal in a French restaurant.

Once they returned to the CID Office, Jim and Al were given an office to work out of while they reviewed a map of France and a list of U.S. Army Air Bases so they could begin to plan their inspection trips. As soon as Jim remarked, "If we don't hear from Colonel Richmond by morning, I say we get on the road and start inspecting every troop carrier group in France," both men stood up when Lt. Colonel Vogel entered the office with another officer.

After introducing the two representatives from the New York CID Task Force to Captain Tommy Savino, Lt. Colonel Vogel faced Major Beauregard and said, "I'm sorry, Jim but we won't be able to run you over to the hospital to visit your son Michael while you're in France." Before Jim could react, Lt. Colonel Vogel continued and said, "Based on what Captain Savino was able to find out, your son Michael left the 203rd General Hospital without being discharged so he could rejoin his unit when they left for Bastogne on the 18th."

Ever since Jim received the letter from his son, that described how he was recovering in a hospital in France, he was looking forward to seeing Michael once he made his way to the ETO. Even if all he was only able to do, was spend a few minutes with his youngest son, it would be well worth it for Jim to take a detour from his official travel plans. As Jim crashed into a nearby chair and he thought about what Michael must be going through, all he could bring himself to say was, "That crazy kid."

When Lt. Colonel Vogel asked Captain Savino if he had any other information to share with the Major, the cop from Providence, Rhode Island who was serving as a CID Agent in Paris responded and said, "Yes, Sir, I do." As Jim stood up and faced the CID Agent who would be assisting him and Al on their manhunt,

Captain Savino continued and said. "According to the Army doctor I spoke to, Sergeant Michael Beauregard of the 3rd Battalion 327th Glider Infantry Regiment sustained a gunshot wound to his right leg that got infected while fighting in Operation Market Garden. The Major's son had two successful surgical procedures to date and was getting ready to be sent for some additional rehabilitation when he left the hospital without being officially released to do so." Then, after pausing briefly while he handed his notes to Jim, Captain Savino added, "You should also know, Sir, that based on what I was told, your son wasn't the only member of the 101st Airborne Division who left the hospital without permission so he could return to his unit."

After thanking Lt. Colonel Vogel and Captain Savino for finding out that his son Michael returned to his unit, Jim removed a cigarette from the pack that he carried in his pocket. As soon as Jim accepted a light from Al Parker, he exhaled a lung full of smoke and repeated his previous comment. "That crazy kid."

As a father who had a son serving in a combat unit, Lt. Colonel Vogel knew what Jim was going through. Having a son serving in a front line unit was bad enough, but having a son who was not fully recovered from a gunshot wound, leave his hospital bed, so he could serve in combat with his fellow soldiers was a lot for any parent to cope with.

After checking his watch, Lt. Colonel Vogel looked at the Major from the New York CID Office and said, "It's almost 1800 hours and there's nothing else we can do until we hear from New York. In the meantime, you look like you could use a drink, Jim. You too, Al."

As soon as Jim remarked, "You're right, Sir. I could use a drink," Al handed the Major his trench coat before he grabbed his own coat.

While Jim and Al put their coats on, Colonel Vogel turned to Captain Savino and added, "You're welcome to join us, Tom. I'm buying."

Long before they crossed the Atlantic Jim Beauregard did his homework on Lt. Colonel Walter Vogel and his CID command in France. As a veteran Atlanta Police Detective, Jim Beauregard learned a long time ago to find out as much as possible about the law enforcement officers he had to work with, especially when he had to operate in another jurisdiction.

According to his contacts in Army CID and the FBI, Walter Vogel was a well respected police captain in civilian life, who commanded a military police unit in North Africa and Italy before he was assigned to Army CID. As soon as he joined CID, Walter Vogel was stationed in two of the most active locations on foreign soil as far as black-market operations were concerned. The fact that Lt. Colonel Vogel also served in the National Guard meant that he and Jim had something else in common besides being cops.

By all accounts, Naples, Italy and Paris, France were Allied occupied territories where crime and black-market related activities flourished. By the winter of 1944, the Colonel's efforts to combat the theft and sale of U.S. military equipment and supplies were legendary among U.S. Army CID Agents.

As soon as they finished their dinner, Jim looked across the table and said, "I thought we had a problem with the black market back in the states until Colonel Richmond told us what you and your men are going through here in France."

After sipping some French cognac, Colonel Vogel grinned a little then remarked, "So you heard about out little war with the local French thieves and deserters?"

"Yes we have, Sir," responded Jim, before he used his Zippo to light a Lucky Strike cigarette. Even Al Parker joined the conversation and said, "Lord knows, Colonel, this is no time for our troops to have to deal with shortages due to a thriving black market."

After seeing that his dinner guests were interested in how he and his men were fighting crime in the ETO, the CID Commander in Paris spoke up and said, "You and Al want'a get sick? Listen to this." While the Colonel removed his pipe and a pouch of tobacco from his jacket pocket, he looked at his guests from New York and said, "According to our best estimates a small army of AWOL American G.I.s are stealing approximately 1000 gallons of gasoline a day from Uncle Sam. In fact, according to one estimate, there are enough thieves in the U.S. Army to form an entire division. Hell, in one detention barracks alone the MPs have over 1300 American soldiers under arrest for various infractions and violations of law, with half of them facing charges for stealing government property. One U.S. Army officer was caught sending over thirty thousand dollars home after earning a small fortune on the black-market. In another case we rounded up 181 officers and 3 enlisted men after they hijacked a military train load of cigarettes, soap and other valuable commodities."[10]

After pausing for a second, the Colonel added, "As shocking as this may sound, every man we arrested in that case had at least five grand in their possession."

"That's a lot'a dough," said Jim before he took a drag on his cigarette and sipped some cognac.

While the Colonel finished filling the bowl of his pipe with tobacco, he nodded his head ever so slightly and remarked, "It sure is."

After enjoying a late supper with Lt. Colonel Vogel and Captain Savino, Jim Beauregard and Al Parker spent most the night walking the streets of Paris, while they talked about their case, the war and their families. Eventually, Jim and Al got tired enough to grab a few hours of sack time before they returned to the CID office after having a light breakfast in a French cafe.

As soon as they arrived at the office, an excited Sergeant Hank Blair met the two members of the New York CID Task Force by the front door and said, "Good news, Sir. We just heard from your office in New York. Colonel Vogel is waiting to brief you and Sergeant Parker before we leave to conduct our interviews."

After hanging up their coats, Jim and Al entered the spacious corner office just as the Commanding Officer of the CID Office in Paris was finishing a phone call. "As soon as I give Major Beauregard and Sergeant Parker the good news, they'll be on their way with two of my men." While Lt. Colonel Vogel used a hand gesture to invite his guests to have a seat, he finished his telephone conversation by saying, "I agree. Thanks again, Harry."

As soon as he hung up the phone, Lt. Colonel Vogel wasted no time in briefing Jim Beauregard and Al Parker before they left for the field. After saying, "Before I get into my conversation with the Provost Marshal at one of the local air bases," the Colonel relayed every major piece of information that was received by the Paris CID Office earlier that morning from their office in New York.

After providing Jim and Al with a detailed briefing about the interview of Lt. Tucker, the Colonel concluded his remarks by saying, "I've also been advised that Lt. Tucker is helping the FBI prepare a new composite sketch of Francis Shorty Mc Ghee. The other good news is that after I received Colonel Richmond's priority cable traffic, I made some inquiries and located Mike Kirby, Billy Davis and the medic who patched up the glider pilot who resembles Shorty Mc Ghee, when he was going through glider training in Texas. According to the Provost Marshal I was speaking to when you walked in, the medic we're looking for is a tech sergeant by the name of Melvin Keller. Both the recently promoted Captain Davis and the medic known as Doc Keller are assigned to Lt. Colonel Kirby's command at the 440th Troop Carrier Group in Orleans, France."

While Colonel Vogel paused to light his pipe, Jim turned to his partner and said, "The fact that the pilot called Shorty was transferred to glider engineering duties means he won't be participating in any resupply missions."

After nodding his head in agreement, Al Parker remarked, "That's true, Sir, but until we fully identify Ivan Larson we risk losing him if he ends up behind the controls of anything with wings."

Even though he agreed with their assessment of the situation, Colonel Vogel wanted to get the conversation back on track and said, "You're both right but for now let's deal with what we know."

After hearing Jim agree, the Colonel continued. "Fortunately, I received this cable traffic early enough this morning to have the Provost Marshal at the 440th get Captain Davis taken off the flying roster so he can be interviewed by CID at 1030 hrs. When the XO complained about this order, the Provost Marshal directed him not to breath a word of this to anyone and promised that he along with Lt. Colonel Kirby would be fully briefed by 1200 hours today."

After pausing long enough to take two quick puffs on his Dunhill straight stem pipe, Lt. Colonel Vogel added, "The Provost Marshal at the air base in Orleans is a Captain by the name of Harry Denton. Harry was a state police sergeant in Montana before the war. He's standing by to help you in any way he can."

As soon as Jim finished lighting a cigarette, he spoke his mind while he looked directly at the Commanding Officer of the CID Office in Paris. "Hopefully, one of these witnesses can also help us identify Ivan Larson."

Once again Lt. Colonel Vogel proved that he knew every detail in the case file that was marked NEW YORK FUGITIVES when he said, "Thanks to the evidence that your partner found in Mike Connely's basement incinerator, Shorty Mc Ghee and Ivan Larson should be stationed on the same air base. That said, if you need to continue your investigation on another base, you can use your orders from the War Department to commandeer any assistance that you require. If you run into any problems, call me and I'll move whatever mountains need to be moved."

After pausing briefly to re-light his pipe, the CID Commander in Paris quickly added, "Since Captain Davis may need to get back to work as soon as possible, I recommend that you interview him first. Besides, according to the statements made by Lt. Tucker, Captain Davis was friends with the pilot who trained in Texas who was called Shorty and resembles the latest rendition of Francis Mc Ghee. That means of all three witnesses, Captain Davis might also know the most about Ivan Larson. The fact that Lt. Colonel Kirby is in the base hospital with a busted ankle means that he isn't going anywhere and can be interviewed at any time."

While Jim tapped the ash from his cigarette in a nearby ashtray, Colonel Vogel continued and said, "You'll also be happy to know that Colonel Richmond is in the process of sending me the list of names of Army personnel who attended the Advanced Glider School at South Plains Army Airfield in Lubbock, Texas in May of '44. Once I receive this list, I'll forward the names to the Provost Marshal's Office at the 440th Troop Carrier Group. If Lt. Tucker is correct, the phony name that Shorty Mc Ghee is using is on this list. If we're real lucky, Ivan Larson was in the same training class."

Jim Beauregard proved that he was confident that they were finally heading in the right direction with the wind in their sails when he remarked, "Even if we're not that lucky, Sir, we believe that if we find one we'll find the other."

After hearing the Colonel agree, Jim asked the CID Commander in Paris how he and his team would be traveling to Orleans.

While Lt. Colonel Vogel ran a pipe cleaner through the stem of his pipe, he looked at his two guests and said, "Since it would be a miserable trip for the four of you to make in a Jeep, you'll be using my staff car. Captain Savino and Sergeant Blair will show you the way and will remain with you for as long as necessary."

As soon as Jim and Al thanked the Colonel for all of his help, the police captain from Colorado who was serving as the CID Commander in Paris stood up, walked around his desk and wished his guests the best of luck.

CHAPTER 7

COME AND GET IT

Fortunately, all ten GC-4A Waco gliders landed without any of the brave pilots who volunteered to fly the second re-supply mission into Bastogne being injured, wounded or killed. Even though these ten gliders were only able to transport a limited amount of cargo, every drop of fuel and every round of artillery ammunition that was delivered in tact would be put to good use by the American troops who were defending the towns in and around Bastogne.

As the last of the ten gliders landed in the snow covered field, the Germans watched as the aircraft that had no engines came to a complete stop within a few feet of an American Tank Destroyer and a handful of paratroopers. The moment Flight Officer William Peterson, who went by the nickname Willie Pete, exited his glider with his co pilot, Flight Officer Russ Schultz called out, "Come and get it!"

As the paratroopers and the men from the 705th Tank Destroyer Battalion jumped out of their makeshift bunker, they were amazed to find that the glider was filled with sixty 5 gallon cans of 80 octane gasoline. Because the enemy was close enough to the landing zone to launch an attack, Sergeant Thomas Verling wasted no time in yelling, "Let's get that glider unloaded. Come on guys, hubba hubba."

As Flight Officer Peterson and his co pilot stood in the snow by the open cargo door of their glider, F.O. Schultz called out in a loud tone of voice and said, "No, smoking boys we're hauling fuel for your vehicles, lanterns and cigarette lighters." Instantly, the men who were smoking took one last drag, before they tossed their cigarette butts into the snow, as they formed a human chain and unloaded the petrol from the crash landed glider.

The moment the mixed contingent of paratroopers and tankers started unloading the glider, Lt. Dan Dixson of the 705th Tank Destroyer Battalion shook hands with the two glider pilots as he said, "You boys couldn't have come at a better time. I'm running on fumes."

Being a team player, Flight Officer Russ Schultz picked up one of the Jerry cans and said, "What are we waiting for, Lieutenant. Let's get you gassed up," as he started to walk toward the American armored vehicle.

While F.O. Schultz and Lt. Dixson trudged through the ankle deep snow carrying two cans of fuel, F.O. Peterson helped stack cans of gasoline in the trailer that was attached to the Jeep, that arrived next to his glider to help transport gasoline to other units. With his M1 Garand slung over his shoulder, a young G.I. from the wheat fields of Kansas smiled wide as he accepted a five gallon can of gasoline from F.O. Peterson and said, "We're sure glad to see you guys, Sir."

After cracking a smile, Flight Officer Peterson proved that he had an excellent sense of humor when he passed another can of gasoline to the Private and remarked, "I'm only sorry we missed your Christmas pageant."

Even a combat veteran like Sergeant Thomas Verling, a man who survived combat in France, Holland and now Bastogne, felt like the Army really cared about him and his men while he admired the sight of ten gliders being off loaded in a large snow covered field under the watchful eyes of the Germans. While two of his men provided security, Sergeant Verling chewed on an unlit cigar stub, as he carried a Jerry can full of fuel over to the tank destroyer that was parked next to his squad's makeshift bunker.

As soon as the war weary squad leader passed the five gallon can of fuel up to Russ Schultz, Sergeant Verling removed the unlit cigar stub from the corner of his mouth and asked, "How much did you bring in, Sir?" While Flight Officer Schultz waited for Lt. Dixson to finish pouring the remains of the second Jerry can into the tank destroyer's fuel receptacle, the glider pilot looked down at Sergeant Verling and said, "300 gallons and more's on the way."

After listening to two of his men discuss the fact that they were incredibly low on ammunition, Staff Sergeant Phil Martin checked his watch and hoped that his squad would be resupplied with small arms ammo and grenades before the Germans launched another attack. When a third G.I. started complaining that he only had three full 20 round magazines of ammunition left for his BAR, Sergeant Martin stood up and said, "What'a you guys want, an egg in your beer? Nothing's changed. If we run into any Krauts make every shot count. If that doesn't work tell your problems to Jesus 'cause the Chaplain went ashore."

As the men in his squad continued to talk among themselves, Sergeant Martin stood vigil on the edge of their defensive position and waited for the Quartermaster Company jeep carrying a resupply of ammo, grenades and rations to arrive. While his men melted snow for drinking water in canteen cups over two small smokeless fires, Phil Martin stamped his feet and clapped his gloved hands together to try and stay warm.

As far as Sergeant Phil Martin was concerned, the only thing that mattered was killing Germans and surviving the hardships of war with his extremities still attached. Even though thoughts of home did their best to creep into his mind, Phil Martin could not become a true blue civilian first class again until his services as a paratrooper were no longer needed. Until then, he was determined to survive and give a good account of himself.

With the air drops came a steady re-supply of ammunition, medical supplies, rations and everything else that was needed to survive in combat, while the bulk of the gliders were used to deliver fuel and artillery ammunition into Bastogne. While in a number of instances air dropped supplies were picked up by individual soldiers and groups of troops, air dropped supplies were also collected and delivered to front line units in Jeeps and other vehicles.

The Jeep from the Division's Quartermaster Company was heard before it was actually observed coming down the road. This was due to the distinctive sound that was made by a vehicle that was driven with a set of chains on all four tires. From a practical perspective, the tradeoff was worth it, because equipping Jeeps with chains gave the most famous compact four wheel drive vehicle of the war even more traction in the snow.

As soon as the Jeep came to a stop where Sergeant Martin and his men were positioned, it was easy to see that the fly boys were working over time by the amount of ammunition and rations that were available for distribution. "Take all you want and put it to good use," said the driver as he jumped out of the front seat of the Jeep and handed Sergeant Martin a copy of a locally printed flier from Division Headquarters and joked, "Hurry, hurry, read all about it."

While the war weary paratroopers got in line to load up on ammunition and rations, Sergeant Martin remarked, "Remind me to thank our commanding general for delivering the morning paper to our front door." After handing Private Harry

Betts an empty musette bag, Sergeant Martin said, "Do me a favor, Kid and grab me anything that doesn't have Lima beans in it and get me a refill of forty five ammo and a few grenades while I catch up on the war news."

As the youngest member of his squad said, "Sure, Sarge," Phil Martin put his right foot up on the front bumper of the jeep, while he continued reading the flier that was provided courtesy of the 101st Airborne Division HQ. By the time Phil Martin finished reading the first half of the flier, Private Betts had four bandoleers of rifle ammunition draped across his chest. Once the skinny Private from Texas finished filling the musette bag with fifty round boxes of .45 ACP caliber ammunition and two fragmentation grenades, he stuffed two boxes of K Ration Dinners in an empty gas mask bag and put two more inside his Heavy Wool Melton Overcoat before he grabbed his M1 Garand rifle.

The moment Private Betts approached his squad leader, Sergeant Martin remarked, "Whatever you do, Kid, don't fall in a puddle." After cracking a smile, the young private proudly reported that he picked up everything his Sergeant requested, including plenty of ammo for his M1A1 Model Thompson. The moment Sergeant Martin took possession of the fully loaded musette bag, he said, "Thanks, Kid," before he began the process of reloading an empty 30 round magazine for his submachine gun.

While Sergeant Martin continued loading round after round of ammunition into the magazine, he looked at his men and said, "I'm sure you'll all be happy to know that we've managed to hold off four German Panzer Divisions, two infantry divisions and one German airborne division."

Just like other new replacements who recently joined the 101st Airborne Division, Private Betts had given a good account of himself in combat. How this young man managed to maintain his innocence during all this carnage continued to amaze Phil Martin and the other old timers in 2nd Squad. When the Private known as The Kid reacted as if he was shocked at the news, he looked at his squad leader and remarked, "That's an awful lot'a Krauts, Sarge."

While responding with a tremendous amount of pride, Sergeant Martin nodded his head in agreement then said, "It sure is, Kid."

As the Jeep driver drove off to his next stop along the lightly held American front line, Sergeant Martin inserted the reloaded thirty round magazine into his Thompson and immediately started loading another empty magazine while he turned to his men and said, "Let's grab some chow before it gets dark." Sergeant

Martin then turned to Private Betts and said, "As soon as we eat I want you to fill that gas mask bag that I gave you with eight round clips from two of those bandoleers. The last thing you want'a do in the middle of a fight with the Krauts is struggle to get to your spare ammo if those cloth bandoleers freeze up in this weather."

After hearing the young Private say, "Will do, Sarge," Phil Martin accepted a box of rations from The Kid and said, "Let's eat."

CHAPTER 8

THE GREAT ESCAPE

While Technical Sergeant Charlie Daniels finished checking the supply of artillery shells and fuses that were packed separately and secured in the back of the glider, Flight Officer Danny Gannon entered the GC-4A known as Chalk 37 in preparation of taking off on a resupply to Bastogne. As Ivan Larson aka Danny Gannon faced Sergeant Daniels, the ammunition specialists remarked, "You're all set, Danny, good luck."

Since Ivan knew that his fate rested in large measure on how well the load he was carrying was secured in his glider, he was sincerely grateful to Sergeant Daniels for doing what appeared to be an outstanding job. After Ivan knelt down and checked the tension on the tie down lines, he looked up and said, "Thanks Charlie. I'll bring you back a Kraut souvenir for a job well done."

While other ground crew personnel worked at a fever pitched pace to finish preparing their gliders for takeoff, Shorty Mc Ghee drove down the flight line with some very disturbing news for his partner in crime. After ignoring Sergeant Daniels, while he drove by in the other direction, a pensive Shorty Mc Ghee waited for a fuel truck to pull away from a nearby C47 before he parked next to Ivan's glider.

As soon as Shorty jumped out of his Jeep, he looked both ways while he walked over to the thirty seventh GC-4A Waco glider in the formation of fifty gliders that were participating in today's mission. While Ivan used a piece of white chalk to write the name Mad Mike in big bold letters on the side of his aircraft, Shorty nervously looked around as if he was being followed. After slipping the piece of chalk in his field jacket pocket, Ivan seemed to be in good spirits when he turned to face Shorty and said, "Mad Mike is ready to fly."

Under the circumstances Shorty was in no mood for small talk or reminiscing about Mad Mike Connely. After nervously looking around again, Shorty stepped closer to Ivan and handed him the most recent edition of The Stars and Stripes Newspaper and said, "I found this copy on a C47 that came in from Membury loaded with spare parts. As far as I know, this is the only copy of the latest issue that made it to this base. According to what I was told, the rest are in England waiting to be delivered once more essential supplies are brought in."

While Ivan continued reading the paper, Shorty went on to say, "Once you read the front page story about us, you'll probably regret putting the old man's nickname on the side of your glider."

Ivan's heart sank the moment he read the feature article that described how Mike Connely was killed in a shootout with members of the New York City based Army CID Task Force. "No wonder we haven't received any mail lately," remarked Ivan as he handed the Army newspaper back to Shorty.

After hearing what Ivan had to say, Shorty came apart at the seams and said, "Did you read the part about us being connected to the famous New York City gangster Mad Mike Connely and how CID recovered evidence in the old man's apartment that indicated that we're masquerading as his nephews and we're hiding out in the Army Air Forces.? Worse yet, they know we're stationed on an air base in France. How long do you think it's gonna take for the people who know us to figure out that we're the two most wanted fugitives in the U.S. Army?"

Rather than continue this conversation on the flight line, Ivan grabbed his friend by the arm and led him into the cargo bay of his glider. As soon as Ivan closed the door, he continued to hold onto Shorty's arm as he scolded him for becoming so upset. "Calm down will ya. I agree this isn't good news, especially the part about us being connected to Mad Mike. Even so, if what you heard is true, we have some time before every air base in France is flooded with copies of the latest edition of The Stars and Stripes. This means that we're safe as long as the push is on to resupply Bastogne."

While Shorty looked directly at Ivan, he spoke like a fast talking New Yorker when he said, "I have more bad news. When I helped unload the supplies from that C47, the crew chief told me that if it wasn't for the Kraut offensive, his crew would have been able to stay in Paris with a white Major from CID and his colored partner. This guy was pissed because their original assignment was to transport these Army cops to air bases all over France so they could search for two fugitives.

Instead, they dropped them off in Paris on the way to Orleans and got sent here to tow a glider on today's mission."

After pausing for a split second, Shorty sounded unusually composed when he continued and said, "That means that the same Major from CID who made those radio broadcasts, along with that colored cop from New York, are bound to visit the 440th and when they do they'll probably end up meeting with Killer Kirby. Even if they don't meet with the CO, there's enough people on that base, including Billy Davis, who can put two and two together and figure out who we really are. The same is true if they come here."

After recovering from the shock of this very troubling news, Ivan shrugged his shoulders and remarked in typical tough guy fashion, "So what. We always knew this day could come. It might as well be today, especially since we're getting ready to take off with forty nine other GC-4As so we can deliver artillery ammo and another medical team to our troops in Bastogne."

"I just wish there was another way," remarked Shorty.

While Ivan took a quick look through the cockpit windshield and the side windows on his glider to make sure no one was near his aircraft he continued and said. "I'm not going through this with you again. My plans haven't changed. Once I do my bit for the war effort, I intend to surrender to the friendliest Kraut I can find. I'm a survivor, Pal, even if I have to do a stint in a German POW Camp to get away from that nigger cop from New York." Then, after pausing for a second, Ivan finished his remarks by saying, "You're welcome to join me if you like. If not, you can stay here and get arrested, unless of course you think you can make a run for it on your own."

After hearing Shorty remark, "Relax, I'm going with you," Ivan reached through layers of clothing and removed his old tags. Once Ivan did so, he replaced his issued set of dog tags with a new set of metal identity tags that identified him as Paul Kraft. As soon as Ivan placed his original set of identification tags in his pant's pocket, he retrieved another set of identity tags and a pair of First Lieutenant bars from his field jacket pocket and handed these items to Shorty as he said, "He's your new dog tags and your new insignia. You just got promoted to the rank of First Lieutenant." Then, after pausing for a split second, Ivan continued and said, "Just to be on the safe side we should hold onto our original dog tags and insignia in case we have to change back to being Flight Officer Danny Gannon and Warrant Officer Gus O'Malley."

While Shorty held the new dog tags and the silver lieutenant bars in his right hand, he had to admit that Ivan was always thinking about the best way to insure that they remained, not one, but two steps ahead of the police. It took two months but Ivan was eventually able to gain access to the otherwise secure office on the air base, where the blank metal identity tags, the embossing machine and the neck chains were kept and used by authorized personnel to replace lost identity tags also known as dog tags.

As Shorty read his new pair of metal identification tags, he looked up at Ivan and asked, "Where did you come up with this name or is that a military secret?" Without hesitating Ivan responded and said, "Lieutenants Gabe Fuller and Paul Kraft were with the 440th Troop Carrier Group and were listed as Missing in Action and presumed dead while flying gliders during the Holland mission. Once I confirmed that these pilots were listed as missing in action, I decided that we should be prepared to adopt their identities in case we had to escape under certain circumstances."

While Shorty replaced his Army issued dog tags with the identity tags that Ivan manufactured, Ivan continued and said, "If anyone including the MPs start checking the glider pilots who land in and around Bastogne, we're better off being Paul Kraft and Gabe Fuller if they're looking for Danny Gannon and Gus O'Malley. Should anyone ask if we know Danny Gannon or Gus O'Malley all we have to say is that we saw Danny Gannon in the briefing room before we headed out to our glider but we haven't seen him since. As far as Gus O'Malley is concerned, we should keep it simple and say we assume he's still back at the base with the other glider engineering officers."

After pausing for a split second, Ivan continued and said, "I even concocted a believable bullshit story in case you get a little nervous about being questioned once we land. All you have to remember is we were both banged up pretty bad when we crash landed in Holland and ended up in a British hospital. Once we heard the Krauts launched their offensive in the Ardennes, we hitched a ride on a C47 back to our base in France and volunteered to fly the next glider re-supply mission. Should we get checked out by MPs or anyone else and they ask if you're alright, all you have to do is hold your stomach and say that you've had the shits ever since we ended up in that Limey hospital. If that doesn't get you some sympathy nothing will."

As soon as Ivan heard Shorty say, "I like it," Ivan continued and said, "Unfortunately, a number of glider pilots on this mission were friends with or knew the real Paul Kraft and Gabe Fuller. Problem number two for us is that most, if not all, of the glider pilots and even some of the tow plane crews on this mission know us as Danny Gannon and Gus O'Malley. There's also a number of glider pilots who flew the previous resupply missions and are waiting to be evacuated from Bastogne who know us as Danny Gannon and Gus O'Malley. We also have to be concerned about someone on the ground in Bastogne becoming suspicious when our glider is the only GC-4A that participates in today's resupply mission that has two pilots on board. This means that it will be in our best interest to get captured as soon as possible after we land."

While doing his best to be a team player, Shorty spoke in a low tone of voice when he asked Ivan a question about their escape plan. "I hate to piss on your parade but what happens if we run into someone who knows us as Danny Gannon and Gus O'Malley while we're using our new names and wearing lieutenant bars?"

Ivan was well aware that his plan was by no means perfect in every sense of the word. As Ivan continued to look directly at Shorty, his tone of voice reflected his own concerns when he said, "I'm just trying to stay one step ahead of the Army cops who seem determined to hunt us down. This is why I think we have more to gain if we adopt new identities, especially if we only need to be Paul Kraft and Gabe Fuller long enough to make our way to the German lines."

While Shorty remained silent, Ivan continued to explain his reasons for adopting the new identities. "Remember, if CID is able to figure out who we are and they suspect or believe that one or both of us participated in a glider resupply mission, they'll contact the MPs in Bastogne to look for Flight Officer Danny Gannon and Warrant Officer Gus O'Malley, not two First Lieutenants by the name of Kraft and Fuller. Besides, remember what I said when I came up with this idea. Once we're picked up by the Krauts, the Red Cross will be notified that Gabe Fuller and Paul Kraft are POW's. That means there won't be any record of Danny Gannon and Gus O'Malley being captured. Who knows, if we get real lucky the Army will consider us missing in action and presumed dead. Once the war is over, we can use the cash that we have stashed, plus the money that Mike's cousins are holding for us, to live happily ever after in Europe with little or no concern about being hunted by the cops."

As Shorty looked at the set of dog tags and the silver lieutenant bars that he held in his right hand, he knew that even though Ivan's plan was far from full proof, it just might enable them to make their escape to the German lines, providing they survive the flight to Bastogne. After seeing the expression on Shorty's face, Ivan was quick to respond and said, "I know what you're thinking and you're right. It's a crap shoot either way. In fact, we would have some serious explaining to do if we use the names Paul Kraft and Gabe Fuller and we end up in the same POW Camp with captured Army pilots who know us as Danny Gannon and Gus O'Malley. The same is true if we used any other names and we run into anyone who knows us as Flight Officer Gannon and Warrant Officer O'Malley."

Once again Ivan paused to catch his breath before he remarked, "I'll tell you what. You call it. You make the decision and I'll go along." Shorty Mc Ghee was shocked that Ivan would trust him with such an important decision. While Shorty stood in the cargo bay of Chalk 37, he considered Ivan's plan. As concerned as he was about being killed in action or taken prisoner, Shorty was deathly afraid of facing a laundry list of felony charges that included participating in a bank robbery that resulted in the death of an off duty cop and the wounding of others.

While Shorty remembered the day when he helped Ivan rob the Lincoln Savings Bank, he wished that he could go back in time and undo what he did. Even though the reason he joined the U.S. Army had nothing to do with patriotism, Shorty ended up adjusting to Army life and felt good about making a valuable contribution to the war effort.

After all that transpired since he became Gus O'Malley, Shorty wondered what his life would be like if he could wake up and have the events of the past turn out to be the results of an exceptionally bad dream. When his thoughts drifted to the last time that he saw his mother, Shorty felt more homesick than ever. If only she could see him now. In fact, the best Shorty could hope for, was that his mother would one day learn that her bank robbing sinner for a son performed such a good deed in time of war while evading the American authorities.

After coming out of a trance like state, Shorty removed a pack of chewing gum from his field jacket pocket and offered a stick to Ivan as he said, "We'll play it your way. We'll go in wearing the new ID tags and rank and hold onto our original dog tags and insignia in case we need to change back to being Danny Gannon and Gus O'Malley."

As soon as Ivan heard Shorty sign on to the final version of his escape plan, Ivan remarked, "That's it then. Next stop Bastogne."

Even though Shorty liked the idea of trying to make something out of himself, if not for his own sake, but for his mother's, the thought of getting shot out of the sky or gunned down by some trigger happy German soldier was not exactly his idea of the perfect escape plan. Regardless of what could have been, it was time to deal with what was happening in the present tense. After Shorty admired the pile of artillery shells that filled the cargo compartment in Chalk 37, he looked at Ivan and said, "My stuff's in the jeep."

While trying not to act like a complete hard ass, Ivan patted Shorty on the arm and remarked, "You stay outta sight. I'll get your gear and stash the jeep."

As soon as Shorty nodded and said, "Thanks," he squatted on the floor of the glider and tried to get as comfortable as possible, while he changed his insignia of rank and adopted his new identity as First Lieutenant Gabe Fuller.

CHAPTER 9

ONE STEP FORWARD
TWO STEPS BACK

A fter getting delayed in heavy traffic while reinforcements moved east, Major Beauregard, Sergeant Al Parker, Captain Thomas Savino and Sergeant Hank Blair arrived in Orleans, France at 1035 hours. As soon as Al Parker stopped the staff car at the front gate, all four occupants of the U.S. Army sedan presented their military law enforcement identification to the military policeman on duty at the entrance to the base. Immediately after the MP presented the two commissioned officers in the staff car with a snappy salute, Major Beauregard asked the MP Private for directions to the Provost Marshal's Office."

After pointing straight ahead, the MP Private looked into the staff car and said, "If you follow this road, Sir, you'll see a sign that will direct you to his office." As soon as the Major thanked the MP Private, Al Parker put the staff car in gear and proceeded to the Provost Marshal's Office at the 440th Troop Carrier Group.

By the time the Major and his three man CID detail arrived at the Provost Marshal's Office, the Group Communications Officer was just leaving after he personally delivered the priority cable traffic to the chief law enforcement officer on base. As soon Jim Beauregard and his team entered the office and met the Provost Marshal, the men from CID received some more good news.

Once the Major finished reading the message, he looked up at the others and said, "This is a list of all U.S. Army personnel who attended the Advanced Glider School at South Plains Army Airfield from April to June of 1944. If Lieutenant Tucker is correct this list contains the name that Francis Shorty Mc Ghee is using. If our fugitives managed to go through glider training together, the name that Ivan Larson is using could also be on this list as well."

Before any interviews were conducted, the decision was made to compare the list of glider pilots who trained in Lubbock, Texas in May of 1944, to the list of glider unit personnel who are currently assigned to the 440th TCG. While the Major and his team made themselves comfortable in a nearby conference room, the Provost Marshal contacted the base personnel officer and requested that he prepare a list of all glider pilots and glider engineering officers, including warrant officers. Before he hung up the phone, the Provost Marshal directed the 440th Troop Carrier Group G1 to have this list ready to be picked up as soon as possible and not discuss this request with anyone else.

With the successful insertion of eleven gliders already completed, the task of mounting a another re-supply mission fell into the hands of the 439th Troop Carrier Group based in Chateaudun, France. To prepare for this mission, ground crew personnel worked throughout the night of December 26th and into the morning of the 27th to load fifty Waco gliders for a morning take off.

At 1025 hours on December 27, 1944 fifty C47s began towing fifty Waco gliders into the air and began flying toward Bastogne in different size combinations of tow planes and GC4As. After reaching an airspeed of 75 mph, Ivan Larson rotated his Waco glider into the air behind a tow plane from the 94th Troop Carrier Squadron at 1043 hours. Once Ivan's glider was towed to a cruising altitude of 2500 feet, he assumed a position slightly above and behind the C47 that was assigned to tow Chalk 37 to a landing zone near the Village of Savy.

While Shorty Mc Ghee remained in the back of the glider, he still had a hard time believing that he and Ivan were flying a combat mission as a way to facilitate their escape from the military police and Army CID. Up until the time they took off, the war was an event that was taking place some distance away from the safety of Allied occupied France. Now things were different, as Ivan and Shorty flew in a glider that was loaded with high explosive artillery ammunition and a box of detonators.

Even though Ivan and Shorty were hoping to avoid being arrested by becoming prisoners of war, they were painfully aware that things did not always work out as planned. Simply put, an awful lot could happen from the time they took off, until the time they made it into German custody as POWs. Still, after considering their situation from every angle, the two fugitives agreed that their options were limited. From a personal perspective, Ivan liked his escape plan because it gave him the chance to participate in a successful combat glider mission, before he got himself captured and sent to a German POW camp.

As confident as Ivan was behind the controls, he also liked the idea of having a co pilot on board, even though his stowaway never completed advanced glider training. Regardless, it was comforting to know that, if anything happened to Ivan, Shorty could take the controls and land the glider in a pinch.

While maintaining the proper position behind and slightly above his tow plane, at a cruising speed of 125 MPH, Ivan enjoyed a spectacular view of the European countryside. Knowing that he was on his way to help resupply a large number of surrounded American soldiers, was an amazing feeling that warmed a spot in Ivan's heart that rarely if ever saw the light of day.

Although he rarely, if ever, discussed his personal feelings, Ivan believed that the world owed him something because he had a tough life as a kid. Ivan also envisioned himself as a Robin Hood style character, who only stole from people who could afford to lose whatever he took from them. Once rationing was imposed, Ivan also had no problem satisfying the needs of those who felt no obligation to abide by the wartime rationing regulations.

Ivan also felt no remorse for killing Tommy Mulray, or Patrolman Murphy, even though the off duty cop turned out to be a war hero. The day Officer Murphy shot and killed his best friend, Ivan reacted with uncontrollable rage when he killed the off duty policeman who was trying to foil a bank robbery. As far as Ivan was concerned, the law of the jungle made it OK for cops and criminals to exchange gunfire and kill each other if need be. The same was true when it came time to shoot and kill the man the newspapers identified as Anthony Giordino. The fact that Anthony Giordino shot at Ivan to prevent his escape, made him fair game as far as the fleeing felon was concerned.

While Ivan's mind was filled with a barrage of thoughts from his past, he felt a twinge of regret for killing Lt. Perkins. Of all the crimes he committed, killing Steve Perkins and making it look like a suicide made Ivan feel tainted and evil. In fact, Ivan had not slept well since he murdered Steve Perkins and made it look like the young Army officer took his own life.

After Ivan glanced back to check on his partner in crime, he cracked a smile when he spotted Shorty curled up on the floor of the cargo bay, while protected from the cold in a U.S. Army sleeping bag. While Ivan faced forward again, he continued thinking about his past actions. After going over and over the reasons why he believed it was necessary to eliminate Lt. Perkins, Ivan became angry with himself for second guessing what appeared to be a good idea at the time.

While Ivan used his Ronson lighter to light a Camel cigarette, he did his best to think about what life would be like if he survived the war. The more Ivan concentrated on his flying duties, the more he began to calm down and become one with his glider. Just like other pilots, Ivan believed that flying was like an elixir that made life worth living. As far as Ivan was concerned, the problems that he had on earth seemed to evaporate once he was airborne and operating in a safe haven where even evil men could find solace. While Ivan became philosophical about the wonders of being a combat aviator, he envisioned his overworked Guardian Angel whispering into his ear as he said, "Perhaps being closer to heaven has had more of an effect on you than you know."

As soon as the list of glider personnel was delivered to the conference room, Major Beauregard sat at the head of the table, while Sergeant Parker along with the two CID agents from the Paris office began cross referencing the names of pilots who were assigned to the 440th TCG, to those who also attended the Advanced Glider School in Lubbock, Texas from April to June of '44. At 1055 hours Al Parker began calling out the names in alphabetical order, while Sergeant Hank Blair and Captain Tommy Savino checked names off the master list that was provided by the 440th Troop Carrier Group G1.

While Al Parker read from the Advanced Glider School list and said, "Ballard, Bowman, Chase, Chicarelli, Dumont, Evans, Gannon, Hart, Jensen, Kingman, Le Clerk, Moran, Nickerson, Olsen, O'Malley," Sergeant Blair called out, "I heard that name before, Sir."

As the former MP who served with Lt. Colonel Vogel in North Africa and Italy before he was transferred to CID flipped through his notebook, Major Beauregard looked at Hank Blair and said, "What is it, Sergeant?"

As Sergeant Blair continued to carefully examine every page, he remained focused on locating the information that he was looking for when he remarked, "I know the name O'Malley, Sir."

While Hank Blair checked his notebook, Captain Savino slid his finger down the list of glider personnel and stopped when he found what he was looking for. "I found him, Sir," said Captain Savino, as he looked up and said, "Warrant Officer Gus O'Malley is an Assistant Glider Engineering Officer with the 440th Troop Carrier Group in Orleans, France."

After checking the list of names from the glider school in Lubbock, Texas, an excited Al Parker looked at Jim Beauregard and said, "I think Sergeant Blair is on to something, Sir." As Al continued, he showed the list from the Advanced Glider School at South Plains Army Airfield to the Major. "According to Lt. Tucker, the glider pilot he knew as Shorty never completed the Advanced Glider School and was transferred to glider engineering duties with the rank of Warrant Officer." While Al pointed to the list, he finished his remarks by saying, "Everyone else on this list holds the rank of Flight Officer, while Gus O'Malley is listed as a Warrant Officer and is the only person who attended glider pilot training in Texas who is serving as an Assistant Glider Engineering Officer."

Just as Jim finished examining the list from South Plains Army Airfield and the list of personnel from the 440th TCG, Sergeant Blair found the entry that he was looking for and said, "I found it, Sir." While gleaming with pride, the young CID Agent referred to his notes as he continued filling everyone in. "I remember this entry because Colonel Vogel asked me to be the duty agent when everyone else was out of the office to execute a series of raids with the French Police. It was late in the day when a call came in from an MP Lieutenant based in Orleans to report that a Glider Engineering Officer by the name of Lieutenant Steve Perkins was the victim of a single self inflicted gunshot wound to the head. In addition to recovering his government issued forty five, the MPs also found a partially burned Dear John letter in the Lieutenant's quarters. The MPs also determined that Lt. Perkins was intoxicated at the time of his death."

As soon as Hank Blair handed his notebook to the Major and said, "Check this out, Sir," Jim Beauregard examined the entry involving the duty call from the MP Lieutenant in Orleans and said, "According to Sergeant Blair's notes, an Assistant Glider Engineering Officer by the name of Gus O'Malley was identified as a close personal friend of Lt. Perkins. In addition to hearing the single gunshot, Warrant Officer O'Malley found the Lieutenant's body. A Flight Officer by the name of Daniel Gannon also responded to the scene when the single gunshot was heard and told MPs that Lt. Perkins was upset after receiving a Dear John letter."

After hearing what was just said, Al Parker pointed to the list from the

Advanced Glider School in Lubbock, Texas and said, "The name Daniel Gannon is also on the list from South Plains Army Airfield, Sir."

Captain Savino was the next to speak when he pointed to the list of glider personnel assigned to the air base in Orleans. "Here he is, Major. Flight Officer Daniel Gannon is also assigned to the 440th Troop Carrier Group."

After hearing what Captain Savino just reported Al Parker remarked, "What are the odds that Daniel Gannon is Ivan Larson and Gus O'Malley is Francis Shorty Mc Ghee?"

While looking at the others, Jim Beauregard wasted no time in saying, "We need to learn more about Mister O'Malley and Flight Officer Gannon and we need to do so as soon as possible. In addition to interviewing Billy Davis, we also need immediate access to the personnel files for these men."

After thinking about the best way to proceed, the Major looked across the table at the rest of his team and said, "Since Gus O'Malley and Daniel Gannon are assigned to this base we can't risk having someone tip them off that CID just pulled their files. This means that we better request a good handful of personnel files at the same time."

As a policeman from Providence, Rhode Island who was performing his national service in time of war by serving in Army CID, Captain Savino knew exactly what needed to be done. "Sergeant Blair and I can handle that, Sir."

Once Captain Savino and Sergeant Blair stood up and prepared to leave, Jim Beauregard thanked the two CID Agents from the Paris office for handling this matter, while he and Al Parker sent for Captain Davis."

As soon as the two CID Agents left the conference room to request additional assistance from the base Provost Marshal, Jim Beauregard turned to his partner, while he removed a cigarette from the pack in his pocket and said, "We're close, Al, real close."

While Al Parker struck a wooden match, he offered Jim a light as he remarked, "Even though I agree, I'm trying real hard not to get too excited until we know more."

After taking a drag on the unfiltered cigarette, Jim Beauregard checked his watch as he stood up and walked over to the door of the conference room and said, "It's time to call our first witness."

Normally, Billy Davis was the life of the party but things were a bit different now that he was temporarily grounded and ordered to remain in his quarters until he was summoned by the military police. As a combat tested Army pilot, Billy Davis did not like being taken off flight status, when his services were needed to re-supply the American troops who were surrounded in Bastogne.

As soon as Captain Davis was escorted into the conference room by MP Sergeant Chris Jacko, the veteran C47 pilot did his best to conceal his frustration about being grounded when he saluted Major Beauregard and identified himself, "Captain Davis reporting as ordered, Sir."

After returning the salute, Major Beauregard produced his CID badge and identification and said, "Captain, my name is Major James Beauregard. I'm a CID Agent from New York." Then, as the Major turned to his left, he introduced Staff Sergeant Al Parker as his partner and added that two CID Agents from Paris will be joining them as soon as they return from the base personnel office."

While Al Parker poured hot coffee into three clean cups, Major Beauregard extended his hand to a nearby chair and said, "Have a seat, Captain, and join Sergeant Parker and I in a cup of coffee while we tell you why you're here."

Between being taken off flight status and being incredibly curious why Army CID Agents wanted to interview him, Captain Davis wasted no time in saying, "Excuse me for asking, Sir, but what the heck is this all about?"

While Al Parker opened his notebook and prepared to document the statements that were made during this interview, Major Beauregard responded to the Captain's question by saying, "I know you'd rather be flying right now, so the faster we get through this, the faster you'll be back in the cockpit of your C47." After seeing a frustrated Billy Davis submit to their authority and take a sip of black coffee, Major Beauregard decided to begin this interview by asking the C47 pilot if he knew an Assistant Glider Engineering Officer by the name of Gus O'Malley.

As soon as Billy Davis responded in the affirmative and said, "Yes, Sir. I know Gus," the Major stood up and walked over to a nearby table where a pitcher of water was located as he asked the Captain to explain how they met.

While the Major filled a glass with water, Captain Davis answered the question in a matter of fact tone of voice. "We met at the Advanced Glider School at South Plains Army Airfield in Lubbock, Texas earlier this year. At the time, I was just back from being stationed overseas. When Lt. Colonel Kirby was a Major he arranged for my transfer to South Plains Army Airfield in April of '44 to help train glider pilots."

After hearing the Major from CID remark, "Please continue, Captain," Billy Davis took a sip of coffee before he went on to say, "When Gus was going through the Advanced School, Major Kirby felt that he had more to offer the glider program if he went to Glider Engineering School and was made an Assistant Glider Engineering Officer. The Major came to this decision because Gus wasn't as comfortable flying as a glider into a crowded LZ as he needed to be, but he did prove to be a talented SOB when it came to repairing gliders and other equipment."

While Major Beauregard continued looking directly at Captain Davis, the veteran street cop from Atlanta wasted no time in asking their witness if Gus O'Malley had any nicknames. After looking at Sergeant Parker who was taking copious notes, Captain Davis turned to face the Major as he responded in a matter of fact tone of voice and said, "There were three pilots in that class who were on the short side so I started calling them Shorty Number 1, Shorty Number 2 and Shorty Number 3. Gus was Shorty 3 because he was the taller of all the short guys. Gus was also called Skinny because he stopped eating when he was worried about flunking outta flight school."

After taking a sip from his coffee cup, Billy Davis added, "I also considered calling Gus "Stitches" after he cut his shaved head open when he recovered a crash landed glider and needed to get stitched up by Doc Keller." Once again Captain Davis paused before he continued and said, "While Gus didn't seem to mind being called Skinny, he hated being called Shorty but so did ever other guy in the Army who was shorter than everyone else."

The time had come to kick this discussion up a notch and ask their witness if Shorty Mc Ghee aka Gus O'Malley was associated with anyone who might match the description of Ivan Larson. After making eye contact with his partner, Jim faced Billy Davis and said, "By any chance was Gus O'Malley friends with anyone else in Advanced Glider School?"

"Yes, Sir, he was," responded Captain Davis who quickly added, "Gus went through all of his Army training from basic training to Advanced Glider School with his cousin, a glider pilot by the name of Danny Gannon."

As soon as Jim asked if Billy Davis knew where they were from, the C47 pilot responded and said, "They were originally from New York City but they moved to Jersey City when they were kids and were raised by their Uncle Mike. I guess that's why we hit it off, Sir. I'm also from New York." Then, in typical Billy Davis fashion, the young C47 pilot remarked, "Even though they moved across the river to Jersey I never held it against them, Sir."

Deep down inside Jim Beauregard and Al Parker were screaming after hearing Billy Davis mention that Danny Gannon and Gus O'Malley were cousins who were raised by their Uncle Mike. As soon as Major Beauregard turned to Al Parker and nodded his head, Al placed a file full of newspaper articles and copies of wanted posters on the table and said, "Captain, have you ever read any of these articles or looked at any of these police sketches before?"

After looking at the file full of newspaper articles and police sketches of the two fugitives, that included a front page article in the latest edition of The Stars and Stripes Newspaper, Billy Davis nodded his head then said, "I read a few of these articles when they first came out and I heard one of the radio broadcasts about this case but I haven't had a chance to read the most recent issue of The Stars and Stripes because this is the first copy I've seen in France. I remember this story, Sergeant, because I'm from Brooklyn. In fact, I've been up and down Nostrand Avenue and Church Avenue a million times and know exactly where the bank that was robbed is located. Sure I remember that story. Why do you ask?"

As Al picked up the most recent edition of The Stars and Stripes Newspaper, he continued while he presented the Army newspaper to their witness. "Would you mind reading this front page article, Captain?"

After shrugging his shoulders, Billy Davis took the paper from Al's hand and began reading the article out loud.

While Captain Davis read the article out loud he felt a strange feeling surge through his stomach. "The fugitives identified as Ivan Larson and Francis Shorty Mc Ghee are wanted for the murder of a New York City Police Officer, bank robbery, assault, possession of unlicensed firearms, the sale of items rationed by the Office of Price Administration and other crimes. Both fugitives were recently identified as close associates of a known gangster identified as Mad Mike Connely. Mike Connely was recently killed in a shootout with New York City Police Detectives assigned to the U.S. Army CID Task Force."

The moment Captain Davis started to show signs of reacting to what he just read, Major Beauregard spoke up and said, "Keep reading, Captain." While Billy Davis continued, he read the article at a faster pace and in much higher tone of voice. "A search of Mr. Connely's residence resulted in recovering evidence that indicates that Ivan Larson and Francis Shorty Mc Ghee are serving in the

United States Army Air Forces under assumed names in the European Theater of Operation and are believed to be stationed on an air base in France. The War Department is asking all U.S. Army personnel to report any information about Army personnel who correspond with anyone named Mike Connely, or represent themselves to be related to an individual by this name to the U.S. Army Criminal Investigations Division, the Provost Marshal's Office, the Military Police or the FBI as soon as possible. Do not attempt to challenge or apprehend these fugitives by yourself. Both fugitives are considered armed and dangerous."

As soon as Billy Davis stopped reading the article, he vaulted out of his chair and remarked, "Mad Mike is the name that Danny Gannon writes on the front of every glider he flies, including the one he flew in the Holland mission." Then, after pausing for a split second, Captain Davis looked at Sergeant Parker then at Major Beauregard and said, "Are you trying to tell me that I was friends with two fugitives who robbed a bank and killed a cop?"

Without displaying any emotion whatsoever, Jim Beauregard motioned Billy Davis to sit back down as he responded to his question. "If you have a seat, Captain, Sergeant Parker and I will be happy to brief you further."

When Billy Davis sat back down, Jim Beauregard addressed the Captain in a business like tone of voice. "For your information, Captain, Staff Sergeant Parker is a New York City Police Officer on military leave assigned to CID to help the Army hunt down these fugitives." After quickly turning to face Al Parker, Billly Davis spoke in a respectful tone of voice when he said, "You're the cop who got a good look at the face of the bank robber after he killed that police officer. That's why you're here. You can identify one of the fugitives."

As soon as Al nodded his head ever so slightly, he quickly confirmed the Captain's suspicions. "That's correct, Captain."

While Billy Davis handed the Army newspaper back to Al Parker, his disposition changed as he thought about the heroism that Patrolman Al Parker displayed during the bank robbery in Brooklyn that cost the life of an off duty policeman. As Al placed the most recent edition of The Stars and Stripes Newspaper on the table, Billy Davis spoke in a very sincere tone of voice when he said, "I'm sorry about what happened to your friend."

Immediately after Al Parker thanked the Captain for his kind words, Major Beauregard asked Billy Davis why he didn't make the connection before. Again, without taking time to consider his response, Captain Davis picked up the most recent wanted poster off the table and said, "Like I said, Sir, after I read the first few articles, I didn't pay much attention to this story. Even when I heard one of the radio broadcasts about this case, I was trying to read my mail and write a few letters before I hit the sack to get some sleep before another day of flying."

After pausing long enough to take another sip of coffee, the Captain continued and said, "I'm sorry, Sir but I never made the connection until I just read that the two fugitives are associated with a gangster by the name of Mad Mike Connely. You see, Sir, in addition to the fact that Danny Gannon wrote the name Mad Mike on every glider that he flew, whenever he and Gus O'Malley received mail it was always from their Uncle Mike. I also never made the connection, because as far as I know, I'm the one who gave Gus O'Malley the nickname Shorty. In fact, as far as I knew at the time, he was never called Shorty before I started calling him Shorty # 3."

While his interrogators remained silent, Captain Davis took another look at the latest issue of The Stars and Stripes Newspaper, before he looked across the table at Al Parker then over to Major Beauregard and said, "I'm just guessing, Sir, but maybe I never made the connection because CID and the MPs were looking for a fugitive who was an orphan. Even his accomplice was a runaway who was turned into the police by his stepfather. I mention this, Sir, because as far as I knew, Danny Gannon and Gus O'Malley were cousins who acted as if they came from a real close family. I also believed them when they told me that after their mothers died when they were young, and they went to live with their Uncle Mike because their fathers were merchant seamen who were away from home for long periods of time. They also said that before the war their fathers got jobs building bases in the Pacific. To tell you the truth, Sir, everyone felt sorry for them when they let it be known that their fathers haven't been heard from ever since the Japs started the war in the Pacific."

After pausing to take another sip of coffee, Captain Davis added, "As you and the Sergeant know, Sir, it's also not hard for Army life to change the way a man looks. For starters, Gus O'Malley has a shaved head, a mustache and is in excellent physical condition. Even though Danny Gannon is taller and thinner than Gus, he's clean shaven, has very short hair and is also in excellent physical condition. I also have to say, Sir, that I met several G.I.s between basic training and my current posting who were made fun of and given nicknames because they are shorter, taller, fatter, stronger, older, younger, smarter or dumber than everyone else."

Because Major Beauregard was convinced that he was dealing with a completely truthful and cooperative witness, he relaxed his demeanor as he tossed a pack of Lucky Strikes on the table and said, "Help yourself to a smoke, Captain, while I ask you a few more questions."

As Captain Davis removed a Lucky Strike from the pack and used his own lighter to light the unfiltered cigarette, Major Beauregard continued the interview. "What about the composite sketches of the two fugitives? In your opinion do they look anything like Danny Gannon and Gus O'Malley?"

After looking at the most recent edition of Stars and Stripes, Billy Davis took a drag on his cigarette before he responded. "Well, Sir, I'd say it's a lot easier to make the connection now that I read this article." After pausing for a second to take another drag on his cigarette, Billy Davis tapped his right index finger on the sketch of Ivan Larson before he continued and said, "I don't know if this helps, Sir, but even though I think there's a stronger resemblance between the fugitive known as Francis Shorty Mc Ghee and Assistant Glider Engineering Officer Gus O'Malley, if you lined up a bunch of glider pilots and you compared their faces to the sketch of the fugitive called Ivan Larson, you'd see enough of a resemblance to pull the pilot I know as Danny Gannon in for further questioning. It would also help if the wanted poster of the guy I know as Gus O'Malley included a mustache and a shaved head."

While Billy Davis paused to take another drag on his cigarette, the enormity of the situation hit him like a ton of bricks. As soon as the decorated C47 pilot realized that he was duped by two bank robbing cop killers, he slumped in his chair and remarked, "They seemed like such nice guys. I feel like a real jerk."

Even though Jim Beauregard and Al Parker were elated to be interviewing such a credible witness, they felt sorry for Captain Davis. After signaling his partner to take over again, Al Parker looked across the table at the highly decorated Army aviator and said, "Don't be so hard on yourself, Sir. Ivan Larson and Francis Shorty Mc Ghee have done an excellent job of staying one step ahead of us, by adopting a new identity and acting like every other patriotic American who's serving in the U.S. Army."

In an effort to be completely thorough in their interview, Jim Beauregard asked the Captain if he knew a Glider Engineering Officer by the name of Steve Perkins. Without taking time to think, Captain Davis sat up straight in his chair as he responded to the Major's question. "Yes, Sir. The Lieutenant was a nice guy. I was sorry to hear that he committed suicide."

After pausing for a split second to stamp his cigarette out in a nearby ashtray, Captain Davis added, "I assume you're asking me, Sir, because Lt. Perkins and Gus O'Malley became friends when they attended Glider Engineering School together. In fact, Gus O'Malley took the death of Lt. Perkins pretty hard."

Immediately after Captain Davis began to describe how everyone, including Lt. Colonel Kirby, thought that Gus O'Malley and Steve Perkins were the most talented glider engineering officers they ever served with, he stopped in mid sentence and said, "They killed him too!"

After seeing their witness react like so many other people who were taken in by criminals, Jim Beauregard remarked, "Sergeant Parker's right. Don't be so hard on yourself, Captain. Ivan Larson and Shorty Mc Ghee had a lot going for them, including the fact that they were helped by Mike Connely. The fact that they were never arrested, fingerprinted or photographed also enabled them to get inducted into the Army and avoid being captured for over a year."

While the Major paused long enough to refill the Captain's cup with hot coffee, he continued and said, "Whether or not Ivan Larson and Shorty Mc Ghee were involved with the death of Lt. Perkins is yet to be determined. All we know is that the military police in Orleans listed Gus O'Malley and Danny Gannon as the Army personnel who found the Lieutenant's body immediately after he reportedly committed suicide with a forty five. What we can prove is that Ivan Larson murdered a truck driver and one of our informants while trying to hijack a truck load of rationed tires, before he robbed a bank and killed one policeman and wounded another. While all this was going on Francis Shorty Mc Ghee provided covering fire with a Thompson Submachine Gun and drove the getaway car. As a result, all that matters is that we capture these fugitives before anyone else gets hurt."

After conducting a long and painstaking investigation Al Parker asked the $64 dollar question. "Captain, are you willing to assist us in locating the U.S. Army personnel who are using the names Daniel Gannon and Gus O'Malley?"

As Captain Davis pointed to the police pencil sketch of Ivan Larson, he wasted no time in responding to Al Parker's question. "Both Danny Gannon and Gus O'Malley are temporarily assigned to the 439th Troop Carrier Group in Chateaudun, France until the first of the year." Then, after pausing long enough to hold up the police sketch of Francis Shorty Mc Ghee, the Captain added, "According to Colonel Kirby, Gus O'Malley is helping Colonel Gately's engineering section get ready for an inspection. The Colonel agreed to detail Danny Gannon to the 439th so he could spend Christmas and New Years with his cousin. Doing so also gave the CO of the 439th access to an extra pilot during any re-supply missions that take place over the holidays."

As soon as Al Parker looked across the table at Jim Beauregard and said, "Once again, Major, we've taken one step forward and two steps back," the Major asked Captain Davis how far it was to Chateaudun, France. Without hesitating Billy Davis remarked, "If we use my C47 I can get you and Sergeant Parker to the 439th in about 30 minutes, Sir, but based on what I know fifty tow plane crews and fifty GC-4A Waco gliders were scheduled to depart our base in Chateaudun sometime this morning to re-supply Bastogne."

After checking his watch Captain Davis continued and said, "They were sched-uled for a 0815 hour departure but I heard take off time had to be delayed due to the 16 degree weather. My guess is that they'll get airborne as soon as it warms up which should be about now. I also think you should know, Sir, that because of the number of pilots who are currently on leave, there's an excellent chance that your fugitive known as Danny Gannon will have no problem volunteering to fly this mission. In fact, if I know Danny Gannon he'll pay another pilot to take his place if that's what it takes for him to get another shot at combat."

While a frustrated Al Parker stood up and began to pace back and forth in the conference room, Billy Davis looked up at the veteran New York City Policeman who joined the Army to hunt down two fugitives in time of war and said, "It won't be easy, Sarge, but you and the Major still have a chance to capture your fugitive if he participated in today's mission." After pausing for a split second, a confident sounding Billy Davis quickly added, "Here, let me show you."

By the time Al Parker sat down, Captain Davis removed an air chart from the inside pocket of his flight jacket and placed the opened map on the table. While Jim Beauregard and Al Parker paid close attention, Captain Davis used his pen as a pointer as he continued speaking. "This is our current position at the 440th Troop Carrier Group in Orleans, France which is designated as A50. A39 is the Army Air Forces designation for the air base in Chateaudun, France where the 439th Troop Carrier Group in located."

Once again Billy continued to use his pen as a pointer, while he traced the flight path that the C47's and gliders would take on today's resupply mission to Bastogne. "As you can see, these fifty tow planes and gliders have to fly past

Orleans just to our north on a heading of East Northeast until they reach Neufchateau. They'll then turn Northeast and fly for another ten minutes before they reach the release point over the Village of Savy, which is about 1 mile northwest of Bastogne."

As soon as Billy Davis put his pen down, he continued while he looked at Al Parker and Major Beauregard. "Even if those fifty gliders got airborne an hour ago, it's still possible to fly to Bastogne and have enough time before it gets dark to continue your search, providing of course that you and your men don't get shot out of the sky in the process. Naturally, the success of your mission will also depend on what happens to Danny Gannon, as well as Gus O'Malley if he stowed away on the same glider."

As a law enforcement officer who began his military career as a soldier during the Punitive Expedition into Mexico, Jim Beauregard knew from experience that you should never go in harms way until you obtain as much intelligence information as possible about your objective. As a result, Jim decided to ask an obvious expert like Billy Davis to give him and Al Parker a no bullshit assessment of the situation, before they went in pursuit of Danny Gannon, if it was determined that their number one fugitive was flying a glider resupply mission to Bastogne.

After looking across the table at Al Parker, then to his left to face Jim Beauregard, Billy Davis responded to the Major's request by saying, "If you and Sergeant Parker determine that you need to pursue Danny Gannon and or Gus O'Malley to Bastogne you need to know exactly what you will be up against. First, you'll have to get equipped to fly a combat mission for over two hours in a Waco glider. You also have to be prepared to deal with the fact, that by the time you arrive over Bastogne, a total of 61 gliders from three different glider missions will have been sent to re-supply our troops in a relatively confined area that is surrounded by a large number of trigger happy German soldiers. This means that many of the best landing zones will likely be crowded with crash landed gliders and the remains of shot down aircraft. The other bad news is that the Germans will be doing everything possible to shoot down C47s and gliders. Needless to say, Sir, this will be even easier to accomplish when the only target in the sky over Bastogne is a single glider that is being towed through the sky by a single C47."

While Billy Davis continued his briefing, he sounded like a man who definitely knew his business when he said, "Another problem involves the size of today's re-supply mission. You see, Sir, these fifty gliders will be towed side by side in different size formations by tow planes from the 91st, 92nd, 93rd, 94th,, 95th and 96th Troop Carrier Squadrons. This means that this entire formation will be spread out for miles. Once the Germans see this airborne supply train coming their way, they're gunners will have plenty of time to determine the altitude and the direction of travel of our aircraft before they open fire."

After pausing to light another cigarette from the pack on the table, Captain Davis added, "It's also important to consider that in certain situations, tow plane pilots will be compelled to deviate from their flight plan in order to evade heavy flak and enemy ground fire. Even though tow plane crews routinely risk their lives to deliver gliders to the proper release point, the simple fact is that gliders can end up landing all over the place. In fact, if enemy anti aircraft fire is intense enough, tow planes and gliders can end up getting badly damaged and shot down with some crews ending up as POW's. All of these factors can impact your ability to capture Danny Gannon."

"This sounds like the deck is stacked against us," remarked Jim Beauregard.

As soon as Captain Davis tapped the ash from his cigarette in a nearby ashtray, he and responded to the Major's comment in a matter of fact tone of voice. "The bottom line, Sir, is that you and your men could end up risking your life to fly into a combat zone that is still under siege with little or no chance of capturing Danny Gannon. As far as Gus O'Malley is concerned, unless he stowed away on Danny Gannon's glider, he should be easy to locate now that you know he's temporarily assigned to the 439th."

When Major Beauregard asked if Billy Davis would be flying the re-supply to Bastogne today if he wasn't directed to be interviewed by CID, the young C47 pilot looked directly at the Major and said, "Yes, Sir, I would. In fact, a total of thirteen tow planes from the 440th were assigned to augment the C47 crews from the 439th. and will be flying to Bastogne at the back end of the formation."

Just as Major Beauregard thanked the Captain for his detailed briefing, the door to the conference room opened as Captain Savino and Sergeant Blair entered carrying an arm full of personnel files. As Captain Savino remarked, "Mission accomplished, Sir," Jim Beauregard and Al Parker stood up and helped the two CID Agents from Paris place the pile of files on the table. While the Major introduced the two Paris based CID Agents to Captain Davis, the files were spread out on the table to make it easier to find the ones that belonged to Gus O'Malley and Daniel Gannon.

The moment of truth came when the two files were recovered and opened in front of Captain Davis. The second Captain Davis examined the photographs that were attached to both files, the young C47 pilot remarked, "That's them, Sir. Danny Gannon and Gus O'Malley."

While Al Parker pointed his right index finger at the photo of Danny Gannon, he took a moment to remember the day when he ripped the nylon stocking mask off Ivan Larson's face during the bank robbery before he remarked, "I don't care how much Army life has changed the way this cop killing son of a bitch looks. That's him, Sir. That's Ivan Larson." Jim Beauregard had been a cop long enough to know when credible witnesses, including a fellow law enforcement officer, were absolutely positive when it came time to identify the perpetrator of a crime.

Being an Army pilot meant that Billy Davis was highly intelligent, very competitive and well trained. As such, he knew that sulking was not going to help the situation. After making some additional calculations, Billy Davis did his best to write off his failure to recognize the two fugitives as he turned to face Major Beauregard and said, "Whatever you plan on doing, Sir, you can count me in." Having Billy Davis on board and at their disposal brought Major Beauregard to pick up a nearby telephone and direct the Army operator to connect him to the 439th Troop Carrier Group.

While waiting for the call to go though, Major Beauregard turned to Captain Davis and said, "Are you ready to do some flying, Captain?" As an enthusiastic Billy Davis said, "Yes, Sir," Major Beauregard turned to Captain Savino and said, "Tom, why don't you and Sergeant Blair head over to the base hospital with Captain Davis and brief Colonel Kirby. Once you fill the Colonel in ask for his assistance. We need a C47 and a glider as well as combat gear for everyone who volunteers to go along. It also wouldn't hurt to have a medic with us on this trip who can also identify Shorty Mc Ghee, so ask Sergeant Keller if he's willing to go with us to Bastogne. We'll meet in the briefing room as soon as I get off the phone with the Commanding Officer of the 439th Troop Carrier Group." After handing an envelope to Captain Savino, the Major added, "These are our orders from the War Department. I doubt you'll need them but take them with you anyway."

"You got it, Major," responded Captain Savino before he left the conference room with Sergeant Blair and Billy Davis.

Once the connection was finally made, the Army Signal Corps operator said, "Go ahead, Major, the 439th is on the line."

After quickly lighting a cigarette, Major Beauregard identified himself to the operator. "This is Major James Beauregard from CID. I need to speak to the Commanding Officer. It's urgent"

After hearing the base operator say, "Yes, Sir," the Major took a drag on his cigarette as he looked at Al and winked his right eye.

A split second later, the Commanding Officer of the 439th TCG came on the line. "This is Colonel Gately."

As soon as the base commander came on the line Jim said, "Sir, this is Major James Beauregard from CID. I have warrants for the arrest of two fugitives who were just identified as using the names Daniel Gannon and Gus O'Malley. These men are wanted for the murder of a New York City Police Officer, bank robbery and other serious crimes."

The stunned Colonel reacted as expected. "What!"

Due to the urgency of the situation Major Beauregard got right down to the matter at hand. "Sir, it's urgent that you place both of these men under arrest and hold them until my men and I arrive at your base. I also suggest that you advise your MPs to consider these fugitives armed and dangerous."

In an effort to comply with CID Agent's request, the base commander responded and said, "I'm sorry, Major, but you're a day late and a dollar short. Flight Officer Gannon is already airborne and on his way to a forward area to deliver supplies. As far as O'Malley is concerned, I can have the MPs hunt him down and take him into custody." When Colonel Gately asked Major Beauregard to hold on, he called out to an aide and said, "Sergeant, have the military police arrest Gus O'Malley and bring his sorry ass to me! And tell them to use caution."

After hearing someone in the background acknowledge the order, Jim Beauregard felt as if some significant progress was being made on their case, when the Colonel got back on the line and said, "OK, Major, the MPs are on the way to arrest Mister O'Malley." While Jim Beauregard continued speaking to the Commanding Officer of the 439th TCG, he assured the Colonel that witnesses working with CID positively identified Danny Gannon and Gus O'Malley as the two fugitives who murdered a New York City policeman and committed other serious crimes.

As much as he wanted to help, Lt. Colonel Gately knew that he had to be the bearer of bad news when he spoke in a matter of fact tone of voice and said,

"I'm sorry, Major but I could have done something about this if you called before today's resupply mission got airborne. Unfortunately, I don't see how I can order the plane towing your fugitive to turn back now that they're on their way to their intended destination. I also hate to say this but your fugitive is carrying 250 rounds of artillery ammunition that is desperately needed by our troops on the ground."

While Jim Beauregard smoked his cigarette and listened to the Commanding Officer of the 439th Troop Carrier Group, Colonel Gately continued and said, "You have to understand, Major. Your fugitive is flying in Chalk 37 which is right behind the mid section of the entire formation. The overall success of this mission could easily be compromised, if I ordered the recall of one tow plane and every C47 flying behind Chalk 37 also turned back to base because they believed that today's mission was canceled."

After pausing for a split second to light one of his own cigarettes, Lt. Colonel Gately remarked, "You should also know, Major, that even if I was able to order the plane towing your fugitive to return to base without compromising this mission, your fugitive will likely become very suspicious when his aircraft is the only glider that gets turned around. If this happens all he has to do is cut the tow line, land in an open field and take off on foot, or hitch a ride in any number of military vehicles that are driving around the French countryside. I also don't mean to tell you how to do your job, but you have a better chance of catching your fugitive if you contact the MPs on the ground where he's expected to land. As long as Flight Officer Gannon doesn't get killed or captured in the process of flying this mission, the MPs should be able to find him and take him into custody."

Under the circumstances, all Jim could say in response was, "I understand, Sir."

When Lt. Colonel Gately continued there was a definite hint of regret in his voice. "I also have to tell you, that it's no secret that CID has been looking for two fugitives who killed a cop and robbed a bank in New York. We just never figured they were here."

Jim Beauregard finished his end of the conversation by asking if Colonel Gately had any other advice or recommendations that might help CID in their manhunt. Without hesitating Colonel Gately responded and said, "I suggest you speak to Colonel Mike Kirby. If anyone can help you it's Mike Kirby. He knows the destination where crews from the 439th and the 440th are headed today and is familiar with every detail of the flight plan. Colonel Kirby can also contact the MPs where Danny Gannon's glider is scheduled to land."

"Two of my agents and a C47 pilot who's assisting us are in the process of doing so, Sir," responded Jim.

Lt. Colonel Gately finished his remarks by saying, "Good luck, Major. I hope you get him."

After thanking the Commanding Officer of the 439th Troop Carrier Group, Jim hung up the phone, looked at Al and said, "Ivan Larson is on his way to resupply Bastogne in a glider that's positioned smack in the middle of the fifty aircraft formation. According to Lt. Colonel Gately, ordering the C47 towing Chalk 37 to return to base could cause the aircraft behind Larson's glider to think the mission was canceled and do the same. The Colonel also sent his MPs after Shorty Mc Ghee."

CHAPTER 10

OFF WE GO INTO
THE WILD BLUE YONDER

While Lt. Colonel Mike Kirby sat in a chair in the briefing room, he took a call from Lt. Colonel Gately and learned that the military police were unable to locate Gus O'Malley. As Lt. Colonel Gately continued, he advised Mike Kirby that one witness reported that he observed Gus O'Malley driving a jeep on the flight line just before take off. A second witness from the ground crew told MPs that a glider pilot drove a jeep from the engineering section down the flight line just before take off and parked the vehicle next to a fuel truck. According to this ground crewman, this glider pilot then ran back to the middle of the formation, just as the tow planes started their engines. Colonel Gately concluded his telephone briefing by adding, "I'm sorry, Mike, but it looks like Gus O'Malley stowed away on Chalk 37 with Danny Gannon."

When Jim Beauregard and the others arrived at the 440th Troop Carrier Command in Orleans, they were wearing Army Combat Uniforms with wool sweaters under their OD Green M43 Field Jackets with a removable liner. The Major also had his Army issue officer's trench coat with him as well. Since they intended to conduct their investigation and hopefully make their arrests on a U.S. Army Air Base, Major Beauregard and his three man team were also only armed with sidearms.

While Major Beauregard, Captain Savino, Al Parker and Sergeant Blair carried an issued Model 1911 .45 ACP caliber pistol with two spare seven round magazines, Al Parker also carried his six shot .38 Special Smith & Wesson Military & Police Model .38 Special revolver with a two inch barrel and a square butt wooden grip in a shoulder holster under his field jacket. In addition, Al Parker carried twenty four additional rounds of .38 Special ammunition, two pairs of handcuffs, his New York City Police Department Patrolman's shield, his military police identification, wanted posters of the two fugitives, the latest issue of The

Stars and Stripes Newspaper and a copy of the arrest warrants for Ivan Larson and Francis Shorty Mc Ghee.

Now that they were preparing to fly into combat, Lt. Colonel Kirby saw to it that Major Beauregard and his team were appropriately equipped. This included issuing the Major and his men a .45 ACP Caliber M3 Grease Gun, a .45 ACP caliber M1A1 Thompson Submachine Gun, several .30 caliber M1 Carbines, a supply of spare magazines and a basic combat load of ammunition, M1 Carbine bayonets and scabbards, helmets, two handie-talkie portable radios, flashlights, waterproof shoe pac boots, K rations, medical supplies, canteens, winter gloves, long underwear, woolen scarves and blankets to make their trip to Bastogne in a GC-4A Waco glider a bit more comfortable.

After thanking Lt. Colonel Gately for his assistance, Mike Kirby hung up the phone and asked everyone in the briefing room to listen up. While Jim Beauregard and the men who volunteered to travel with him to Bastogne stopped preparing their weapons and equipment for their mission, Lt. Colonel Kirby spoke once he knew that he had everyone's undivided attention. "According to Colonel Gately, the MPs can't find Gus O'Malley. Based on what two witnesses said, it looks like that little prick stowed away on his friend's glider. That means that if you still want to pursue your fugitives using a glider, you'll have to get airborne as soon as possible."

Even though he was still limping from his leg wound, Sergeant Michael Beauregard was just as gung ho as the other glider infantrymen and paratroopers who reported for duty. Unfortunately, making the 107 mile trip from Camp Mourmelon in France to Bastogne, in the back of an Army truck in the dead of winter, was no easy task for the young squad leader who was still recovering from two surgical procedures.

After several days and nights of living in a freezing cold front line defensive position, Sergeant Michael Beauregard was limping even more and using a walking stick made from a broken tree branch to get around. In order to remain with his men, Sergeant Beauregard would toss his walking stick aside whenever an officer inspected their position or met with squad leaders from his platoon. In addition to being an outstanding squad leader, Michael Beauregard was also an inspiration to his men because he didn't have to be where he was. This was the case because

Michael left a warm hospital bed to rejoin his unit, even though the wound that he sustained while fighting in Holland was not fully healed.

After checking his watch, Lt. Colonel Kirby looked at the mismatched posse that consisted of Major Jim Beauregard, his three man team from CID, Doc Keller and two MPs from the 440th TCG who volunteered to go along and said, "I have a few things I'd like to say before you leave on what has to be the most unusual glider mission of this war. First, I wish I could go with you but between my duties as the Commanding Officer of this base and my bad ankle I'm unable to do so. Second, when you catch your fugitives kick 'em in the ass once for me."

After breaking the tension in the room, the Colonel continued and said, "I have a C47 being fueled and a glider being prepared for take off. There's a truck outside that will take you to your glider. I'll meet you on the flight line as soon as I call the tower to clear you for immediate take off. Good luck, men."

As soon as Lt. Colonel Kirby used a pair of crutches to navigate his way off the elevated platform in the briefing room, Major Beauregard approached the Commanding Officer of the 440th TCG and asked if Captain Davis could go along with him and the others in the glider? After listening to the Major from CID explain that Captain Davis could prove to be a big help because he was able to identify both fugitives, Lt. Colonel Kirby removed a cigar from his flight jacket pocket as he faced Billy Davis and said, "Can you fly a glider as good as you can handle a C47?" As soon as Billy Davis responded and said, "Yes, Sir," Lt. Colonel Kirby turned to face Major Beauregard and said, "He's all yours, Major. I'll get someone to fly right seat in the Captain's plane." Then, after pausing long enough to light his cigar, Lt. Colonel Kirby remarked, "You boys are crazy but I hope you get 'em."

While the Major and the others grabbed their gear and started to walk out of the briefing room, Billy Davis remained behind to have a private chat with Mike Kirby. "I thought you gave those things up for chocolate bars?"

As soon as Mike Kirby removed the cigar from the corner of his mouth, he looked at his favorite C47 pilot and remarked, "I tried that but it didn't work, so I'm back on cigars again. In fact, I intend to puff away until you and the rest of your posse returns from your manhunt with that bank robbing little prick Gus O'Malley and that murdering piece of shit Danny Gannon in handcuffs."

The day Hans Sigmann observed decorated World War I veterans being carted off to Nazi concentration camps because they were Jewish, was the day that he began to privately question the sanity of the regime. Even though there wasn't much difference between serving Hitler's government as a policeman or as a soldier, Hans volunteered to leave his 20 year police career so he could serve in a Volksgrenadier unit.

Because of his age and his prior combat experience in World War 1, Oberfeldwebel (Master Sergeant) Hans Sigmann was like a father figure to his men. The fact that Hans was a police sergeant with the Munich Police Department gave him an even greater status among the platoon of Feldgendarmie (Military Police) from the 26th Volksgrenadier (VGD) Division that he commanded for some time. Unfortunately, between the number of men who were needed to guard American POW's during the early days of the Ardennes offensive and the casualties that his unit sustained, Hans Sigmann's field command was now comprised of one seasoned corporal and fifteen young Feldgendarmie.

During the opening days of the offensive, Sergeant Sigmann was like a proud father when he observed the reaction of the new men when they experienced their first victory. Even Hans was initially impressed by the success of the campaign and allowed himself the luxury of enjoying one more illusion, before he was forced to face the fact that the winter offensive in the Ardennes was doomed to fail.

Even though he was a policeman by profession, Sergeant Hans Sigmann knew enough about modern warfare and American History to admire the American soldiers who defended their positions from being overrun. While other Germans believed that cut off and encircled American Army units would eventually accept defeat, Hans knew that the Americans would develop a "Remember the Alamo" mentality and would continue to fight rather than surrender.

Despite the initial success of the German winter offensive, the Americans proved to be savage fighters when they were out numbered, short on supplies and lacked air support. Now that the Americans were receiving tactical air support, while also being resupplied by air, they were more determined and capable than ever of defending their positions from being overrun.

As far as Hans was concerned, the Americans were like a fighter in the ring who goes down but gets up on the count of nine and beats his opponent with a shot to the solar plexus followed by a sucker punch to the kisser. Even though he kept his opinions to himself, Hans Sigmann was convinced that the enemy would survive the current offensive and eventually win the war. The foolish dreams of victory were now being extinguished by the sights and sounds of a battle, that was being waged within a relatively short distance from the position that Hans Sigmann and his men were ordered to secure.

After surviving another bombardment by Allied planes, Hans patted the youngest member of his unit on the back and sounded more like a concerned father than a non commissioned officer when he said, "Are you all right, Jurgen?"

As soon as the young private smiled then said, "Yes, Sergeant," he had no idea that Hans Sigmann had taken a personal liking to him because he looked a lot like the son he lost on the Eastern Front.

After removing his wallet from his pocket and admiring two pictures of his family, Hans spotted a reinforced squad of SS troops moving into position inside the wooded terrain that was closer to the American lines. According to his superiors, this particular reinforced squad of SS troops were directed to conduct reconnaissance missions in close proximity to the American lines.

Sergeant Sigmann was interested in the arrival of this SS unit, because they would be occupying a section of the forest that was adjacent to the position that was under the control of the 26th Volksgrenadier Division. One reason for his concern was because Hans and his men would be responsible to direct traffic and take care of American Prisoners of War, once the redirected attack on the American defensive positions proved successful. Since there were rumors spreading that SS troops committed atrocities during the recent fighting in Malmedy, Hans had good reason to keep an eye on anyone from an SS unit.

While the members of this reinforced squad of SS troops funneled into position, SS Sergeant Claus Werner made eye contact with Hans Sigmann and acknowledged the military policeman with a simple nod of his head. After returning the nod, Hans instinctively knew that things were about to go from bad to worse in their section of the front line.

As the SS troops walked toward the American held perimeter, that was located west of Longchamps, Hans heard one of the youngest teenagers in his unit remark, "I told you they wouldn't forget us. I'll bet the Fuhrer personally ordered that SS unit to reinforce our left flank."

After Hans mumbled a derogatory remark about Nazis under his breath, he turned to the contingent of young military policemen under his command and said, "Check your equipment. I want a full accounting of your ammunition, food and water so we can reacquisition additional supplies as needed."

While his men complied with his order, Hans turned to his second in command and spoke as he pointed to a position in the wooded terrain southeast of their position. "Willie, I want you and Peter to keep and eye on that SS unit. Once the shooting starts the Americans will likely retaliate with artillery and another air attack."

As soon as Corporal Willie Prost nodded his head in a respectful fashion and said, "Yes, Sergeant," Private Peter Deitrick checked the bolt on his Mauser Karabina 98 Mauser rifle and jogged off with the corporal to assume their new position.

CHAPTER 11

IN HOT PURSUIT

While Jim Beauregard stood next to the glider that would take him and his team to Bastogne, he shouldered his M1A1 Paratrooper Model .30 Caliber Carbine with the side folding metal stock and buttoned the collar on the Army issued officer's trench coat that he wore over his field jacket. When Jim noticed that Al Parker appeared to be lost in thought, he walked over to the rear of the glider to have a private conversation with his partner. "You OK, Al?."

As Al Parker turned around to face Jim Beauregard, he spoke in a sincere tone of voice when he said, "The only thing I've been thinking about for the last year is getting my hands on Ivan Larson and Francis Shorty Mc Ghee and here we are getting ready to fly in a glider, so we can continue our search in a town that's surrounded by the German Army." While Al rubbed his gloved hands together and stamped his waterproof boots on the ice cold tarmac, he concluded his remarks by saying, "I'm just worried that more good men will get hurt or killed trying to take these bastards into custody."

While ground crew personnel finished refueling the C47 that would tow them to Bastogne, Jim looked directly at Al and said, "I know how you feel, Al, but the way I see it bad things happen to good people all the time and when that happens men like us willingly place our lives in danger to make things right. That includes the men who volunteered to go with us to Bastogne to find Larson and Mc Ghee."

When Jim continued he sounded like a man who had tremendous faith in their mission. "Don't forget what the Bible says, Al. Ask The Father anything in My Name and you shall receive. Now it's time to see if our prayers are gonna be answered."

After hearing Jim's words of encouragement, Al Parker nodded his head in agreement and remarked, "Amen."

A split second later a ground crewman removed the fuel hose from the wing of the C47 and called down to Billy Davis. "She's ready to fly, Captain."

While Jim patted Al on his back and said, "Our chariot awaits," Al Parker pointed at the approaching jeep and remarked, "Here comes Colonel Kirby."

After being driven out to the flight line in a canvass topped Jeep, Colonel Kirby motioned his driver to stop next to the tail section of the glider where Jim Beauregard and Al Parker were standing. By the time the Colonel's Jeep came to a stop, Flight Officer Steve Dickenson was concluding his pre-flight check of the GC-4A that would take the Major and his men to Bastogne.

Immediately after Jim and Al exchanged casual salutes with Lt. Colonel Kirby, the Commanding Officer of the 440th Troop Carrier Group wasted no time in relaying some good news. "The MPs in and around Bastogne have been notified to locate and arrest Danny Gannon and Gus O'Malley. I also made arrangements for MPs to meet you and your men when you land. In addition, I had some small arms ammo, medical supplies and rations put on board your glider. I'm sure everything we bring in will be put to good use."

After thanking Lt. Colonel Kirby for all of his help, Jim Beauregard and Al Parker saluted the Commanding Officer of the 440th Troop Carrier Group, while the other members of their search team boarded the glider. As soon as the Colonel returned the salute, he looked at Jim Beauregard and Al Parker and said, "You boys come back in one piece and that's an order." Then, as the Colonel motioned his driver to proceed, he remarked, "Take me to my office, Sergeant, we have work to do."

While Flight Officer Larry Allbright strapped himself into the co pilot's seat of the C47, Billy Davis went over the changes that were made to the flight plan before he wished Lt. Andy Archer and hi co pilot good luck. As soon as Billy Davis left the cockpit and called out, "Happy landings boys," his crew wished him good luck as he made his way through the cargo bay of the C47. Once he left the aircraft, Billy Davis patted the side of the fuselage and said, "You be careful, girl" before he jogged over to the glider that was being hooked up to his C47 by a 350 foot nylon tow rope.

Once Billy Davis entered the glider, he closed the door before he looked at the seven passengers who were seated in the back and called out, "Next stop, Bastogne."

While Al Parker stood in a slight crouch in the front of the cargo bay, he presented the C47 pilot with an M1 Carbine, that was loaded with a fifteen round magazine and had two spare fifteen round magazines strapped to the wooden stock in a khaki colored cotton canvass pouch. "This is for you, Captain. It might come in handy when we get where we're go'in."

Immediately after Captain Davis said, "Thanks Sarge," the sound of C47 engines coming to life signaled that it was time to get airborne. Without wasting any time, Captain Davis put on his flak suit and helmet before he strapped into the co pilot's seat, while Flight Officer Steve Dickenson prepared for take off.

Now that the Americans were being re-supplied by air and an armored relief force was fighting its way toward the Town of Assenois, the cut off and surrounded U.S. Army troops were becoming more aggressive in their defense of Bastogne. This included having the ability to be more liberal with the use of artillery ammunition to defend U.S. held positions. Even when the U.S. Army experienced supply problems after the D Day Invasion at Normandy, the U.S. Third Army alone fired approximately 76,000 rounds of artillery ammunition per day by late December of 1944.[11]

When the C47 towing Chalk 37 approached the LZ on the outskirts of the Village of Savy, a German gun crew hit the mark and peppered the cockpit of the tow plane with anti aircraft fire. The second the tow plane was hit with a burst of flak, the aircraft reeled to the left like a punch drunk fighter heading for the ropes. As the mortally wounded pilot slumped over dead in his seat and the less seriously wounded co pilot regained control of the shot up C47, another burst of flak blew a chunk out of the number one engine and started a blazing fire that quickly spread across the wing. After telling the surviving members of his crew to bail out of the burning aircraft, the incredibly brave co pilot continued to hold his course and delivered the glider known as Chalk 37 to the proper release point.

Now that they were flying closer to their intended landing zone, it no longer made any sense for Shorty to remain hidden. After hearing Ivan call out, "Up front! Standby to take the controls if I get hit," Shorty got up off the floor and buckled himself into the co pilot's seat. As Shorty watched two crewmen bail out of the burning tow plane, he turned to Ivan and yelled, "Whoever's in the cockpit of that C47 is doing one hell of a job of bringing us closer to the release point."

No matter how may times Ivan heard stories about men behaving bravely in combat, nothing compared to witnessing an act of heroism under fire take place with your own eyes. While Ivan watched the fire continue to spread over the fuselage of the C47, he couldn't help but admire the brave son of a bitch who was risking his life to deliver Chalk 37 to the LZ in Savy.

After quickly glancing over to Shorty before he continued looking straight ahead, Ivan spoke in a raised voice to insure that he would be heard. "We're approaching the Village of Savy. Bastogne is on the right to the south. If we're lucky we'll land in an area of the LZ where the other gliders have already been unloaded. As long as no G.I.s are around, we'll take off for the German lines!"

Whether he was resigned to die or he felt comfortable being in a tight spot with his partner in crime, Shorty called out and said, "Got it," while he continued to remain focusedon his duties as an unofficial member of the cockpit crew.

As the fire spread down the fuselage to the tail section of their tow plane, Ivan called out, "This is it! Here we go!" Whether it was luck or his skill as a pilot, Ivan reached for the tow line release mechanism and pulled down to separate his glider from the burning tow plane at just the right time. In order to avoid a sky full of falling debris, Ivan instinctively banked his glider to the right, as he made his decent seconds before the burning C47 exploded and fell to the ground in pieces.

Francis Shorty Mc Ghee proved that he was an excellent co pilot when he pointed to the left and called out, "There's a smaller open field due north of the LZ with wooded terrain on the west, east and south side. There's not a glider or any vehicles or troops in sight. Even I could land in there."

"That's it, then," remarked Ivan who quickly added, "Good choice. It looks secluded enough."

As Ivan continued to glide Chalk 37 into the smaller snow covered open field that was due north of the larger LZ, he spoke without taking his eyes off his duties. "If we were landing on sand or dirt this would be a piece'a cake. Since this field is covered with snow we might not be able stop in time before we hit those trees so hang on because he we go!" After hearing what Ivan had to say, all Shorty could do was tighten every muscle in his body as he prepared himself for what would happen next.

While Ivan continued to control the decent of his glider, he became one with his aircraft as he glided Chalk 37 toward the smaller open field that was due north of the designated landing zone. The moment Chalk 37 flew over the edge of the field, Ivan executed a textbook cross wind landing using the right amount of slip and crab. With no other gliders in the area, Chalk 37 came to a stop facing a row of trees that were located approximately forty yards away.

The fact that Ivan and Shorty landed in a location where a battle was being fought, became evident the moment Chalk 37 came under enemy small arms fire. By the time Ivan Larson and Francis Shorty Mc Ghee unbuckled their seat belts, German bullets were hitting the mark with more intensity. Because they were under fire, the two fugitives had no choice but to belly crawl out of the crash landed glider while still wearing their flak suits.

As a barrage of enemy bullets continued to penetrate the plexiglass windshield and the plywood fuselage, the two fugitives took cover on the starboard side of the glider behind a mound of ice covered snow in order to keep from getting hit. While Ivan instinctively cycled a round of ammunition into the chamber of his Thompson, Shorty remained face down in the snow as another burst from a German MP40 Submachine Gun struck the ground nearby.

As soon as the German patrol left the cover of the treeline, they held their fire while they stopped and called out, "Endaho, Americana." While the Germans patrol stood out in the open off to the right about thirty yards away Ivan looked at Shorty and said, "I guess my plan is working. Are you ready?"

Without giving any indication that he intended to move first, Shorty shouted, "Don't shoot, I surrender," as he stood up with his hands in the air and faced a squad of German soldiers dressed in white camouflage.

While Shorty wondered whether he would be taken prisoner or summarily executed, Ivan remarked, "Ah, what the heck," as he laid his Thompson Submachine Gun in the snow before he stood up with his hands raised at chest level. As soon as the German Sergeant ordered one of his men to assist him in capturing the two pilots, a squad of American soldiers were spotted advancing quickly across the open field toward their position. The second the American paratroopers opened fire on the German patrol, Ivan and Shorty fell face down in the snow next to their glider.

As much as he wanted to be taken prisoner by the enemy, something took hold in Ivan Larson that motivated the soldier in him to use his Tommy Gun to engage the Germans who were firing at the advancing American patrol. While Ivan got up on one knee and fired burst after burst from his submachine gun, Shorty called out, "This isn't part of the plan," as he drew his government issued 1911 pistol and emptied the entire seven round magazine at the escaping enemy troops. Whether Ivan and Shorty were responsible for killing the German Sergeant and two of his men didn't really matter, because for a brief period of time the two fugitives felt more like soldiers than wanted men.

By the time Ivan and Shorty dropped their flak suits in the snow, a group of American paratroopers, including a few who wore white bed sheets as a way to camouflage themselves in the snow covered landscape, advanced closer to their position. When the G.I.s got within 20 yards of the crash landed glider, a paratrooper from the 101st Airborne Division by the name of Staff Sergeant Phil Martin called out, "Hundred and First! Are you guys all right?"

While Ivan and Shorty finished reloading their issued weapons, Shorty turned to his partner in crime and whispered, "Now what?"

As soon as Ivan shouldered his Thompson, the fugitive who was wanted for killing a policeman and other serious crimes waved at the approaching American troops as he remarked, "Whatever you do act grateful."

After directing his men to fan out and secure the area, Sergeant Martin reloaded his Thompson Submachine Gun, while he identified himself and thanked the two lieutenants for helping out. As soon as Ivan greeted Sergeant Martin with a hearty handshake and said, "Lieutenant Paul Kraft," and Shorty Mc Ghee introduced himself as Lieutenant Gabe Fuller, Ivan continued and said, "Thanks for bailing us out, Sarge. If it wasn't for you and your men my co pilot and I would be on our way to a POW camp."

"Don't mention it, Lieutenant," responded Sergeant Martin, who quickly added, "My men and I were on our way to the Village of Savy to pick up small arms ammo and rations when we saw you come in for a landing. After I sent our driver into town to get some additional help, my men and I got here as fast as we could. As soon as we get your glider unloaded and your cargo is transported to the ammo dump, we'll get you and your co pilot a ride to the division assembly area."

Ivan knew that in order for him and Shorty to make their escape to the German lines, they needed to know the location of the American units, as well as the position of the enemy units that surrounded Bastogne and the neighboring towns. While doing his best to sound like a curious U.S. Army aviator, Ivan asked Sergeant Martin to give him and his copilot an update on how things were going on the ground.

Immediately after Sergeant Martin slung his Thompson over his right shoulder with the barrel pointing toward the ground, he pointed to the dead Germans who were lying in the snow near the edge of the treeline as he began his briefing. "The German patrol that tried to capture you and your co pilot were probably scavenging for supplies. If I had to guess, I'd say those Krauts were operating in the unoccupied terrain between this area on the outskirts of Savy and our positions to the east or the north."

While Sergeant Martin pointed due east, he continued and said. "The area beyond those trees is a bit of a no mans land, that runs into the Jacques Forest where the 506 PIR is positioned across from the Village of Foy. On their right flank, the 501 PIR is holding the line across from Neffe." While pointing his right index finger in an arch that ran from the east to the south Sergeant Martin added, "We also have armored units, glider infantry and airborne engineers holding a perimeter that runs all along our eastern perimeter to the south."

As Sergeant Martin turned and pointed first to the northeast then to the northwest he said, "It's a little over two miles to our northern perimeter. If you stay off the main road and take the scenic route between here and Recogne you'll find more snow covered open fields and wooded terrain. On the other side of the line along our northern perimeter you'll also find Waffen SS troops, Panzergrenadiers and Volksgrenadier troops. My unit, the Five O Deuce, is holding the line from the northeast all the way over to northwest. Our CP is south of Longchamps in Rolle. The 327th Glider Infantry Regiment is holding the line to the extreme northwest, the west and part of the south side of our perimeter and is facing more Kraut armor and Panzergrendiers."

As soon as Sergeant Martin finished describing the lay of the land to the two pilots, he sounded more serious when he continued and said, "You and your co pilot should know, Sir, that based on what my men and I observed from the ground, it looks like your glider was the last one to land inside our perimeter." Fugitive or not, Ivan Larson was shocked to hear that such large number of gliders failed to make their way to the correct LZ near Bastogne. Even Shorty felt a strange feeling in the pit of his stomach when he heard the distressing news.

"But there were fifty gliders in this resupply mission," remarked a shocked Ivan Larson.

"I'm sorry, Sir," responded Sergeant Martin who quickly added, "Just before you came in for a landing we heard our Pathfinder unit confirm that only thirty three gliders made it in today."

While Ivan remarked, "Fuckin Krauts" he removed a pack of Camel cigarettes from the left side breast pocket of his field jacket and offered one to Sergeant Martin and Shorty before he took one for himself.

After accepting the cigarette, the veteran squad leader snapped open his Zippo and offered the pair of friendly glider pilots a light before he lit his own Camel and said, "The good news, Lieutenant, is that yesterday lead elements of the 4th Armored Division under the command of General Patton's 3rd Army broke through the German lines from the south and secured enough of an open corridor to enable all Army Air Corps personnel who landed inside our perimeter to be evacuated with the wounded in the morning."

As soon as Sergeant Martin finished his briefing, the sound of approaching vehicles brought Ivan to remark, "Here comes our ride." While Shorty wondered what their next move would be, a Major from an airborne artillery battalion drove up in a Jeep, while a 4x4 Dodge weapons carrier and a second Jeep arrived a moment later.

As the Major approached the two glider pilots, he extended his right hand and said, "Welcome to the Village of Savy. I'm Major John Grimacki from the 377th Parachute Field Artillery Battalion (PFAB)."

While Ivan identified himself as Lieutenant Paul Kraft, Shorty shook hands with Major Gramacki as he introduced himself and said, "Gabe Fuller, Sir." Immediately after Major Grimacki thanked Sergeant Martin and his men for coming to the rescue of the glider crew, the airborne artillery officer directed the driver of the Dodge truck to tow Chalk 37 to the other side of the LZ and stop as close to the paved road as possible.

Once the two glider pilots, as well as the other Americans and Chalk 37 were transported closer to the road that connected Bastogne with Savy, the paratroopers and the men from the 377th PFAB unloaded the Waco glider that displayed the number thirty seven and the name Mad Mike on the side of its cockpit. While his glider was being off loaded, Ivan turned to Shorty and said, "I think it's time we made a few friends before we have to object about being transported to the assembly area."

As soon as Shorty asked Ivan what he had in mind, Ivan explained that he brought two musette bags along that contained various hard to obtain items that could make life in a combat zone more bearable. "Besides," said Ivan, "Once we get captured the Krauts are gonna take everything of value in our possession, so we might as well put this stuff to good use right now. If we're lucky these goodies will buy us some time so we can make our escape on our own terms."

Once again Shorty was impressed that his partner was always thinking ahead. As a native New Yorker, Shorty was also well aware that handing out gifts and gratuities at the right time could make friends out of strangers. Besides, even though there was a war on, everyone liked receiving thoughtful gifts over the Christmas Holidays.

After hearing Shorty remark, "I hope you have a Plan B if your Santa Claus act doesn't work 'cause we won't last thirty seconds if we end up in the division assembly area," Ivan asked one of the airborne artillerymen to retrieve the two musette bags from the cockpit of his glider. As soon as the two bags were removed from Chalk 37 and handed to Ivan, the glider pilot now known as Lt. Paul Kraft and his co pilot Lt. Gabe Fuller walked over to where Major Gramacki was standing by the side of his jeep.

As soon as the Major remarked, "What's up, Lieutenant," Ivan responded as he handed one of the musette bags to the airborne artillery officer. "My buddy and I brought a few things along in case we had to camp out for a while in Bastogne. Now that it looks like we'll be getting pulled out tomorrow, we'd like you and your men to have this stuff, Sir. Hopefully, the contents of this musette bag will make your stay in this frozen paradise a little more bearable."

While the airborne artillery officer looked inside the musette bag, that contained a fruit cake, two one ounce cans of instant coffee, four packs of hard to get Lucky Strike Cigarettes, two packs of equally hard to get Camel cigarettes, two packages of pipe tobacco, a brand new BBB (Best British Brand) Pipe and four chocolate bars Ivan continued and said, "We also have a few things we'd like to share with Sergeant Martin and his men for coming to our rescue after we landed."

As soon as Major Gramacki thanked the two glider pilots for the generous gifts, Ivan and Shorty looked across the snow covered field toward the German lines like starving men admiring a steak dinner through a restaurant window. While Ivan and Shorty turned back to face the artillery officer, the two fugitives felt the weight of the world lifted from their shoulders when Major Grimacki said, "I know you glider pilots are supposed to report to the division assembly area after you land but you're welcome to spend the night in our CP. It's not the Waldorf but it's a lot more comfortable than the accommodations at the assembly area that's jam packed with dozens of pilots who are waiting to be evacuated."

While Major Gramachi helped himself to a Lucky Strike cigarette from a pack in the musette bag, he continued and said, "After you spend the night with us, I'll have someone drive you over to the assembly area in the morning after chow. Besides, when my CO sees this pipe tobacco he'll want'a thank the two of you in person because he ran out two days ago." Under the circumstances, the two fugitives didn't have to act when they appeared sincerely grateful and they accepted the Major's kind offer.

Once the last of the artillery ammunition was loaded on the Dodge weapons carrier and the box of detonators were placed in the back of the second jeep, Ivan and Shorty walked over to thank Sergeant Martin and his men for coming to their rescue. After handing the squad leader the musette bag, Ivan remarked, "It's not much, Sarge, but we'd like to thank you and your men for pulling our chestnuts out of the fire after we landed."

As soon as Sergeant Martin looked inside the bag, he was one grateful para-trooper when he took a quick inventory of the sought after items that were placed inside. While Sergeant Martin thanked the two glider pilots for the goodies that he promised to share with his men, the vehicles carrying the artillery shells and the detonators drove off in the direction of the ammunition dump. After saying goodbye to Sergeant Martin and his squad of paratroopers, the two fugitives walked over to Major Gramacki's Jeep.

As the squad of paratroopers left the area in their truck, Major Grimacki took a quick drag on his Lucky Strike cigarette before he turned to the two glider pilots and said, "Hop in, gentlemen." While Ivan and Shorty climbed into the back of the Jeep, Major Gramacki sat in the passenger seat and offered his driver a Lucky

Strike cigarette and a light from his Zippo. "Free smokes, Johnny. It doesn't get any better than this," remarked the airborne artillery officer as he slipped the pack of cigarettes and his Zippo lighter in the breast pockets of his field jacket.

As soon as Private John Reader thanked his commanding officer for the cigarette and he put the Jeep in gear, Major Gramacki pointed in the direction of their command post and said, "Back to the barn, Johnny, and take the scenic route." While the two fugitives sat in the back of the Jeep and looked at each other, Ivan did his best to sound reassuring when he leaned closer to his partner in crime and remarked, "So far so good."

CHAPTER 12

WELCOME TO BASTOGNE

While Jim Beauregard looked around the interior of the glider, he made a mental note of the members of his search team who had some form of combat experience and who didn't. Even though some of the men on board had never been under fire or engaged another human being in mortal combat, Jim knew that this could change before the day was over. Jim was also grateful that an experienced medic was traveling with him and the others to a location that was still surrounded by the enemy.

After sitting back and getting as comfortable as possible. Jim decided to close his eyes and think about Beatrice and their two sons. Jim was especially concerned about his youngest son Michael, a young man who was serving in a combat unit even though his leg wound was not fully healed. As concerned as he was as a father, deep down inside Jim knew that his son Michael did exactly what he would do if he found himself in the same situation. His son Peter made a similar decision, when he decided to remain in combat and postpone taking advantage of his "survivors leave" after his PT boat was sunk in the Solomon Islands. As much as Jim hated to admit it, he loved them both for the way his sons took their responsibilities seriously.

The moment the glider bounced around in some light turbulence, Jim opened his eyes and leaned into the isle, as he looked up front to the cockpit and thought to himself, "I'm still gonna have words with that kid for leaving his hospital bed. Then I'm gonna give him a hug he'll never forget."

As soon as the crew chief in their tow plane flashed the First (Red) Warning Light, Billy Davis held up all ten fingers to signal the men in the back of the glider that they had ten minutes to go. After quickly checking his watch, Jim nudged Al

Parker with his elbow before he held up ten fingers to let his partner know that they would be over Bastogne in ten minutes. As soon as Al nodded his head, he leaned forward in his seat while he held onto his M3 Grease Gun and prepared for what was about to happen. Throughout this entire flight Al did everything from pray to think about his family. He also thought about his service during World War I and how his single foray into no mans land to rescue a white Army officer by the name of Patrick Murphy Sr. brought him to experience this very moment.

While Al Parker continued to cradle his M3 Grease Gun in his arms, he allowed the hatred that he had for the two fugitives to warm the cockles of his heart. Just like other good street cops, Al Parker was always incredibly calm, cool and collected whenever he went in harms way. Today was no different.

As a sense of peace and tranquility came over Al like a warm blanket, he looked up to where he envisioned heaven to be and wondered if Pat Murphy Jr. was looking down and wishing him well. Now that Al felt ready to face whatever came his way, he offered a stick of gum to Jim Beauregard and cracked a smile before he slipped a piece of Wrigley's into his own mouth.

Even though Captain Billy Davis and Lt. Andy Archer altered their flight plan, to avoid taking the same route as the aircraft that flew the previous mission, there were enough German gunners on the ground to challenge the presence of a single American C47 and glider flying over the battleground below. The moment the German gunners opened fire, Billy Davis kept his hands ready to take the controls if Flight Officer Dickenson became incapacitated or required his assistance.

While Billy Davis checked his watch and did some calculations in his head, he knew that they were very close to the release point. As Billy called out, "Standby for the white light!," he watched the C47 being flown by Lt. Archer fly directly into a sky full of flak. Billy Davis proved that his calculations were correct, when the Second (White) Warning Light was flashed from the tow plane, to alert the glider crew that they were one minute away from reaching the release point.

As proud as Billy Davis was that Andy Archer was holding the proper heading and altitude, the veteran C47 pilot was equally concerned about the safety of the crew that was towing him and the others to a landing zone that was surrounded by enemy troops. Both Billy Davis and Steve Dickenson also knew, that at their current altitude and airspeed it wouldn't be very hard for the Germans to hit what they were aiming at.

The second a German cannon shell pulverized their number one engine into a pile of useless parts, Lt. Archer called out, "Feathering Number One... Larry, kill the fuel switch." Even though he was trained as a glider pilot, Flight Officer Allbright had enough twin engine time to know how to react during an inflight emergency. While F.O. Allbright turned the switch to stop the flow of fuel to the destroyed engine, Andy Archer checked his watch before he called out, "Standby, Chief. Forty-five seconds more then let'em go!"

While the crew chief prepared to signal the glider pilot to cut lose from the tow plane, Andy instructed his co pilot to take the controls, while he picked up the phone that connected his aircraft to the GC-4A that he was towing to Bastogne. Despite the circumstances, Flight Officer Dickenson sounded remarkably calm when he remarked, "I guess I don't have to tell you that your number one engine has been shot to shit."

Andy Archer's voice was heard loud and clear, when the young man who was flying his first mission of the war as a pilot in command of a combat aircraft remarked, "Release point coming up. LZ in sight. Standby for the Green Light." Then, in true Andy Archer fashion, the young Army pilot who developed his sense of humor under the tutelage of Billy Davis added, "I should'a told this before we took off but Billy Davis doesn't have a pilot's license. I've been covering for him ever since Holland." A second later the line went dead as the tow plane was hit with another burst of German anti aircraft fire.

Because they were the only target in the sky, the German gunners had the American C47 that was towing a glider over the outskirts of Bastogne bracketed on both sides. The next volley of German anti aircraft fire perforated the tow plane's undercarriage, while another burst violated the integrity of the glider's cockpit and sent shards of steel into the left side of Flight Officer Dickenson's face, left hand and left leg.

Whether it was professional pride or heroism, Steve Dickenson's initial reaction was to remain in command of his glider, despite the fact that the left side of his body was riddled with shrapnel. As a veteran of combat glider missions in Southern France and Holland, Steve Dickenson knew that if he was the only pilot on board, he would have no choice but to land his glider despite his painful shrapnel wounds. Since he was fortunate to be flying with an accomplished Army aviator, Steve continued to remain on the controls until the pain from his shrapnel wounds made it too uncomfortable to hold the controls with both hands. The second Billy Davis observed the green colored light being flashed from the tow plane, he called out, "Green Light! Green Light!" Flight Officer Dickenson relinquished the control of his glider to his co pilot.

The moment Billy Davis assumed command of the glider, the number two engine on the C47 tow plane stopped turning. While Billy Davis called out, "Here we go," he reached up and pulled the release lever that cut the tow line, just as the C47 began to descend to the ground in what was called a dead stick landing.

As tempted as he was to look to his left to check on the status of his C47 crew, Billy Davis concentrated on his duties and did an excellent job of controlling the descent of the GC-4A Waco glider. Despite the fact that he was wounded, Steve Dickenson proved that he was still a vital member of the cockpit crew, when he pointed off into the distance with his good hand and said, "LZ coming up at One O'clock. There's an opening on the northwest side of the field."

While Billy Davis called out, "You know how to pick 'em, Steve," the veteran C47 pilot prepared to land the GC-4A Waco on the only section of the crowded landing zone that had room for one more glider.

While Oberfeldwebel (Master Sergeant) Hans Sigmann wondered why a single American glider was in the process of landing closer to Bastogne, he couldn't help but focus his attention on the C47 that was descending to the ground with both engines out. Because the events that he was observing were taking place some three miles away from his present position, Hans assumed that the American transport plane was able to make an emergency landing because no explosion was observed off in the distance, After watching the single American C47 and glider make their descent over the heavily contested battle space, Hans lowered his field glasses and suggested that his men concentrate on their duties, while they waited for the next phase of the offensive to begin.

As soon as Billy Davis flew over a road and a wire fence, he skillfully landed the GC-4A in a snow covered landing zone that was used by one of the earlier resupply missions and was occupied by a number of crash landed gliders. The fact that the other gliders in this LZ were already unloaded made this particular landing zone a lonely place to be. Regardless, this part of the snow covered field would have to due.

Once the GC-4A Waco glider came to a stop, Billy Davis called for their medic to come forward to care for Flight Officer Dickenson. While Billy Davis helped Steve out of his flak suit, Al Parker opened the side door of the Waco glider, just as Major Beauregard instructed Captain Savino to have the men secure the immediate area and keep an eye out for the MPs who are supposed to transport them into Bastogne. While Al Parker led the way, Captain Savino stood by the open door of the glider and said, "Will do, Sir."

Sergeant "Doc" Mel Keller proved to be a first rate combat medic when he briefed the Major while he treated his patient. "Shrapnel wounds, Sir. We'll be ready to travel as soon as the MPs arrive. If we have to travel on foot we'll have to carry Flight Officer Dickenson."

As soon as Billy Davis finished removing the flak suit that he was wearing, he picked up his M1 Carbine before he faced Major Beauregard and said, "I can give Doc Keller a hand, Sir."

After taking the time to admire the way that Doc Keller was caring for his patient, Major Beauregard remarked, "I'll be outside waiting for our ride into town. Call if you need anything."

The sight of two jeeps and a half track driven by American military policemen coming their way was a sight for sore eyes. After sizing up the situation and sensing the obvious tension among the men, Al Parker broke the silence and remarked, "Who said there's never a cop around when you need one."

As Jim Beauregard grinned, he checked his watch then turned to Al and asked when the Air Corps said the sun would set?"

As Al knelt in the snow, while facing the open terrain to the east he called out, "1658 hours, Sir."

"That doesn't give us much time to find these pricks before it gets dark," responded Jim Beauregard as the three MP vehicles from Bastogne pulled along the right side of their glider.

Because American soldiers were not required to salute a superior officer in a combat zone, for fear of alerting enemy troops who their commanders were, the military police lieutenant in the lead jeep simply nodded his head in a respectful fashion when he addressed the Major from Army CID. "Major Beauregard, I'm Lieutenant Chester Wright from the 101st Airborne Division. Lt. Colonel Kirby asked us to look out for you and your men." Then, after wiping the snot from his runny nose with his gloved left hand, Lt. Wright quickly added, "I have to say, Sir, you and your men made quite an entrance."

"You should've seen it from our end," remarked Jim Beauregard.

As Lt. Wright continued he gave the Major some good news, "I'm sure you and your men will be happy to hear, Sir, that some of our guys picked up all five crew members from the C47 that towed your glider to Bastogne and crash landed not far from here. We had all five transported to the hospital to get checked out, even though only two of the crew sustained minor wounds."

After expressing his gratitude about the status of the C47 crew, Major Beauregard called Captain Savino and Al Parker over so he could introduce them to Lt. Wright. "Lieutenant, this is Captain Savino from the CID office in Paris. Staff Sergeant Parker is on military leave from the New York City Police Department and is assigned to CID. The Sergeant and I have been working this case for over a year. He's also one of the few people who can identify Ivan Larson, the fugitive who adopted the identity of Flight Officer Danny Gannon."

While the MP Lieutenant made eye contact with Captain Savino and Staff Sergeant Parker and remarked, "Welcome to Bastogne," both Al Parker and Captain Tommy Savino responded almost in unison and said, "Thanks, Lieutenant."

Unlike other G.I.s who came from down south or back east, Lt. Chester Wright was from the small border town of Deming, New Mexico. As a result, he didn't have many dealings with Negroes. Where he was from Mexicans and Indians were the people who ranked lower on the totem pole than white folks. Even though this was the case, Chester Wright was color blind when he heard about an act of bravery that was performed by a fellow police officer, including a Negro policeman. This especially applied to Al Parker, the New York City Policeman who enlisted to help hunt down two fugitives who joined the U.S. Army to facilitate their escape.

When Major Beauregard asked the young MP officer how the search for Danny Gannon and Gus O'Malley was going, Lieutenant Wright wasted no time in giving the CID Officer in charge of the fugitive manhunt a detailed briefing about the status of the search for the two fugitives. "As soon as we were notified that the two fugitives were heading this way, we started checking the dog tags of every pilot who landed in this area. We also have MPs and medics checking casualties in an effort to locate the subjects of your manhunt."

After removing a map from his field jacket pocket, Lieutenant Wright continued as he opened the map and showed it to Major Beauregard, Captain Savino and Al Parker. "This is a map of Bastogne and the surrounding area, Sir. My CO asked the G2 to circle every landing zone that's been used by gliders, including the one that was used today near the Village of Savy. As you can see, Sir, while a number of gliders landed in the immediate area, we also received reports that other gliders from today's mission landed in or near Sibret, Flamierge, Tillet, Nimbermont and the Bois des Hales de Magery Forest. This means that a number of glider pilots have likely been captured or killed. We also have to face the fact, Sir, that the presence of various German units around Bastogne and the surrounding area will not help our efforts to locate and arrest the two fugitives."

After being briefed in the field, Jim Beauregard, Tommy Savino and Al Parker were very impressed with Lt. Wright. Simply put, the young MP officer appeared to have his shit together. Once the MP Lieutenant finished giving them a quick run down of the situation, Major Beauregard removed his M1 Carbine from his shoulder and held it in his right hand as he responded in a sincere tone of voice. "It sounds like you and your men have everything under control, Lieutenant."

As much as the MP Officer appreciated the compliment, he knew it was time to move out before the Germans took an interest in their meeting and started lobbing shells on their position. After quickly scanning the area around the landing zone, Lieutenant Wright faced the Major from Army CID as he relayed a word of caution. "We should be going, Sir, before the Germans take an interest in our presence in this open field."

"You're right, Lieutenant, we need to get go'in," responded Jim before pointed to the Waco glider that delivered him and his team to an LZ on the outskirts of

Bastogne and said, "Unfortunately, one of our pilots got hit on the way in and is being patched up by our medic. Once he's ready to travel we can move out. In the meantime we have some some small arms ammunition, rations and medical supplies that need to be unloaded from our glider."

When Captain Davis and Doc Keller emerged from the glider with Steve Dickenson, Lt. Wright instructed one of his military policemen to bring a stretcher over. While the MP Private removed the stretcher from the M3 Half Track and delivered it to Doc Keller, Jim Beauregard turned to Captain Savino and said, "Tom, can you see to it that the supplies we brought with us get loaded into the half track?"

After acknowledging the order, Captain Savino led Al Parker, Sergeant Blair and the two MPs from the 440th Troop Carrier Group into the Waco glider to unload the ammo, rations and medical supplies, while Doc Keller and Captain Billy Davis placed Steve Dickenson on the stretcher and covered him with an Army blanket. Once the stretcher was placed over the back of the second MP Jeep, Doc Keller climbed in and stayed with his patient.

Even though they never met before they departed on this mission, Jim Beauregard considered Steve Dickenson to be one of "his" men. As soon as Jim Beauregard walked over to the second MP jeep with Lt. Wright, he handed a Lucky Strike cigarette to the wounded glider pilot.

While Jim used his Zippo to light the unfiltered cigarette, he spoke in a concerned tone of voice when he said, "Hang on, Steve. Our first stop will be the hospital in Bastogne." As soon as the wounded glider pilot apologized for holding everyone up, the Major patted Steve Dickenson on the top of his right shoulder and said, "If it wasn't for crazy pilots like you and Billy Davis, along with the crew in our tow plane, my men and I would still be stuck in France."

After hearing Captain Savino call out, "We're ready to go, Major," Jim Beauregard waved to the CID Captain from the Paris office, while he stood in the back of the half track with Sergeant Blair and the two MPs from the 440th TCG. As soon as Lt. Wright introduced himself to Captain Billy Davis, the Major gave Billy the good news about the crew from his C47 that survived being shot down and crash landing in an open field.

As soon as he heard the good news, Billy Davis returned his attention to the mission at hand and asked Major Beauregard if he could ride with Doc Keller in case their medic needed help caring for Steve Dickenson. From the moment they first met, Jim Beauregard liked Billy Davis. Even though Billy could have let

Sergeant Keller watch over his patient on his own, the Captain was concerned enough about a fellow aviator, to volunteer to help their medic care for the first member of their search party to be wounded in battle. After nodding his head in agreement, the Major remarked, "OK, Billy. Sergeant Parker and I will ride with Lt. Wright. After we take Steve to the hospital, you and Doc Keller can follow us to the Division CP."

Once Jim walked back over to Lt. Wright's Jeep, he faced the young MP Officer and said, "I need a favor, Lieutenant."

"Name it, Sir," remarked the MP Officer.

While Jim stood by the front passenger seat of the Lt. Wright's MP Jeep, Jim continued and said, "My youngest son Michael is a Sergeant with the 3rd Battalion 327th Glider Infantry Regiment. I was told he left his hospital bed in France to rejoin his unit when he heard about the German offensive. If it's not too much trouble I'd like to try and see him while I'm in Bastogne. Can you find him for me?"

"Can do, Sir," responded the MP Lieutenant as he sat behind the wheel of the Jeep and started the engine.

As soon as Al Parker climbed into the back of the lead jeep, Major Beauregard thanked the MP Officer before he sat in the front passenger seat and remarked, "Lead the way, Lieutenant."

While Lt. Wright turned the lead jeep around and drove back to his command post, Major Beauregard continued filling the MP Officer in about the case at hand. "Captain Davis is a C47 pilot who met Ivan Larson and Shorty Mc Ghee when they were going through advanced glider training in Texas. He helped us track the two fugitives to the 439th Troop Carrier Group in Chatteaudun, France but they managed to take off on today's glider resupply mission before I was able to ask the CO to have the MPs take them into custody."

After pausing to light a cigarette, Major Beauregard continued and said, "Doc Keller also met Shorty Mc Ghee when he was going through advanced glider training in Lubbock, Texas. Doc Keller patched up a nasty gash on the head of the fugitive who's masquerading as Gus O'Malley when he cut his head open while recovering a crash landed glider. We're lucky to have him along."

While Lt. Wright drove the Willy's Jeep across the snow cover LZ and onto the paved road, he shared his personal thoughts about this case with the Major and Al Parker. "It's hard to believe, Sir, that two cop killing bank robbers are on the loose right here in Bastogne."

As soon as Jim Beauregard finished taking a drag on his cigarette, he spoke in a friendly tone of voice as he turned to his left and said, "Just think of them as frontline fugitives, Lieutenant."

CHAPTER 13

ON THE GROUND IN BASTOGNE & SAVY

As soon as they arrived at the 377th Parachute Field Artillery Battalion (PFAB) Command Post, Major Gramacki introduced Lt. Paul Kraft and Lt. Gabe Fuller to his commanding officer. After telling Lt. Colonel Paul Defoe about the hair raising events that took place when the two pilots landed their glider, the Major made the Colonel's day when he informed his CO about the 250 rounds of artillery ammunition that the two pilots safely delivered to an LZ near Savy. As an avid pipe smoker, Lt. Colonel Defoe was especially grateful when Major Grimacki handed him a two ounce package of Prince Albert Crimp Cut Pipe and Cigarette Tobacco and explained that the contents of the musette bag were gifts from the two glider pilots.

Immediately after Major Gramacki explained that he invited the two pilots to be their guests for the night, Lt. Colonel Defoe packed the bowl of his pipe with tobacco while he called out to his driver and said, "Landy, front and center." When Private Alan Landy from Mobile, Alabama reported as ordered, Lt. Colonel Defoe finished lighting his pipe before he said, "These officers will be spending the night with us. See to it that they get settled."

As soon as Private Landy acknowledge the order, Major Gramacki finished placing the items from the musette bag on a nearby empty ammunition crate, before he tossed a pack of hard to get Camel cigarettes to the Colonel's driver and said, "The smokes along with these other goodies are from these pilots so take good care of 'em, Alan."

After Private Landy responded and said, "Yes Sir," Lt. Colonel Defoe turned to his two guests and invited them to join him for dinner.

Even though Ivan and Shorty did their best to sound grateful when they accepted the invitation, they had no intention of remaining in the Colonel's

117

command post any longer than necessary. As far as Ivan was concerned, he and Shorty were too close to the German lines to risk delaying their plans to escape, just so they could have supper with Lt. Colonel Defoe or anyone else on his staff.

When the battalion communications officer called out that he had a message from 101st Airborne Division G4, Lt. Colonel Defoe remarked, "Excuse us, gentlemen, duty calls," before he and Major Gramacki walked over to the other side of the CP where the radio operator was located.

Immediately after Private Landy thanked the two glider pilots for the hard to get premium brand cigarettes, Ivan remarked, "Don't mention it, Private." When the Colonel's driver asked if the two Lieutenants would like a cup of freshly brewed coffee, Ivan put on a friendly face as he responded and said, "Coffee sounds good, Private. Lead the way."

While Ivan and Shorty followed Private Landy over to the wood burning stove that was installed in the barn to provide heat and a way to boil water, all the two fugitives could think about was making a successful escape to the German lines. After checking his watch, Ivan began calculating how long it would take him and Shorty to make their way to enemy held territory before sunset. The problem wasn't the distance to German held territory but what they might have to go through in order to get captured by the enemy.

After contacting the 327th Glider Infantry Regiment and learning that Sergeant Michael Beauregard was wounded in a recent combat action, Lt. Chester Wright grabbed his helmet and his M1 Carbine as he spoke with a sense of urgency and said, "I found your son, Sir. He knocked out a German tank with a bazooka after he was hit with some shell fragments. He's waiting to be evacuated from one of our field hospitals."

After being told that Michael was wounded again, Jim turned to Captain Savino and said, "Tom, take over. Sergeant Parker and I will be back as soon as I check on my son." While the Captain from the CID office in Paris responded and said, "Yes, Sir," Jim Beauregard and Al Parker followed Lt. Wright out of the command post to an awaiting Jeep that was being guarded by a military policeman.

As soon as they arrived at the aid station that was set up in a large garage, Lt.

Wright volunteered to remain with their Jeep, in order to comply with the military police directive that U.S. Army vehicles in Bastogne could not be left unattended. After telling Lieutenant Wright that he wouldn't be long, Major Beauregard said, "Let's go, Al," as he hopped out of the Jeep followed by his partner and walked into the makeshift field hospital.

After meeting with the surgeon who removed the shrapnel from his son's left arm and shoulder, Jim was taken to see Michael. While Al Parker stood nearby, Jim's eyes began to swell with tears, as he knelt by his youngest son's side and gently stroked his short blonde hair with his right hand. As he did so, all Jim could think about as he looked at Michael sleep, was how glad he was that Bea wasn't present to see their youngest son in his current condition.

As much as Jim did not want to wake Michael up, he knew he might not get another chance to see his son before he got evacuated to an Army hospital in France or England. After hearing a medic say, "It's OK to wake him up, Sir. I'll be back as soon as I check on some other patients." Jim leaned closer to his son and said, "Michael, it's Dad. Can you hear me, son."

While Michael began to come around, he thought he was dreaming when he heard his father's voice calling his name. The young squad leader was twice as surprised when he opened his eyes and he found his father kneeling over him.

"I can't believe your here, Dad," remarked Michael who quickly added, "How'd you get through?"

When Jim responded he pointed to his partner and said, "Sergeant Parker and I tracked those fugitives I told you about in my last letter to a glider unit in France. As soon as we learned that the subjects of our manhunt participated in today's glider mission, we had a C47 tow us to Bastogne in a GC-4A so we could continue our search. A few CID Agents and MPs, as well as two of our witnesses came along to help out."

The moment Michael heard what his father had to say the young glider infantryman remarked, "Mom is not gonna be happy when she finds out that you flew into this hell hole in a glider just to make an arrest."

After cracking a smile, Jim couldn't resist and said, "Speaking of your mother... wait 'till she finds out what you did."

When Michael asked his father if he was upset with him for returning to his unit, Jim did his best to control his emotions when he responded and said, "As long as you believe that you did the right thing by leaving that hospital bed, so you could rejoin your unit, you made the right decision."

As soon as Michael reached out and grabbed his father's left hand, the young squad leader explained why he took the action that he did. "I couldn't let my squad go into action without me, Dad. You understand...don't you? You wouldn't let Sergeant Parker and the other men look for those fugitives without being with them...right Dad?"

Jim had been a father long enough to know that his son was looking for validation after making a decision that could have cost him his life. When Jim answered his youngest son he spoke from the heart. "I can't lie to you, son. I'd do the same thing if I was in your shoes. I guess that makes us who we are."

As soon as the medic returned, Jim changed the subject as he looked at Michael and said, "The doctor said you're gonna be OK. If you're not evacuated later today you should be outta here by tomorrow." Then, as Jim straightened up, he turned to the medic who was standing nearby with a tray containing fresh bandages, sulfur powder and a syringe and said, "I'll be out of your way in a minute, Doc."

Even though the father in him would like nothing more than to remain by his son's side, Jim knew that it was time for him and Al to get back to work. As soon as Jim removed two packs of Lucky Strike cigarettes, a pack of chewing gum and two chocolate bars from his pockets, he placed the items on his son's good side and said, "This should hold you over until you get to a hospital."

"Thanks, Dad," responded Michael.

While Jim did his best not to get choked up, he looked at Michael and said, "Sergeant Parker and I have to go, son. We have two fugitives to catch and you need your rest."

After trading places with the Major from CID, the Army medic spoke as soon as he began to tend to his patient. "Don't worry, Sir. We'll take good care of him."

As the experienced combat medic began to cut the bandages that needed to be replaced from his son's wounded body, Jim stood over his youngest son and said, "I'll do my best to visit you before I return to the states." While Jim continued, he pointed his right index finger at Michael. "In the meantime, you get better, that's an order."

When Al Parker leaned over and handed the youngest of the Beauregard boys three additional chocolate bars, the man who also had two sons in uniform smiled then said, "You better take these with you, Sergeant. If I keep eating candy bars I won't be able to keep up with your father."

While Michael thanked Al Parker for the extra supply of chocolate, the Army medic helped his patient to sit up so he could remove the large bandage that was wrapped around his chest and left shoulder.

As the young squad leader looked up at his father and his partner, he sounded like a very concerned son when he said, "Dad, promise me that you and Sergeant Parker will be careful out there. The Krauts are playing for keeps and so are the two fugitives you're chasing."

After saying "We will son," Jim sounded more like a typical father when he remarked, "Don't forget to write your mother, your brother and your grandparents and tell 'em that you're OK and that I said hi."

As soon as Michael said, "I won't forget, Dad," Jim smiled one last time as he made eye contact with his youngest son before he turned to his partner and said, "Let's go, Al."

The last person that Jim Beauregard and Al Parker expected or wanted to run into when they arrived at the 101st Airborne Division Command Post in Bastogne was General Nathan Tremble. While the hard ass one star general put his hands on his hips, he looked at the Major from CID and his Negro partner and remarked, "Well, if it isn't the Lone Ranger and Tonto."

Under the circumstances, Jim did his best not to behave in a disrespectful fashion when he responded. "Sir, Sergeant Parker and I are looking for two fugitives who are in this area. We really need to be going, General."

As the General stood in front of the entrance to the Division CP, he looked directly at Jim Beauregard and said, "You know, Major, I've been looking for my driver ever since you and your partner bumped him off that flight to England."

In an effort to diffuse a situation that had all of the trappings of a full fledged confrontation, Jim saluted the General and said, "It was nice to see you again, Sir," before he entered the CP with Al Parker.

While the speechless General stood with his hands on his hips, Lt. Wright said, "Excuse me, General," as he walked by and entered the 101st Airborne Division HQ CP.

As the two military policemen standing guard by the entrance stood at attention and continued looking straight ahead, General Tremble remarked, "Cops in a combat zone. What's this war coming to," before he turned and walked over to his jeep.

Both Jim Beauregard and Al Parker knew that managing a police manhunt in the average size American city was hard enough, but trying to find two fugitives masquerading as soldiers in a combat zone was a seemingly impossible task. This manhunt was even more complicated by the fact, that everywhere you looked in Bastogne all you saw was a sea of American troops who were dressed and equipped for war.

During his time as an Army MP, Lt. Chester Wright handled everything from drunks to actual combat, including while helping to defend Bastogne. Even though chasing fugitives was new to him, he was beginning to enjoy the experience. After all, it wasn't every day that a cop in the Army had the opportunity to hunt down two wanted men in the middle of a major battle. The Lieutenant also knew that they had nothing to show for their efforts, despite everything that was being done by the military police in the vicinity of Bastogne to capture the two fugitives. This was confirmed when Lt. Wright was handed a message that stated that none of his men had any contact with any glider pilots using the names Gannon and O'Malley who matched the description of the two fugitives.

As soon as Lt. Wright handed the message to Major Beauregard and the Major passed the bad news to the other key members of his search party, the young officer remarked, "It sounds like we need to get lucky, Sir."

Jim Beauregard had been cop long enough to know exactly how to respond to the young military policeman from New Mexico. After making eye contact with Al Parker and Tommy Savino, Jim Beauregard turned back to face the young MP officer and said, "Lieutenant, a good cop makes his own luck."

It had been some time since Chester Wright heard that particular piece of advice. While the MP officer thought about the days when he used to sit in the sheriffs office back home and listen to the various members of his family who were lawmen talk about police work, Jim Beauregard remarked, "By the look on your face it seems that you've heard that saying before, Lieutenant."

"Yes, Sir," I have," responded Lt. Wright who quickly added, "My father gave the same advice to several lawmen back home, including my older brother." Then, in an effort to explain himself further, the young officer continued and said, "You see, Sir, my father was elected Sheriff of Luna County, New Mexico after he retired from the state police. Two of my uncles and my older brother are with the state police and my grandfather is a retired state police captain."

After leaning over the table Jim examined the map of Bastogne as he remarked, "Tell me Lieutenant. What else do we need to know that can help us find our fugitives?"

While using a sharp pencil to point to different positions on the map, Lt. Wright wasted no time in giving Major Beauregard, Captain Savino, Captain Davis, Staff Sergeant Parker and Staff Sergeant Blair a more detailed description of the situation at hand. "This is a larger map of the area that contains much of the same information that's listed on the smaller map that I gave you after you landed, Sir. As I said earlier, Sir, while the destination for today's glider resupply mission was a landing zone next to the Village of Savy, a number of gliders, including the one that you and your men came in on, landed in other locations in and around Bastogne. I should also mention that some of the gliders that landed too close to the German lines, were towed by vehicles to a location were it was safer to off load the supplies that were brought in."

After Lt. Wright looked up at the Major and the others, he continued his briefing while pointing at different locations on the map. "This is the LZ where you and your men landed and this is the open field where your C47 tow -plane crash landed. This map also contains the location of every command post in and around Bastogne. I mention this, Sir, because as gliders came down, they would likely be met by G.I.s from the units holding positions in these areas, as well as by members of our Quartermaster Company."

After pausing to slip his pencil into his field jacket pocket, Lt. Wright continued and said, "You and your men also need to know, Sir, that Colonel Gray, our Division G2, received a report from one of our Pathfinder Officers that thirty three gliders were counted landing inside our perimeter out of the fifty that participated in today's resupply mission. Our G2 also reports that the reinforcements that penetrated the German lines to our south are widening that corridor. This means that the two fugitives could try and make their escape through this open corridor to the south, because no one will be stopping to search the trucks or the ambulances that will be transporting Army Air Corps personnel and the wounded out of Bastogne. The other bad news is that even though reinforcements and supplies are pouring into this area, we're still surrounded on three sides by the German Army."

While Major Beauregard examined the map of the area, he spoke up and said, "Let's go over what we know. Ivan Larson volunteered to fly the glider resupply mission that left the 439th Troop Carrier Group earlier today. We also know that Larson was assigned to Chalk 37 which departed Chatteadun, France just before 1100 hours. Even if that Pathfinder Officer from the 101st is right and only thirty three gliders landed in this area, until we prove otherwise, we have to operate under the assumption that Chalk 37 landed inside the perimeter that is under the control of the 101st Airborne Division. We also know that Francis Shorty Mc Ghee was no where to be found when the MPs conducted a thorough search of the 439th Troop Carrier Group. If Shorty Mc Ghee stowed away on Chalk 37 with Ivan Larson, it wasn't to fly a combat mission so he could go home with a chestful of medals. If they flew this mission together, it was to evade arrest and either hide out in Allied territory or get captured by the enemy. Needless to say, if they end up in a German POW Camp, we'll have our hands full trying to find them when this war is over."

"Is there anything I'm missing?" asked Jim Beauregard.

Captain Billy Davis once again proved to be a valuable member of the Major's search team when he spoke up and said, "I have a few points to make that I think might help, Sir."

While all eyes focused on Billy Davis, the experienced C47 pilot needed no coaxing to say what was on his mind. "It's also important to remember, Sir, that the fifty gliders that took off earlier today from the 439th did so with only one pilot on board. Even if no one made the connection at the time, there's bound to be some G.I.s who had contact with a glider from today's resupply mission that had two people on board. This means that there are G.I.s in this area who know where we can find Chalk 37 and may also know where the two fugitives are located."

While he removed his pipe and a pouch of Half and Half Tobacco from his flight jacket pocket, Captain Davis added, "We also have to consider that we're looking for something as large as a GC-4A Waco glider that has the name Mad Mike and the number thirty seven written in white chalk on the side of its fuselage. Finding that glider could prove very helpful, Sir."

As soon as Major Beauregard asked Billy Davis if he had anything else to add, the young Captain sounded like a man who knew what he was talking about when he said, "I also think I can shed some light on the chances of Chalk 37 being able to make its way to a landing zone within the vicinity of Bastogne. You see, Sir, it's quite possible that Chalk 37 made it down safely if other gliders in front of its position were shot down or forced down elsewhere. The best way to find out which gliders made it to landing zones in and around Bastogne, is to debrief the glider pilots who are waiting to be evacuated from the division assembly area. We especially need to speak to the pilots who flew Chalks 34, 35 and 36, because these gliders were the only GC-4As that were towed to the LZ near the Village of Savy along with Chalk 37 by C47s from the 94th Troop Carrier Squadron. In fact, the pilot who flew Chalk 36 is the one we should talk to first, because he should've arrived over this area at the same time as Chalk 37."

After thanking Billy Davis for the contribution that he just made to their discussion, Jim Beauregard turned to Lt. Wright and said, "Tell me, Lieutenant. Are there enough MPs available to launch a thorough search for Chalk 37?"

"No, Sir, there aren't," responded Lt. Wright.

Without wasting any time the Major asked a followup question. "And I also assume we don't have enough MPs to search every fox hole, gun position and command post along the front lines to locate G.I.s who had contact with Chalk 37 when it landed?"

Once again Lieutenant Wright sounded disappointed when he said, "No, Sir, we don't. The truth is we're stretched pretty thin, Sir. We just don't have enough MPs to perform our regular duties, while also searching the entire perimeter. I'm sorry, Sir, but I don't know what else we can do."

After lighting a cigarette, Major Beauregard looked over to Al Parker and said, "Any ideas, Al?" Ever since his run in with General Tremble, Al Parker had a lot on his mind. Despite the fact that it felt good to watch the Major run interference for him, Al was deeply troubled that he had to deal with such bullshit at his age. Most of all, Al wondered how long he had to continue to prove himself before he would be treated as an equal by White America.

While Al did his best to ignore the complexities of life in the land of the partially free and the home of the brave, he looked directly at Jim Beauregard when he responded to the Major's question. "Well Sir, since we have to operate under the assumption that Larson and Mc Ghee are still alive and since the MPs in Bastogne can't be expected to search every possible location where the two fugitives could be hiding out, I think it's time we recruit some professional help to assist us in our search."

By this time in their relationship, Jim Beauregard knew Al Parker well enough to know that he was a hard charging street cop, who proved to be an excellent investigator, even though he only held the rank of Patrolman with the N.Y.P.D. As a result, Jim Beauregard could tell by the sound of Al's voice that he had something worthwhile to say. Due to the urgency of the situation Jim reacted quickly to Al's last remark and said, "What do you have in mind, Al?"

While speaking in a very confident tone of voice, Al Parker made eye contact with Staff Sergeant Blair as well as the four officers who surrounded the makeshift mapping table as he presented his idea. "Just like Captain Davis said, Sir, we have a small army of glider pilots who reported to the division assembly area after landing in and around Bastogne. I say we recruit every glider pilot who can identify Larson and Mc Ghee to help us find these bastards, Sir."

As strange as their partnership appeared to others, Jim knew that he and Al were a good team. They worked well together and exchanged ideas without trying to upstage each other. No one counted who made the last good suggestion or called a certain play with complete accuracy. What one did right was enjoyed by the other, as if the victory was shared by all and not just by the originator of a particular idea.

Even though Jim Beauregard had every intention of interviewing the glider pilots, who were assembled in the former Belgium Army barracks that was being used to temporarily house the Army aviators who landed in Bastogne, the Major never actually thought of using glider pilots to help locate the two fugitives. Clearly, it was a brilliant idea.

After hearing Lt. Wright compliment Al Parker for making an excellent suggestion, Jim Beauregard remarked, "You win another box of cigars for that one, Al." Seeing Al Parker smile was all that it took to make Jim feel as if they were back on track again as a team after their run in with General Tremble.

Since they were running out of daylight, the Major sounded anxious to proceed when he turned to Lt. Wright and said, "Lieutenant, we need you to kick things off by getting every swinging dick wearing a set of glider pilot wings assembled out back. Tell 'em what's going on and that we need their help. Captain Savino and Captain Davis along with Sergeant Blair will help you organize this effort."

Without hesitating Lieutenant Wright remarked, "Yes, Sir," as he retrieved his M1 Carbine from the top of a nearby wooden ammo crate before he headed for the back door of the command post. As the MP Lieutenant left the Division CP, Jim Beauregard turned to the others and said, "In addition to sending search teams to look for a glider that has the number thirty seven and the name Mad Mike written on its fuselage, our teams also need to make contact with as many G.I.s as possible, especially in any location where Chalk 37 is located."

While Al Parker re-lit his cigar and blew a plume of smoke off to the side, Jim faced Captain Davis and described in detail exactly what he needed in the way of assistance from the combat tested C47 pilot. "Captain, we need you to coordinate the debriefing of the glider pilots that are being assembled outback. Since we have no time to interview them individually we'll have to do it as a group. Once you select locations that need to be searched, Captain Savino, Lt. Wright and Sergeant Blair will be responsible to put the teams together and send them into the field with one MP or one CID Agent assigned to each team. Al Parker and I will meet you out back in a few minutes."

As soon as Captain Davis, Captain Savino and Sergeant Blair acknowledged their orders and left the command post, Al Parker took a look at the rather large gathering of glider pilots who were assembling behind the Division Headquarters. After he closed the door, Al walked over to the makeshift table where the Major was reviewing the map of the area and said, "Our new posse is starting to assemble out back."

While Al stood next to the makeshift map table, Jim pointed to various positions on the map and said. "Check this out, Al. According to this map, it's a good two to three miles from the various locations where gliders landed in this area, to front line positions that are being held by various U.S. Army units. Even though some of this terrain is more desolate than others, Larson and Mc Ghee will have to go through check points and heavily defended positions along the front, before they'll be able to cross over into German held territory I'm not saying it can't be done. All I'm saying is that it won't be as easy as they might think, especially if they don't know the disposition of the U.S. Army units in this area."

After pausing to take a puff on his cigar, Al pointed to the position on the map where the 101st Airborne Division Headquarters assembly area was located and said, "They also have to deal with the fact that the Hundred and First Airborne HQ has ordered every glider pilot to be transported to the division assembly area. That means that glider pilots have no reason to be traveling on foot or in a vehicle in any direction that takes them away from this building."

While Jim continued to examine the map of the area he remarked, "You're right, Al. Captain Davis and Lt. Wright also made some valid points. The question is, how can we make it impossible for Larson and Mc Ghee to run into a G.I. without being challenged?' After pausing for a split second, Jim seemed to come to life as he turned to face his partner and said, "I have an idea, Al and I hope it works 'cause we're running out of daylight."

As Jim walked over to the communications officer who was seated by the radio operator, he spoke as he began to open his map of the area. "Excuse me, Lieutenant."

The moment Lieutenant Benjamin Carver put down a well worn copy of Life Magazine, the airborne signals officer picked up his note book and pen and remarked, "How can I help, Sir?"

While Major Beauregard showed the communications officer his map of the area, he addressed the signals officer in a tone of voice that was laced with a sense of urgency. "We're currently conducting a search for two fugitives in this area who are masquerading as glider pilots. While we interview the glider pilots who are assembled out back, we need you to contact every command post in this area, starting with the units located northwest and north of Bastogne, to let them know that CID and the MPs are looking for two fugitives masquerading as glider pilots who are wanted for killing a policeman and other serious crimes. We also need every command post to contact the units under their command, to see if any U.S. Army personnel have had any contact with a glider that displayed the name Mad Mike and the number thirty seven on the side of its fuselage by the cockpit."

After waiting for the signals officer to finish taking his notes, the Major continued and said, "It's also critical to let every command post know that every glider that landed earlier today was only supposed to have one pilot on board. As a result, we need to know if any U.S. Army personnel had contact with a glider that contained two crewmen. We also need to know if any glider pilots are currently staying with any U.S. Army personnel, especially with units positioned closest to the German lines and we need this information yesterday. In addition, we need any glider pilots who are not in the presence of CID Agents or MPs to be immediately disarmed and transported under guard to the 101st Airborne Division Headquarters Command Post as soon as possible. Any U.S. Army personnel who have any information regarding any of these questions should contact this command post, so the information can be immediately relayed to CID Agents and MPs."

After taking copious notes, the communications officer looked up at the Major and remarked, "I'll get on this right away, Sir."

As Major Beauregard folded his map of the area, he thanked Lieutenant Carver for his assistance and finished his remarks by saying, "Staff Sergeant Parker and I will be out back. Let us know if you come up with anything."

CHAPTER 14

IT'S TIME TO GO

As far as Ivan was concerned, if they had any intentions of making their way to the German lines they had to do so before it got dark. After watching Lt. Colonel Defoe drive off to meet the Division G4 at the ammunition dump, Ivan checked his watch then said, "If we're gonna take off we better do so before that Colonel comes back."

While Ivan removed a map from his field jacket pocket, he continued as he showed it to Shorty. "As I see it, our best course of action is to make our way to the German lines as fast as possible. In order to do so we have to leave this command post, preferably without raising any suspicions. We also need to make this trip in a Jeep because we won't get very far on foot, not if that paratrooper from the Five O Deuce is right and the German lines are roughly two to three miles away in any direction."

After pausing to make sure they were still alone, Ivan continued as he pointed to his map of the area. "In order to go east from here on a paved road we'd have to travel south through Bastogne, then take the road to Bizory or to Luzery then on to Foy, both areas that are crawling with our troops. I also doubt it will be any easier for us to travel to Neffe or Marvie. There's also bound to be a small army of MPs in and around Bastogne, so going that way makes no sense to me." When Ivan continued he looked directly at Shorty and said, "As I see it our options are to head northwest to Champs, north to Longchamps or northeast to Recogne. Of those three choices it's more of a straight run for us if we go to Longchamps."

While Shorty looked at the map of the area, he did his best to make a valid contribution to the conversation because his life, as well as the life of his partner, depended on their ability to make a successful escape to the German lines. "Unless we get lucky twice in the same day and we run into another Kraut patrol on our side of the line, we're gonna have to travel through some open pastures and wooded terrain, or on a paved road to make our way to enemy held territory."

As Shorty continued, he looked up from the map and said, "If we drive on a paved road we'll make better time but we'll also risk having to go through one or more check points in order to reach the German lines. If we take the scenic route, we could still run into some of our patrols and have to explain what two glider pilots are doing driving around the countryside." After pausing for a split second, Shorty added, "There's also the Germans to worry about, especially if we get caught out in the open during an artillery barrage."

After considering their options, Ivan folded his map of the area and slipped it back into his field jacket pocket as he looked at Shorty and said, "There's another option that we need to consider, but it might not be all that easy to pull off and it could involve us having to tangle with some of our own troops."

As soon as Shorty asked what his partner had in mind, Ivan responded and said, "Do you remember what the Colonel's driver said about those L4 liaison pilots when he joined us for a cup of Joe by the stove? Private Landy may have given us a way outta this mess, when he mentioned that two L4's that are spotting for artillery units happen to be based in an open field due east of where we came in for a landing."

Despite the fact that Ivan knew that Shorty would not be very supportive about an escape plan that involved another plane ride, even if that plane had an engine, he spoke his mind anyway and said, "If we can get our hands on an L4, we can be over German held territory in a matter of minutes." While it was true that stealing a small single engine L4 Piper Cub observation aircraft offered them the fastest way to make their escape, the thought of flying over another battlefield, where they risked getting shot at and possibly shot down, did not sit well with Francis Shorty Mc Ghee.

Just as Ivan expected, Shorty responded without mincing words. "While it would be great if we could use our status as pilots to get the hell outta here, I'd rather take my chances on the ground, than take another ride in another small plane that's bound to become an easy target for every Kraut with a rifle once we get airborne. Besides, there's no guarantee that these planes will be ready to fly when we show up. We could also waste valuable time that we don't have making our way out to this unimproved field, only to find out that these planes are airborne or down for maintenance. What do we do then...hang around and wait?"

After Shorty took a few steps off to the right, he turned and walked back over to Ivan as he continued. "Even if an L4 is available for us to steal, what do we do when the pilot and his observer, as well as the ground crew personnel, object to us using one of their planes to fly a one way mission to German held territory? Are we prepared to start shooting our own guys? There's also the issue of our presence at a makeshift base for grasshoppers and puddle jumpers in the ass end of nowhere, when we're supposed to be waiting to be evacuated with other glider pilots at the division assembly area."

Ivan had to admit that Shorty just made a number of valid points. In fact, instead of being upset with Shorty for questioning his proposed escape plan, Ivan reacted as if his buddy just gave him an excellent idea how they should proceed. As soon as Ivan perked up and said, "You just gave me a great idea how we're gonna get outta this mess."

While Shorty looked a bit confused, he paid close attention when Ivan went on and explained what he had in mind. "You're right about the pros and cons of driving on a paved road versus traveling off road. You're also right about us using our rank as Lieutenants and our status as pilots to get us right up to the German lines without raising any suspicions."

After pausing to remove a pack of gum from his pant's pocket, Ivan offered a piece to Shorty as he continued and said, "We'll head due north from where we landed and stay off the paved roads for as far as we can go. If we run into any MPs or G.I.s along the way, we'll tell 'em we're members of an Air Support Party that's been sent up to the front-line to coordinate bombing and strafing missions by Allied aircraft. That should enable us to get as close to the German lines as possible so we can spot enemy positions. When the time is right, we'll make a run for it and get ourselves captured by the Krauts."

After slipping a stick of gum into his own mouth, Ivan added, "If we can't get captured by the Krauts before this day is over, we might have to go to Germany to become POW's, because the reinforcements that are pouring into this area are gonna drive the German Army back to the Fatherland in short order. That means we don't have much time to pull this off."

Even though Shorty wasn't looking forward to getting captured by the enemy, he knew their options were limited. "I agree. It's a great idea and it's probably the only way we'll be able to get through any checkpoints or past any patrols that we meet along the way, as long as we don't run into any real Air Support pilots who are directing air attacks against enemy positions."

"You're right. This plan is no more foolproof than any other idea that we can come up with," said Ivan who quickly added, "If we're lucky and we put on a good show, we can probably buy ourselves a few minutes with a front line unit before they notice that we're not directing our fighters and bombers to knock out German positions. Once that happens we'll have to roll the dice and hope for the best."

As soon as Ivan heard Shorty agree with his plan, he casually looked around to make sure that they were still alone before he faced his partner in crime and said, "When we go back inside the CP I'm gonna start looking for my Ronsen lighter. While I'm looking around, you tell Major Gramacki that I'm going nuts because I lost my lucky lighter that my father gave me and that you think it might be on the floor of our glider along with our sleeping bags. I then want you to ask that artillery officer if we can borrow a jeep, so we can run over to our glider to retrieve our sleeping bags and look for my lucky lighter before it gets dark. When I see you light a cigarette I'll come over and keep up the act."

Shorty only had one question for his partner in crime. "What happens if the Major says that he can supply us with plenty of blankets for tonight and he'll make sure that we stop at our glider in the morning to look for your lighter before he delivers us to the Division CP?"

As usual Ivan was a confident son of a gun when he looked at his buddy and said, "We're Lieutenants remember. If need be we'll tell the soldier guarding the vehicles in front of this CP that Major Gramacki gave us permission to borrow a Jeep so we can return to our glider before it gets dark. If that doesn't work we'll steal a Jeep at gunpoint. Either way, we're making a run to the German lines before it gets any later in the day."

While Captain Billy Davis and Sergeant Blair continued talking to the group of glider pilots, Captain Savino walked over to Major Beauregard when he exited the command post with Al Parker and Lt. Colonel Gray, the G2 from the 101st Airborne Division. As Colonel Gray, Major Beauregard and Staff Sergeant Parker stood behind the building, Captain Savino reported his findings. "While none of these glider pilots have seen the Army personnel they know as Danny Gannon and Gus O'Malley since they landed in Bastogne, the pilot from Chalk 36 reports that he observed the C47 towing Chalk 37 get hit pretty bad on the way to the release point. According to this pilot, Chalk 37 cut lose from his tow plane seconds before the C47 exploded and went down in flames. While Chalk 37 made its descent toward the designated LZ near the Village of Savy, Chalk 36 headed west and landed south of the Bastogne-Flamierge Road at about 1234 hours."

After pausing long enough to point to a glider pilot who was speaking to Captain Billy Davis, the CID Captain from Paris continued and said, "Captain Davis is talking to another pilot who observed a GC-4A cut loose from a burning tow plane and land north of Bastogne in the vicinity of Savy. Captain Davis believes that due to the time of day when this sighting was made, it's safe to assume that the glider this pilot observed coming in for a landing was Chalk 37. A number of other pilots who were at the division assembly area also said they observed a glider cut loose from a burning C47 seconds before this particular tow plane exploded and fell to the ground in pieces. The general consensus, Sir, is that Chalk 37 landed north of Bastogne in or near the LZ at Savy at approximately 1235 hours."

While Captain Savino completed his briefing, he handed the Major a map of the area and said, "Captain Davis marked the areas on this map where he believes we should concentrate our initial search for Chalk 37. I made the same notations on my map as well, Sir."

After saying, "Thanks, Tom," Jim Beauregard looked at the group of glider pilots who were assembled behind the Division CP before he turned to Lt. Colonel Gray and said, "They look like a rough bunch, Sir." "That they are, Major," responded the 101st Airborne Division Intelligence Officer who quickly added, "And they're pissed off to boot now that they know who Danny Gannon and Gus O'Malley really are."

Jim Beauregard then turned to Al Parker and said, "OK, Al, call 'em to order."

Without wasting any time Staff Sergeant Parker stepped forward as he held up his right hand and called out in a raised tone of voice and said, "Gentlemen, the Major has something to say."

As soon as Jim began to speak, he could see that he had the undivided attention of every glider pilot assembled behind the command post. While speaking in a slightly raised voice, Jim began his briefing by saying, "My name is Major James Beauregard. I'm assigned to CID in New York. By now you all know why my men and I are here. Even though I hate to ask any of you men to stick your necks out again after all you've done, CID and the Military Police need help locating the fugitives known as Danny Gannon and Gus O'Malley."

The first two pilots to step forward were Flight Officer Pete Peterson and Russ Schultz. As the glider pilot known as Willie Pete remarked, "Count us in,

Sir," other men began sounding off as they agreed to help in any way they could. After asking for a show of hands, Jim Beauregard felt even better about Al's plan to use glider pilots to help locate the two fugitives,when every pilot in the group acknowledged that they could identify the two fugitives.

By having his posse expanded to include a small army of glider pilots, Jim Beauregard could flood the area with teams of heavily armed men who could help MPs and CID Agents locate the two fugitives. While he held up his right hand, Major Beauregard called out, "OK, you're all deputized but remember this is a CID and Military Police manhunt not a lynch mob. Every effort should be made to take the two fugitives into custody alive. See Captain Savino and Lt. Wright for your assignments and get to your assigned area as soon as possible. "Watch your ass and good hunting."

Flight Officer Vincent Mancuso was a tough kid from Boston who flew combat glider missions in Normandy, Holland and now Bastonge. While F.O. Mancuso cradled his Thompson Submachine Gun in his arms, he spoke up and said, "Pardon my French, Major, but what do we do if these son's a bitches resist arrest?" Without mincing words Jim Beauregard looked at the young glider pilot and called out, "Send 'em to hell!"

While Ivan made it appear that he was carefully searching the area in the command post by the stove, he looked over to Shorty as he called out, "Hey, Gabe have you seen my lighter?"

Just as they planned Shorty MC Ghee played his part perfectly when he turned to Major Gramacki and said, "We're in trouble now, Sir. The last time Paul misplaced his good luck lighter we were up to our arm pits in Germans while fighting in Normandy. Fortunately, he found his lighter before we got pulled out or we'd still be there looking for it."

Seeing the artillery officer grin was a clear indication that the show they were putting on was working. As Shorty continued the charade, he spoke while he stood next to Major Gramacki. "His Dad gave him a Ronson lighter when he got his wings. Paul's father was one of the last Pan Am Clipper pilots to leave Wake Island before the Japs launched their attack and captured all those Marines. His Dad's a great guy. I met him once when we went on leave together."

The moment Shorty offered Major Gramacki a Camel cigarette and he took one from the pack for himself, Ivan came over as soon as he saw his buddy put the flame of his Zippo lighter to the tip of his cigarette and said, "It's gone, Gabe. I looked everywhere."

"Your buddy told me how important your lighter is to you," responded Major Gramcki who quickly asked, "When was the last time you used it?"

Without hesitating to think about the question, Ivan remarked, "I've had two smokes since we landed, Sir. Sergeant Martin gave us both a light after our close call with that Kraut patrol and Gabe offered me a light when we had a cup of coffee by the stove. I'm positive, Sir, that the last time I used my Ronson was when I had a smoke before we cut loose from our tow plane."

While playing his part perfectly, Shorty turned to Major Gramacki and said, "We came in pretty hard, Sir. Maybe Paul's lighter fell on the floor of our glider."

Ivan also continued to give a command performance when he remarked, "If it's not on the floor of our glider, I'll bet it's in the damn snow where we took cover when that Kraut patrol tried to take us prisoner."

Once again Shorty played his part when he held up his right hand and said, "Relax Paul. I promise we'll find your lighter."

Shorty then turned to Major Gramacki and said, "Excuse me, Sir, but could we borrow a Jeep so we can run out to our glider to look for Paul's lighter. We also have two sleeping bags stashed on board that might come in handy tonight."

Without hesitating Major Gramacki said, "You can take my jeep but only if you limit your search to the area in and around the current location of your glider. If you can't find your lighter where your glider is parked, we'll search the area where you came in for a landing tomorrow morning before I run you over to the Division CP."

After hearing Ivan remark, "Thank you, Sir," Major Gramcki called his driver over.

As the enlisted man approached, Major Gramacki looked at the two glider pilots and said, "Gentlemen, you remember Private Reader." While Private Reader stood next to a stack of ammo crates that Major Gramacki used as a makeshift desk, the senior airborne artillery officer relayed his instructions to his driver. "Johnny, I want you to run the two Lieutenant's over to their glider so they can pick up their sleeping bags and look for a personal item of great value to Lieutenant Kraft. You're not to go any further than the current position of their glider."

As soon as Private Reader acknowledged his orders, Ivan picked up his Thompson Submachine Gun, while Major Gramacki checked his watch before he looked at all three men and said, "While you're gone I'll use the Command Car to check on our gun positions. We'll meet back here in a bit."

"Yes, Sir," said Ivan.

Shorty also sounded like an Officer and a gentleman when he turned to Private Reader and said, "Lead the way, Private," and all four men left the artillery unit's command post.

The moment Jim Beauregard spotted Lt. Carver coming his way at a fast pace, he knew the communications officer had good news to share with the men from CID. As soon as the communications officer arrived by the Major's side, he spoke with a sense of urgency in his voice when he filed his report. "I just spoke to the Five O Deuce, Sir. One of their rifle squads went to the aid of two glider pilots who came under fire when their glider landed near the Village of Savy. Based on what I was told, a rifle squad led by Sergeant Phil Martin saved the two glider pilots from getting captured by a Kraut patrol."

While Jim paid close attention to everything that was being said, Lt. Carver continued relaying the rest of the message from memory. "Once the surviving members of the Kraut patrol withdrew from the area, the glider was towed closer to the road where it was unloaded. The artillery ammo on the glider was then transported to the ammo dump by the 377th Parachute Field Artillery Battalion. I should know more, Sir, once I hear from Sergeant Martin."

After pausing to catch his breath, Lt. Carver went on to say, "The other good news, Sir, came from the radio operator at the 377th who confirmed that two glider pilots just left their CP with Major Gramacki's driver to get some gear from their glider, but they're supposed to return to have dinner with the CO. Unfortunately, both Colonel Defoe and Major Gramacki are currently away from their command post so I was unable to run any of your questions by them."

"We definitely need to talk to Colonel Defoe and Major Gramacki," responded Jim Beauregard.

When Lt. Carver continued the communications officer continued and said, "We will, Sir," before he added, "I also spoke to the S2 at the 321st Glider Field

Artillery Battalion CP in the Village of Savy. According to Captain Monroe, the last glider to land during today's resupply mission landed just after 1230 hours in the field just north of the large LZ near the Village of Savy. The Captain also said that when this glider came to a stop, it came under fire but a squad of paratroopers drove the Germans off after a brief exchange with the Krauts. Captain Monroe also confirmed that this glider was towed closer to the road that runs through Savy before it was off loaded."

Once the signals officer completed his report, Lt. Wright proved that police work ran in his veins when he enthusiastically volunteered to take a patrol to the 377th PFAB to follow up on this lead. After telling the MP Lieutenant to standby, Jim turned to Lt. Carver and said, "Lieutenant, I need you to notify the 502nd PIR and the 377th that we need Major Gramacki and Sergeant Martin to meet a contingent of CID Agents, MPs and a glider pilot who can identify the two fugitives along the road in Savy where glider number thirty seven is parked. I also need you to notify both units to alert their personnel that the two glider pilots they met earlier today, who landed in a glider bearing the number thirty seven and the name Mad Mike, need to be disarmed and taken into custody."

As soon as Lieutenant Carver acknowledged his new orders and returned to the command post, Major Beauregard turned to Colonel Gray and said, "Sir, can you help us get our hands on some additional transportation, so we can take some of these glider pilots who can identify the two fugitives with us into the field?"

Even though he had a war to fight, the Division Intelligence Officer was committed to doing everything possible to help the visiting CID Agents capture the two fugitives. As soon as Colonel Gray remarked, "Let me see what I can do," the intelligence officer headed back into the Division CP.

After thanking the Division Intelligence Officer, Major Beauregard turned to Captain Savino and said, "Tom, I need you and Private Garcia to follow Lt. Wright and one of the glider pilots who can identify Larson and Mc Ghee up to the LZ near the Village of Savy. Once you locate Chalk 37 do what you can to find Major Granacki's driver and the two fugitives, As soon as we get some additional transportation, we'll meet on the side of the road where Chalk 37 is located. If anything changes we can keep in touch via radio." Immediately after Jim Beauregard told his men to be careful and he wished them good luck, the four men got in their jeeps and left for the Village of Savy.

The last thing that Colonel Gray wanted to do was tell Jim Beauregard that his request to utilize the services of glider pilots to assist in the search for the two fugitives was denied. Even Jim's written orders from the War Department, could not be used to override the standing order, that directed glider pilots to be transported back to their Troop Carrier Squadron as soon as it was feasible to do so. As Colonel Gray continued, he explained that assembly areas, also known as collection points, were established so glider pilots would remain in one location, preferably out of direct combat, where they could perform support duties until they could be evacuated. This policy existed to insure that highly trained glider pilots would be removed from harms way as soon as possible, so they could be made available to fly other missions.

After hearing what Colonel Gray had to say, Jim had no choice but to continue the search without utilizing the services of glider pilots who could identify the two fugitives. Even Flight Officer Mancuso had to be returned to the division assembly area, as soon as it was possible to get a message to Captain Savino and Lt. Wright.

When two paratroopers driving a pair of Jeeps pulled up behind the Division CP, Colonel Gray pointed to the two vehicles and said, "I couldn't get you any glider pilots but I was able to commandeer a pair of Jeeps, including one that's fitted with a belt fed machine gun. I also had some extra small arms ammo, grenades, rations and blankets put in the back of each Jeep in case you and your men end up operating in the field longer than expected."

As soon as the two paratroopers were driven away by an MP driving another Jeep, Colonel Gray pointed to his personal vehicle that was parked nearby and said, "You can also take my Jeep and my driver. In addition to being one hell of a soldier, Corporal Polanski knows the way to every command post, drop zone, LZ and town in this area that you might have to visit when you conduct your search."

After thanking the Colonel for all of his help, Jim checked his watch before he turned to Al Parker and the others and said, "We'll give Lt. Carver two minutes to get in touch with Major Gramacki. After that we're outta here. We also need Lt. Carver to get a message to Lt. Wright to drop Flight Officer Mancuso off at the first available unit so he can be returned to Bastogne."

As soon as Captain Davis said, "I'll handle that, Sir," the C47 pilot walked toward the rear entrance of the command post and entered the building.

After Jim turned to face Al Parker he looked at his partner and said, "We're close, Al...real close."

The moment their Jeep came to a stop behind a U.S. Army truck and a pair of Jeeps, Ivan swallowed hard and tightened his stomach muscles when he heard the sound of a siren coming up from behind. While Ivan experienced a flashback of that night in Brooklyn, when the sound of an approaching siren caused him to panic and kill Tommy Mulray, his partner in crime turned sideways in his seat and looked to the rear as he said, "Here comes another meat wagon."

As the ambulance raced by their jeep, Ivan tried his best not to let Shorty or Private Reader know that he was having a panic attack. After glancing back to see if Private Reader noticed his reaction to the unnerving sound of the ambulance siren, Ivan looked at Shorty and said, "Give me a smoke, Gabe."

While Shorty reached into his pocket and removed a pack of Camels, he could tell that Ivan was worried about something. After tapping a cigarette partially out of the pack, Shorty leaned closer to Ivan and offered his friend a smoke, followed by a light from his Zippo, as he remarked, "Are you all right?"

Instead of responding right away, Ivan took a long drag on the unfiltered cigarette and exhaled before he said, "I'm fine."

While Ivan did his best to shake off the effects of the flashback, he continued driving back to the LZ once the traffic started moving again. As soon as Ivan glanced to his right and said, "Sirens give me the creeps. They remind me of what happens when you screw up a landing in a glider."

"I know what you mean," remarked Shorty.

While Ivan followed a truck from the Quartermaster Company that was delivering ammunition to units positioned along the front, he turned to his right again and said, "Thanks for the smoke. I feel better already." Shorty knew that Ivan's troubles began the night he thought that he was being set up and he shot Tommy Mulray in the face at point blank range to avoid being taken into custody. Even though the siren that Ivan heard that night turned out to belong to an ambulance, his instinct to survive proved to be correct because the feds and the cops were waiting to arrest him once he took possession of a truck load of stolen tires.

As soon as Ivan pulled off the road and parked the borrowed Jeep next to Chalk 37, he instructed Private Reader to sit tight and have a smoke while he and Shorty retrieved their sleeping bags. While the Private sat in the back of the Jeep and smoked a cigarette, Ivan and Shorty entered Chalk 37 to discuss how they were going to escape to the German lines while being saddled with the presence of Private Reader.

While standing inside Chalk 37, Shorty forgot how cold he was when he turned and looked out one of the windows at the Jeep where Private Reader was sitting and said, "What do we do about him? If we leave him behind it won't take Private Reader very long to get word back to Major Gramacki that we stole his Jeep. We sure as hell can't take him with us and I for one don't want to see any harm come to him."

Ivan knew the moment that Major Gramacki instructed his driver to accompany the two pilots to the location where their glider was parked, that his presence in the Jeep would prove to be a complication that they didn't need to deal with. After giving the matter some thought, Ivan decided on a compromise. "We'll take the Private with us while we head due north and leave him in the ass end of nowhere before we make the rest of the trip on a paved road. If we have to we'll tie him to a tree." After pausing for a second Ivan added, "Who knows maybe he'll come in handy if we get into a tight spot."

Since Shorty didn't have any better ideas, his only concern was how to break the news to Private Reader that they intended to disregard Major Gramacki's orders by taking an unauthorized trip in his Jeep. After all, the airborne artilleryman seemed like a good kid who was smart enough to know, that a direct order from a Major could not be countermanded by a Lieutenant. Unless exigent circumstances were involved, even an order from two Lieutenants would never pull enough weight to get a good soldier to ignore a previously issued direct order from a superior officer. The fact that Private Reader was armed with a Thompson Submachine Gun also meant that he had the means to resist if push came to shove.

Ivan Larson proved that he was still in charge when he looked directly at Shorty and said, "The second we hand these sleeping bags to the Major's driver I want you to use your forty five to relieve Private Reader of his Thompson and his pistol belt. While you keep him covered, I'll take the wheel. We have a plan and we're sticking to it unless the situation changes. Any objections?"

Shorty didn't have to think twice before he responded and said, "I'm right behind you," as he bent over and picked up his sleeping bag.

CHAPTER 15

THE NOOSE TIGHTENS

Shortly after Lt. Wright, Flight Officer Mancuso, Captain Savino and MP Private Garcia took off in a pair of Jeeps, Lt. Carver called out, "Major," as he ran out of the command post with an important update for the Commanding Officer of the CID led patrol. "I just spoke to Major Gramacki and boy is he pissed, Sir. According to the Major, he and his men watched glider number thirty seven come in for a landing in a smaller field located due north of the primary land zone near Savy. While a rifle squad from the 502nd PIR led by Sergeant Martin saved the two glider pilots from getting captured, the Major and his men drove out to the LZ to off load the ammo just as the surviving Germans were falling back. Rather than risk another encounter with the Krauts, the glider was towed closer to the paved road that runs through Savy. After the glider was unloaded, two glider pilots identified as Lt. Paul Kraft and Lt. Gabe Fuller were transported to the 377th PFA Battalion CP where they were invited to have supper with the CO. According to Major Gramacki, the two glider pilots left his CP a few minutes ago with his driver and his Jeep so they could retrieve their sleeping bags from their glider."

After hearing Lieutenant Carver's last remark, Flight Officer William Peterson called out, "That's impossible, Major," a comment that was quickly followed by Flight Officer Russ Schultz saying, "Willie's right, Sir."

As soon as everyone turned to face the two glider pilots, Flight Officer William Peterson continued without being asked to do so. "Paul Kraft and Gabe Fuller are friends of ours, Sir. They were both listed as Missing in Action when their gliders went down during Operation Market Garden."

After hearing this interesting tidbit of information, Jim Beauregard turned to Al Parker and said, "This has to be them."

The next to speak was Colonel Gray who asked Lt. Carver if the two glider pilots ever returned to the 377th CP with Private Reader. Even though he was only recently asked to assist in this manhunt, Lt. Carver felt as if he was making a valuable contribution at a critical time in this investigative effort when he responded and said, "No, Sir, they're not back yet."

When Jim Beauregard addressed Lt. Carver he removed a map of the area from the inside pocket of his field jacket and said, "Standby, Lieutenant." Once Jim unfolded the map and placed it on the hood of Colonel's Gray's Jeep, he found the location of the 377th Parachute Field Artillery Battalion CP, then ran his right index finger to the landing zone next to the Village of Savy. The fact that Savy was located just over a mile north of Bastogne meant that it wouldn't take very long to reach the search area.

While the Major relayed his instructions to Lt. Carver, he knew that this was the closest they have ever been to capturing the two fugitives. "Lieutenant, we need you to get a message to Lt. Wright and Captain Savino and let them know that Major Gramacki just confirmed that the two fugitives left the 377th Command Post and are heading back to their glider with the Major's driver. Also, let them know the names the two fugitives are using and that the rest of us are on the way."

After hearing Lt. Carver acknowledge his orders, Major Beauregard finished relaying his instructions to the communication officer by saying, "We also need every command post in the area to pass the word that two fugitives using the names Gannon, Kraft, O'Malley or Fuller are masker-aiding as glider pilots and might try to make a run for the German lines in a stolen Jeep."

As soon as Lt. Carver said, "Will do, Sir," the communications officer returned to the command post.

Colonel Gray extended his right hand and said, "Good hunting, Jim. I'll try to get some help out to you as soon as I can."

"Thanks again, Sir," responded Major Beauregard before he relayed his orders to the remaining members of his search team. "Captain Davis and Sergeant Jacko will take the Jeep that's equipped with the M1919, while Sergeant Blair and Doc Keller will bring up the rear in the other Jeep. I'll lead the way with Al Parker and Corporal Polanski. Let's go!"

As soon as everyone took their positions, Jim Beauregard sat in the passenger seat of Colonel Gray's Jeep and said, "You're in charge, Corporal. Take us to the LZ in Savy and put a rush on it."

After starting the Colonel's Jeep, Corporal Raymond Polanski worked his way through the gears as he drove away from the Division CP at a high rate of speed.

Following close behind was Captain Davis, MP Sergeant Chris Jacko, Sergeant Hank Blair and Doc Keller.

After being briefed over the radio, Captain Savino and Lt. Wright drove directly to location where Chalk 37 was located and visible from the side of the paved road. Knowing that Major Gramcki and Sergeant Martin, along with the other members of the CID led patrol, were converging on the same location, meant that they would have a suitable number of armed personnel to conduct a search of the area. Rather than leave Flight Officer Mancuso on the side of the road, Captain Savino decided to take the glider pilot to the LZ, so he could walk to the Village of Savy to catch a ride back to Bastogne.

The sight of a paratrooper sitting in the back of a Jeep, that was parked next to a Waco glider that was parked on the side of the road, was a clear indication that they were moments away from locating Chalk 37 and possibly even the two fugitives. As Flight Officer Mancuso downshifted and slowed the Jeep to a crawl, Lt. Wright called out, "Either Major Gramacki beat us here, or that's his Jeep and his driver which means the two fugitives are close by."

Ivan Larson hadn't taken more than a few steps out of his glider, when he spotted a pair of MP Jeeps slowing down as they approached the location where Chalk 37 was parked by the side of the road. The moment the two vehicles came to a stop and Ivan spotted Flight Officer Vincent Mancuso point his way and call out, "That's him," Ivan knew that it was time to transition back to his persona as a wanted man. After dropping his sleeping bag in the snow, Ivan yelled, "Get the Jeep," as he removed the Thompson Submachine Gun from his shoulder and fired a long burst at the lead MP jeep that contained a glider pilot who knew him as Danny Gannon.

As the occupants of the two MP Jeeps took cover behind their vehicles and began to return fire, Ivan knelt in the snow by the side of his glider and continued firing a succession of short bursts. While Ivan provided covering fire, Shorty made his way to their getaway vehicle and ordered Private Reader at gunpoint to place his Thompson and his pistol belt on the front passenger seat of the Jeep. Shorty's next command was to tell the dumbfounded paratrooper to sit on the floor of the Jeep facing backwards and place his hands on top of his head.

"What's going on, Lieutenant?," asked the shocked airborne artillery soldier.

Shorty kept his response simple, "Sorry, Pal, but we're wanted by the MPs. If that Major of yours didn't make you come along we'd be long gone by now, so sit tight and we'll let you go when the time is right."

As soon as Shorty holstered his pistol, he picked up the Thompson Submachine Gun and leaned on the front passenger seat of Major Gramacki's Jeep to let the MPs see that he was much better armed while he held Private Reader hostage.

When Flight Officer Mancuso aimed his Thompson at Gus O'Malley and said, "Scratch one Assistant Glider Engineering Officer," Lt. Wright put his gloved left hand on the barrel of the glider pilot's submachine gun and said, "Hold your fire. You might hit that paratrooper."

As soon as Ivan Larson saw the Army cops and Flight Officer Mancuso hold their fire, he stood up and reloaded his Thompson, while he called out and said, "We're leaving and we're taking Private Reader with us. All we want is to have one of your MP Jeeps lead the way due North, to insure that we make it to an area along the front line in Longchamps. I want the other MP Jeep to fall in behind our Jeep to make sure that no one takes a shot at us along the way. We'll let Private Reader go once we cross over to the German side of the line. That's the deal! Take it or start shooting again and we'll end this right here and now."

The exchange of gunfire on the road that ran north from Bastogne through the Village of Savy caused quite a commotion and brought a number of military policemen and armed troops to converge on the area. One of the Army officers who responded to the sound of shots being fired was Captain Monroe, the S2 from the 321st Glider Field Artillery Battalion. As soon as Captain Monroe stopped his Jeep on the other side of the road from where Major Gramacki's Jeep was parked, the S2 from the 321st GFAB remarked, "So that's the famous Glider Number 37.

In order to control the situation, Captain Savino stood up and placed his M1 Carbine in the back of his jeep, before he instructed Lt. Wright to do the same and accompany him into the middle of the road. As Captain Savino showed the two fugitives that he wasn't holding any weapons in hand, he identified himself to everyone present. "My name is Captain Savino from CID. Lt. Wright is with the Hundred and First. I'm ordering everyone not involved in this incident to leave the area."

In an effort to assist the Captain from CID, Lt. Wright waved his right hand in the air as he called out, "You heard the Captain. Return to your units. Move out! Let's go!" Lt. Wright then turned to the two military policemen who responded to the area and said, "Let's get this traffic moving!"

When Captain Monroe identified himself to Captain Savino and asked if he needed any additional assistance, the CID Agent from Paris asked the S2 from the 321st Glider Field Artillery Battalion if he could standby and give the two MPs directing traffic a ride back to town, because he intended to commandeer their Jeep. After hearing the S2 agree to provide transportation for the two military policemen, Captain Savino called Flight Officer Mancuso over to where he was standing.

As far as Captain Savino was concerned, he had to stop Major Beauregard and Sergeant Parker from being spotted by the two fugitives. Captain Savino felt this way because Larson and Mc Ghee would never believe that the two cops who have been pursuing them for the last year would allow them to escape. In order for the plan that he had in mind to work, Captain Savino needed to keep a few cards up his sleeve.

As soon as Flight Officer Mancuso arrived by his side, Captain Savino said, "I need you to commandeer that Jeep from the MPs who are directing traffic and head back to Bastgone. It's imperative that you stop Major Beauregard and Sergeant Parker from responding to this location. If the two fugitives find out that Major Beauregard and Sergeant Parker are in this area, they'll never believe we're serious about letting them escape to the German lines to save the hostage. Tell the Major that I'll be sending someone back to explain everything in more detail as soon as I can. I also want all other traffic except for ambulances stopped for ten minutes. Now go."

While Shorty continued to hold Private Reader hostage, Ivan Larson stood with his Tommy Gun in hand by the driver's side of Major Gramacki's Jeep. When Ivan saw Flight Officer Mancuso leave the area in a different Jeep, he wasted no time in calling out, "Hey, Captain. Where's that glider pilot going? Do we have a deal or not?"

Once again Captain Savino sounded like an officer who was in complete command of a difficult situation when he called out and said, "Calm the fuck down, Larson and let me do my job so we can get this show on the road." As someone who spent enough time as a cop in Providence, Rhode Island to know how to deal with bad guys, Tommy Savino quickly added, "For your information, tough guy, Flight Officer Mancuso was sent back toward Bastogne to stop traffic from heading north for a few minutes, so we don't end up with another group of G.I.s taking a personal interest in this situation."

The last thing that the two fugitives wanted to see was a Dodge WC-57 4x4 Command Car driven by Major Gramacki swerve to a stop behind the two MP Jeeps, while the area around the standoff was being cleared of troops and passing vehicle traffic. As soon as Major Gramacki introduced himself, Captain Savino explained the situation while Shorty Mc Ghee continued to hold Private Reader hostage.

As much as Captain Savino wanted to end this standoff, he had good reason to be concerned that Ivan Larson would rather go down fighting than submit to arrest. Even Shorty Mc Ghee had a well documented reputation for having no compunction about shooting at law enforcement officers and innocent bystanders with a Thompson Submachine Gun. The fact that CID had every reason to believe that Larson and Mc Ghee also murdered Lt. Perkins, meant that the two fugitives had no problem killing a fellow soldier if doing so served their purpose.

Once again an arrogant sounding Ivan Larson stood by the driver's side of the stolen Jeep and called out, "What's it gonna be, Captain or should we be dealing with the Major since he out ranks you?"

Just like he did before, Captain Savino stood his ground and did his best to remain in control of the situation, when he responded in a commanding tone of voice and said, "I'm not gonna tell you again, Larson. Hold your fucking horses. Once I brief Major Gramacki and Captain Monroe we'll be heading north, so until then sit tight and don't do anything stupid."

As soon as the airborne artillery officer remarked, "Now what, Captain?" the CID Agent from Paris explained what he had in mind. "Under the circumstances, Sir, I think the best course of action is to play along until we're in a better position to take action without having any harm come to Private Reader."

When Major Gramacki suggested that they get some sharpshooters to end this standoff with two pulls of the trigger, Captain Savino responded as if he had given the same idea some consideration. "As much as I would like to have two expert marksman finish these guys off right here and now, I'm concerned that even if they hit the mark with their first shot, the fugitive identified as Francis Shorty Mc Ghee could still kill or seriously wound Private Reader. For this reason, Sir, I recommend that Lt. Wright should lead the way and I'll fall in behind the two fugitives while we head north to Longchamps."

When Captain Savino heard Major Gramacki say that he was going along to make sure that nothing happened to Private Reader, the CID Agent from Paris tried to sound as diplomatic as possible when he presented Major Gramacki with a much better way for him to be involved in this case. "Sir, you could help us a lot more if you left the area and drove south toward Bastogne where you'll find Major James Beauregard and other members of the CID led search team on the side of the road waiting for us to head north. We need Major Beauregard and the men who are with him to make their way to Longchamps by traveling off the paved road for as long as possible. In the meantime, Lt. Wright and I will do everything possible to delay our arrival along the front line in the vicinity of Longchamps. Once we're in position, we'll communicate via radio before we make our move. My plan is to offer myself as a hostage and change places with Private Reader. Ten seconds after I begin to cross over into enemy territory with the two fugitives, I want two sharpshooters to open fire the second they see me hit the dirt. I know this plan is risky but I don't see any other way for us to handle this situation."

After pausing for a split second, Captain Savino made one last statement to reinforce the severity of the situation at hand. "I assure you, Sir, that Ivan Larson and Francis Shorty Mc Ghee will do whatever they feel is necessary to facilitate their escape. Unless other opportunities present themselves, we need to stick to a plan that offers us the best chance of preventing any harm from coming to Private Reader, while also preventing the escape of the two fugitives."

After hearing Captain Savino lay out his plan, Major Gramacki said, "As far as I'm concerned you're in command here, Captain. I'll also let Major Beauregard know that I approve of the way that you're handling this situation."

When Captain Savino wished the airborne artillery officer good luck, he presented him with a casual salute before he added, "We'll see you in Longchamps, Sir."

While Major Gramacki got back in his Dodge Command Car and drove away, Captain Savino walked in front of Lt. Wright's Jeep to confer with the two fugitives and Private Reader. When the Captain from CID spoke, he sounded like a veteran street cop who was willing to play ball with the two fugitives, as long they agreed to comply with his rules of engagement. "Major Gramacki has decided to return to his command post and let CID handle this situation. This means I'm still in charge and you have a deal but understand this. You and Shorty Mc Ghee better enjoy your time in a Kraut POW Camp because once this war is over Army CID will not rest until the two of you are hunted down and taken into custody."

While Captain Savino continued he looked directly at Ivan Larson as he said, "Now that I got that off my chest we're ready to take you where you want to go. Lt. Wright will lead the way and make sure that you and your accomplice along with Private Reader will arrive safely along a front line position in Longchamps. I'll bring up the rear in my Jeep. Since there's still a war on we need to give ambulances and resupply convoys the right of way. For safety purposes we will also proceed at a reasonable speed to be set by the lead MP Jeep. Since we don't have all that far to go this trip should not take long."

So far Captain Savino was doing an excellent job of delaying the trip north, so Major Gramacki could meet up with Major Beauregard and the others and execute a flanking maneuver to an area along the front line in the vicinity of Longchamps. As Captain Savino removed a stick of gum from his field jacket breast pocket, he paused long enough to remove the wrapper and slip the piece into his mouth before he continued addressing the two fugitives. "Whatever you do don't panic and start shooting if we run into any legitimate delays along the way. Remember, we're still surrounded on three sides by the German Army so anything could happen, including an enemy air attack, an enemy artillery barrage or a ground attack. If anything does happen to delay our arrival in Longchamps, either Lt. Wright or I will approach your vehicle unarmed to explain the situation before we move on. As soon as we reach a forward area along the front, all military police and CID personnel except me will remain with their vehicles. Once I take the place of Private Reader as your hostage, my presence will insure that you'll be able to cross over to the German lines under a flag of truce. After we travel a safe distance from our lines, I'll return to the U.S. side of the line, while you and Mc Ghee turn yourselves over to the enemy to be taken as Prisoners of War."

As much as Ivan wanted to be escorted to the closest Air Liaison unit so he and Shorty could use a single engine L4 or L5 to make their escape, it actually made more sense to cross into German held territory on foot under a flag of truce, than risk getting shot down by enemy anti aircraft fire. Ivan also knew that a handful of pissed off Army cops would have no problem preventing them from being able to take off once they released their hostage. After Ivan considered every possible option, he nodded his head in agreement and said, "OK, Captain. Whenever you're ready."

As soon as Captain Savino advised the two fugitives that they would be leaving momentarily, the CID Agent from the Paris Office walked over to where Lt. Wright was standing to go over the real game plan. "I want you to take the lead because you know the way to Longchamps. I'll send Private Garcia over to be your driver. Just make sure you take your sweet time getting us to our intended destination."

After instructing Private Garcia to accompany Lt. Wright and drive the lead MP Jeep, Captain Savino continued briefing the MP Lieutenant from New Mexico in a low tone of voice. "Once we reach the vicinity of Longchamps, I want you to delay our arrival along a front line position. If possible, make a bit of a scene when you confer with MPs or any other troops in the area, especially if we have to pass through a checkpoint. I then want you to use your handie-talkie radio to call me over to your Jeep. I'll handle the rest and will explain to the two fugitives that due to enemy activity it isn't as easy as they think to drive up to the front line without getting shot at." After hearing the Military Police Lieutenant from the 101st Airborne Division acknowledge his orders, Captain Savino remarked, "Good luck, Lieutenant. Move out."

Before he sat in his Jeep, Captain Savino thanked Captain Monroe for lending a hand by transporting the two MPs back to town. After wishing the CID Agent good luck, Captain Monroe walked across the road to give the two MPs a lift back to Savy. With nothing else to do except get this show on the road, Captain Savino sat in the driver's seat of his Jeep and started the engine in preparation of heading north.

While Flight Officer Mancuso returned to Bastogne in the commandeered MP Jeep, Major Gramacki briefed Major Beauregard and his team on the side of the road just south of the Village of Savy. After pointing northeast, Major Gramacki continued and said, "The best way for us to make our way north to Longchamps without running into your fugitives, is to travel off road through open snow covered fields and wooded terrain for as long as possible. If everything goes according to plan, Lt. Wright and Captain Savino will find a way to delay their trip up north, so we can get into position to stop your fugitives from escaping without any harm coming to Private Reader."

Once Major Gramacki finished his briefing, Major Beauregard asked if anyone had any questions. When no one had anything to say Jim remarked, "I'll ride with Major Gramacki and Al Parker. Everyone else fall in behind." Without wasting any time, Al Parker got behind the wheel of the Dodge 4x4 Command Car, while Jim Beauregard jumped into the back seat and Major Gramacki sat up front.

After quickly lighting a cigarette, Jim leaned forward and called out, "OK, Al, take us to 42nd and Broadway and put a rush on it."

"Yes, Sir, 42nd and Broadway coming right up," responded Al as he drove the Dodge Command Car off road and headed north.

Just as MP Private Garcia was about to lead the three vehicle convoy north, Lt. Wright stopped him from doing so, when MP Sergeant Mike Mulligan and Sergeant Phil Martin drove up in a jeep that came to a stop on the west side of the road. As soon as Sergeant Martin stepped out of the MP Jeep with his Tommy Gun in hand, the veteran paratrooper immediately made eye contact with the two glider pilots who were the most wanted men in the U.S. Army. In fact, if looks could kill, Ivan Larson and Francis Shorty Mc Ghee would have died on the spot.

In order to avoid a potential confrontation, Captain Savino jumped out of his Jeep and met Sergeant Mulligan on the driver's side of his vehicle. Once Sergeant Mulligan introduced himself and explained that he was ordered by Colonel Gray to deliver Sergeant Martin to this location, Captain Savino said, "Make a U Turn, Sergeant and fall in behind my Jeep. We're heading back to Longchamps."

As Sergeant Mulligan complied with his instructions, Sergeant Martin was left standing on the west side of the road staring at Ivan Larson and Francis Shorty Mc Ghee. The second a pissed off sounding Ivan Larson spotted Sergeant Martin, the angry fugitive called out and said, "He's not part of our deal, Captain."

After hearing what Ivan Larson had to say, Captain Savino had to physically restrain Sergeant Martin from lunging at the fugitive when the paratrooper screamed, "You're no Lieutenant. You're a cop killing bank robbing piece of shit and so's that short fuck who's masquerading as your co pilot."

Once again Captain Savino proved to be an officer who knew how to take command of a situation and be respected in the process. While speaking in a friendly but firm tone of voice Captain Savino spoke as he let go of the paratrooper's right arm. "Take a seat in my Jeep, Sarge. I'll handle this."

After hearing the squad leader from the 502nd PIR acknowledge the order, Captain Savino took a step closer to Ivan Larson and said, "As an experienced squad leader with the 502nd Parachute Infantry Regiment, Sergeant Martin knows the terrain along the northern perimeter of our lines better than anyone else in this convoy of vehicles. As a result, I suggest you disregard his outright hatred for you and your partner, because he just might make it possible for us to find a place where you can surrender to the Krauts without getting all of us killed in the process." Without saying another word, Captain Savino turned and faced Lt. Wright and motioned him to proceed as he said, "Move out, Lieutenant."

CHAPTER 16

THE SHORT AND LONG WAY
TO LONGCHAMPS

T he trip to Longchamps in off road snow covered conditions was made a lot easier by the fact that the 4x4 Dodge Command Car and the U.S. made Jeep were incredibly rugged all terrain vehicles. The fact that the Jeeps were also fitted with chains made it even easier to drive in off road conditions.

While making some good time as they headed north, Jim Beauregard briefed Major Gramacki on their case that included explaining Al Parker's reason for being involved in this manhunt. After hearing what Major Beauregard had to say, the airborne artillery officer turned to his left and said, "Don't worry Sarge. We'll get 'em."

While MP Private Garcia remained behind the wheel of the lead Jeep, Lt. Wright put on a command performance when he met with the pair of MPs, who were guarding the turn off that led to the 502nd PIR Command Post at the Chateau Rolle. While quickly explaining the situation to the two military policemen, Lt. Wright repeatedly pointed north before he purposely used a raised voice to argue his case to be allowed to pass through the checkpoint.

After quietly telling the two MPs what he planned to relay to the two fugitives, Lt.Wright returned to his Jeep and picked up his portable handie-talkie radio. Just as they rehearsed, Captain Savino arrived by the MP Officer's side and played along as he listened to Lt. Wright's plan to delay the two fugitives from going any further for at least a good fifteen minutes.

As soon as Captain Savino approached the driver's side of the stolen Jeep, he ignored the fact that Ivan Larson was holding his Thompson in his lap with the barrel pointed in his direction. "The Germans that you and Shorty Mc Ghee are determined to surrender to just tried to probe our defensive positions between Champs and Longchamps. According to the MPs manning this check point, we have to sit tight for about fifteen minutes before we can proceed."

Ivan Larson knew that he and Shorty had no way of knowing if Captain Savino was telling the truth about enemy activity in the area. As soon as Captain Savino observed Ivan Larson look at his watch, the CID Agent from the Paris Office remarked, "Don't worry, Larson. You'll still be able to cross over before it gets dark."

While Ivan looked up at Captain Savino, he asked his partner in crime what he thought about this delay. As Shorty Mc Ghee sat sideways, while he continued to point a Thompson Submachine Gun at Private Reader, he sounded content when he responded and said, "Fifteen minutes isn't all that long to wait."

After hearing Ivan Larson concede to the delay, Captain Savino pointed to the side of the road and said, "We'll pull our vehicles over and wait for the word to move out. Until then sit tight."

As Captain Savino walked back to meet with Lt. Wright, he called out, "Let's pull these Jeeps over until this checkpoint is open."

While Ivan watched Captain Savino meet with Lt. Wright, he removed a Camel cigarette from the open pack that he had in his field jacket breast pocket and asked Shorty what he thought about the Captain from CID. Without taking his eyes off their hostage, Shorty responded and said, "So far so good but this Captain from CID is still an Army cop which means I don't trust him."

After lighting his cigarette, Ivan turned and looked at Private Reader and said, "I'm sorry you got involved in this, Private. Like my buddy said before. If your Major didn't order you to accompany us back to our glider none of this would have happened." When Private Reader asked if he could smoke a cigarette Ivan said, "Sure Pal," as he produced his Ronson lighter and offered their hostage a light.

After taking a long drag on an unfiltered Camel cigarette, Private Reader thanked Ivan for the light then said, "Are you guys really gonna let me go once we reach the front?"

While Ivan Larson continued to keep an eye on the Army cops, he answered the airborne artillery soldier's question by saying, "You heard what that Captain from CID said. As soon as we get to a location along the front line, he's gonna take your place, while we cross over into German held territory under a flag of truce. All you have to do is sit tight and go along for the ride."

After meeting with an MP Lieutenant and Captain Rico Cabrerra, the S2 for the 502nd PIR, the plan was set in motion for the two fugitives and their hostage to be escorted to a position that was relatively close to the front line. Before doing so, Captain Savino asked if it would be possible for a few shots to be fired off in the distance without drawing any return fire from the Germans. When Captain Savino made this request, he explained that he would use the sound of gunfire to further delay their departure to the proposed take down area by another ten minutes.

Captain Savino also asked the S2 to raise Major Gramacki or Major Beauregard on the radio to check on their status and make arrangements to escort them into the area where they planned to prevent the escape of the two fugitives. Captain Cabrerra was also asked to alert patrols and fixed positions from the Five O Deuce to be on the lookout for Major Gramachi, Major Beauregard and the other Army personnel who were traveling to Longchamps via the off road route.

The sound of gunfire off in the distance proved to be an effective rouse that convinced Ivan Larson and Shorty Mv Ghee that the paratroopers from the Five O Deuce were still mopping up the German effort to prob the American lines near Longchamps. As soon as Captain Savino notified the two fugitives that paratroopers from the 502nd PIR were in the process of securing the area, he produced his map and showed Ivan Larson the location that the S2 believed would be the best place to cross over into enemy held territory.

While Captain Savino folded his map and slipped back it into his field jacket pocket, he finished his remarks by saying, "We'll be moving out as soon as Captain Cabrerra and Sergeant Martin inspect the location along the perimeter where you and Mc Ghee can cross over to the German lines under a flag of truce."

As Captain Savino walked away, Shorty removed the set of dog tags that identified him as Lt. Gabe Fuller and tossed them out of the Jeep as he said, "I hope you don't mind but I kind'a got used to being Gus O'Malley."

Immediately after Ivan nodded his head and remarked, "What the heck," he replaced the dog tags that identified him as Lt. Paul Kraft with the set that identified him as Daniel Gannon. Once Ivan replaced the set of lieutenant bars that he wore on his field jacket with his Flight Officer insignia, he covered their hostage with his Thompson while Shorty repeated the same process and became a Warrant Officer again.

After observing the two fugitives change dog tags and their insignia of rank, Private Reader remarked, "Excuse me for asking but you guys aren't Lieutenants?"

"My real rank is Flight Officer," responded Ivan who continued and said, "My buddy's a Warrant Officer who also happens to be the best Assistant Glider Engineering Officer in the Army Air Forces. We joined the Army back in 1943 as a way to get away from the cops after we broke a few laws. After basic training and a brief stint in an infantry unit we applied for the glider program."

While Ivan continued to keep an eye on the military cops who were huddled around the checkpoint, he continued and said, "To be quite honest, Private, my buddy and I ended up liking the Army and were hoping to make a fresh start in Europe once this war was over. Unfortunately, the Army cops caught up with us just as we were preparing to take you for a ride so you wouldn't be able to let anyone know which way we went to make our escape. Naturally, we were gonna let you go before we crossed over into German held territory."

As soon as the reinforced squad of SS troopers finished camouflaging their L shaped fighting position, Sergeant Claus Werner decided to inspect the area near the American lines. While leading a two man patrol, Sergeant Werner walked to the edge of the treeline, that overlooked the open snow covered terrain, that separated the American side of the front line from German held territory. Even though nothing appeared to be out of the ordinary, Sergeant Werner instructed his men to remain behind good cover, while they continued to observe a section of the American held perimeter.

Both Ivan Larson and Shorty Mc Ghee felt as if they were getting closer to making their escape, when they observed Sergeant Martin and the intelligence officer from the 502nd PIR drive off to inspect the location along the front, where they would be allowed to cross over to German held territory. What the two fugitives didn't know, was that Captain Cabrerra and Sergeant Martin were actually on their way to escort Major Gramacki and the members of the CID search team to the location along the perimeter, where the terrain features offered the Army cops the best chance of protecting the hostage while preventing the escape of the two fugitives.

Once they arrived in the location that was selected by Captain Cabrerra to set the trap for the two fugitives, the paratroopers who were normally positioned in this area took cover in woods on the American side of the front line. This was done to make the two fugitives believe that this particular sector was quiet enough for them to release their hostage, while they escaped to the German side of the line.

As soon as these paratroopers, minus two men who were directed to handle security, were called over to the assembly of parked Army vehicles, Captain Cabrerra introduced Lt. Chuck Graham and Sergeant Martin to Major Beauregard and the others. Once the introductions were out of the way, Captain Cabrerra continued and said, "Lt. Graham and his men have already been briefed about this situation and will be available to provide assistance as required."

After thanking Lt. Graham and his men for helping out, Major Beauregard looked through the treeline across the open field and said, "I'm curious, Captain, but what makes this location more suitable for our needs than any other."

While Captain Cabrerra stood next to Major Gramacki's Dodge Command Car, the intelligence officer from the 502nd PIR responded like a combat tested soldier who knew his business. "In addition to allowing us to conceal you and your men, this position provides us with enough open terrain to maneuver and engage the two fugitives once the hostage is outta the line of fire. In order to be prepared for every possible contingency, Sergeant Martin and I brought a bolt action '03 with a scope along, in case it becomes necessary to engage the two fugitives with precision rifle fire. Lt. Graham and his men are also crack shots and can help out in this regard as well."

As Captain Cabrerra continued, he turned and pointed toward German held territory. "You should also know, Sir, that while Waffen SS and Panzergrenadier units are active along our perimeter to the east of this position, the German side of this particular sector is controlled by the 26th Volksgrenadier Division. Since we're in a position to pick the spot to make the exchange, I figured we'd be better off operating along a perimeter that's under the control of a Volksgrenadier Division that has taken some heavy casualties. The alternative, Sir, would be to intentionally operate in an area that is under the control of a fanatical SS unit."

After pausing to turn back to face the Major from CID, the Captain finished answering Major Beauregard's question by saying, "Either way, Sir, the Germans can be counted on to retaliate to any increased level of activity or aggressive behavior by our troops, especially if we move against the two fugitives after they enter the German side of the line under a flag of truce."

After thanking the intelligence officer for providing such a detailed response to his question, Major Beauregard remarked, "This is one hell of a mess. Even if we manage to capture or kill Larson and Mc Ghee without any harm coming to their hostage, we risk having to fight the German Army in order to do so." While continuing to address the mixed compliment of troops who were assembled behind good cover in wooded terrain, the Major continued and said, "Captain Cabrerra is also right about the issue of us engaging or pursuing the two fugitives once they display a flag of truce."

Under any other circumstances it would seem a bit strange that a white Army officer would seek the advice and council of a Negro non commissioned officer but in this case everyone present was familiar enough with the situation at hand to know who Al Parker was and why he was present. Because they were dealing with a time critical situation, Jim turned to the veteran street cop that he served with for over a year and asked if he had any ideas how they should proceed.

As far as Al Parker was concerned, he and Jim Beauregard had come too far to see Larson and Mc Ghee escape into enemy held territory so they could end up becoming Prisoners of War. After all, it would be a daunting task to continue this manhunt once the two fugitives were liberated from a POW Camp and they were able to make a new life for themselves in post war Europe.

When Al Parker responded to the Major's question, he did so like a man who had already given this issue a great deal of thought. "Well, Sir, I think there's a good chance that once those Jeeps arrive in this area, the Germans will become real curious when they see U.S. Army Military Policemen involved in a standoff with other U.S. Army personnel. Quite frankly, Sir, I think we can use this to our advantage."

As soon as Jim remarked, "You mean this rather unusual event will make the Germans curious enough to wait and watch rather than attack and fight?" "That's correct, Sir," said Al who continued and said, "In fact, I believe that our only hope of pulling this off is if we make our move before Ivan Larson or Francis Shorty Mc Ghee display a flag of truce. After all, if we saw the Krauts engaging their own men we'd probably sit still and watch as well."

"I agree," remarked Major Beauregard who quickly turned to Major Gramacki and said, "Major, can we borrow your Command Car?"

"She's all yours," responded Major Gramacki.

After turning back to face his partner, Jim Beauregard explained to Al Parker what he had in mind. "The two of us will be using the Command Car to drive across this open field as fast as possible, once Larson and Mc Ghee release Private Reader and Captain Savino dives to the ground after he offers himself as a hostage. We've been chasing these bastards long enough to know that they're resourceful, desperate, dangerous and determined to escape justice. That means we can't trust them to make the exchange as planned."

While the Major continued, he turned to Captain Cabrerra and said, "Captain, I need you to find two expert marksman who can put an '03 and an M1 Garand to good use, if either of the two fugitives try to harm Captain Savino or Private Reader. I also need these riflemen to open fire if Larson and Mc Ghee take off running. To make this work I want one rifleman positioned off to the right and one off to the left, so those of us using vehicles can cross the open terrain without being in the line of fire."

Corporal Polanski was the first to volunteer. "I'd like to do more than drive a Jeep, Sir. I'm a crack shot with an M1."

"You're hired," responded Major Beauregard before he continued and said, "All we need now is someone to handle the '03."

In addition to the fact that one of his men was being held hostage by the two fugitives, Major Gramacki had no love for the two criminals who represented themselves to be U.S. Army Lieutenants. As someone who wanted to do more than observe the action, Major Gramacki spoke up and said, "I shot expert with an '03 in OCS. I also carried one in North Africa and put it to good use."

After thanking Major Gramacki for volunteering, Jim looked at the airborne artillery officer then at Corporal Polanski and said, "If they can be wounded fine... if not..kill 'em both."

Major Beauregard then turned to Sergeant Hank Blair and MP Sergeant Chris Jacko and said, "Hank, I want you and Sergeant Jacko to cut across this open field on the right side of the Command Car, while Sergeant Jacko prepares to provide covering fire with that belt fed machine gun. But remember, don't open up unless the fugitives make a run for it or the Krauts launch and attack."

Once both men acknowledged their orders, Captain Davis spoke up and asked how he could be of service. While doing his best to be diplomatic, Jim Beauregard answered the Captain's question by saying, "I'd say you did more than your fair share just by making it possible for us to get to Bastogne. I'd like you to sit this part out."

Jim should have known better than to try and keep a New Yorker out of the action. The second Major Beauregard finished speaking, Billy Davis objected to being left out and let his feelings be known in a very forceful but respectful fashion. "I'm sorry, Sir, but with all due respect I think I can help in more ways than one. In addition to bringing another gun to what will likely turn out to be a gunfight, I believe that seeing me involved in this action will be very upsetting to both fugitives"

Because Jim liked Billy Davis he was willing to hear what he had to say and asked, "How so, Captain?"

When Billy Davis responded he sounded like a man who was incredibly sure of himself. "In addition to the shock value of seeing you and Sergeant Parker show up in all places but the front line of a European battlefield, the two fugitives are also gonna be shocked to see me as well, Sir. After all, I was friends with those guys and they have to know how pissed off I must be now that I know who they really are. That sense of shock could buy us an extra split second or two and just might make it possible for us to prevent the escape of the two fugitives."

While Jim Beauregard considered what Billy Davis had to say, Sergeant Martin spoke up and said, "Excuse me, Sir, but I think the Captain is onto something. Even though these fugitives are real tough guys, they seemed a bit rattled when they saw me arrive in an MP jeep where their glider was parked near the Village of Savy. You should also know, Sir, that Captain Savino sent me with Captain Cabrerra, because my presence back at the checkpoint was making the taller fugitive who said his name was Lieutenant Kraft very uncomfortable."

After hearing what Captain Davis and Sergeant Martin had to say, Major Beauregard looked at Billy Davis and said, "OK, Billy, you ride with me and Al."

Jim then turned to Sergeant Martin and said, "If you're willing to volunteer I'd like you to ride with us as well, Sergeant."

Immediately after Sergeant Martin remarked, "My pleasure, Sir," the radio crackled with a report that the fugitives were tired of waiting and wanted to move out.

After instructing Doc Keller to get ready to drive out in the other Jeep if his services were required, Major Beauregard turned to Captain Cabrerra and said, "Captain, I need you to do two things for me, when you return to the checkpoint to escort Captain Savino and the others to this location. First, I want the two fugitives to hear you tell Captain Savino and Lt. Wright that you were delayed because you dropped Sergeant Martin off with his rifle squad because his services were no longer required. That should increase the shock value of having Sergeant Martin with us when we move in to capture Larson and Mc Ghee."

As the Major continued he said, "I also want you to find a way to have a private chat with Captain Savino and Lt. Wright before they follow you through the checkpoint and let them know how we intend to handle this situation once they arrive in this area. I want Captain Savino to insist that the two fugitives should wait until he's on his way back to our side of the line, before they display a flag of truce, or he might end up in the same POW Camp with them if they're captured together. Captain Savino needs to remind Larson and Mc Ghee that this would not serve the best interest of their rather elaborate escape plan."

As soon as the confident sounding intelligence officer responded and said, "Will do, Sir," he picked up his handie-talkie radio and notified Captain Savino that he was on his way back to the checkpoint.

While the intelligence officer from the Five O Deuce returned to the checkpoint, Major Beauregard turned and addressed Lt. Graham. "Lieutenant, I'll leave it up to you to deploy your men in their new positions."

After acknowledging his instructions with a nod of the head, the young airborne officer remarked, "We're here if you need us, Sir."

Major Beauregard then made eye contact with the others and said, "Let's get into position. They'll be here soon."

As Jim removed his Paratrooper Model M1A1 Carbine from the Dodge Command Car, he cycled the charging handle to load the chamber in case it became necessary to engage the two fugitives or the Germans. After getting into the passenger seat, Jim turned to Al and said, "Promise me you'll be careful."

Al Parker appreciated the fact that the man who was his commanding officer and his partner cared enough to be concerned that he might do some exceptionally crazy, when he finally came face to face with the two fugitives. While Captain Davis and Sergeant Martin sat in the back of the Command Car, Al looked to his right and said, "I'll behave if you do."

CHAPTER 17

THE DOUBLE CROSS

When Sergeant Werner observed a U.S. Army officer drive by his position at a high rate of speed, he wondered what the Americans were up to. In order to prepare for any probing actions or attacks in his area of operation, Sergeant Werner decided to establish an ambush site in a location that commanded an excellent view of the road that ran past his unit's L shaped fighting position.

While on the way back to meet with his men, Sergeant Werner tied his tattered scarf at chest level around a tree trunk on the east side of the road. He did so to mark the location where he wanted his forward element to position themselves. Once he returned to his reinforced squad, Sergeant Werner explained his plan to Corporal Spitzer and the other members of the ambush team. The SS Sergeant then instructed two of his riflemen to lay enough phone wire, to cover the several hundred yards between their L shaped fighting position and the ambush site.

After telling his men that he tied his scarf around a tree branch to mark the spot where he wanted them to establish the ambush, SS Sergeant Werner handed the extra field phone to his favorite Corporal as he continued his briefing. "Call me as soon as the field phone is operational to make sure the equipment is working properly. Position your men to engage any Amis who advance down that road. Once it is safe to do so, send your men back to this position, while you remain in the general vicinity of the ambush site to see if any additional Americans come our way. Remember, Carl, you're my eyes and ears so keep me posted at all times."

As soon as Corporal Spitzer acknowledged his orders and he began to lead his men to their new position, Sergeant Werner called out, "Carl, don't forget to untie my scarf from that tree and put it around your neck to keep warm."

After seeing his corporal turn and call out, "Thank you, Sergeant," Claus Werner waved his right hand as he watched the best corporal he ever had jog off after the other members of the ambush team.

Despite the fact that the Ardennes Offensive did not go according to plan, SS Sergeant Claus Werner continued to have high hopes for Germany. As he recently told his men, "This war is not over. We can still win and we will win because we are stronger than the Allies and have proven we are because they have more of everything yet they have been unable to defeat us."

After receiving a report from his scouting party, Sergeant Hans Sigmann was interested in everything that was happening along their sector of the front line. Clearly, the Americans were up to something, especially when a single Jeep that was driven by an American Army Officer drove away from this particular sector as if he was in a hurry. After telling his men to be prepared to move out without any warning, Sergeant Sigmann reverted back to being a father figure to the young military policemen under his command, when he suggested that they get something to eat while they waited to see what developed.

After laying enough wire to cover several hundred yards through the forest, the field phone was made operational while Corporal Spitzer positioned his Panzerfaust 60 operator and his MG42 gun crew. As soon as he tied the Sergeant's scarf around his neck, Corporal Spitzer tested the field phone to make sure that he had a good connection with his squad leader.

"I assume you found my scarf," asked Sergeant Werner while he spoke on the field phone that was positioned on top of the L shaped fighting position.

"Yes, Sergeant, I am much warmer now thanks to you," responded Corporal Spitzer.

"Good hunting, Carl," remarked, Sergeant Werner before he hung up the phone.

While Ivan Larson followed the lead MP Jeep to a remote location along the front line, he turned to Shorty and said, "I hope you realize that this will probably not go down as planned."

Even though Shorty knew that Ivan was right, he proved that he was trying to keep a positive attitude when he said, "At least that Major from CID and that colored cop from New York never made it to Bastogne. Hostage or not, those cops would have never let us get this far."

"You're right about that," said Ivan who quickly added, "So what'a you think? Do we go along for the ride or change the plan?"

While Shorty continued to hold a Thompson Submachine Gun on their hostage, he looked directly at Private Reader when he responded and said, "You think that Captain from CID is planning a double cross?"

"I would if I was him," remarked Ivan, while he followed the lead MP Jeep past several defensive positions that were manned by paratroopers from the 502nd PIR.

When Shorty said that he would go along with any Plan B that his partner came up with, Ivan offered his buddy a cigarette and a light before he took one for himself. After lighting his own cigarette, Ivan told Private Reader that he would be a free man in a matter of minutes as long as he did as he was told.

Rather than provoke the two fugitives, Private Reader limited his response to saying, "All I want is to get back to my unit. You won't get any trouble from me."

As Ivan glanced back and forth at Private Reader, he continued and said, "That Captain from CID said he's gonna change places with you once we get to a location where we're gonna be allowed to cross over to German held territory. Since I don't believe that CID or the MPs are gonna make it easy for us to escape, I think it's better for us and safer for you, if we double cross the Army cops by heading into the forest off to our right. After all, the Krauts currently control the terrain north of this entire area. That means my buddy and I should have no problem running into some German soldiers no matter where we cross over into enemy held territory."

Once again Ivan took his eyes off the road long enough to relay some instructions to Private Reader. "To make sure that nothing bad happens to you, I want you to jump outta this Jeep the moment I give you the word."

Under the circumstances the young airborne artilleryman who fought in Holland before arriving in Bastogne did his best to sound appreciative when he said, "Yes, Sir. Just say the word and I'll hit the silk."

As soon as Ivan Larson scanned the terrain to his right, he quickly glanced back and said, "Get ready, Private, 'cause here we go."

Captain Savino felt as if he had been duped the second he spotted Ivan Larson turn the Jeep that he was driving to the right and race across the snow covered field toward the German lines. The fact that the two fugitives fled from their escorts meant that there were a limited number of good guys available to give chase.

As soon as Lieutenant Wright and MP Private Garcia raced off after the two escaping fugitives, Captain Savino stopped his Jeep, jumped out and looked at Sergeant Mulligan as he waved his right hand and said, "Go with him! I'll be along as soon as we call for help!"

While MP Sergeant Mulligan raced off after the lead MP Jeep, Captain Cabrerra met with Captain Savino by the driver's side of the MP Jeep to plan their next move. As soon as Captain Savino asked Captain Cabrerra to let the rest of the CID search team know where the two fugitives crossed over into enemy territory, the CID Agent from the Paris Office jumped in his Jeep and joined the pursuit. By the time Captain Cabrerra ran back to his Jeep and made contact with Major Gramacki, the Jeep being driven by Captain Savino crossed over into enemy held territory.

All Lieutenant Wright could think about, while he and Private Garcia pursued the two fugitives, was that Ivan Larson was one shrewd son of a bitch. The MP Lieutenant was even more frustrated when he observed Private Reader sit up on the back seat of the Jeep, because doing so made it too risky to shoot at the escaping vehicle without hitting the hostage.

Once the Jeep carrying the two fugitives traveled deeper behind enemy lines, Ivan glanced back and said, "This is it, Private...jump!"

The second the hostage was observed jumping clear of the stolen Jeep, Lieutenant Wright wasted no time in putting his M1 Carbine to good use. While Ivan Larson drove the stolen Jeep like a New York cabby with a hot fare, .30 caliber bullets snapped overhead and struck the back of the vehicle.

As far as Ivan was concerned, he and Shorty had come too far to get shot in the back of the head by a military policeman, especially since it was just a question of time before they ran into a German patrol. While doing his best to swerve the stolen Jeep back and forth on the road that ran through the forest, Ivan turned to Shorty and screamed, "How 'bout putting that Tommy Gun to work like you did when we robbed that bank in Brooklyn!"

Once it became obvious that whoever was shooting at them probably stopped to reload, Shorty turned sideways in the passenger seat and opened fire with the submachine gun that he liberated from Private Reader. The second Shorty Mc Ghee began firing, Private Garcia reacted by slowing down and swerving out of the line of fire, while burst after burst of .45 caliber bullets struck the front of the MP jeep and nearly missed hitting the occupants.

When Shorty stopped to load a fresh thirty round magazine into the Thompson, Lieutenant Wright returned fire with his M1 Carbine. Whether it was luck or good marksmanship, five of Lieutenant Wright's bullets struck Shorty Mc Ghee in his right arm, right shoulder and the right side of his chest when he turned to open fire again.

While Shorty moaned and slumped over, Ivan reached out and screamed, "Hang on," as he pulled his badly wounded buddy back in his seat. As bullets from Lieutenant Wright's M1 Carbine continued to wiz overhead and strike the stolen Jeep, the two fugitives drove deeper into enemy held territory at a high rate of speed.

While kneeling on the side of the road and looking through his binoculars, Corporal Spitzer was shocked to see one group of U.S. Army troops pursuing two of their own men. This event was even more bizarre because the Americans were shooting at each other.

Without wasting any time, Corporal Spitzer picked up the field phone and briefed his squad leader about the unusual situation that was taking place on their side of the line. While under normal circumstances all American troops were considered viable targets, in this case Sergeant Werner decided to try and capture the soldiers who were fleeing from their own people. This meant that the initial ambush would be directed against the U.S. Army personnel who were pursuing two of their own soldiers behind the German lines.

After hearing what his trusted corporal had to say, Sergeant Werner directed Carl Spitzer to allow the first American Jeep heading in their direction to pass his position and open fire on all other U.S. Army personnel who came within range. As soon as Corporal Spitzer hung up the field phone, he relayed Sergeant Werner's instructions to his Panzerfaust 60 operator and the MG42 gun crew. Corporal Spitzer then directed the two riflemen who laid the phone wire to provide security for the ambush team.

In order to prepare for the second phase of the ambush, SS Sergeant Werner directed two of his men to take positions on both sides of the road and wait for his command to open fire on the American Jeep that was heading their way. As the two SS troopers moved into position, Sergeant Werner instructed his men to make every effort to disable the American vehicle without killing its occupants. Sergeant Werner then turned to his troops who were still positioned in the L shaped fighting position and said, "You men hold your fire unless the Americans resist or attempt to flee."

While standing on the side of the road, Sergeant Werner reminded the two men on his ambush team that once the Americans were captured, they needed to reload and prepare to engage any other enemy troops who might come their way. After using his binoculars to look down the road that ran through the forest, Sergeant Werner remarked, "Take cover and standby to fire on my command."

As soon as the Jeep being pursued by three American Military Police Jeeps raced by their position, Corporal Spitzer waited until the first target came into range before he tapped the Panzerfaust operator on the top of his left shoulder and yelled, "Fire!" The second the projectile from the rocket launcher made contact with the front of Lieutenant Wright's jeep, the explosive charge detonated with enough force to pulverize the front end of the vehicle.

At the exact same time that the MG42 gunner opened fire, Sergeant Mulligan down shifted and applied the brakes to his Jeep. Fortunately, Sergeant Mulligan avoided being hit when he swerved his shot up Jeep to the left and skidded to a stop behind the wreckage of Lieutenant Wright's vehicle. While MP Sergeant Mike Mulligan took cover behind his vehicle, Corporal Spitzer stepped out into the roadway and emptied half of a thirty round magazine from his 9mm MP40 at Captain Savino's Jeep.

When a 9mm bullet put a gash in the left side of his face, the CID Agent from Paris turned the shot up Ford GPW to the right and crashed into the edge of the treeline. While another burst of enemy machine gun fire raked the area, Captain Savino took cover behind the back of his vehicle and cursed the two fugitives for getting away. As far as Captain Savino was concerned, the sound of small arms fire off in the distance could only mean one of three things; the two fugitives were dead, wounded or captured by the enemy.

After executing a successful ambush, Corporal Spitzer instructed his men to return to the L shaped fighting position in the forest. As soon as his men started back, Corporal Spitzer picked up the field phone and repositioned himself further away from the ambush site, while remaining close enough to keep an eye on the Americans.

Ever since that fateful day in Brooklyn when Terry was killed, Ivan and Shorty became running mates and successfully managed to elude the police for well over a year. The fact that they made it this far without being arrested, made Ivan Larson and Francis Shorty Mc Ghee feel as if they deserved to be included in The Fugitive Hall of Fame.

As much as Ivan wanted to get captured by the Germans, he knew that anything could happen in a combat zone, especially if he and Shorty ran into a trigger happy group of enemy troops. Ivan also knew that until they made their way to a POW Camp, they could be attacked by Allied aircraft or caught in the middle of an Allied artillery barrage. Regardless, anything was better than being arrested by U.S. Army MPs and CID Agents and being shipped back to New York City to face a litany of felony charges.

Ivan also didn't have to be a West Point graduate to know that he and Shorty just drove through a German ambush and were lucky to be alive. Since they were no longer being pursued by U.S. Army MPs, Ivan decided to downshift the manual transmission and slow the Jeep to a crawl. The second Ivan did so, three SS troops in camouflage clothing opened fire from their positions of cover on both sides of the tree lined road.

As a fuselage of bullets shot up the radiator and the front tires, Ivan Larson instinctively turned the disabled Jeep to the left and crashed into a row of trees. The second the SS Squad leader and his men stepped out onto the road, Sergeant Werner called out, "Hande Hoch... Hands up, Americans. Surrender or we will not miss when we open fire again!"

Even though he was still startled by the ambush and the impact of the crash, Ivan immediately raised his hands to signal that he was submitting to being captured. As soon as Ivan turned to face Shorty, he knew that his buddy was in bad shape when he observed the condition of his blood soaked field jacket.

The moment Shorty began to come around, he looked up at Ivan and had trouble breathing when he remarked, "I feel like I got run over by a truck."

While Ivan held his hands at chest level, he responded as he watched the Germans approach their disabled vehicle. "We've got company and they're not wearing U.S. Army uniforms."

CHAPTER 18

BEHIND ENEMY LINES

A fter picking up Private Reader, Major Beauregard, Major Gramacki, Captain Cabrerra, Sergeant Al Parker, Captain Billy Davis, Sergeant Hank Blair, Sergeant Phil Martin, MP Sergeant Chris Jacko, Doc Keller and Corporal Polanski proceeded to the ambush site. As soon as they arrived, Major Beauregard jumped out of the Dodge Command Car and instructed Captain Cabrerra to post a security detail, while he checked on casualties with Major Gramacki and Doc Keller.

Once Major Beauregard, Major Gramacki and Doc Keller made their way over to the remains of the destroyed MP Jeep, they found Sergeant Mulligan providing security, while Captain Savino did his best to comfort Lieutenant Wright. Lying nearby was the dead body of Private Garcia.

Immediately after the three men knelt down next to Captain Savino and Lieutenant Wright, Doc Keller injected the mortally wounded MP Officer with a morphine syrette. The fact that Lieutenant Wright sustained devastating wounds to his lower extremities meant that he would not last much longer. Once Doc Keller administered a second morphine syrette, he faced Jim Beauregard and said, "I'm sorry, Sir," to let the Major from CID know that there wasn't anything that could be done for the young Army Officer.

While Lieutenant Wright remained sitting up against the mangled remains of a destroyed Jeep, Jim wondered how this young man could be so horribly wounded and still be alive. As Lieutenant Wright looked up, he spoke just above a whisper when he relayed his last request to the Major from CID. "Please tell my family that I died thinking of them. They'll appreciate hearing from you, Sir."

After swallowing the lump in his throat, Jim patted the Lieutenant's left hand as he responded in a soft tone of voice and said, "Don't worry, Chester. I'll personally visit your folks when I get back to the states."

Hearing Major Beauregard make such a promise comforted Lieutenant

Wright a great deal. Like other soldiers who died in battle, Chester Wright was more concerned about how his family would react to the news of his death than he was about dying. Knowing that someone would write or visit your family, to fill in all of the blanks that were left out of a sparsely worded Western Union Telegram, meant a great deal to a soldier who was about to leave this world for the hereafter.

As soon as Lieutenant Wright closed his eyes and passed away, Major Beauregard remained kneeling while he looked at the others and said, "Chester Wright was a fine young man. From the moment we met he impressed the heck out of me. It was an honor to know him. He certainly didn't deserve to die like this. Neither did Private Garcia. He was another good kid who died too damn young."

Once Jim finished speaking from the heart, he stood up followed by Major Gramacki, Doc Keller and Captain Savino. Being the good medic that he was, Doc Keller wasted no time in suggesting that Captain Savino take a seat in one of the Jeeps so he could take a look at his wound. While Captain Savino held a blood soaked handkerchief against the left side of his face, he clenched his jaw to minimize the level of pain that he experienced when he remarked, "Not now, Doc. I have to brief the Major."

"OK, Captain," responded Doc Keller, who continued as he gently removed the blood soaked handkerchief from the Captain's hand and replaced it with a sterile gauze compress, "In the meantime, Sir, use this clean bandage to keep pressure on that wound."

Even though Captain Savino needed medical attention, Jim Beauregard also knew that Tommy Savino was an outstanding CID Agent who was anxious to share what he knew about the ambush and the status of the two fugitives. Under these circumstances, Jim turned to Doc Keller and said, "Give us a minute, Doc. We'll meet you over by Colonel Gray's Jeep."

"Yes, Sir," responded Doc Keller before he knelt back down and removed one of Lieutenant Wright's dog tags from the chain that hung around his neck.

While Major Beauregard, Major Gramacki and Tommy Savino walked over to the Colonel's Jeep, the Captain kept pressure on his wound as he clenched the teeth on the left side of his face and said, "Once Larson and Mc Ghee took off, Lt. Wright waited until Private Reader jumped to safety before he opened fire on the two fugitives. While we chased them deeper behind enemy lines, Shorty Mc Ghee returned fire with a Thompson. Thanks to Lieutenant Wright, Mc Ghee was hit in the exchange and stopped firing."

After pausing to spit a mouthful of blood onto the snow covered ground, Captain Savino picked up where he left off. "As soon as we reached this position, the Germans fired one of their rocket launchers or a bazooka at Lieutenant Wright's Jeep. Lieutenant Wright was mortally wounded when his Jeep caught a direct hit. As far as I know, Private Garcia was killed instantly. A second later the Krauts opened up with a machine gun. Sergeant Mulligan survived because he swerved to the left and stopped behind the wreckage of Lieutenant Wright's Jeep. I got hit when a Kraut opened up on my Jeep with a burp gun." Captain Savino concluded his remarks by saying, "Even though they initially got away, it sounded like the two fugitives ran into another ambush further down the road."

After thanking Tom for the detailed briefing, Jim Beauregard motioned Doc Keller over to Colonel Gray's Jeep before he turned back to face Captain Savino. "Sit tight, Tom. It's time to let Doc Keller patch you up."

As soon as their medic arrived to treat Captain Savino, Jim offered Major Gramacki a cigarette before he took one out of the pack for himself. After accepting a light from the airborne artillery officer, Jim looked around the ambush sight while he smoked his cigarette.

After taking a drag on his cigarette, Major Gramacki remarked, "The two fugitives that you've been chasing for over a year must have nine lives to have survived this long."

Under the circumstances Jim Beauregard wasn't in a very talkative mood. Instead, Jim limited his response to saying, "If they had nine lives they just used them all up."

Even though his original mission was to observe the American side of the front line that extended west of Longchamps, Sergeant Werner knew that he and his men would never be criticized for capturing two Americans, who were involved in a running gun battle while fleeing from their own troops. Sergeant Werner also knew that if the Americans continued to pursue their two soldiers behind the German lines, he and his men might get the chance to kill or capture more Amis before this day was over.

While two of his men prepared to provide covering fire, Sergeant Werner approached the shot up American Jeep, where a number of shell holes and bomb craters made the forested landscape look more like the pock marked surface of the moon than the Ardennes. Just as Sergeant Werner was about to reach the shot up Jeep, the men from the ambush team returned to the L shaped fighting position. At the same time a call was received on the field phone.

While the men from the ambush team assumed their previous positions, the SS Private who was manning the field phone approached his squad leader to relay some important information. "Excuse me, Sergeant, but Corporal Spitzer just called to report that the two Americans you just captured were being pursued by American military policemen. The Corporal also reports that other Americans including military police and paratroopers just arrived in the area."

After instructing the young private to continue manning the field phone, Sergeant Werner ordered Ivan Larson to step out of the Jeep with his hands on top of his head. The moment he did so, Sergeant Werner grabbed the lanky American prisoner by the collar of his field jacket and dragged him over to the passenger side of the vehicle where his wounded friend was writhing in pain.

Seeing a captured American soldier breathing heavy, while he wondered how he would be treated, was not a new experience for Claus Werner. After slinging his 9mm MP40 Submachine Gun over his right shoulder, Sergeant Werner pointed to the silver wings that Ivan wore on his field jacket while he spoke in English and said. "You are a pilot, yes?"

Even though Ivan became concerned when he spotted the SS insignia on the German Sergeant's collar, he did his best not to appear afraid when he responded to the question in a respectful fashion. "Yes, I'm a pilot." When Sergeant Werner asked if his friend was also a pilot, Ivan almost succumbed to the temptation to turn around and check on Shorty. Instead, Ivan remained facing forward with his hands on top of his head when he said, "Yes, my friend's a pilot."

While Sergeant Werner relieved Ivan of his sidearm and he tucked the captured pistol in his belt, he instructed the youngest SS trooper in his unit to search the wounded pilot who was sitting sideways and a bit slumped over in the passenger seat of the Jeep. "Search him good, Gunther."

"Yes, Sergeant," responded the 16 year old private as he proceeded to take possession of Shorty's pistol belt, two packs of Camel cigarettes, a Zippo lighter, a Chocolate Field Ration known as a D Bar and a pack of chewing gum.

As soon as the young Private finished searching Shorty, he removed the two Thompson Submachine Guns and a second pistol belt from the Jeep. After passing the captured weapons and equipment to other members of his squad, the young SS Private remained standing guard over the badly wounded American prisoner.

After Sergeant Werner unbuckled Ivan's pistol belt and let it drop to the ground, he continued questioning his prisoner while he patted him down and relieved the captured pilot of his wristwatch, cigarettes, Ronson lighter and a small cardboard box containing five morphine syrettes. "Why did the American military police pursue you and your friend into our lines? Why did your military police shoot your friend and why did your fellow pilot shoot at your own soldaten? You are deserters, yes?"

Ivan didn't have to think twice about what to say. As a street wise criminal, Ivan was able to produce a believable response that fit just about any scenario on a moments notice. While giving the command performance of his life, Ivan looked directly at the SS Sergeant and said, "No, Sergeant, we're not deserters. My friend and I got in a fight with some paratroopers who were beating two German Prisoners of War in Bastogne because they were captured wearing U.S. Army issued scarfs, gloves and boots. When I ordered them to stop and my friend tried to pull one of the paratroopers off one of the German prisoners, another paratrooper pulled his boot knife on my buddy. When the paratrooper refused to drop his knife, I shot him in the leg to keep my friend from getting stabbed. When the military police arrived, they didn't want to hear anything about paratroopers mistreating German POW's. Instead, they ordered us to surrender our weapons and submit to arrest. That's when my friend slugged an MP Lieutenant and we stole his Jeep and took his driver with us at gunpoint to get away."

After pausing to catch his breath, Ivan continued and said, "Once we took the MP Lieutenant's driver hostage we made a deal to let him go, if the MPs escorted us to an area along the front line so we could cross over into your territory and get captured by German soldiers. We figured we'd be better off spending the rest of the war in a German POW camp, than end up in the stockade for shooting one of our own men and striking an MP Lieutenant. We let the soldier we took hostage jump out, when we double crossed the MPs and we headed north about a mile from where we were supposed to make the exchange. Quite frankly, Sergeant, you and your men did us a favor getting those MPs off our tail."

Sergeant Werner knew that his superiors would be very interested in the propaganda value of capturing two American pilots who were forced to flee from their own military police, because they protected German POWs from being mistreated by U.S. Army paratroopers in Bastogne. Sergeant Werner also believed that since the American pilots went to such lengths to be captured by German forces, they should also prove to be very cooperative during questioning.

After grabbing Ivan by the collar, Sergeant Werner was less than gentle when he removed the American Army pilot's identification tags and read them out load "Daniel Gannon... Catholic." When the German SS Sergeant let the dog tags fall against Ivan's field jacket, he looked directly at his prisoner and said, "Other Americans will be angry yes, if they learn that you shot another American to protect German Prisoners of War?"

As Ivan did his best to sound like a man with strong convictions, he wasted no time in responding in a confident tone of voice. "I don't care what anybody says. All prisoners of war deserve to be treated with respect. Those German POWs did what they had to do to survive. No more, no less. There was no reason for those paratroopers to abuse German POWs just because they're pissed off that the war didn't end by Christmas."

While Doc Keller finished treating the gunshot wound that put a deep gash across the Captain Savino's face, Captain Cabrerra approached Major Beauregard and said, "Sir, I just spoke to Lt. Carver on the radio in the Command Car. According to Lt. Carver, Colonel Gray is on his way to Longchamps to do what he can to help out. The Colonel also wants you to know that Major Gramacki is needed back at his command but Sergeant Mulligan, Sergeant Martin, Corporal Polanski and I can continue to assist you and your men. The Colonel also directed Lt. Carver to remind the Major that all U.S. Army personnel assigned to CID and assisting CID must return to our side of the line before sunset."

After thanking the intelligence officer for the update, Jim checked his watch before he looked into enemy held territory and wondered if they still had a chance to capture Ivan Larson and Francis Shorty Mc Ghee.

After receiving the order to return to his unit, Major Gramacki agreed to drive Captain Savino to the closest aid station on his way back to the 377th PFAB.

While Major Gramacki stood by the driver's side of the Dodge Command Car, the airborne artillery officer looked at Jim Beauregard and said, "Private Reader requested permission to remain behind to assist in the search. If you can use him he's all yours."

While Jim extended his hand, he sounded very appreciative when he responded and said, "Thanks for everything, John, and thanks for letting Private Reader give us a hand. Lord knows we need all the help we can get."

While Major Gramacki climbed in behind the steering wheel, he turned to face the Major from CID and said, "If I ever get caught speeding in Georgia I'll mention your name."

When Captain Savino refused to be transported to an aid station, Major Beauregard addressed the wounded CID Agent from the Paris office in a very concerned and friendly tone of voice. "I'm worried about you, Tom. That's a nasty wound that you have on the side of your face. It must hurt like hell. You're also lucky to be alive."

Even though it wasn't easy to talk with such a painful wound on his face, Captain Savino held the left side of his chin as he grit his teeth and said, "I'm going with you, Sir."

Throughout his career Jim Beauregard worked with a number of law enforcement officers who routinely went above and beyond the call of duty to apprehend dangerous criminals. Al Parker was one of these exceptionally brave men and Tommy Savino was another. Having such a fine Army officer, who deserved to be removed from the field of battle, volunteer to remain in action gave Jim Beauregard a badly needed boost to his morale.

"OK, Tom, you can stay, but make sure you keep that wound of yours clean and properly bandaged," responded Jim Beauregard who quickly added, "I also want Captain Cabrerra to handle the radio for you."

Despite the pain that he was in, Captain Savino did his best to respond while he held his jaw and said, "Thank you, Sir."

As soon as Major Gramacki drove away with the covered body of Private Garcia, the troops who were eager to continue to pursue the two fugitives checked their weapons in anticipation of heading deeper into German held territory. Even though Captain Billy Davis was a C47 pilot, he seemed to take to ground combat like a fish to water and proved it when he approached Jim Beauregard and said, "Sir, I asked Sergeant Parker to recover Private Garcia's weapons and ammo and place them in Colonel Gray's Jeep. Lieutenant Wright's weapons were too badly damaged to be put back in service. I also took the liberty of having the extra ammo and grenades that Colonel Gray had loaded in the back of these Jeeps distributed to the men."

After thanking Billy Davis, Major Beauregard reached into the Jeep where the weapons that were taken from Private Garcia were located and removed the MP Private's Thompson and pistol belt. As soon as Jim called Private Reader over, he presented the airborne artilleryman with the submachine gun and the pistol belt that contained a .45 caliber pistol, two spare pistol magazines, a medical pouch, a canteen and a cotton canvass pouch containing three spare Tommy Gun magazines. "Here you go, Private. This might come in handy where we're going."

CHAPTER 19

I GOT A BAD FEELING ABOUT THIS

As soon as the members of the CID led search and arrest team started to take positions in the available vehicles, Jim Beauregard turned to Al Parker and said, "I can't explain it, Al, but I got a bad feeling about this." After stepping out of the lead Jeep, Jim faced his men and called out, "Change in plans. We're going the rest of the way on foot. Assemble on me."

As the men in the CID led patrol assembled around the lead Jeep, Jim turned to Al Parker and said, "Keep an eye out for Germans while I talk to the men."

"Yes, Sir," responded Al Parker as he stood facing enemy held territory with his M3 Grease Gun in hand.

Once Jim had everyone's undivided attention, he posed a question to Captain Cabrerra. "Tell me, Captain, what's the effective range of a German bazooka?"

Without hesitating the airborne intelligence officer responded and said, "The Panzerschreck has a maximum range of 150 meters. The newer model can shoot a little further but not by much." When the Major from CID asked about the effective range of the German Panzerfaust, Captain Cabrerra answered the question with complete confidence. "From thirty to a hundred meters depending on the model, Sir."

After thanking the airborne intelligence officer, Major Beauregard continued as he made eye contact with the entire assembly. "If the Krauts in this area are armed with a Panzerschreck or a Panzerfaust we better not give them any other vehicles to shoot at." The Major then looked directly at Captain Savino and said, "Tom, I want you to nod your head if you agree with Sergeant Mulligan."

As soon as the Major turned to face Sergeant Mulligan, he asked the military policeman how much time passed after the Krauts opened up on their vehicles when he heard small arms fire off in the distance.

"Less than a minute later, Sir, probably closer to thirty seconds," responded Sergeant Mulligan."

As soon as Captain Savino nodded his head in agreement, Jim asked Sergeant Mulligan how fast he estimated the fugitives were traveling and how much of a lead the fugitives maintained throughout the chase.

Once again Sergeant Mulligan responded with confidence. "We were never able to catch up to them, Sir, because they had a rolling head start when they took off toward the German lines. I'd say they maintained a good twenty five to thirty yard lead in front of Lieutenant Wright's Jeep but that lead got even larger when one of the fugitives opened fire with a Thompson. To answer your other question, Sir, I'd say we probably averaged 40 to 50 miles an hour during the chase with all of us going airborne a few times."

Immediately after Captain Savino nodded his head in agreement, Major Beauregard continued as he looked at the men who were assembled around his Jeep. "If Larson and Mc Ghee were traveling at anything close to flank speed in a Jeep and small arms fire was heard off in the distance shortly after the Germans executed an attack at this location, the second ambush site can't be all that far away. We also have to consider that the Germans had to take an interest in seeing two American soldiers fleeing from their own people. The Germans had to be twice as convinced that Larson and Mc Ghee were worth taking alive, if they saw one of them shooting at American MPs with a Thompson Submachine Gun. There's also a good chance that the Germans are waiting to ambush any other American MPs who advance deeper into their lines to continue the pursuit. As a result, I believe we'll be better off if we use the forest for cover and move ahead on foot. If I'm right we're gonna spot a shot up Jeep not all that far from here. If we get real lucky we'll find two dead fugitives."

After pausing for a split second, the Major turned to Captain Cabrerra and spoke quickly as he relayed his instructions to the airborne intelligence officer. "Captain, I want you, Captain Savino, Sergeant Blair, Sergeant Jacko, Corporal Polanski, Private Reader and Doc Keller to bring up the rear. We'll use hand signals when appropriate or the handie-talkie radios to communicate. It's also imperative that we maintain good separation between the two groups."

As soon as Captain Cabrerra acknowledged his orders, the Major turned to MP Sergeant Mike Mulligan as he pointed to the last Jeep in line and said, "I know it's a pain in the ass to lug around but I'd like you to volunteer to carry the M1919A4 that's mounted in the back of that Jeep. Even though it doesn't have a tripod, a belt fed machine gun can come in very handy if we get into a gunfight behind enemy lines."

Being the team player that he was, the muscular XXL size 101st Airborne Division MP responded and said, "You got it, Major."

Jim Beauregard then turned to Billy Davis and said, "Captain, I want you and Sergeant Mulligan to fall in behind me and keep that machine gun loaded with a belt of ammo and ready to go. I also need you to serve as Sergeant Mulligan's loader and carry any extra ammo that you can find for that gun."

As soon as Billy Davis acknowledged the order, he and Sergeant Mulligan went to work removing the belt fed M1919A4 from the pedestal mount in the rear compartment of the number three Jeep.

After turning to Al Parker and Sergeant Martin, the Major continued. "Al, I want you and Sergeant Martin to fall in with me as soon as you pull these vehicles off the road."

As soon as the two sergeants acknowledged the order, they started parking the operational Jeeps as close to the side of the road as possible, or off the road wherever there was a break in the tree line.

When Jim Beauregard continued he finished addressing the men under his command by saying. "Remember, our mission is to pursue the two fugitives a reasonable distance behind enemy lines, while making sure that we return to our side of the line before it gets dark. If anything happens to me Captain Cabrerra will assume command, while conferring with Captain Savino on all matters of interest to Army CID or the Military Police." With nothing else to do except advance deeper into German held territory, Jim Beauregard looked at his men and said, "Move out."

Jim Beauregard was just about to lead the way when Al Parker remarked, "I'll take point, Sir."

A split second later Sergeant Martin spoke up and said, "If you don't mind, Sir, I'd like to keep Sergeant Parker company."

After making eye contact with Al Parker, the Major looked at Sergeant Martin and nodded his head once before he remarked, "OK, lets go."

Before Al Parker took point he handed the Major a khaki colored cotton cloth musette bag that contained several fifty round boxes of ammunition and two additional hand-grenades. "Just in case," was all Al said as he made eye contact with the man he worked with for well over a year to locate Ivan Larson and Francis Shorty Mc Ghee. As soon as Jim thanked Al for the extra ammo, his partner from the P.D.N.Y. led the way with Sergeant Martin following close behind.

Once the lead element started to advance deeper into German held territory, Captain Cabrerra motioned his men to spread out, while maintaining the proper separation between the two groups. Even though his face hurt like hell, Captain Savino refused a shot of morphine so he could participate in the search for the two fugitives. While Doc Keller kept an eye on the Captain from CID, he wondered how long the wounded officer would be able to endue a march through snow covered wooded terrain behind enemy lines in the dead of winter.

Just when the conversation with the American pilot was getting interesting, Corporal Spitzer emerged from the treeline and jogged over to where his squad leader was standing. When Sergeant Werner ordered his prisoner to remain silent and not move, Ivan Larson made the mistake of saying, "Excuse me, Sergeant, but my friend is badly hurt. He needs a doctor."

Before Ivan could say anything else, Sergeant Werner grabbed his prisoner by the throat, as he grit his tobacco stained teeth and said, "I said silence or you will end up like your friend!" As soon as Sergeant Werner released his grip on Ivan's throat, he forcibly relieved his prisoner of his U.S. Army issue woolen scarf before he turned to listen to his Corporal's scouting report.

While his prisoner coughed a few times and rubbed his sore throat, Sergeant Werner tucked the liberated scarf around his neck as he addressed Corporal Spitzer in German and said, "Go ahead, Carl."

As the Corporal faced his sergeant, he also spoke in German when he filed his scouting report in a clear and distinct fashion. "An eleven man American patrol that contains military police, paratroopers and one medic is coming this way through the woods. They're armed with infantry weapons and a belt fed machine gun."

After instructing Corporal Spitzer to keep an eye on the advancing American patrol, Sergeant Werner spoke in a stern tone of voice when he faced the American pilot identified as Flight Officer Daniel Gannon "An American patrol consisting of military police and paratroopers is coming this way. We can assume they are looking for you and your friend. If you wish to remain our prisoner you must remain silent and do as ordered. If you disobey you will be shot." Then, without warning, the SS Sergeant drew the captured pilot's .45 caliber automatic from his belt and pistol whipped Ivan Larson across his forehead, the result of which knocked the fugitive off his feet and rendered him unconscious.

After looking toward the American lines, Sergeant Werner pointed to a large bomb crater that was situated in a clearing next to the road and said, "Put the two Americans in that bomb crater so we can keep an eye on them. They could prove to be very useful if the other Americans come looking for them."

Once an unconscious Ivan Larson was dragged over to the side of the road and dropped into the bottom of the crater, Shorty Mc Ghee was removed from the shot up Jeep with no regard for the fact that he was badly wounded. After Shorty passed out while being manhandled in this fashion, his body was rolled into the bottom of the same bomb crater.

Before he walked over to his unit's well concealed fighting position, Sergeant Werner bent down and picked up the pistol belt that he removed from his prisoner's waist. Immediately after he draped the pistol belt over his left shoulder, Sergeant Werner instructed his men to take cover and prepare to engage the Americans on his command.

As soon as Corporal Spitzer made his way back to his unit's well concealed fighting position, he informed Sergeant Werner that the Americans were coming their way. After receiving the report from his favorite scout, Sergeant Werner looked through his binoculars while he remarked, "These Americans seem to know what they're doing and have good separation between their two groups." Once he lowered his binoculars, the SS Sergeant remained facing forward when he added, "Even though we're fairly evenly matched, we have the advantage of fighting from a well camouflaged fortified position that is located on slightly elevated terrain."

After hearing what Sergeant Werner just said, Corporal Spitzer remarked, "We also have the element of surprise to our advantage, Sergeant."

"That is correct, Carl," responded Sergeant Werner who went on to say, "Unfortunately, the forest is filled with large bomb craters and smaller shell holes, as well as a number of felled trees that can be used by the enemy to take cover once we open fire. This is why it's critical that when we initiate the ambush we do so with ferocity."

After checking his watch, Sergeant Werner turned to Corporal Spitzer and said, "I want you to take command of the men on the west side of our fighting position. The first priority for our MG42 gunner is to engage any Americans who come out into the open to inspect that Jeep or search for the two prisoners. His second priority is to engage the American machine crew. I also want you to pass the word for the men to stay down...no noise....Have Private Dietz use his rifle and save our last Panzerfaust in case an American armored vehicle comes down the road."

As soon as Corporal Spitzer acknowledged his orders and he left to carry out his duties, Sergeant Werner took another look through his binoculars at the American soldiers who were cautiously heading his way. After getting a good look at the enemy troops, Sergeant Werner spoke just above a whisper and said, "This is working out better than I expected."

After stopping to scan the area ahead and to the left of their current position, Al Parker spotted a Jeep that looked as if it swerved off the road and crashed into the edge of the treeline. While Al used a hand signal to alert the Major to come forward, Sergeant Martin looked through his field glasses to scan the area around the crashed Jeep.

As soon as the Major arrived by their side, Al spoke just above a whisper and said, "There's a crashed Jeep about seventy yards from here on the west side of the road, Sir."

Immediately after Sergeant Martin handed his field glasses to Major Beauregard, the paratrooper remarked, "I'll bet a month's pay that Jeep belongs to your two fugitives, Major."

While Jim Beauregard carefully scanned the area with the Sergeant's binoculars, he responded in a low tone of voice and said, "Either the Krauts took the two fugitives prisoner and left the area or they're waiting for us to arrive."

While Ivan huddled over his seriously wounded friend, any romantic notions that he had about being a hero before he was captured by the enemy were now gone.

Once Ivan and Shorty narrowly escaped being arrested by the military police, they became men without a country and fugitives on the run, where even the enemy could not be counted on to comply with the terms of the Geneva Convention. The simple truth was, that Ivan Larson experienced all of the glory that he would ever know in his troubled life, when he successfully delivered 250 rounds of artillery ammunition to the American troops in Bastogne.

For the last year Ivan assumed that once he and Shorty were captured by the enemy, they would be immediately shipped off to a Prisoner of War Camp. Now that Ivan was lying at the bottom of a bomb crater next to his badly wounded friend, he was at a loss for words about what to do next. Seeing Shorty writhing in pain, while he gripped the side of his chest and had trouble breathing made a bad situation worse for both fugitives.

While Ivan held his khaki colored handkerchief over the bloody cut that ran across his forehead, he looked at Shorty and whispered, "We can't get a break no how."

Under the circumstances, all Shorty could bring himself to say was, "That SS Sergeant is using us for bait."

As dazed as he was after being hit across the forehead with his government issued 1911 pistol, Ivan Larson was painfully aware of the fact that he and Shorty were in big trouble. One thing was certain. Even though Shorty was badly wounded, his chances of surviving the war as a POW would have increased if he received the proper medical attention. Unfortunately, SS units had a well deserved reputation for being the most feared troops in the Nazi Party dominated German Armed Forces.

Ivan Larson never sounded more frustrated than when he looked directly at his badly wounded buddy and said, "If that Kraut Sergeant didn't take the morphine that I've been carrying since the Holland mission, I'd be able to give you a shot and make you feel better."

After Shorty paused to spit up blood, he used his left hand to point to his pair of waterproof M1944 Snow Pac Boots as he whispered, "Unlace my right boot and check inside."

While Ivan knelt over Shorty, he continued speaking in a low tone of voice. "You were right about the Krauts. I'm sorry I got you into this. We should'a stole a fully fueled C47 and flew to Switzerland rather than risk trying to get captured by some friendly Krauts."

As surprised as Shorty was to hear Ivan apologize, he knew that every escape plan had its pros and cons. Had they deserted and tried to hide out in Paris, they could have just as easily been captured by now. Even if they stole a fully fueled aircraft and tried to fly to a neutral country, they could have been shot down along the way.

Even though Ivan was a glider pilot and not a medic, he was well aware of the fact that the right dosage of morphine would alleviate Shorty's pain and help him die in peace. Instead of finding morphine syrettes, Ivan was surprised to find a blue steel Colt Model 1908 .25 ACP Caliber Pistol concealed inside his friend's right boot.

As Ivan Larson looked at Shorty, he sounded a bit dumfounded when he said, "I thought you had some morphine stashed in your boot. What the hell am I supposed to do with this pea shooter?"

While Shorty leaned back against the snow covered wall of the bomb crater, he did his best to respond for someone who had a hard time breathing. "I bought it from a glider pilot who was unlucky in cards. I thought it might come in handy, so I stashed it in my boot."

Ivan had to admit, Shorty found a clever way to conceal a hideout pistol that might prove useful before the day was over.

After pausing again to catch his breath, Shorty continued and said, "The Kraut who searched me never checked my boots. Maybe he didn't want'a lean over me 'cause I'm covered in blood. Either way, that pistol is better than nothing." Once again Shorty paused when he had trouble breathing. When he continued, Shorty pointed to his left foot and said, "Now check my other boot." As soon as Ivan unlaced Shorty's left Snow Pac Boot, he found a spare magazine loaded with six rounds of ammunition tucked up against Shorty's heavy wool sock.

"I'll ask again," remarked, Ivan. "What am I supposed to do with a .25 caliber pistol and twelve rounds of ammo, while we're surrounded by heavily armed Krauts and a bunch of Army cops and paratroopers?"

Without speaking, Shorty reached out and picked up Ivan's hand that gripped the pistol. The moment Shorty placed Ivan's hand that held the pistol next to the side of his head, he looked at his partner in crime and said, "One shot should do it."

For the first time in their relationship Shorty saw the look of sheer terror on Ivan's face as he reeled back and said, "I can't do that!"

While Shorty labored to breathe, he spit up more blood and said, "I can't take my own life. I'm Irish Catholic. Please, I'd do it for you." Once again Shorty paused to catch his breath before added, "If you can't make a run for it, tell the Krauts I shot myself when you were passed out."

Even though there were times when Ivan lost his patience when Shorty screwed up, he always managed to hold it together and press on with his partner in crime by his side. After all they had been through, Shorty wasn't surprised to hear Ivan sound like a man who had a heart, when he leaned closer to his badly wounded buddy and whispered, "I know you're hurting but once these storm-troopers ambush the Army cops who are coming this way, they're bound to take you to a Kraut doctor. All you have to do is hold on for a few minutes."

Seeing Shorty struggle to breathe was a clear indication that his sidekick was dying a miserable death. After Shorty closed his eyes he whispered. "One shot and I'll be on my way."

"Are you sure you want me to do this?" asked Ivan in almost a pleading tone of voice.

After shaking his head ever so slightly up and down, Shorty had an even harder time breathing when he whispered, "I can't breath and it hurts like hell."

As Ivan's eyes began to swell with tears, he tried to sound as upbeat as possible when he asked, "What's my name?"

By now Shorty was almost gasping for breath when he looked up at Ivan and said. "Danny Gannon."

After Ivan cracked a smile, he whispered, "It's about time you got it right."

While Ivan racked the slide on the small caliber pistol to load the chamber, Shorty began to pray and ask God to forgive him for his sins. As Ivan slowly placed the small caliber pistol next to his mortally wounded friend's head, Shorty reached out and patted Ivan's trembling right hand as a way of letting him know that it was OK to pull the trigger. With tears streaming down his face, Ivan could barely speak as he held Shorty's hand and whispered, "Goodbye Shorty."

As Shorty spit up more blood, he closed his eyes and said, "Bye Ivan."

A split second later Ivan Larson fired one shot into the side of his friend's head then screamed, "NO!!!!!!"

The second the shot was fired a stern faced Sergeant Werner turned to the youngest member of his squad and whispered, "I told you to search the wounded

American." As the embarrassed SS Private lowered his head, Sergeant Werner used his binoculars to scan the forested terrain across from his position.

After hearing the shot fired, the Americans quickly dispersed and took positions of cover behind a number of felled trees and inside a number of bomb craters. Now that the enemy was properly dispersed and stopped advancing toward the crashed Jeep, Sergeant Werner was frustrated beyond belief by the unusual turn of events that were unfolding in front of his unit's fighting position.

CHAPTER 20

GUNFIGHT

While Jim Beauregard took cover with Al Parker and Sergeant Martin behind some trees, the Major spoke just above a whisper and said, "That sounded like a shot from a small caliber handgun."

"You're right about that, Sir," responded Al Parker before he pointed toward the northwest and said, "It sounded like that shot came from one of the bomb craters near that crashed Jeep."

When Sergeant Martin spoke up and said, "I wonder who did the screaming after that shot was fired?"

"I doubt it was a German soldier," responded Jim Beauregard.

After signaling Captain Davis and Sergeant Mulligan to stand fast, Jim Beauregard looked through the leafless trees and said, "You would think a shot fired behind enemy lines would bring every German in this area over to investigate."

While Sergeant Martin continued he scanned the area ahead of their position. "Like you said before, Sir, maybe the Krauts are already here and they're just waiting for us to show ourselves before they open up."

As soon as Jim Beauregard remarked, "I don't like it," and Al Parker added, "Me either," Sergeant Martin glanced back at the Major from CID and said, "Now that we all agree, Sir. What's our next move?"

Before advancing any further, Jim used a hand signal to motion Captain Cabrerra, Captain Davis and Sergeant Mulligan to come forward. As soon as Captain Davis, Sergeant Mulligan and Captain Cabrerra arrived by his side, Major Beauregard sounded like a superior officer who knew exactly what needed to be done when he addressed his men. "Even though whoever fired that shot and let out that scream was probably not a German soldier, we have to proceed with caution when we take a closer look at the area near that crashed Jeep."

While Major Beauregard continued, he pointed to a location that was northwest of their current position. "In order to take advantage of the best cover available, my section will advance to the left at an angle and take cover in the two large bomb craters that are located inside the treeline along the edge of the road. I'll also put one of my men in that smaller shell hole that's located off to the right of those positions behind those uprooted trees. That'll put us a few yards away from the bomb crater in that clearing that's fairly close to the crashed Jeep."

As soon as Major Beauregard turned back to face Captain Cabrerra, he quickly added, "Once we get settled, I'd like you to position your squad off to our right. Before we move any further, I'll relay the plan to you over the radio. If need be, I'll send a runner to your position with a more detailed message." After Captain Cabrerra wished the Major and his men good luck, Jim responded and said, "Good luck to you and your men as well, Rico."

While Captain Cabrerra returned to his half of the CID led patrol, the Major faced the men in his section and said, "I'll go first. Wait for my hand signal before you follow. As soon as Captain Davis and Sergeant Mulligan set the machine gun up in the bomb crater on my right, I'll signal Sergeant Martin and Sergeant Parker to come ahead." After pausing for a split second, the Major turned to Al Parker and said, "Al, you take cover with me."

In order to give a combat veteran like Sergeant Martin some leeway, as far as where he should position himself, Major Beauregard looked directly at the squad leader from the 101st Airborne Division and said, "That uprooted tree in front of that smaller shell hole should give you some decent cover but if you find a better spot take it."

As soon as Jim was finished relaying his instructions, he stood up in a slight crouch with his paratrooper model M1A1 .30 Caliber Carbine in hand and said, "Though I walk through the shadow of the valley of death I fear no evil for You are with me. Your rod and Your staff comfort me." After finishing his favorite verse of the 23rd Psalm, Jim Beauregard jogged off in a low crouch toward the northwest corner of the treeline near the side of the road, while Al Parker and the other members of his section prepared to provide covering fire if necessary.

Just as Sergeant Werner was whispering to his men to standby to open fire, Ivan Larson never felt more alone in his entire life. In addition to being on the verge of becoming sick to his stomach after killing Shorty, Ivan's head hurt like hell and was dripping blood down the side of his face.

As soon as Ivan heard movement coming from the wooded area that was south of his position, he slowly peered over the top of the bomb crater. The moment he did so, he spotted what appeared to be an ambush in the making, when he observed an American soldier taking cover in a bomb crater that was located along the edge of the nearby treeline. Once Ivan slid back down into the bomb crater, he spoke just above a whisper to Shorty Mc Ghee as if he was still alive and said, "We got company."

Ivan Larson was caught between the proverbial rock and the hard place, as long as a unit of German SS troops blocked his ability to flee, while he was being pursued by a contingent of U.S. Army personnel who were determined to take him into custody. While Ivan waited for the shooting to start, he tried as hard as he could to suppress the fear that was interfering with his ability to think clearly. After coming to his senses, Ivan decided that once the shooting started he would be better off if he made his way deeper into enemy territory, so he could be taken prisoner by a less fanatical group of German soldiers.

In an effort to time his escape with the outbreak of hostilities, Ivan slowly inched his way up to the top of the bomb crater, so he could check on the status of the approaching American MPs and paratroopers. The second he did so, Ivan became paralyzed with fear, when he spotted Al Parker wearing the combat uniform of a U.S. Army MP taking cover next to a white G.I. in a bomb crater that was only a few yards away.

The moment the three adversaries spotted each other, neither Al Parker, Jim Beauregard or Ivan Larson initially reacted to meeting face to face at fairly close range on a battlefield in Europe. Once the shock of finally running into Ivan Larson wore off, Al Parker screamed, "I got you you son of a bitch!" before he fired a burst from his M3 Grease Gun, just as the fugitive recovered from the encounter and ducked down out of sight. A split second later, the reinforced squad of German SS troops opened fire on the U.S. Army CID led patrol.

How Al Parker wasn't wounded or killed in action can best be described as a combination of being in the right place at the right time and an Act of Divine Intervention. Jim Beauregard wasn't so lucky and was wounded when a 9mm bullet fired from a German MP40 Submachine Gun penetrated his right shoulder. While the rest of the men in the CID search team provided accurate covering fire, Al Parker pulled the Major into the bottom of the bomb crater that they were using as a fighting position.

As soon as Al inspected the Major's wound, he spoke loud enough to be heard over the sound of gunfire. "It looks like the bullet went clean through. I'll call Doc Keller as soon as I get some sulfur powder and a bandage on that wound."

While Al removed a packet of Sulfanilamide powder and a bandage from his Carlisle medical pouch, Jim responded as a steady stream of bullets wizzed overhead and impacted the ground around their position. "I'll be OK, Al. Get back on your gun."

"I'm almost done, Sir" responded Al as he sprinkled five grams of sulfur powder on the front and back of the Major's wound.

As soon as Al placed a clean bandage over the bullet hole in the Major's shoulder, an excited Jim remarked, "Did you see that son of a bitch, Al? Talk about being close. We'll get that prick yet."

"First we have to patch you up," responded Al, as he looked at Jim and quickly added, "Try to keep some pressure on that bandage until Doc Keller get's here."

Once Al picked up his M3 Grease Gun, he looked to his right and called out, "Medic! Medic!" A split second later Al was blasting away at the enemy. As soon Al paused to reload, Jim stopped putting pressure on his shoulder wound, long enough to use the handie-talkie radio to notify Captain Cabrerra that Ivan Larson was in one of the nearby bomb craters.

Even though the belt fed M1919A4 wasn't mounted on a tripod, Sergeant Mulligan made effective use of the machine gun and killed the SS Private who destroyed Lieutenant Wright's Jeep with a Panzerfaust and one of the SS Privates who laid the phone wire to the original ambush site. When Sergeant Mulligan went through the first belt, Captain Davis wasted no time in reloading the gun with another hundred rounds of 30.06 caliber ammunition. While working as a team, Sergeant Martin raked the enemy position with well aimed bursts, as Captain Davis served as his loader and insured the reliable feeding of the ammunition into the M1919A4 machine gun.

As soon as the Germans initiated their ambush, Captain Savino appreciated the reason why Major Beauregard divided their mismatched unit into two sections. Once the shooting began, Captain Cabrerra directed the men under his command to put down a base of fire, that concentrated on engaging the Germans located from the center to the east side of the enemy fighting position. Doing so, left the Major and his men to focus their efforts on engaging the Germans located from the center to the west side of the well camouflaged position.

The first piece of good news came when Captain Cabrerra and Captain Savino heard the Major confirm that Ivan Larson was located in the large bomb crater that was closest to the crashed Jeep. Even though they were involved in a firefight with a squad of Germans, this was exceptionally good news because it meant they still had a chance to complete their mission.

The second casualty on the American side of this engagement was Corporal Polanski. Fortunately, the German rifle bullet that penetrated his pistol belt and grazed the left side of his torso wasn't serious enough to take him out of the fight. Once his wound was inspected and bandaged by Doc Keller, the young paratrooper continued to engage the enemy from behind a felled tree.

Staff Sergeant Blair was hit next, when a burst of 9mm bullets fired from a German MP40 Submachine Gun stitched up the ground where he was kneeling behind a tree while he fired his M1 Carbine. The moment his left foot was hit by a single 9mm bullet, Sergeant Blair fell back behind cover for a few seconds before he continued firing. Even when Doc Keller ran over to check on the CID Agent from the Paris Office, Sergeant Blair called out, "Hold on, Doc," while he fired his M1 Carbine until it needed to be reloaded again.

Private Reader was also wounded when a German bullet perforated his left hand. This left MP Sergeant Chris Jacko, Captain Cabrerra and Doc Keller as the only combatants in the second half of the CID led patrol team who were not wounded in some way. However, despite their wounds, everyone in the second half of the CID search team continued to engage the enemy.

Even though Doc Keller had cared for plenty of casualties while flying on C47's, this was the first time that he served as a medic in a ground combat action. Despite this fact, Doc Keller had no problem making the transition from being an Army Air Forces medic, to functioning like an Army Ground Forces medic when circumstances dictated that he do so.

Just about the time that Doc Keller finished taking care of Private Reader's wounded hand, he scurried past Captain Savino when he heard Al Parker calling again for their medic. By the time he reached the Major's side, Doc Keller remarked, "Sorry, I'm late, Sir, but I had three house calls to make." When Jim asked about the status of the other casualties, Doc Keller reassured the Major that Corporal Polanski, Sergeant Blair and Private Reader were still in the fight.

As soon as Doc Keller inspected the Major's wound, he called out, "I'll have you back in action as soon as I bandage you up, Sir. Just try not to move around too much."

After hearing what the experienced medic had to say, the Major remarked, "I'm sorry, Doc, but I'm too pissed off at the Germans right now to give a shit about my situation."

While Doc Keller placed a fresh bandage on the Major's shoulder wound, Captain Davis belly crawled behind the cover of the felled tree from his fighting position to the bomb crater that was occupied by Al Parker and Jim Beauregard. As soon as he reached the edge of the Major's fighting position, Captain Davis looked inside and said, "I thought you should know, Sir, we're almost down to the last can of machine gun ammo."

"Hold on, Doc. I gotta hand this ammo to the Captain," said Jim as he relayed instructions to the C47 pilot, while he used his left hand to pass the musette bag up to Billy Davis. "Save the machine gun ammo in case the Krauts rush us, or we need to use it to cover our withdrawal. In the meantime, use your carbines. Leave one box of forty five ammo and the grenades and pass out the rest."

"Yes, Sir," was all that Billy Davis said as he quickly complied with the Major's order. Once Captain Davis returned to his fighting position and he relayed the Major's instructions to Sergeant Mulligan, the XXL size MP acknowledged the order and transitioned to using his M1 Carbine to engage the enemy. Captain Davis then removed two fifty round boxes of .30 caliber ammunition from the musette bag and placed them on the leading edge of the bomb crater. As soon as Captain Davis removed a fifty round box of .45 ACP ammunition from the musette bag, he carefully looked over the east side rim of the bomb crater and called out, "Ammo resupply, Sarge. Standby to catch."

After tossing the fifty round box of ammo into the smaller shell hole off to his right, Billy Davis ducked back down and picked up his M1 Carbine, while Sergeant Martin called out, "Thanks Captain."

The CID led patrol sustained another casualty, when a German bullet grazed Sergeant Martin's armpit between his left arm and his upper chest while he fired his Thompson. As soon as Captain Billy Davis spotted Sergeant Martin get hit, he climbed out of his bomb crater and went to the aid of the wounded paratrooper.

After inspecting Sergeant Martin's wound and reassuring him that he would be OK, Captain Davis used his teeth to rip open a packet of sulfur powder. While Sergeant Martin sat back against the best cover available, he tried as hard as he could to ignore the pain as he said, "Thanks for stopping by, Captain."

"Don't mention it," responded Billy Davis before he called for their medic while he sprinkled sulfur powder on Sergeant Martin's wound.

The moment Jim Beauregard heard Captain Davis call for their medic, he turned to Doc Keller and said, "You better go, Doc." After telling the Major to take it easy, Doc Keller grabbed his medical bag and left to treat another casualty.

While Doc Keller bandaged the paratrooper's wound, Captain Davis reloaded Sergeant Martin's submachine gun with a thirty round magazine and said, "What'a day, uh, Sarge?"

"You said it, Captain," responded Sergeant Martin as he took possession of his reloaded Thompson, while Doc Keller finished bandaging his wound.

Just before he scrambled back to his fighting position, Billy Davis remarked, "I'll be next door if you need me."

As Billy took off, Sergeant Martin called out, "Thanks again, Captain!"

"You're welcome!" responded the C47 pilot as he returned to his fighting position and engaged the enemy with his M1 Carbine.

Once Doc Keller did all he could for his patient, the medic grabbed his medical bag in preparation of leaving and said, "That should hold you for a while, Sarge."

While Phil Martin pulled himself up in preparation of getting back in the fight, he called out, "Keep your head down, Doc," as the medic crawled away under fire and returned to his half of the CID led patrol. A split second later, Sergeant Martin tucked the wooden stock on his Thompson into his right shoulder, as he stood up and fired three bursts at the enemy. After ducking back down behind cover, Sergeant Martin got back up and fired another three bursts at the Germans.

While doing his best not to cause himself anymore discomfort than he was already in, Jim Beauregard raised his body enough to get back into the fight. Fortunately, M1A1 Paratrooper Model of the M1Carbine was lightweight, easy to wield, easy to operate and soft shooting, especially for someone who was wounded. It also helped that Jim Beauregard was proficient with firearms and was able to shoot left handed. He managed to do so, by placing the metal folding stock against his left shoulder while he continued firing at the enemy.

The moment Larson's head popped up above the rim of the bomb crater again, Al ducked behind a nearby tree stump when the fugitive fired two shots in his direction from a small caliber pistol. With his blood boiling, Al Parker quickly aimed his M3 Grease Gun at the cop killing fugitive and fired a quick burst to motivate Larson to get back in his hole.

While Jim Beauregard reloaded his M1 Carbine, Al did his best to keep an eye on Ivan Larson in between firing short bursts at the Germans with his M3 Grease Gun. When Al stopped to reload his M3, he turned and called out, "Are you OK?"

While Jim yelled, "I'm OK, keep shooting," he rested his M1 Carbine on top of a felled tree that was positioned along the leading edge of the bomb crater and fired four quick shots at the enemy.

Seeing his wounded partner and commanding officer in action motivated Al Parker to get even more excited and scream, "The Krauts don't have a chance now that you're back in action."

As much as Jim Beauregard appreciated Al's kind words, he limited his response by repeating himself and saying, "Keep shooting."

After calling out, "Yes, Sir," Al continued firing burst after burst at the well entrenched enemy troops.

So far, the Major and his mixed compliment of Army cops, paratroopers, a C47 pilot and one medic were holding their own. The question was, how long would they be able to do so before they ran out of ammunition and fell to the mercy of the enemy? What the Major didn't know at the time, was that he and his men had inflicted several casualties on the enemy that included two dead and two wounded.

CHAPTER 21

DESPERATE TIMES CALL FOR DESPERATE MEASURES

While Ivan ignored the throbbing pain from the long cut that ran along his scalp line, he knelt next to his dead friend and said, "You're not gonna believe it but that nigger cop from New York just shot at me with a fucking Grease Gun." As Ivan continued to face Shorty, he spoke to his dead buddy as if he was still alive and said, "If I ever get out'a this mess I'll find a way to let your mom know that you were a good soldier."

As much as it bothered Ivan to leave Shorty, he knew that he had no choice but to try and flee deeper into enemy territory, or face being killed or captured by that crazy colored cop from New York. Even if the Germans managed to wipe out the U.S. Army personnel who pursued him and Shorty behind enemy lines, Ivan did not like the idea of being taken prisoner by the SS Sergeant who pistol whipped him with his own gun. Ivan also felt that it was unforgivable that the Germans made no attempt to render first aid to Shorty as soon as they were captured. The fact that the Kraut Sergeant stole the morphine that Ivan carried, that could have been used to ease his friend's pain, was another reason why he held a grudge against anyone who wore the SS insignia on their uniform.

While a battle raged overhead, Ivan Larson could not believe that a Negro cop and his white partner managed to hunt him down all the way from Brooklyn to a position behind enemy lines in Belgium. With nothing left to lose except his miserable life, Ivan Larson prepared to make a run for it, or die trying when he heard the angry voice of Al Parker call out, "You're a fucking dead man, Larson. You better pray the Krauts get their hands on you before I do."

While Ivan held Shorty's Colt pistol in his right right hand, he mustered up the courage to respond in a similar tone of voice and screamed, "Come and get it copper!"

Even though the Germans were perfectly positioned on slightly elevated terrain, Jim Beauregard was proud of his men for performing so bravely in the face of a determined enemy. Jim was especially grateful to have Al Parker serve by his side during such a violent combat action. In fact, Jim regretted not having a combat cameraman along on this mission, to capture the way that Al Parker performed under fire.

While Jim reloaded his M1 Carbine, he had high hopes that things would be different back home, once the American people learned that Negro troops fought just as heroically as the white troops in battle. Whether Al was fearless because he had a tremendous need to prove himself, he was born brave, or both, he was incredibly calm, cool and collected when he engaged the forces of evil. Al was also loyal and proved it when he pulled Jim behind the best cover available, immediately after he was wounded during the opening salvo of the German ambush.

In between keeping an eye on the bomb crater where Ivan Larson was located and defending against the German ambush, Jim's mind was working overtime while he tried to think of a way to accomplish their mission without getting anyone else under his command wounded or killed. Like it or not, as long as the Germans were well armed and behind good cover, Jim Beauregard and his men were in no position to do much more than fall back to the American lines or face being killed or captured. Jim also knew that if he and his men withdrew from contact, they might never find out what happened to Ivan Larson and Francis Shorty Mc Ghee.

After firing a few more rounds at the Germans, Jim spoke in a raised tone of voice and said, "If we stay put they'll whittle us down to nothing. If we pull back, we'll lose Ivan Larson and never find out what happened to Shorty Mc Ghee." Then, after pausing for a second, Jim looked at Al Parker and said, "I'm sorry, Al but we might have to settle for tossing a few grenades into that bomb crater and hope for the best before we fall back to our side of the line."

Under the circumstances, Al knew that Jim was right. The fact that the American troops who volunteered to hunt down the two fugitives were using up their supply of ammunition, while also sustaining one casualty after another, made it clear that this fight needed to be ended as soon as possible. Even though many years had gone by since he saw combat in the First World War, Al Parker knew that something had to be done to turn the tide of this battle, before everyone in the CID led patrol was wounded, killed or taken prisoner.

After checking to see if Ivan Larson was still in the nearby bomb crater, Al Parker turned to Jim and said, "I have an idea. If it works we can get our hands on Ivan Larson and find out what happened to Shorty Mc Ghee. If it doesn't work, you can toss two grenades into that bomb crater and get everyone back to our lines before it gets dark."

After Al paused long enough to check on Ivan Larson, he turned around to face Jim again and said, "I know you're not gonna like what I have to say but I think I can flank the Kraut position if I make it look like I'm deserting under fire. To make this work I can't have any covering fire. Instead, I need everyone to stop firing and call me every name in the book when I take off and head back toward our lines. If I'm right, the members of the so called Master Race will enjoy watching a colored American soldier turn tail and run. Once I get far enough away, I'll circle back then cross the road northwest of here and attack the Krauts from behind. If you approve I'll move out as soon as you brief the others about the plan."

Even though Al's plan was incredibly brave and dangerous, Jim knew that losing the opportunity to capture the two fugitives was one thing but losing Al Parker after all they had been through would be too much for him to bear. The moment that Al saw the look of concern on Jim's face, he leaned closer to the man who was his partner and his commanding officer and said, "I'm not leaving without Ivan Larson and Shorty Mc Ghee. I have to do this, Jim. I can't explain it but I know I can pull this off."

After hearing what Al had to say, Jim nodded his head in agreement before he remarked, "OK, Al. Get ready while I pass the word."

The only thing that seemed to comfort Jim Beauregard while he prepared to brief the others, was the fact that during his police career he became a firm believer in the ability of a good street cop to develop his instincts. If Al believed that his plan would work, Jim had no choice but to go along, if for no other reason than he had worked with Al Parker long enough to know that he had excellent instincts.

After pulling himself up to the edge of the bomb crater, Jim called out, "I'll be right back," as he made his way over to the next bomb crater to have a face to face briefing session with the other members of his squad. As the bullets kicked up the ground and streaked overhead, the pain from the Major's shoulder wound proved to be too much to take and forced Jim to collapse face down on the ground halfway to his destination.

After seeing the Major go down, Captain Davis called out, "Medic!" as he went to his aid and dragged Jim back into the relative safety of the large bomb crater where Al Parker was continuing to engage the enemy. A moment later Doc Keller arrived and immediately went to work on his patient.

As Al Parker paused to reload his M3 Grease Gun he glanced to his right and called out, "How is he, Doc?"

While Doc Keller removed the blood soaked bandage from the Major's right shoulder, he proved that he had a tremendous sense of humor under fire, when he responded while never taking his eyes off his patient. "The Major didn't follow his doctor's orders." A split second later Doc Keller looked up at Al and called out, "He'll be OK."

While Doc Keller finished patching up his patient, Jim turned to Captain Davis and said, "Billy, I have something to say that I want you to relay to Sergeant Martin and Sergeant Mulligan. I also need you to listen to this as well, Doc, so you can relay my instructions to Captain Cabrerra and the others." Once he saw that he had their attention, Jim continued and said, "Al has a plan that just might make it possible for us to complete our mission and get back to our lines before it gets dark. I'm not crazy about this plan but I approved it because our options are limited."

After being offered a cigarette and a light from Doc Keller, the Major thanked his favorite combat medic for the smoke before he continued his briefing. "When Al takes off and looks like a deserter going over the hill, I want everyone to stop firing and call him every name in the book as he runs by. When I say every name in the book, I mean every name in the book. Tell everyone that in order to make this work, we have to put on a good show for the Germans. Once Al gets far enough away, he'll double back and cut across the road northwest of here and hit the Krauts from behind. In order to avoid hitting Al when he moves in, we need to direct our fire at the center and right side of the German fighting position. If for any reason this plan fails, I'll toss two grenades in the bomb crater where Ivan Larson is hiding, before I order everyone to fall back to our side of the line. I'll also be staying behind to cover the withdrawal with the machine gun."

While the Major looked up at Sergeant Keller, he reached out and grabbed the medic's left arm when he continued and said, "Doc, I need you to tell Captain Cabrerra and Captain Savino that it has to be this way." Then, after asking everyone to check their watches, the Major said, "On my mark Al takes off in five minutes......
mark!"

Doc Keller had been in the Army long enough to know that a good officer never gives an order that needs to be debated or discussed. After nodding his head, Doc Keller kept his response short and remarked, "Don't worry, Sir, I'll deliver the message." Doc Keller then looked over to Al Parker who was reloading an empty Grease Gun magazine from a spare box of ammunition and said, "Good luck, Al."

As soon as Al called out, "Thanks, Doc," Doc Keller climbed up and out of the bomb crater and scurried off under fire to relay the Major's instructions to Captain Cabrerra and Captain Savino.

After taking one last drag on his Lucky Strike, Jim crushed the cigarette butt in the side of the bomb crater, while he made eye contact with Captain Davis and said, "If this doesn't work I want you to give Captain Cabrerra and Captain Savino a hand and make sure the others get back in one piece."

As much as the civilian in him wanted to discuss the pros and cons of this rather bold plan, Billy Davis had been in command of a C47 crew long enough to know what it was like to give an order and expect it to be carried out without question or hesitation. After checking his watch, the combat tested C47 pilot looked at the Major and remarked, "Four minutes and counting, Sir," before he wished Al good luck and returned to his fighting position.

After Al handed his reloaded M3 Grease Gun and two spare 30 round magazines to the Major, he removed his pistol belt and filled his pockets with three hand-grenades and two spare .45 caliber pistol magazines. Al then racked the slide to load his Model 1911 before he applied the thumb safety and tucked the pistol inside his pants' belt in a cross draw position. As soon as Al finished checking to make sure that the Smith & Wesson revolver that he carried in a shoulder holster was fully loaded, Jim handed his partner his .45 caliber pistol and said, "Here, take this. It might come in handy."

While Al racked the slide to load the chamber, he looked at Jim while he slipped the extra pistol in the small of his back as he said, "I'm loaded for bear now."

After hearing Jim remark, "We're gonna play this your way but only if you promise to be careful."

While sounding as sincere as possible Al responded and said, "You have my word on that."

While Jim checked his watch, Al removed the bone handle folding knife from his pants pocket and admired the gift that Pat Murphy Jr. gave him on that fateful day back in 1943. It was hard to believe that so much had transpired since then.

As soon as Al slipped the treasured gift back in his pant's pocket, he looked at Jim and said, "I just want you to know that I'm not crazy about you staying behind to cover the withdrawal if things don't work out as planned."

When Jim stopped checking his watch, he seemed to be a man who was at peace with his decision when he looked at Al and said, "First of all, if you can do something crazy so can I. Second, if I go home without you, your wife will kill me and I'll never eat one of her delicious home cooked meals again." After exchanging friendly smiles with his partner, Jim checked his watch and was all business when he remarked, "Thirty seconds."

When the Major began to count down from ten, Al turned to face the direction of the American lines and was off running the moment Jim said, "Three, two, one..go!"

The moment that Al Parker climbed out of the bomb crater, he tossed his MP helmet aside and started screaming, "Pull back! Pull back! We're all gonna die!" as he ran through the forest in the opposite direction of the battle. The second he did so, the other men in the CID led patrol stopped shooting and began calling Al Parker every name in the book from coward to various racial slurs.

By the time Al ran by Captain Savino's position, the Germans stopped shooting as well when they spotted the only Negro soldier in the American patrol deserting under fire. The plan proved to be working when Sergeant Werner stood up and yelled, "Look at the nigger run!" By the time Al vanished from sight, the Germans began laughing and insulting the Americans for allowing Untermenschens (Sub Humans) to serve in their army.

After running through the woods in the direction of the American lines, Al Parker circled back and crossed the road far enough away from the ambush site, to insure that his actions weren't observed by the SS troops who were ordering the Americans to surrender. When Al heard Jim Beauregard call out and said, "Drop dead," he knew that the Major was intentionally provoking the Germans, so they would continue firing and make it easier for him to flank their position from behind.

While the Major and the others risked annihilation, Al made his way through the snow covered forest until he was a good 30 yards northwest of the enemy position. What no one including Al Parker knew at the time, was that Sergeant Hans Sigmann was leading his unit of military policemen through a nearby section of wooded terrain, that overlooked the fighting that was taking place between the SS unit and the American patrol.

As soon as Ivan Larson said goodbye to Shorty, he crawled up the side of the bomb crater and looked over the top in anticipation of making a run for it. The moment Ivan spotted Al Parker cross the road from the northwest and head toward the rear of the enemy position, he jumped up and frantically tried to warn the enemy that they were about to be attacked from behind.

As the sounds of the battle drowned out Ivan's attempt to warn the enemy, Jim Beauregard fired a two round burst from Al's M3 Grease Gun and just missed hitting the mark, when Ivan Larson slipped and fell on the snow covered ground. Immediately after Ivan frantically emptied the Colt .25 Automatic at the Major from CID, Jim fired a second burst that hit the fugitive in his right buttocks when he started to stand up. Once again Ivan fell, only this time he dropped the empty pistol in a slushy mixture of ice cold mud and snow.

The second another burst fired by Major Beauregard kicked up the ground nearby, Ivan managed to belly crawl over to the driver's side of the shot up Jeep. While Ivan Larson continued to crawl along the driver's side of the crashed Jeep, Al Parker quietly made his way behind the German L shaped fighting position. As soon as Al Parker vanished from sight, Ivan Larson began to head deeper into German held territory.

Once Al made his way to an area of the forest that was behind the west side of the enemy position, he knelt down and placed the three grenades on the ground. As soon as Al pulled the pin, he tossed the first hand-grenade into the far left side of the enemy position. Just before the first grenade exploded, the second grenade was falling through the air and landed in the middle of the enemy position. A split second later, Al tossed the third grenade into the far right side of the enemy fighting position. Immediately after the last grenade exploded, Al Parker stood up and called out, "Who are you calling a nigger?" as he stepped closer to the enemy position and used a pair of .45 caliber pistols to engage several wounded German soldiers, including SS Sergeant Werner and Corporal Spitzer.

Despite his multiple shrapnel and bullet wounds, SS Sergeant Claus Werner had enough fight left in him to drop his empty submachine gun and draw the captured

American pistol from his belt as he turned to face his attacker. The second he did so, Al Parker tossed the two empty .45s aside and quickly drew his Smith & Wesson revolver from his shoulder holster. As soon as Al Parker aimed and fired, he riddled the storm trooper's torso with six rounds of N.Y.P.D. issue .38 Special ammunition.

After ordering his men to halt, Sergeant Sigmann split his squad in three sections. While the largest section was instructed to flank the American patrol from behind and take them prisoner if possible, Sergeant Sigmann directed one of his men to intercept the wounded American who was making his way deeper into the German lines, while he led the remaining member of his squad to capture the brave Negro MP who single handily took on the SS unit.

The moment Al Parker saw Jim stand up and call out, "He's heading north," Al holstered his revolver, as he jumped into the right side of the slit trench where the dead bodies of the MG42 machine gun crew were located. After pushing the body of a dead German aside, Al picked up the MG42 and fired a short burst that stitched up the snow covered ground next to the escaping fugitive before he screamed, "You're under arrest you son of a bitch!"

When a frantic Ivan Larson did his best to limp faster, Al fired another short burst that brought the fugitive down when a bullet grazed his right ankle. While Ivan Larson cursed out loud and remained on the ground, Al Parker spotted Major Beauregard and the others being led out of the forest and onto the road, with their hands up after being taken prisoner by German soldiers. As soon as Al turned and faced the enemy with the captured machine gun in hand, Jim Beauregard ordered Al to hold his fire. A split second later Al heard the distinctive sound of a rifle bolt being cycled from behind, as a German soldier speaking perfect English remarked, "I wouldn't do that if I were you, Sergeant."

Rather than risk being shot in the back, Al dropped the MG42 and raised his hands to chest level, as he turned and faced a middle aged German sergeant armed with a 9mm MP 40 Submachine Gun and a young German Private armed with a bolt action K98 rifle. Once Al was relieved of his .38 caliber revolver, a seemingly friendly Sergeant Hans Sigmann pointed to the road below and said, "Shall we join the others?"

Ivan Larson was living his worst nightmare when a German soldier ignored his pleas to be separated from the other Americans and marched him at gun point back down the road. By the time Al Parker joined the other members of the CID led patrol, Ivan Larson arrived with his German escort prodding him along from behind.

Even the Germans could tell by the look on Ivan Larson's face and his obvious reluctance to approach the other Americans, that he was more petrified of his own countrymen than being captured by the enemy. Al Parker further convinced his captors that they were right in their assessment, when he lunged at Ivan Larson and began to beat the wounded fugitive senseless until three German Military Policemen managed to pry them apart.

Even when two young German soldiers continued to hold him back, Al Parker pointed his right index finger at Ivan Larson and screamed like a wild man when he said, "If I can't bring you back I'm gonna kill you with my fucking bare hands the minute I get the chance you cop killing son of a bitch!"

As soon as his men turned to see how their sergeant would handle this unusual situation, Hans Sigmann stepped forward and spoke in a businesslike tone of voice when he addressed Al Parker and said, "What is this all about, Sergeant?"

Without wasting any time Al faced the enemy non commissioned officer and answered his question while speaking fluent German. "This man is wanted for murder in New York City. He killed a policeman during a bank robbery in Brooklyn. I know because I was there."

While acting both surprised and very interested in what the Negro American Military Policeman had to say, Sergeant Sigmann complimented Al Parker in English and said, "Your German is excellent, Sergeant."

When Sergeant Sigmann continued, he pointed to Ivan Larson and said, "You say this man is wanted for killing a policeman in New York?"

As soon as Al nodded his head in agreement and said, "That's correct," Ivan Larson went berserk while he balanced himself on one foot and screamed, "He's lying. Who you gonna believe. Me or this nigger?"

In an effort to back up his partner, Major Beauregard stepped forward while he braced his wounded shoulder with his left hand and said, "Sergeant Parker is telling the truth. We have a warrant for this man's arrest for killing a New York City Police Officer and other serious crimes. The other fugitive we've been hunting is in the bottom of that bomb crater. My men and I are with the Criminal Investigation Division and the Military Police. Captain Davis, Sergeant Martin and our medic are witnesses who can identify the two fugitives that Sergeant Parker and I have been pursuing since 1943. Captain Cabrerra, Sergeant Mulligan, Corporal Polanski and Private Reader are paratroopers who were assigned to assist us in our search."

The moment Sergeant Sigmann turned to his corporal and said, "Search the Americans. I wish to see their identification," his men went to work and produced identification cards, arrest warrants, several pairs of handcuffs and various wanted posters. The most interesting piece of personal property taken from the Americans, was the silver metallic New York City Police Department Patrolman's shield that was removed from Al Parker's pants pocket.

Hans Sigmann had not experienced this much intrigue since he left the Munich Police Department and joined the German Army as a military police sergeant. Immediately after Sergeant Mulligan turned to Major Beauregard and remarked, "These guys are Kraut MPs, Sir," Sergeant Sigmann cracked a smile and said, "That's correct, Major. My men and I are military policemen just like you and your men."

While Ivan Larson tried in vain to tell the Germans that they were required to comply with the terms of the Geneva Convention and take him prisoner, Sergeant Sigmann examined Major Beauregard's CID credentials and read the arrest warrants found on Al Parker before he handed everything except the silver patrolman's shield back to Jurgen and said, "Return these items to the Americans, Jurgen." Sergeant Sigmann then stepped over to where Ivan Larson was standing on one foot and said, "Setzen," as he pushed the cop killer to the ground.

As Sergeant Sigmann turned to face Al Parker, one of his men ran down the road from the direction of the American lines and called out, "Sergeant, the Americans are coming. Several vehicles supported by infantry."

Despite the report that an American column was heading in their direction, Sergeant Sigmann appeared to be in no hurry when he stepped closer to Al Parker and pinned his New York City Police Department Patrolman's shield through the open button hole on the collar of his field jacket. Sergeant Sigmann then handed a surprised Al Parker his revolver and a pair of handcuffs as he spoke in a friendly tone of voice and said, "You'll be needing these when you take your prisoner back to New York."

As dumbfounded as he was, Al Parker spoke in English for all to hear and said, "You mean you're turning the prisoner over to us?"

While Sergeant Sigmann took a step back, he snapped to attention and bowed his head ever so slightly before he looked up and said, "Sergeant Hans Sigmann... Munich Police...at your service."

When Al remarked, "You're also a cop in civilian life?" Sergeant Sigmann turned to his left and saluted Major Beauregard as he said, "With your permission, Major, my men and I will withdraw from the area."

Much like his partner and the other Americans in the CID led patrol, Jim Beauregard was shocked by the unusual turn of events that were unfolding before his eyes. While Jim returned the salute, he expressed his appreciation when he responded in a very sincere tone of voice and said, "Thank you, Sergeant."

As the sound of the approaching jeeps and armored vehicles got louder, Hans Sigmann ordered his squad of young German MPs to fall back. The moment the German Military Police Sergeant began to follow his men, Al Parker lifted Ivan Larson off the ground and searched him for weapons before placing handcuffs on his wrists. While Ivan Larson lowered his head and submitted to arrest, the lead elements of the American relief force arrived in the area.

CHAPTER 22

COPS IN A COMBAT ZONE

When the Jeep leading the column came to a stop and the driver aimed his M1 Garand at the retreating German MPs, Jim Beauregard placed his left hand on top of the soldier's rifle and ordered him to hold his fire. As the shocked American paratrooper lowered his M1 Garand, Major Beauregard remarked, "Trust me, Private. It's a long story." A moment later, Sergeant Hans Sigmann turned and tossed the Americans a casual salute before he vanished into the snow covered forest.

While Staff Sergeant Hank Blair leaned on Captain Savino and remarked, "They'll never believe this back in Paris, Sir," Jim Beauregard looked into the bomb crater where Shorty Mc Ghee was located and instructed Sergeant Jacko and Sergeant Mulligan to recover the body. The Major then faced Captain Davis and Captain Cabrerra and asked the two officers to check on the Germans they engaged and recover any valuable intelligence information they might possess."

While Al Parker reloaded his revolver, the Major asked Sergeant Martin about his wounded arm. "Doc Keller said I'll be OK, Sir," responded the wounded paratrooper before he looked at Ivan Larson and added, "Besides, it was worth getting hit to help capture that cop killing piece'a shit."

Jim Beauregard knew exactly how the wounded paratrooper felt and proved it when he remarked, "I feel the same way, Sarge."

While Sergeant Martin was helped over to one of the responding Jeeps by a fellow paratrooper, Captain Davis returned with a captured 9mm German P38 pistol tucked in his belt while holding a pair of 1911s in his hands. As Billy handed one 1911 pistol to Major Beauregard and the other to Sergeant Parker, the C47 pilot said, "Captain Cabrerra and I found these forty fives on the ground when we checked on the Krauts, Sir. They're SS and they're all dead. We also reloaded the forty fives for you and Sergeant Parker."

After thanking Billy Davis, the Major tucked the 1911 in his M36 pistol belt,

208

while Al Parker slipped the pistol in his waistband as he remarked, "Here comes the rest of the cavalry."

While the main body of the relief force arrived in the area, Billy Davis took a long hard look at their prisoner. The moment Ivan Larson turned away, the C47 pilot who helped capture the most wanted fugitive in the United States Army remarked, "I better walk away, Sir, before I do something I won't regret." After facing Major Beauregard and Al Parker, Billy nodded his head in a respectful fashion and said, "I'll be around if you and the sergeant need me, Sir." As soon as Jim thanked Billy for all of his help, the C47 pilot walked over to join the others.

This day was full of surprises when a pair of familiar faces arrived in the area, while a heavily armed contingent of U.S. Army paratroopers and military police-men fanned out and provided security in the area. The moment Jim Beauregard spotted General Tremble walking their way, he leaned closer to Al and remarked, "Not this guy again."

While Doc Keller and two other medics helped the wounded men over to an M3 Half Track, General Tremble and Colonel Gray approached Jim Beauregard and Al Parker, while Al held their wounded prisoner by the arm. When Jim slipped his last Lucky Strike cigarette in between his lips, he turned to his partner and said, "Gimme a light, will ya, Al."

As Al reached into his field jacket pocket for a box of matches, Jim crumpled the empty pack and tossed it to the ground, just as the cantankerous General Tremble produced his own Zippo lighter and remarked, "I got it, Sergeant. You have your hands full."

After accepting a light from the seemingly more pleasant one star general, Jim Beauregard exhaled a long plume of smoke, while he stood next to his partner and their prisoner and said, "Sir, Sergeant Parker and I have taken the fugitive Ivan Larson into custody." While Sergeants Mulligan and Jacko, along with two medics, placed the lifeless body of Shorty Mc Ghee on a stretcher, Jim added, "We also recovered the dead body of the fugitive Francis Shorty Mc Ghee, Sir."

While Colonel Gray wasted no time in congratulating Jim Beauregard and Al Parker, the General stood with his hands on his hips as he nodded his head up and down in approval. In an effort to break the obvious tension, Colonel Gray spoke up and said, "When General Tremble heard you might need some help he volunteered to come along."

Jim Beauregard knew there was such a thing as taking a feud too far. When Sergeant Chris Jacko and Sergeant Mike Mulligan returned and went to take custody of the prisoner, Al Parker protested and said, "That's all right. I can handle it from here."

Without offering an explanation for his previous crude behavior, General Tremble took a step closer to Al Parker and looked directly into the Negro policeman's eyes as he remarked, "Colonel, I'm placing my driver and my jeep at Sergeant Parker's disposal. See to it that he and Major Beauregard are assisted in every way possible and get the Major and this prisoner the proper medical attention."

As soon as Colonel Gray responded and said, "Yes, Sir," he turned to the pair of MPs and nodded once as his way of telling them to take the prisoner to the General's Jeep.

While Al Parker and Jim Beauregard snapped to attention, the two Army cops sounded like professional soldiers when they responded in unison and said, "Thank you, Sir."

Colonel Gray then faced the wounded Major from CID and said, "Come on, Jim, let me give you a hand," as he guided him over to a nearby Jeep, while Al Parker remained facing the General at attention.

As the two men from different worlds faced each other in silence, Al Parker was tempted to ask the General why he had the change of heart. Instead, Al remained straight faced as he presented the General with the snappiest salute he ever received. After returning the salute, General Tremble sounded more like his old self again, when he removed an expensive cigar from his jacket pocket and presented it to Al and said, "Cops in a combat zone. What's this war coming to?"

At approximately 1645 hours (4:45 PM) on December 26, 1944 the lead elements of the 37th Tank Battalion and the 53rd Armored Infantry Battalion of the U.S. 4th Armored Division broke through the German lines along the southern perimeter of Bastogne and ended the siege. Even though it would take until December 28th to completely secure the road leading to the southern route into Bastogne, the arrival of an American armored relief force, along with the continued presence of Allied air support, signaled the beginning of the end of the German offensive in the

Ardennes. Although the American troops were no longer completely surrounded they still had German troops positioned on three sides.[12]

As Al Parker walked down the stairs of his new command, it seemed like yesterday that he returned to New York City with his prisoner and was promoted to the rank of Detective 3rd Grade. After being told to wait for Captain Murphy before he headed home for the day, Al Parker decided to stand in the corner of the roll call room, while the 4X12 tour prepared to turn out for their eight hours on patrol in Harlem.

Immediately after Captain Patrick Murphy Sr. entered the 32nd Precinct in the company of Major James Beauregard, Detective Frank Angelone and Detective Johnny Mc Donald, the desk sergeant stood up and said, "Detective Parker is waiting for you in the roll call room, Sir."

As Captain Patrick Murphy Sr. waved his right hand and said "Thanks Sarge," the desk sergeant smiled because he knew the real reason why the most famous captain in the police department was in his precinct with an Army officer and two detectives.

The moment the Captain and his entourage entered the roll call room, Captain Murphy called out, "Hey, Al," when he spotted his old friend standing off to the side. After turning to face his visitors, Al Parker smiled as Captain Murphy, Jim Beauregard, Frank Angelone and Johnny Mc Donald walked his way in an obvious hurry.

The moment Jim Beauregard extended his hand said, "How the hell are you, Al?," Captain Murphy patted Detective Parker on the back and remarked, "Look who I ran into downtown."

It had been almost two months since they returned to the States with their prisoner. During that time Jim Beauregard recuperated at home from his wounds and made a trip to New Mexico to pay his respects to Lieutenant Wright's family. After the Major was transferred to CID Headquarters, he returned to New York to watch Ivan Larson get sentenced after pleading guilty to all charges.

Unlike Pat Murphy Sr, Frank Angelone and Johnny Mc Donald who continued to see Al Parker on a more regular basis, Jim Beauregard had more limited
contact with the only Negro cop he ever served with. Even though this was the
case, both Jim Beauregard and Al Parker cherished their friendship and all they
accomplished while working together.

As soon as Al asked how his shoulder wound was coming along, Jim
responded as he slowly rotated his right shoulder ever so slightly back and forth.
"Even though I'm still a little stiff, I managed to convince an Army doctor to clear
me to return to duty with CID."

Now it was Jim's turn to see how his Army buddy was doing. While Jim
admired the shinny gold detective shield that hung from Al's lapel, the Major
teased his former partner by saying, "You made one lousy arrest and they made
you a detective."

"And in Belgium no less," joked Johnny Mc Donald as he patted Al on the
back, while Frank Angelone remarked, "Talk about being off post and getting
rewarded for it."

The sight of a dozen patrolmen and one sergeant assembled in the roll call
room brought Captain Murphy to interrupt and remark, "Come on, boys. You
can break each others balls later. Right now we've got some official business to
attend to."

As Captain Murphy guided Al to the front of the room, Al wondered what
was going on when Major Jim Beauregard stood at attention while facing the
front of the formation. While Al Parker stood in between Captain Murphy and
Jim Beauregard, the roll call supervisor called everyone to attention before he
saluted the two superior officers and said, "The four to twelve tour is all present
and accounted for, Sir."

Immediately after the Captain and the Major returned the salute, Pat Murphy
Sr. addressed the room full of cops in a friendly tone of voice. "Men, you all know
that Detective Parker recently served with the military police and was assigned
to Army CID under the command of Major James Beauregard. For those of you
who don't know, Major Beauregard is on military leave from the Atlanta Police
Department, so give him your undivided attention because he has something very
important to say to us today."

Immediately after Jim thanked Captain Murphy for the introduction, he
removed a leather covered box from his pocket as he faced Al Parker and said, "On

behalf of the President of the United States it gives me great pleasure to award Staff Sergeant Alvin Parker The Silver Star for gallantry in action. While operating behind enemy lines, Staff Sergeant Parker single handily rescued his unit from a German ambush on December 27, 1944 near the Town of Longchamps. As a direct result of this combat action, Staff Sergeant Parker and other U.S. Army personnel were able to complete their mission and capture the fugitive identified as Ivan Larson."

The moment Major Beauregard presented his Army buddy with the third highest decoration in the land and said, "Congratulations, Al," the room full of police officers, many of whom were Negroes, began to applaud and cheer. When a proud Captain Murphy stepped forward and congratulated his old friend, Al Parker thought to himself that he would gladly trade his detective badge and his medal to have young Patrick Murphy Jr. still be alive. After thanking Jim Beauregard and Captain Murphy, Al admired his medal before he looked up and said, "I guess this means the drinks are on me."

As soon as everyone got comfortable at a table in a local Harlem nightclub, Jim removed an envelope from his inside uniform jacket pocket and handed it to Al as he said, "I didn't want'a give this to you in front of a roomful of cops in case you weren't interested."

While Al read the contents of the letter from the War Department, he could not believe that this official correspondence was addressed to him. The first to notice Al's reaction was Captain Murphy. After looking across the table and seeing the smile on Jim's face, Pat Murphy Sr. turned his attention to his old friend and said, "They either want to give you another medal or the bastards are drafting you to serve in the same Army for a third time. Which is it, Al?"

Even though he was still in state of shock, Al handed the letter to Captain Murphy as he spoke up and said, "I can't believe it, Captain. The Army wants to make me a First Lieutenant assigned to the CID Office in Paris."

While Detective Frank Angelone and Detective Johnny Mc Donald helped the waitress deliver a round of drinks to the table, Jim Beauregard spoke up and said, "After you pulled that crazy stunt in Belgium that saved us from that SS unit and enabled us to complete our mission, General Tremble of all people said that you deserved a lot more than a medal for bravery. When Colonel Gray asked the General what he had in mind, his exact words were, "That cigar smoking New York City cop deserves a damn battlefield commission and I intend to see that he gets one."

As soon as Jim paused to light a cigarette, he continued and said, "When I told the General that I tried to get you a commission when you volunteered to serve in CID but the Army denied my request, he looked at me and said, "Forget about the past, Major and get me that recommendation."

After taking a quick drag on his cigarette, Jim went on to say, "Once I wrote up the recommendation, I had endorsements from General Tremble, Colonel Gray, Colonel Richmond, Captain Savino, Captain Davis and Captain Cabrerra. I also picked up another endorsement when we arrived at the CID Office in Paris with Ivan Larson in custody and Colonel Vogel agreed to sign off on my recommendation on one condition."

By now everyone at the table was paying close attention to everything that was being said, as if they were listening to their favorite radio program. When Al asked what Colonel Vogel wanted in return for his endorsement, Jim wasted no time in saying, "The Colonel wanted me to agree to take command of the CID Office in Paris, because he was being rotated back to Washington. He also said he wanted to turn his command over to the best team of CID Agents in the Army and hoped that you would accept the commission so we could pick up where he left off. Apparently, the black market in France is still a major problem. There's also a large number of deserters to round up and plenty of crimes to investigate."

After pausing for a second to tap the ash from his cigarette into an ashtray, Jim continued and said, "I also put Captain Savino in for a promotion. He's a Major now and will be my second in command. If you agree to accept this commission, you'll be my liaison officer to the French Police. I also got Hank Blair promoted to Master Sergeant and recruited Sergeant Mulligan and Sergeant Jacko into CID. Colonel Vogel also agreed to see if he could get Frank's son and Joe Coppola's son transferred from their MP units to the CID Office in Paris."

"Oh, I almost forgot," said Jim, who paused long enough to put his cigarette out before he continued and said, "I also managed to get an MP Sergeant who was decorated for the way that he and his men captured three German infiltrators at the Ambleve River Bridge check point promoted and made a CID Agent."

Al couldn't believe his ears and said, "You got my son Cal in CID?"

Without hesitating the man who helped Al Parker pursue Ivan Larson and Francis Shorty Mc Ghee all the way to the front lines during the Battle of the Bulge remarked, "Staff Sergeant Parker is in Paris right now, Al."

As a former commissioned officer in the United States Army, Captain Murphy knew the significance of the Army's offer and said, "A battlefield commission. That's quite an honor, Al. One that's hard to pass up."

While Al looked across the table at Captain Murphy, he sounded like a man who needed some good advice from a close friend. "I don't know what to do, Captain. I just made detective after all these years on the job. As much as I'd love to go back to Paris and serve in CID with Jim as my CO, as well as with my son Cal and the men who made it possible to capture Ivan Larson, I hate to give this up."

After all they had been through together, Captain Murphy wasted no time in saying, "Take the commission, Al. You deserve it." Frank Angelone and Johnny Mc Donald also agreed and encouraged Al to take the Army up on their offer to make him a First Lieutenant.

When Detective Frank Angelone saw that Al still looked a bit confused about what to do, the Italian American First Grade Detective spoke up and said, "As my grandmother used to say. When it comes to things changing for the better, things happen little by little. Take the commission, Al. This job will be waiting for you when you get back."

While Al considered what he should do, he turned to Jim and said, "Since the Army is being so generous I hope they didn't forget you."

After cracking a smile, Jim responded as he pointed to one of the ribbons on the left side of his uniform and said, "Not only are they gonna make me a Lieutenant Colonel but your Yankee Army gave me the DSC for leading that mixed bag of G.I.s behind enemy lines."

While Al continued to look as if he was struggling with his decision, Captain Murphy spoke up and said, "If you accept the commission you'll still be a member of this department on military leave. Once the war's over and you return home, you can put your suit back on and serve in the squad as if nothing's changed."

As soon as Al removed a cigar from his suit jacket pocket, Jim Beauregard offered him a light and said, "What'a you say, Al?"

After taking a few puffs on his White Owl cigar, Al raised his glass of whiskey and said, "Paris here we come."

After being processed back into the U.S. Army, the newly minted First Lieutenant Al Parker and the recently promoted Lt. Colonel James Beauregard boarded a flight to England with priority orders in hand to catch a connecting flight to Paris, France. By the time they arrived at the Paris CID Office, the Allies were preparing to launch the Invasion of Germany.

Even though the end of the war was near, there was still a great deal of fight left in the German Army. As a result, it was imperative that U.S. Army CID Agents, in conjunction with their counterparts in the military police and the local civilian police, prevented the theft of critical supplies and equipment that were needed by Allied troops to win the war in Europe.

The end of Book II
To be continued

NOTES

1 *Seven Roads to Hell* by Donald R. Burgett and *G.I.* by Lee Kennett.

2 *Green Light* by Martin Wolfe

3 *Green Light* by Martin Wolfe

4 *Remembering the Bulge Part Three* by James H. Farmer

5 *Green Light* by Martin Wolfe

6 *Remembering the Bulge Part Three* by James H. Farmer

7 *Silent Wings* by Gerard Devlin

8 *Remembering the Bulge* by James H. Farmer

9 *Silent Wings* by Gerard Devlin

10 *Battle - The Story of the Bulge* by John Toland

11 *Hitler's Last Gamble - The Battle of the Bulge, December 1944-January 1945* by Trevor N. Dupuy, David L. Bongard and Richard C. Anderson Jr.

12 *A Time For Trumpets* by Charles B. Mc Donald & *Silent Wings* by Gerard M. Devlin

FOOTNOTES

Footnote for Chapter 5 and 10: In the actual incident that took place that was documented in Gerald Astor's book A Blood Dimmed Tide Private First Class Charles W. Lawrence, PFC George Sensanbach and PFC Clarence van der Werth became Gunter Billing, Wilhelm Schmidt and Manfred Pernass. Once the three German infiltrators were taken prisoner they were transported to a barracks that was fifteen miles from Liege where they were found guilty of being spies and were executed by firing squad.

Footnote: Chapter 14 & 15. The Book titled Pulse And Repulse written by H. Rex Shama was used as a reference material to accurately represent certain aspects of the combat glider operations during the Battle of the Bulge, including the identification of specific Troop Carrier Squadrons that towed GC-4A Waco gliders to Bastogne, specifics about the flight from France to Bastogne, enemy opposition to this resupply mission to include the descriptions of battle damage to U.S. Army aircraft, the number of gliders that were able to land in and around Bastogne, the identification and the description of the locations and the type of terrain where gliders landed, the activities of glider pilots once they landed, contact with the enemy and other aspects related to airborne glider operations.

Footnote: Green Light – A Troop Carrier Squadron's War From Normandy to the Rhine by Martin Wolfe and Into The Valley – The Untold Story of USAAF Troop Carrier In World War II by Colonel Charles H. Young are two other general reference sources that I relied on to become more familiar with combat glider operations in the European Theater of Operation.

Footnote: NYPD A City And Its Police by James Lardner and Thomas Repetto is a well written and easy to read book that gave me an additional insight into the history of the New York City Police Department. This included information about the employment of African American police officers in the early days of the 20th Century.

Footnote: Brothers In Arms by Kareem Abdul–Jabbar and Anthony Walton is an excellent book to read if you are interested in the history of the 761st Tank Battalion, an armored unit comprised of African American enlisted personnel, six white officers and thirty African American commissioned officers. Brothers

In Arms proved to be an excellent general reference source that described the problems of racism that African American U.S. Army personnel faced during World War II.

Made in the USA
Middletown, DE
08 November 2022

14395209R00129